"It's tough to raise the stakes in crime fiction, but Cliff Burns's Zinnea and Nightstalk really up the ante. This detective duo plays for keeps."

David Galef, *author of* Turning Japanese *and* Flesh

Sex & Other Acts of the Imagination (1990)

"This is a book of hot dreams and frozen nightmares. It floats on a plane few writers achieve, where the imagery is raw but the insights are tender. The people in these stories will stay with me for a long time to come."

Timothy Findley, author of *Not Wanted on the Voyage*

"At last Canada has found a literary equivalent to David Cronenberg..."

Strange Adventures (U.K.)

"Burns writes like Hitchcock directs, producing gooseflesh without monsters. And that is the scariest writing there is."

Factsheet Five (USA)

The Reality Machine (1997)

"Burns's writing is sparse, minimalist, but his words are as sharp as knives, dissecting our universe with astonishing precision. *The Reality Machine*, as sharp and memorable as a paper cut, is a real find. These stories have teeth, and they bite. You will not leave unmarked."

Corey Redekop, author of *Shelf Monkey*

So Dark the Night

(A Zinnea & Nightstalk Mystery)

by Cliff Burns

Best wishes,

[signature: Cliff Burns]

Cover Art: "Midnight Randevouz" by Ado Ceric
(http://www.adoceric.com)

Book cover design: Chris Kent

Published by: Black Dog Press
(blackdogpress@yahoo.ca)

Author website: http://cliffjburns.wordpress.com

Printed by: Lightning Source

"Psalm" and "You Were" by Paul Celan appear in *Paul Celan: Poet, Survivor, Jew*; Translations by John Felstiner, Yale University Press (1995)

The excerpt from *Practical Guide for Private Investigators* by Edward Smith was reprinted with permission from Paladin Press.

Quotes from H.P. Lovecraft, John Whiteside Parsons, Aleister Crowley, Italo Calvino, etc. are included under the terms of "fair use".

ISBN: 978-0-9694853-3-9

for my Creator

Contents:

Book I

April - May

"For wisdom is the property of the dead,
A something incompatible with life; and power
Like everything that has the stain of blood,
A property of the living; but no stain
Can come upon the visage of the moon
When it has looked in glory from a cloud."

"Blood and the Moon" by W.B. Yeats

"For the thing which I greatly feared
is come upon me, and that which I was
afraid of is come unto me."

The Book of Job

I want to confess.

This is a mystery, isn't it, and in most whodunits doesn't someone break down, sooner or later, seeking to rid themselves of an insupportable burden of guilt or, at the very least, rationalize their bad behavior? For others, it's a golden opportunity to gloat over nefarious deeds and bask in the glory of their criminal genius. They clearly relish the retelling and don't mind thoughtfully summarizing their twisted schemes for the folks who lost the thread somewhere around Chapter Eight.

Whatever their motivation, clearing the slate seems to come as something of a relief to the majority of wrong-doers. Naming their sins, acknowledging ownership of their crimes (without necessarily taking responsibility for them).

I want to make one thing clear: this is a confession, not an apology. I have no regrets when I admit, freely and with hand on heart, that I fell in love with Cassandra Zinnea the moment I set eyes on her.

You'd understand if you met her. The woman had an unbelievable presence, a movie star quality. Effortlessly exotic, the life force radiating from her creating an intoxicating aura of grace and elegance and sensuality.

The combination of beauty and that otherworldly charisma was irresistible to anyone who was on the receiving end. Including me. Especially me.

I've described our initial encounter before[1] so I won't repeat myself. Suffice to say, she made quite a first impression. Framed in the narrow doorway, a six foot-two-inch Amazon, wearing a chocolate brown, cashmere blazer and dark slacks, cut thin to accentuate the longest legs I have ever seen.

It's funny. At the time, I'd been with After Hours Investigations nearly six months. I had seniority, plenty of on the job experience...and yet right from the start, she was the one in charge. I deferred to her automatically; she was a natural born leader while I filled the role of adoring follower and/or brutal sidekick.

In the two years we were together, we found ourselves in some pretty hairy situations. I soon came to rely on her exceptional mind, physical courage and pluck...along with other talents not specifically mentioned in her curriculum vitae.

---

[1] "The Long Nap" (*The Casebooks of Zinnea & Nightstalk, Volume I*)

It was part of my job to write up daily reports for our employer. Once Cassandra Zinnea came on board, those reports expanded and I began keeping more detailed notes, especially when a case was odd or unusual for one reason or another. I suppose it could be argued that my efforts were an attempt to preserve some sort of historical record. There is also ample evidence to suggest that my Casebooks amount to little more than an extended love letter to my partner.

Gradually those archives, kept in heavy-duty, three-inch binders, expanded to impressive proportions. It seemed like every investigation warranted at least a few pages; understandable, perhaps, in light of the type of clientele our agency seemed to attract.

We had our share of duds, no question, but there were quite a few thrills and chills along the way too. There is, however, one particular case that found us at the very top of our game. Simply put, it had everything: murder, mayhem, supernatural creatures and demon spawn galore. Yeah, it was pretty far out, even by our standards.

There were hints, numerous signs and portents. The cats, of course. And maybe there's something to that "lines of energy" theory. Invisible strands of magical power converging on one spot. All I know for certain is that for a short period of time the city of Ilium was the focal point for a bizarre series of events, culminating in a thrilling battle with the forces of darkness and chaos that left over twenty people dead and many others permanently scarred by the experience.

And I was there, ladies and gents, right in the thick of things, so I'm in a good position to offer my version of what took place, who was involved, etc. I couldn't be everywhere at once so those scenes and exchanges I didn't personally witness, I've reconstructed. Certain details have been added (or omitted) for the purposes of clarity.

That said, in my opinion this is the only accurate account of the circumstances leading up to the "bombing" of the Leiber Building currently available. After all, the official story is that some kind of radical terrorist group was responsible for the carnage. Well, I suppose they had to say something...

The reality, as you're about to discover, is far more fantastic and shocking than anyone has been willing to acknowledge. And since I am a living witness, a survivor, as it were, I suppose it's up to me to set the record straight.

Evgeny Davidovitch Nightstalk

I

"We have a great deal to do," he said sharply, "even before we leave this house. It's pretty dark—and there's a Thing in the garden."

Aleister Crowley, *Moonchild* (Samuel Weiser, Inc.; 1992) [2]

It was a few minutes before midnight. The witching hour.

Late for some, still early for others. Those who shun daylight and its bright attractions, venturing out only after the sun goes down.

People like me.

"Shades", "nighthawks"…call us what you want. Nocturnal souls, temperamentally unsuited for the humdrum, nine-to-five existence of the "Gray" world. Some individuals are just wired up differently, tuned to other frequencies. You'll find us in all walks of life: convenience store clerks, cab drivers, E.R. nurses, security guards. Hell, I heard even the President is a closet Shade. Or maybe it's his guilty conscience keeping him awake.

Creatures of the night, every one of us. Our senses and reflexes heightened, eyes adapted to the dark. Because once dusk descends, you need all the advantages you can get. The smart ones go where the shadows are deepest. They know…

There are those who prefer to hunt by night.

Alone or in packs, alert for any movement, attacking without warning, killing without conscience. Predators, born and bred…

The three cars drew scant notice. They were, apparently, dark in colour, blue or maybe green, it was hard to tell because of the street lights. The way they wash everything out. Expensive, possibly foreign. License plates? You must be joking. Scores of witnesses about but no one paying attention to street traffic; they had other things on their minds. Thus the

---

[2] Most quotes courtesy Cassandra Zinnea

convoy of cars motoring past left nary a ripple in its wake, barely registering at all.

The lead vehicle slowed, signaling a right turn into St. Andrew's Park. The second and third cars followed close behind. Sightseers or visiting businessmen, out for a scenic cruise around Erie after a night on the town. But a few hundred meters inside the park the cars turned again, away from the water, into a tangle of lanes that led to the picnic area, tennis courts and three separate parking lots. In the daytime, people came here to jog, eat their lunches or toss a football around. At night it's a different story, the trees and hedges providing cover for drug deals, sexual assaults, cruising...anything your heart desires. Desperation the only prerequisite.

The cars' headlights pointed the way, the procession moving at a steady, unhurried pace. Finally the first car's brake lights flashed, the other two slowing immediately and pulling in behind it.

Five or six men got out. They approached the middle vehicle, surrounding it and smoothly extracting one of its occupants, closing ranks around him.

No indication of fear or resistance on his part. He seemed to be moving of his own volition, walking among them without displaying any outward signs of anxiety. No one saying anything. Very professional, this crew, all business.

They escorted him to the nearest bench. At one time the benches were made of wood, repainted every spring. But then the fuckin' skateboarders showed up and basically smashed them to splinters. Doing their stupid tricks and stunts. Now the benches are metal, practically indestructible and uncomfortable as hell.

They chained him down, binding his feet first, cinching them good and tight. Then they secured his wrists, shackling them to the steel support behind him. One of the men sauntered over, opened a trunk lid and returned with what looked like a gas can.

It *was* a gas can.

He proceeded to empty it over the chained man, drenching him.

Now someone else emerged from one of the vehicles. Tall and bald. Pale, thin face, Max Schreck without the teeth and stuck-on ears. Wearing a long, flowing cape, believe it or not. Very commanding presence. Towering over the captive man, throwing his arms in the air and reciting something that sounded like a record being played backward.

The guy on the bench was shaking his head, groaning, the gasoline burning his eyes. He spat on the ground, regarding the bald guy blearily, listening to his weird chatter. He had to know what was going on, what

6

was about to happen. But did he try to talk his way out of it, make deals, offer to divulge sensitive information? At least yell for help?

Nope. I don't see him doing that.

But was he brave...or resigned?

With a final flourish, the caped figure stepped back and nodded to his accomplices.

They never hesitated. They had a job to do and they did it.

They set him on fire.

It was a terrible thing to behold but none of them seemed the slightest bit fazed by what they were witnessing. The sight of flesh melting and unraveling in thin strips like tissue paper. The smell of burning hair, charred meat and viscera.

And, of course, the *screams*...

It wasn't long before the cops started receiving calls about strange goings on in St. Andrew's Park. A unit was dispatched to check out reports of a suspicious fire and, at the same time, show the colours to any freaks in the vicinity. The patrol car made its way through the park. At one point the two policemen noticed people running, cutting across the grass boulevards and crashing through the low brush and hedges. The cops pulled over and followed on foot, pushing through a ring of gawking bystanders, all too aware that they were outnumbered and a long way from home.

One look at the feature attraction and the boys in blue were on the horn, yelling for backup. Within minutes, the place was swarming with five-o.

The scorched grass was steaming, the body still smoking, most horribly from the eye sockets and gaping mouth. One cop loudly inquired if anyone had brought marshmallows. A rookie spewed triple-glazed doughnuts onto the grass in front of him. The senior officer present tried to maintain order, keep everyone back, doing his best to preserve the integrity of the crime scene until the investigating detectives arrived. Wojeck and Faro were on call, the assholes. One car left to resume its patrol. They were short-handed again and couldn't spare the men. Cutbacks were a bitch.

To kill time, the cops took turns laying bets, most tending to the view that this was a gangland thing. A settling of scores. Someone mentioned the Colombians, they were big on sending messages. Or the Asians— maybe some kinda weird *tong* shit?

On one point everyone was unanimous: *whoever* was behind this and whatever their motivations, it sure was one lousy fucking way to die.

"Listen to this, Nightstalk," Cassandra Zinnea said, "and tell me what you think."

I was seated opposite her, on my (neater) side of our shared desk. Which was really just a big, oak table that took up most of the center of the room. It had once resided in a school classroom and sported hand-carved hearts and daggers, fading graffiti along the lines of *Leticia V. gives good head* and *Fuck all teechers.*

I was unsticking the keys of my ancient Underwood typewriter for the umpteenth time in the past hour. Struggling to catch up on paperwork, my brain going too fast for my fingers. We were *years* behind and my partner, while an otherwise excellent operative and top-flight investigator, couldn't be bothered with mundane tasks like typing progress reports and filling out expense forms. So that was left up to me. And let me add, for the record, that liquid paper is the greatest invention since consensual sex.

Not to belabor the point or anything, but it was *her* fault I was reduced to using the manual monster in the first place. Her body's crazy electrical field wreaked havoc on computers, fax machines, copiers, etc., relegating us to the Stone Age, technologically speaking.

She read from the book she was holding:

> "No one kneads us again out of earth and clay,
> no one incants our dust.
> No one.
>
> Blessed art thou, No One.
> In thy sight would
> we bloom.
> In thy
> spite.
>
> A nothing
> we were, are now, and ever
> shall be, blooming:
> the Nothing-, the
> No-One's-Rose..." [3]

---

[3] From *Paul Celan: Poet, Survivor, Jew* (Translation by John Felstiner)

She looked up. "There's more but...I wanted you to hear that part."

"Cripes," I muttered, plucking apart two more keys with black-tipped fingers, "and I thought *I* was cynical. That guy takes the cake."

"Cynical...*hmmm*."

"It's pretty bloody bleak, you have to admit."

"It's called 'Psalm' and it's written by Paul Celan. Brilliant, amazing poet. His family died in a concentration camp but somehow he survived."

"Is it from our collection?" I indicated the bookshelves lining the wall to my left. They went all the way to the ceiling and were crammed with hundreds of mystical, occult, and metaphysical tomes covering everything from the arcane to the ridiculous. I'm talking about mouldering books of spells, philtres and potions dating back millennia vying for space with *Bullfinch's Mythology* and Frazer's *Golden Bough*. Graves' *White Goddess*. Colin Wilson's *The Occult*. A copy of *The Protocols of the Elders of Zion* (excellent bathroom reading). At least four unauthorized biographies of Michael Jackson. Every single Charles Berlitz book. I kid you not.

Instead of answering, she fixed her attention on the telephone. "Excuse me," she said, a beat or two before it started ringing. She grinned, knowing how much I hated that particular parlour trick.

"*After Hours Investigations*: 'Solving mysteries while the competition sleeps—' *What?* Could you repeat that? Yes, that's what I thought you said. Well, now...." She leaned back in her chair. "Let's be clear on this. Exactly how *big* is it? Because I have to tell you, sport, with me size *definitely* counts. I've had experiences with some seriously well-hung—"

I reached over and jammed my thumb down on the button. "I wish you wouldn't do that. It only encourages the perverts." It was a variation of a rebuke I'd delivered on at least a dozen prior occasions. "If the Old Man would spring for it, we could get call display and then I'd find out who these creeps are, drive over and lay a serious hurtin' on 'em."

She was more forgiving. "It livens things up around here. And if I can give some poor loser a thrill, I say why not? Besides, if *you'd* answer once in awhile--"

"Ah *ah*." I waggled an ink-stained finger at her. "Let's not go there. We have a clear division of responsibilities in this organization. Not only that," playing the martyr card, "I have to do all the grunt work around here so answering the phone is the *least* you can do."

"Gee," she said, arching one meticulously plucked eyebrow, "I seem to recall an occasion or two when I've done a good deal *more* than my fair share. Like the time I saved your butt from a vicious, man-eating *striga* in that fleabag hotel in Phoenix. The one you were just about to...you know. You remember *that* particular incident, don't you?" [4]

I winced. It hadn't been one of my finer hours and she knew it. "I think people like it better when a woman answers. It's more, uh, reassuring."

"Bull."

"The Old Man said so?" I ventured hopelessly.

She sniggered.

I suppose I could have pulled rank since I had seniority and was, ergo, her superior. In reality, that amounted to a small hill of rotting lima beans. When it came to sheer brain power, natural talent, education, social standing and just about every other important criterion you care to name, Cassandra Zinnea left me eating her dust.

She had a sharp mind, the moves and agility of a champion athlete and the face of a super model. I told her once she was a cross between Carolyn Jones (the original "Morticia Addams") and Uma Thurman. Then I made the mistake of asking what actor or character *I* brought to mind and she hardly gave it any thought before replying: "I'd have to say Bob Hoskins. Yeah. A short, mean, hairy, hard-headed cannonball, that's you. Ferociously loyal and not nearly as dumb as he lets on. The best friend and asskickingest sidekick a girl could ask for."

I took it as a compliment so I wouldn't have to kill her.

The phone buzzed. I pointedly kept typing and picking apart keys. Finally she gave in and answered, though I could feel the heat of her disapproving gaze on my bald spot.

"Yes, sir?" The call originated from the inner office, about twenty feet and a locked door away. Cassandra scribbled on a pad, jotting furiously as she tried to keep up. "Right. Yes, sir, will do. And we have nothing more at this point? Uh huh. So is this an official case then? I mean, is there an actual client or--yes, I understand. Very good, sir." Her hand shook as she hung up. Talking to the Old Man did that to you.

"What did he say?" My heart had speeded up and every detail in the room seemed more vivid.

"The usual: find out what we can and do what's necessary."

---

[4] "The Phantom in Room 306" (*The Casebooks of Zinnea & Nightstalk, Vol. II*). Observant readers will note how often in the course of our adventures I fall prey to succubus-like creatures. *See*: "The Mystery of Crooked Lake" (The *Casebooks of Zinnea & Nightstalk, Vol. I*), "The Lady and the Stake" (*Casebooks, Vol. I*); "Dirty Deeds Done Dirt Cheap" (*Casebooks, Vol. II*), "Bloody Harvest" (*Casebooks, Vol. II*); "The Girl With the 1-900 Eyes" (*Casebooks, Vol. III*); etc.

"So…what exactly are we dealing with?"

"Something bad." She read off the notes she had ticked down: *midnight…St. Andrew's Park…man burned…no suspects at this time…*

I didn't like the sound of it and said so. Then: "I wonder how he heard." I checked my watch. "It's not even twelve-thirty. Who's his source? How did he know? Does he have a police scanner? Maybe he uses a fucking Ouija board--"

"Who knows? He has his ways, that's why he's the Old Man. We'd better get going." She marked her place in the Celan book and stood, stretching sinuously. It was a breath-taking sight. "To St. Andrew's Park, Jeeves." I unhooked my jacket from the back of my chair. "Shouldn't be too hard to find. And if all else fails, we'll just let that trusty nose of yours show us the way…"

Strange, but true: I possess a special faculty that enables me to locate crime scenes almost by innate instinct. [5] I just drive around and gradually feel myself drawn to a certain area, then a certain street, an otherwise nondescript house in the middle of a seemingly ordinary block…

Within fifteen minutes I was signaling to turn into the park, passing a row of short, neo-Soviet apartment blocks on the left. "Lego architecture," my partner sniffed, with evident disdain.

After that, it was easy. We actually followed the coroner's meat wagon right to the spot. There were a number of cops milling about, looking very serious and official. You could see they were spooked.

They had affixed yellow crime scene tape to everything in sight and considerately draped a plastic tarp over the crispy critter on the bench. There were a good number of bystanders and rubber-neckers, as well as a TV news crew that were about to deliver their first "Live" report from the scene. *Vultures.*

It didn't take long to get ourselves up to speed, mainly by tapping the news hounds. They were giddy, thrilled at scooping their rival station, high-fiving one another after finishing their brief segment.

The victim was as yet unidentified and details were still sketchy but it was almost certain that he had been alive and conscious when set ablaze. Heaving forward in those chains, screaming until the blood and tissue boiled in his throat—

I was glad the breeze was blowing the other way.

---

[5] As highlighted in "The Affair of the Scotsman's Kilt", "Who Framed Roger Radek?" (*The Casebooks of Zinnea & Nightstalk, Vol. I*); "The Curse of the Danish", "Marlowe's Last Case" (*Casebooks, Vol. II*); etc.

Killing someone by setting them on fire. What in the name of whatever god currently in vogue had this man done to deserve such treatment? The extreme nature of the act suggested a grudge, an old score settled. Then again, sometimes druggies did crazy things to each other for no reason at all. But the Old Man wouldn't interest himself in something like that. As usual, it was up to us to fill in the blanks.

First things first: who was the dead guy and what was his story (and they always had one)? If we were lucky there might even be eyewitnesses, although from past experience I knew our chances on that front weren't great. For most people the distinction between a cop and a private dick is an extremely fine one. What it comes down to is *they don't want to get involved.*

Cassandra was chatting up a uniformed rookie with vomit stains on his pant cuffs. She rewarded him for one particularly interesting tidbit with her phone number. From the expression on the kid's face you'd have thought he'd just won a lottery. And, in a way, I guess he had.

I gritted my teeth and tried to find something else to look at. Unfortunately, the first two things my eyes settled on were the distinctive figures of Detectives Dennis Wojeck and Stanley Faro, closing in on me like a couple of famished wolves.

"Well, well, if it ain't Dr. Watson," Faro sneered. He was as big and ugly as a Yeti with mange. About as smart too. "I was just telling my partner here how *weird* you Shades get after awhile. Must be from never seeing the sun." He eyed me up and down. "You're a fuckin' waste, Nightstalk, you know that? Always playin' second banana to her. Easy to see which of you is the brains of the operation." It was a pitiful crack, what passed for wit down at the cop shop. Faro had allegedly been demoted to the graveyard shift as punishment for hassling an attractive hooker (i.e. undercover policewoman) for a free blowjob. You could tell he'd never catch on to the unique rhythms of the night.

"I thought I told you to mind your own business, shit for brains." Wojeck had an old grudge to settle with me and wasn't one to forgive and forget. Fine with me. As long as they kept the peace and didn't make a nuisance of themselves, I promised myself I wouldn't grab the two of them and wring their necks like a couple of corn-fed chickens.

I could see they were getting ready to run me off. Before it got to that point Cassandra arrived, radiating positive vibes and clouds of enticing pheromones. "*Hel-lo*, boys," she purred. "Funny how our paths keep crossing, isn't it?"

Wojeck scowled. "Goddamnit, woman, tell the Old Man to stay outta this. Let us ordinary, hard-working cops handle it and you bunch fuck off. Make sure you pass that along."

"Roger, wilco, A-okay," Cassandra affirmed, saluting briskly. "Now be a good boy and tell me: who was the guest of honour at tonight's barbeque? Seems like a lot of trouble to go through to kill somebody. Why not just shoot the guy? Come on, Dennis," she pouted, practically fluttering her eyelashes at the ugly mug. "You can tell me..."

Wojeck looked like he was about to say something. He opened his mouth but Faro jabbed him with an admonitory elbow. Wojeck glared at Cassandra. "Don't think you can fuck with me. You screw up this investigation, either one of you, and I'll nail you up like Jesus at Easter."

She rolled her eyes. "Will you at least tell us--"

"I'm telling you, it's *nothing*. Forget about it." Wojeck yawned, clearly bored with life in general. "Likely just another gangbang thing. This guy'll turn out to be some shitbag dealer who got in too deep and got taught a very important lesson."

"Which was?" This I had to hear.

Either my eyes were deceiving me or he actually smiled. "Don't play with matches."

Faro guffawed. "Good one, Den. Right below the fuckin' waterline. "

"Thanks for your help," Cassandra called as they trudged off, slapping each other on the back, too busy or too tired to get into it with us.

"So what do you think? Was he right about this being gang-related?"

At first I thought she was going to play it inscrutable and not answer. "I'd say there was a definite purpose to this. Burning him, the suffering it would inflict..." She sounded distant, dreamy. "It's close to my period so I feel extra sensitive tonight. Can you feel it, the energy?" Closing her eyes. "What happened here? Who was this guy to leave a signature like that?"

"Cass?"

She rubbed her forehead. "This place is still hot...wow, the residuals are just...the air is practically *buzzing*."

I didn't hear any buzzing. Then again my teeth were chattering so loud it was hard to hear anything. It was cold and getting colder. Not good for my arthritis. My poor hands were aching and I'd forgotten my calfskin gloves in the car. Meanwhile, the tarp had blown or slipped off the body. Someone in the thinning crowd moaned. It wasn't a pretty sight.

She turned to me. "Can you get some readings? I'm curious to see what the equipment says."

The problem was I couldn't get close enough to take accurate measurements. Which meant that eight grand worth of paranormal gear in my trunk was, for all intents and purposes, useless. I did my best, going to work with the tri-field meter, testing for electrical and magnetic activity in the area. I paced about the perimeter—there were definite "hot" spots, unexplained spikes worthy of further investigation. I started jotting down numbers, noting the location of my findings on a rough sketch I made of the crime scene.

"Take a look. You're right about one thing: mucho E-M energy was released here tonight." I showed her what I had. The unit was about the size and shape of a cell phone. She read it over my shoulder.

"Well, well..." She paused, absorbing the figures. She knew the numbers and math better than I did but didn't seem inclined to share her impressions.

"We should get going," I urged. Faro was glaring in our direction. "I don't think there's much more to learn here."

She didn't answer right away. "Sorry...I was kind of drifting a bit." A wan smile. "Wow, I feel just *zapped*. Whatever caused this..." She thrust her hands into her coat pockets. "*Brrr*. First, let's take a few discreet pictures, have a word with some of these people. Find out if anyone saw anything."

"I wouldn't bet on it." I trailed after her. "Then what?"

"I'll make some calls. I think it's time to consult an expert."

I winced, knowing what that probably meant. "So which crackpot do you intend wasting our time and money on this time? Keeping in mind the Old Man has been paying closer attention to our expenses of late and asking some pointed questions." Not that my protests would make the slightest impression. It didn't matter that I was a *guy*, a full-fledged alpha male with the excess body hair to prove it. In the end, she usually got her way.

"I want to talk to Eva Jauch."

"You mean *Madame* Eva, don't you? Why not Sanjay, that asshole astrologer guy or Perry, the sheep entrails dude? At least they're mildly amusing."

She shook her head stubbornly. "Eva *knows* things."

"Eva is nothing but a two-bit, crazy old dope fiend, a fraud in every sense of the word. You've seen how she operates."

She chuckled. "You're just mad because she blabbed about how madly in love with me you are." I blushed from head to toe. "It's okay, Nightstalk, you big palooka," she cooed. "I love you too."

The number of spectators had dwindled, the cold taking its toll on even the hardiest ghouls. "This is a waste of time and you know it. Nobody'll know anything, nobody saw anything--"

"Use a little charm and persuasion," she suggested. Then she glanced at me. "On second thought," she amended, "maybe you'd better let *me* do the talking..."

I'd had my share of run-ins with Eva Jauch and wasn't anxious to repeat the experience. Ours wasn't what you'd call a warm and fuzzy relationship. We maintained a mutual dislike that was based, in part, on the fact that we hated each other's guts.

I considered her nothing more than a crafty charlatan who preyed on the gullible and stupid. She operated out of a tiny storefront in a neighborhood that was in the process of being "reclaimed". The yuppies hadn't chased the junkies and whores out yet but it was only a matter of time. Yuppies are like the creature in "The Thing": once they start multiplying, you're fucked.

We got there just after ten the following evening. The lights were on, her sandwich board propped out front. "*Readings and Consultations: By Appointment Only.*"

I didn't have much truck with mediums and psychics and "Madame" Eva was one of the reasons why. She claimed all sorts of extrasensory powers but I suspected her "gift" had more to do with reading a person's body language, a relatively commonplace talent. She'd tell you a bunch of general stuff and based on how you reacted (she could detect the subtlest twitch), she'd either pursue a point or back off and try something else.

"All that crap she spouts about being able to read people's auras--"

"She *can*," my partner insisted.

"Yeah, right. Supposedly she sees different colours and shit? So, what, if your aura's purple you need to get laid and if it's orange you should eat more fiber..."

Needless to say, Cassandra turned a deaf ear to my complaints. She put an inordinate amount of faith in Eva. And I have to admit that on at least one occasion, during our search for the Riverdale Stalker, she did provide a valuable clue that aided in the apprehension of the homicidal, ax-murdering DJ, Ronnie Cummins. [6]

---

[6] An account I dubbed "Killing Them Softly With His Song" (*The Casebooks of Zinnea & Nightstalk, Vol. III*)

Eva was ushering out a shell-shocked client--apparently the news from beyond wasn't always good--when we showed up.

As soon as you walked in, you found yourself in a small sitting room. It contained a couple of over-stuffed armchairs, a hideously ugly floor lamp, a round table and four fold-up metal chairs.

Eva ignored me but greeted my partner warmly. "Cassandra, my dear, let me look at you. You're simply *gorgeous*. Helen of Troy only *wished* she had your cheekbones." She finally grudgingly acknowledged my presence. "So...she brought you. Mr. Personality." Her eyes narrowed as she pretended to access her special faculties or whatever. "Still in love with her, I see, and not doing anything about it. How pathetic." I fumed, enduring the humiliation while at the same time visualizing wrapping my fingers around her wattled throat and *squeezing*. "What are you waiting for, lover boy? You think she respects a man who won't come and *take* her? That's not the way of her kind."

"That's enough, Eva," Cassandra chided her. "Nightstalk promised he'd be nice."

"You're not man enough for her," Eva concluded, and I fought the urge to introduce her to the fucking spirits, up close and personal.

Because we all knew it was true. Every word of it.

"Madame Eva," Cassandra, trying to keep things from turning ugly, "this is a professional visit. Last night, just after midnight, something happened--"

"Don't you think I know that?" Eva swayed, suddenly faint, and Cassandra helped her over to one of the armchairs. It vented a cloud of dust and cat hair as she settled into it. "I felt it about midnight, as you say," she whispered hoarsely, "like a cold, sharp knife going right through my heart. There was a shock wave, ripples in the ether like—like--"

"A disturbance in the Force?" I suggested innocently.

Cassandra frowned but Eva pretended not to have heard.

Despite my uncouth behavior, Eva agreed to assist our investigation. Cassandra said she didn't trust cards, finding them too "amorphous and inexact" (I nearly laughed out loud). Instead she gave Eva a small baggie of soil we'd collected from the park.

Within moments of thrusting her chubby fingers into the dirt, a spasm went through Eva's body and she began to moan and sway from side to side.

"...smoke...terrible stench...*ugh*...there's only one thing that smells like that...burnt offerings for Moloch...it begins...an evil tide, washing over us...*no one will escape*..."

"Is there a message?" Cassandra asked, but the spirits weren't interested in a dialogue, preferring the stream of consciousness approach.

"...bright days will pass...soon comes the cold and dark...streets running with blood...they're coming...*they're coming*..."

Pretty standard stuff, a verbal salad of cryptic utterances and unconnected phrases that were supposed to pass for visions or prophesies. It was all I could do to keep from rolling my eyes.

"...so much suffering and death...word from the Black Tower...*time to cull the herd*...hunger...fury...fiends with ancient faces...old...old beyond time..."

And so on.

I probably should have been taking notes but, frankly, couldn't be bothered. As far as I was concerned, we might as well have put our questions to one of those magic eight balls.

Eva trailed off and showed signs of rejoining us in the non-spiritual realm. Once back, she regarded us vacantly, as if trying to remember who we were and what we were doing in her tacky sitting room. *Oh, brother.* "I felt a strong connection tonight." She appeared exhausted by her exertions, serving as a living conduit between two separate dimensions. "Everything is in flux, there's much turmoil and confusion over there."

"Is that why nothing you told us made a lick of sense?" I asked.

She didn't like that. "You are a stupid man with a closed, ugly mind. But *she* understands," indicating Cassandra, "so it doesn't matter what you think."

"Tell us about it, Eva," Cassandra urged.

Eva shook her head. She dragged the hassock over with one foot so she could prop up her thick, hairy legs. Something had been at the hassock, either a cat or a playful werewolf. "I can only describe bits and pieces. Impressions. I get a sense of great upheaval. We're at a pivotal time right now, there are changes coming, something there, just over the horizon."

"Can you be a *wee* bit more specific?" I requested. "'Something over the horizon. Changes coming.' That seems kind of...*vague*. Is it just me or is that vague?"

"Nightstalk..." Cassandra warned.

"I mean, *come on.*" My patience evaporated like desert rain. "You people are all the same. 'You'll find the body near water.' 'The child will be found by a man with a limp'." I flung up my hands in exasperation. "We came here looking for some hard evidence, something we can use. Instead we get...fuckin' mumbo-jumbo."

I could feel my partner's eyes on me. If her glare got any hotter, I'd end up with a sunburn.

Eva, however, refused to be goaded. She hauled herself to her feet and tottered toward a beaded curtain that led to her living quarters. "You must be careful, my dear. Beware the counsel of fools like this one. I sense great danger. Please, I'm very tired. I can tell you nothing more tonight. If you prefer to pay with a credit card, let me know. I keep the slips in the back." The curtain parted with a dry rattle and she disappeared from view. Soon afterward, I could smell pot smoke.

"Hey, could I get a receipt for that?" I called after her. No answer. I tugged a couple of twenties out of my thin wallet and left them on the table. "I guess she's too busy recharging her batteries."

Cassandra didn't find my smart-ass attitude funny at all. She said it was one of my least attractive qualities. Far worse than the premature balding thing.

After leaving Eva's, we drove around, stopping whenever we spotted anybody we knew and who owed us for past favours. We spent several hours buttonholing various weirdos and fuckups, learning little of value. It put me in a foul mood, itching to make like Picasso on someone's face.

Sadly, no opportunity presented itself. Instead it was back to the office in the wee hours to type up my nightly progress report, a task which, if I was lucky, I'd be able to complete by sunrise.

Bellied up to my ancient, round-keyed Underwood. I've tried other manual typewriters but they can't stand up to the pounding. I have what you might call a heavy touch.

Setting things down on paper helped put my thoughts in some semblance of order. The Old Man liked reports to be clear and concise. I had specific instructions to avoid unnecessary detail and speculation. That I saved for the *Casebooks*.

As I worked away, my partner was busy raiding our bookshelves, creating an architecturally unsound pile of books on her side of the desk. She was a speed-reader with almost perfect recall and could devour a book in the time it took most people to use the john.

Yet as far as I knew, my partner had never even *peeked* inside one of my *Casebooks*. I tried to convince myself it didn't bug me. My style was likely too hard-boiled for her tastes. She preferred "literary" authors. The more depressing the better. Celan the latest in a long line.

I cobbled together a summary of our consultation with Eva, playing up the invaluable insights we had gained, making a mountain out of an anthill. Hey, I wanted that forty bucks back, receipt or no receipt.

I stuck the carbon copy of the report in a file I'd begun, as yet unnamed. The original I slipped under the Old Man's door.

It was after five a.m. and I was winding down. "Any idea where this is leading? I've got my own theory," I offered cagily, "but I'm probably way off base. So if there's something you want to tell me--"

She was stuffing books into her bag. I noticed a few with Latin titles. "It's late, Nightstalk, nearly closing time. Let's call it quits. Go grab some breakfast and give your brain a rest. I'll see you back here tonight and we'll find out what the Old Man's turned up in the meantime."

"Do I take it we're working overtime on this one?" Usually we were on from Tuesday to Saturday but when something heavy came up, that schedule tended to go out the window.

"I think you can make that assumption," she confirmed. "Knowing our employer, he'll want this wrapped up as soon as possible." She hoisted her bag.

"You *know* something, don't you?" I accused her. "You've got a hunch but you're holding out on me."

"Stop being so paranoid." She blew me a kiss from the door. "Ta ta, Nightstalk. Don't stay up too late." She left, taking all the life in the room with her.

It was getting light outside. I watched from the window as she walked up the street, playing my accustomed role of ineffectual voyeur. She held her head high and her step was lively and confident. She looked like she was about to break out into a song and dance routine. I lowered the blinds on the dirty windows; the ones facing south we'd papered over with three layers of aluminum foil.

I slipped a plastic sheath over the Underwood. Thought I heard it groan in relief.

I pulled on my coat, making sure I had my gloves. Turned off the lights on the way out.

Time to head home to the bachelor apartment/crypt where I spent the daylight hours. There was no air conditioning, no swimming pool, but it *did* come equipped with about a hundred cable channels. Any distraction was welcome, as long as it kept me from brooding about who Cassandra was with and what she was doing. That sort of thing could drive a guy around the bend.

It was hard being in love with a woman like Cassandra Zinnea. She was brilliant and bedevilled, both saint and sinner. The finest human being I had the pleasure of knowing and, also, the most haunted. She was her own worst enemy and try as I might to protect her, against such a clever and willful adversary my chances were, I knew, somewhere between slim and none.

As usual, I beat Cassandra to the office. Punctuality was *not* among her many virtues. It was 8:30 p.m. on the dot when I slid my key into the lock and pushed open the door.

After Hours Investigations
"While the competition sleeps..."

The Old Man was never able to hire a receptionist who lasted more than a week. The kind of clients our outfit attracted, the stuff we had to deal with relating to the otherworldly, uncanny or just plain *wacky*...well, it tended to have a negative effect on impressionable minds.

When we weren't around, an ancient (i.e. *pre*-digital) Duophone answering machine took our messages. I checked as soon as I got in, rewinding the tape to the beginning and letting it play. Three of the callers were heavy breathers, hoping to catch Cassandra in. One guy wanted us to fly to Iraq with him and recover the last remaining copy of the *Necronomicon* before agents of the Dark Lord Asmodeus beat him to it and--

Ho hum.

We got a lot of calls like that.

One time we even took up the chase although, admittedly, that very peculiar affair ended in tragedy all around. [7]

A few months previously the Old Man had left a memo saying he wanted to advertise us as "paranormal investigators" but Cassandra and I talked him out of it. We had a hard enough time getting respect from other private dicks as it was. We put up with a lot of "Mulder and Scully" crap and that shit wore thin *real* fast.

Dealing with clients was bad enough. No wonder the receptionists bailed. Some of the people who walked through our door were real lu-lu's. "Renfields", Cassandra called them, after the fly-eating lunatic in *Dracula*. In some instances it was all too appropriate.

---

[7] "The Bad Book" (*The Casebooks of Zinnea & Nightstalk, Volume I*)

During a free moment, I'd done a quick count and determined that in the two years we'd worked together, Cass and I had handled over 90 cases. I won't say our success rate was perfect but we won a helluva lot more than we lost. Having a genius for a partner helped, but it was more than that. We had chemistry. Together, we were a *machine*. Brain and brawn. Beauty and the beast.

Read the *Casebooks*, gentle reader, it's all there. The many great adventures of Cassandra Zinnea and her steadfast companion-in-arms Evgeny Davidovitch Nightstalk. Our numerous crazy high jinks and miraculous escapes...that helped make the petty, tedious, day-to-day stuff easier to bear. *Most* of the time.

It was hard getting a handle on this latest deal. The Old Man thought it was important and Cassandra was definitely acting keyed up. But maybe it really *was* nothing, a botched drug deal or what have you. Of no concern to us, just the boss waving his dick around, Cassandra and me running hither and yon like a couple of headless chickens, trying to solve a case that existed only in his convoluted mind.

Cassandra came floating in twenty minutes later and right away I noticed the fresh welt on her throat, visible despite the high collar of the turtleneck she had taken great care selecting. She hastily adjusted the collar but the damage was done.

My partner had some rather, ah, odd proclivities for someone so beautiful and intelligent. She liked to walk on the wild side, as the saying goes. When that hag Eva snipped that I wasn't man enough for Cassandra, what she meant was that I lacked the strength and cruelty necessary to satisfy her bent desires. As I discovered early in our relationship, while investigating *The House on High Street*,[8] Cassandra's tastes ran to the extreme, involving practices that to certain prudish-minded people might seem...well, it would be indiscreet if I went into more detail than I already have.

Man enough? Let's see: I was short, balding on top, hairy as a binobo ape everywhere else and boring to boot. I had an irritable bowel and the beginnings of arthritis in my hands and lower back. I plodded along cheerlessly through life, no close friends or meaningful relationships and would have been lonely except that for the most part I didn't much *like* people. Cassandra made great leaps of logic (I connected the dots). She had brainstorms (I chased red herrings). She was sexy and exciting and

---

[8] Included in *The Casebooks of Zinnea & Nightstalk (Volume I)*

Cassandra. I was me. You didn't need second sight to know it would never work out.

I made coffee the way we both liked it, strong enough to raise the dead. She took a tentative sip of the infernal brew. "Oooo, that's *perfect*, Nightstalk." Coming over with her cup, leaning down to give me a hug, careful not to spill. She had managed to squeeze in a shower and smelled good, no spunky after aroma. I got a close up look at the hickey. There was another two inches below it. I wondered where the trail led.

"Good grief, woman," I burst out, "who are you dating, Bela Lugosi?"

She pulled away and walked back to her side of the desk. Once seated, she didn't touch her coffee and seemed ill at ease. Then she looked directly at me. "Do you forgive me?" Plaintively. "Tell me you do. Better yet," she corrected herself, "tell me you love me. That no matter what, I can always count on the knowledge that you'll never be ashamed of me. That you won't accuse and punish me if I...fall off the high wire every once in awhile. Okay? Nightstalk?"

I cleared my throat. "The Old Man dug up some stuff for us to look over. I highlighted a few things I thought we should—"

"*Say* it, Nightstalk." I avoided her eyes, they were scary with need. "Absolve me. Make me feel *clean.*"

"—some items of interest--"

She was trying to work magic with those eyes, which had changed colour again, to a shade close to amber. "*Say* it."

"—no identification so far of our John Doe in the park. According to the Old Man's sources, the cops don't know much about him except that he was white, male and in his early to mid-thirties--"

"*Nightstalk...*"

I closed myself off as best as I could, shoring up my mental defenses, raising every shield I had. "There's also an analysis of the readings and soil samples we took at the scene." My voice sounded squeaky. "They confirm a massive expenditure of EM energy. We've definitely tweaked the Old Man's interest with this one. He says we're to drop everything else and refuse any new cases." She was giving me the evil eye. I hoped it wasn't the real thing, they could be nasty. I tuned out her displeasure and disappointment, hurting with intent. "So why is it," I continued, "that when Mr. X becomes Johnny the Human Torch there's such a big, honkin' energy burst? This guy went off like a fuckin' supernova--"

"It tells us he wasn't just some low-life druggie. Which means everything that happened was premeditated and carefully choreographed. There's an intention behind this, a design waiting to be revealed." She simply couldn't resist the opportunity to talk about the case. "It's even plausible that it's part of a ritual or magickal working. Don't forget, this all took place just after midnight on May Eve, Beltane, a very significant date on the occult calendar." She glanced over and saw the look on my face. "Something wrong?"

"Goddamnit, Cassandra, you've been sitting on this all along," I complained. "This Beltane stuff--"

"It's just something that occurred to me," she protested. "I was planning on telling you."

I shook my head. "So toasting our guy releases a humungous amount of energy...so what? What does that get them?"

"It's possible someone was seeking to gain power by channeling or absorbing it in some way."

My heart speeded up. "But who would need that sort of energy?"

She nodded, trying (I thought) not to look smug. "Who indeed?"

Then it hit me. "Oh, shit. *Shit.*" I closed my eyes. "This is black arts crap, isn't it? *Fuck.* I should've known."

"Well done, my dear Watson," she congratulated me.

"*Quit that.* It's like you're patronizing me." I was still seething about the love tattoos. "I *hate* occult shit. Those people are fuckin' psychos."

"I'm sorry, Evvie," she said, sounding very timid and contrite. "And I *don't* patronize you. I want you to know that I respect you and value your insights and opinions." She radiated peaceful, calming vibes but they just bounced off me. "The police think this killing was underworld related. What nonsense. Not with those readings."

I couldn't resist a dig. "And let's not forget what Eva told us. All that shit about disturbances in the ether. There's all the confirmation we need right there."

"Don't be such a bitch, Evgeny." She was definitely mad. She hardly ever swore.

I tried to joke it away. "I certainly don't wish to offend you by impugning the integrity of such a highly respected and unimpeachable expert on the so-called—"

"Forget it," she snapped.

I could smell ozone. "Okay, okay..." I decided I'd pushed things far enough. "I'll keep my opinions about Eva to myself from now on. Promise."

"*And?*"

I was stumped...and then realized what she was after. "Oh...and I, uh, love you."

"*What?*" She cupped a hand beside her ear. "I didn't hear you."

"Damn it, woman, I—I love you, all right? Are you satisfied? I worship the toilet seat you perch on. I worship the holy tampon you—"

"That will be sufficient."

The air was clear again and we were back on the same page. I suspected she'd used some kind of glamour or enchantment on me but, of course, could prove nothing. Then again, she hardly needed ancient spells and burnt toenail clippings to win me over.

I was hers, body and soul, and would be 'til the day I died.

Afterward, she insisted we take a drive down by the lake. She needed to get away. No way to claim mileage for it, money right out of my pocket but, never mind, off we went. I'd parked about a block from our building and as soon as we were within sight of the car I heard her go "Uh oh".

And then I saw why.

Some *idiot* had crammed his vehicle into the space right behind the Taurus, effectively wedging me in. There were other places available but he had chosen, of his own free will, to plant himself right flush against my rear bumper.

I growled.

"No, Evvie, *please...*"

Fuck that. I went behind his car, got hold of his rear bumper and lifted. It was one of those Buick Centuries, a decent-sized car, so I had to really put my back into it. My shirt ripped under my armpit but I managed to lift and drag the ass end of the Century into the street then went around and did the same to the front. When buddy got back, he was in for a big surprise...if the city hadn't hauled his car off to the impound lot in the meantime.

My partner was waiting for me in the Taurus. She knew better than to say anything, merely clucked her tongue and shook her head at such immature antics.

A long, curving road took us past the marina and the old docks. I kept going and finally pulled off and parked beneath the rusting skeleton of the 45th Street Bridge. I took the key from the ignition and was about to ask her the purpose of our pleasure cruise, when she abruptly opened her door and got out.

She walked down to the water's edge, getting toxic and likely radioactive sludge all over a nice pair of shoes. She didn't seem to notice, her eyes fixed on the dark water, her thoughts elsewhere. The bridge takes you to Parmeter Island, where you can check out the landfill, walk around the grounds of the old territorial prison or visit the mass grave of the people who died during a cholera epidemic right after WW II. Too many to count apparently. The place is creepy, over-run with ghosts and bogeys. Cass and I hated it when a case took us out to the island. It was sort of like our version of "Chinatown".[9]

I spit into the dark. A superstition of mine. "Do you want to talk about it? Bare your soul and all that crap." I waited. "You seem, I dunno, kind of blue or something."

"Not now," she answered, "maybe later."

"Is it something I said?"

"Nightstalk...." She sounded tired.

I kept plugging. "Sometimes when you talk about stuff it doesn't seem like such a big deal."

"It's nothing. *Really*. I just needed to get out of the office."

"Should I wait in the car?"

She answered without turning around. "Suit yourself. I only need a few minutes."

Twenty minutes later she was still in the same position. I had wandered up the shore a ways, chucked some stones, counted the stars and had pretty much run out of things to do. Then I decided enough was enough and went back to roust her. I cleared my throat, letting her know I was there. "Uh, it's getting kinda late. You need more time?"

She didn't reply right away, kept looking out at the island. I could see lights, a few dots of yellow and white. Maybe the squatters' camp. The city administration was supposedly negotiating a deal with Gregory Fischer, the real estate tycoon, to redevelop the entire area--the old docks, the island—putting up luxury towers and condominiums, restoring the waterfront, sinking a couple billion dollars into a giant pipe dream. And, as always, the taxpayers would end up footing the bill.

"I can't shake this feeling." Wrapping her arms around herself. "There's something about this case that bothers me. I've never felt like this."

"It's a terrible thing, burning somebody like that. It got to me too." A rare admission.

She came toward me, leaving septic footprints behind her, standing close enough for me to smell the muck...and the alluring tang of her perfume. It was a potent combination. "I think I've wrecked my shoes."

---

[9] See: "The Unusual Suspects", "Dead on Revival" (*The Casebooks of Zinnea & Nightstalk, Volume I*); "Sorry, Wrong Caliber"; "Hell on Wheels" (*Casebooks, Vol. II*)

"No kidding."

"They're soaked through." She kicked them off. "*Ewww*, look at my feet."

"Hey, don't be walking around here like that." I scooped her up in my arms. "There might be needles and shit."

"Oh, Nightstalk," she said, her voice going all delicate and fluttery, "you are *such* a gentleman." She curled into me. I bore her easily back to the car, taking my time getting there.

"This is ridiculous. I wonder how many other partners put up with this."

But we both knew it was just hot air.

I convinced her to go home early and dropped her off at her apartment building, near the old campus. Kind of a rundown place, the neighborhood none too friendly. I waited until she was safely inside before taking off.

Picked up coffee and a cruller on the way back to the office. Tried not to think about her, how it felt holding her in my arms. It was no use. I found myself literally counting the ways I loved her, a menace on four wheels as I navigated the early morning streets.

Once my report was done (it didn't take long), I decided to update my *Casebook* notes. I took the opportunity to revisit old cases, flipping through the binders, pausing over the ones that provoked the fondest memories. By the time I finished, the sun was threatening to beat me home. Still I lingered, taking in all the personal touches that brought to mind my partner, the gorgeous and maddening Cassandra Zinnea.

There was her mug ("*A witch is a woman who knows what she wants!*"), a pack of breath mints, some hair clips, lip balm, a badly gnawed pencil. Her half of the desktop was a brilliant mess: notes and newspaper clippings and dog-eared, broken-backed books stained with yellow highlighter; takeout containers, food scraps and coffee slops...in stark contrast to the prissy order and tidiness that delineated my area. I spotted the Celan volume amid the debris, picked it up, opened it. My eyes falling on a short, blunt stanza at the top of the page 233:

> "You were my death:
> you I could hold
> while everything slipped from me."

I closed the book, suddenly two hundred and twenty pounds of prickling gooseflesh. I stuck my report under the Old Man's door and paused, listening for any sounds from within. Nothing. I pulled on my jacket, closed and locked the door behind me. No alarms necessary, my partner's protective spells and hexes took care of that.

I started down the stairs just as Maude Dreyfuss came out of her store. She'd spent most of the night doing inventory (one of the many perks of owning a small, family-run business). She was a former dominatrix now plying her trade as the hardest working purveyor of sex toys in the Greater Ilium area. Thanks to her tireless efforts, *The Tool Shed* (open 5:00 p.m. – 1:00 a.m.) was a going concern. She rented the upstairs to the Old Man cheap with the understanding that we would keep an eye on her shop which, until we moved in, had been robbed more times than Wells Fargo.

Maude's next words were music to my ears. "Hey, I think your movies might be in. We got a bunch of boxes delivered late yesterday afternoon. I haven't had a chance to go through them yet. On your way home, huh? Well, ask Tara about them tonight."

"Yeah, uh, Tara." I hesitated before saying it. "Nice girl. But…I was wondering. She's such a shy little thing. Aren't you worried about her working in, y'know, such an unusual environment? The kind of people that come in here, especially at night. She seems…uncomfortable at times."

"She's *seventeen*, Nightstalk. It's not like she's an innocent. If one of my customers wants to buy a twelve inch rubber cock with a spring-loaded chicken on the end, she can bloody well grin and bear it."

I summoned a weak smile, remembering the cheap rent. "Sure, okay. And—and obviously you know best," I finished lamely, reaching for the outside door.

"But let me know if she gives you or Cassandra any trouble. You know, service-wise."

That brought me up short. "So…Cass frequents your establishment as well?"

She looked at me slyly. "*Nightstalk*. You know as well as I do that the privacy of my clientele is my number one priority. Discretion guaranteed." She winked as she passed me, calling back: "You have a great day."

Thanks to the arrival of those movies, things were definitely looking up. At that moment, I was probably as *happy* as it's possible for me to get. Because I had something to look forward to and that didn't happen nearly often enough.

I never brought people home with me or encouraged what few acquaintances I had to drop by for visits.

It was a conscious decision I made *not* to humiliate myself.

Basically I lived in a single room apartment. A minuscule living room, alcove kitchen and closet-sized bathroom. That was it. Home sweet fucking home. I slept on a fold out couch I'd had since Christ was a youngster. Most of the time I didn't even bother opening it up. The windows, a small one in the kitchen and another in the can, were both blacked out. Tin foil and duct tape. Rubber stripping tacked around the edges of the door. When I turned out the lights I wanted it *dark*.

My TV rested on one of those blue plastic milk crates restaurants are always leaving by their back doors. A CD player and a combination DVD/ VCR console—good quality stuff, lacking only serial numbers—sat on another crate beside it. *Voila!* That was my entertainment unit.

Not much in terms of personal touches or mementos. A couple of TV trays, some ratty-looking movie posters thumbtacked to the walls: "Eraserhead", "Clockwork Orange", "The Wild Bunch". Books piled everywhere; lots of mysteries, Golden Age SF, true crime. Others I'd borrowed or pinched off my partner. She didn't begrudge me, maybe getting a kick out of a lunkhead like me slogging through Camus' *Myth of Sisyphus* or Anthony Storr's introduction to the theories of Jung. The only problem was she insisted that we talk about the books afterward, *discuss* them. Mostly I kept mum but every so often I'd open my big mouth and blow it by saying something totally stupid and irrelevant. A half-bright hick spouting off about the "contemporary resonances" one could find in *Heart of Darkness* or *Jude the Obscure*.

Christ.

One time, when we were returning from an out of town trip, I made an off the cuff comment about a particularly funky sexual act I'd come across in a memoir penned by some ex-porn queen.

"Oh, I've done that," she responded breezily. "It's not as difficult as it sounds. Having good balance is the key." It took all of my self-restraint to keep my hands on the wheel. She looked at me, twigging to the sudden awkwardness. "Hey, different strokes for different folks, Nightstalk."

Most of my off-duty hours were spent availing myself of the programming offered by the building's communal satellite dish. The package tenants received included scores of channels, everything from Toons to Euro porn. Fuck, you name it, I had it.

Even at 5:30 a.m. you were guaranteed to find *something* worth watching. An old "Star Trek" episode, a Portuguese soap opera or a classy French skin flick. And if I couldn't find anything to yank my chain, I could always turn to my personal stash. There were tall stacks of videotapes and DVD's beside the TV. I had some mainstream stuff but for the most part it was porn. Soft and hard. Something for every mood. Loosely subdivided into "Cheerleaders", "Spanking", "Oriental Girls", "French Maid", etc.

Women of all ages, shapes and sizes, each of them ready, willing and eager to please.

Oh, and I forgot to mention Tree. My house pet and/or built-in home security system. If you haven't met, introductions are in order:

Tree sat in a white ceramic planter on the far side of the couch. Upon casual inspection, you'd think she was one of those miniature palms. Good, sturdy trunk and long, lush green leaves with razor thin edges and sharp, tapering points.

Cassandra gave me Tree right after we crossed paths, nearly fatally, with the arch villain and Nobel Prize winning mathematician Angus Podgorny. He resented our pivotal role in bringing about his downfall and swore his revenge as he was being led from the dock. [10]

Much of Podgorny's network was left intact after his conviction and Cass thought Tree might come in handy in case a bunch of his beastie boys busted in on me some night. I was kind of touched and also insulted, if you know what I mean. It was like *she* was trying to protect *me*. Despite initial misgivings and one or two minor incidents that nearly cost me some fingers, for the most part Tree and I got along pretty well. She was good company and as a personal watchdog, er, sentinel, I couldn't have asked for anything better.

The first thing I did when I got home was go to the fridge and fetch a fresh hamburger patty. It couldn't be frozen and it had to be lean and pink. Any brown spots and there could be dire consequences. I stood on one side of the couch and sort of lobbed the patty in Tree's direction—

--flinching as the fucking thing *erupted* into life, snapping the patty out of mid-air, the long, green fronds actually disguised jaws and teeth. In two quick gulps the quarter pound of meat was gone and a placated Tree subsided into stillness and, I hoped, dormancy.

Cass told me Tree was the perfect companion for someone like me. She didn't require any special care or attention, just a hunk of meat once a day. No light, no other food, fertilizer or water needed. Oh, and I should avoid smoking, she hated that.

She?

Of course Tree was female. Couldn't I tell?

Er, no, actually, I couldn't.

---

[10] "The Death of Pi" (*The Casebooks of Zinnea & Nightstalk, Vol. III*)

I made damn sure I obeyed my partner's instructions to the letter, resisting the urge to over-feed Tree ("I can't emphasize what a mistake that would be") or substituting anything other than fresh ground meat ("not advisable under *any* circumstances"). The daily feeding ritual still scared the piss out of me. The sheer *speed* of the thing was incredible. But I liked the fact that she was cheap and almost maintenance-free. She would be a formidable adversary for any housebreakers. Very territorial. I'd hate to have that old girl mad at *me*, that's for damn sure...

The building was humming with activity. Early risers firing up showers and getting their breakfasts ready, while shift workers stumbled home, bleary-eyed and cranky, their body cycles and bio-rhythms hopelessly screwed up, not used to keeping a vampire's hours.

Me, I've always been a night person. A natural Shade. Same with my father and my sister Constance. Cassandra too—she said she only really came to life after midnight. Her peak hours were between one and four a.m. That's when she was practically unstoppable, especially if the moon was waxing.

I watched CNN for awhile but then I got lucky and came across some sumo wrestling. I finished one beer and started another. Those fat bastards were amazingly quick and agile. They *hurtled* at each other, colliding with a sickening thud of flesh. Very primal.

After that ended, it was time to get down to business.

I couldn't make up my mind. Was I in the mood for horny sorority girls or a horny stewardess with a hankering to join the "mile high" club in style...

Instead I reached for a tape I'd watched over and over again, catching the flick on Channel 68 one morning, only managing to record the last half. There were no end credits so I never got the movie's title or even the name of the actress. The one who bore such a startling resemblance to...well, not *startling*. From certain angles, perhaps, when the lighting was just right—

Every time I played the tape I felt strange. Like I'd crossed a line. The actress was tall, blonde, with just the right mix of sauciness and elegance. She had a slight accent, it sounded Scandinavian to me. It was hard to tell, she didn't have many lines. Just a near-perfect butt that she accentuated with microskirts and eye-grabbing thongs. She was very enthusiastic and convincing during sex scenes, making eager noises, urging her lover on, her climaxes monumental and seemingly authentic. I wondered if she'd studied under Strasberg (so to speak).

When the movie was over and I finished I felt...bad. Depressed. Wishing I'd had the courage to throw a blanket over Tree so she wouldn't be a witness to my transgression. Sure, I knew she didn't have eyes *per se* but there must be some kind of visual receptors involved. A sensory organ that could detect my presence in the room and track a hunk of meat thrown in her direction.

I indulged in a brief bout of self-loathing before finally nodding off. And so ended another far from perfect day in the life of Evgeny Davidovitch Nightstalk, mediocre sleuth and pervert extraordinaire. Not much of a life, surely. But it was the one I'd been given and, being the strong, silent type, it would have been out of character for me to complain.

II

"The bright day is done, and we are for the dark."
William Shakespeare, *Romeo & Juliet*

Monday, May 3rd

As soon as the sun went down, I was a new man.

When the sky darkens and street lights start winking on, a city takes on a different character, transformed into something mysterious, dangerous, spooky. A place of jagged, reaching shadows, half-concealed faces, secrets and surprises.

For a detective, it's the perfect atmosphere.

Have you ever seen a film *noir* where most of the action takes place in the daytime? Or a horror flick? My partner pointed out that for uncounted thousands of years humankind has feared the night because our most trusted sense, sight, is neutralized, near useless, once we lose the light. That kind of thinking always makes me scratch my bald spot in irritation. To my mind, a nocturnal existence actually *improves* your chances of survival, especially if you happen to be one of the hunted. For one thing, there are a lot more places to hide in the dark.

I ate a late supper at *Mother's*, a joint not far from my apartment. Claimed my usual spot at the counter, sugar, salt, napkins and condiments within easy reach. It's a small establishment and Sam Mother runs the place basically by himself. He doesn't appreciate cracks about his name, by the way. Matter of fact, there isn't much Sam *does* appreciate, except maybe the sound of his cash register ringing merrily away. The man is a workaholic, open 365 days of the year, including Christmas. It's a neighborhood joke: his two sons ran off and joined the army to escape his autocratic ways. True story. Sam's still pretty bitter about it so it's wise not to bring it up.

Sam took my order, walked through a set of swinging doors to the kitchen and started preparing my meal. A real one-man operation.

The supper rush was over. The only other patron was a guy sipping cold coffee by the window. He looked like someone who'd lost his soul in a loaded game of three-card monte. There were big, fat zeroes where his eyes should have been. Life can do that sometimes.

Sam makes a killer Greek salad. Lots of feta cheese and olives saltier than the Dead Sea. Followed by a club sandwich and free coffee refill. And the best part of it was that I'd been frequenting the place for *years* and in all that time scarcely ten words had passed between us. Mainly we communicated via grunts and gestures. Showing our true roots.

When I hit the street again I felt spectacular, like a regular *flanneur*, a citizen of a modern city of wonders, graced with tall towers and teeming with life, a veritable microcosm of human endeavor (see what working in close proximity to Cassandra Zinnea could do to a person?). I exited the parking lot and within five minutes was angling for the on-ramp. I drove in to mid-town and even though I was forced to take Finlayson Drive, which was *still* under construction, and had to put up with three different detours, I never lost my temper once. My partner would've been proud of me.

Midtown empties out after five o'clock. A mass exodus to the suburbs. Good riddance. More room for the rest of us. There are a couple of under-rated blues bars and plenty of ethnic places to eat. Joints the Grays...er sorry, I mean the white collar, daytime crowd, don't even know exist.

I saw some people I recognized, emerging for the first time in twelve hours. Lots of visible minorities, single women, unemployed; Shades by virtue of their low standing in the socio-economic pecking order. Scrubbing toilets and shampooing carpets and cleaning the big office towers from sunset to sunup to put food on the table because, contrary to popular belief, people *do* starve to death in this country.

I pushed through the door of *The Tool Shed* and found some guy giving grief to poor Tara.

"—ordered that Slippery Suzie doll over *five* weeks ago, goddamnit! That's *five weeks*. There's a minimum expectation of service here, isn't there?" Buddy was wearing a good quality army parka but when I got close enough I saw he was shivering like a dog pissing razor blades. Ex-dope fiend of one kind or other. I knew him, vaguely, disliked him instinctively. People like him give porn a bad name.

Tara looked stricken, taking his bullshit personally. "I'll check our records again but I'm sure it'll be here as soon as—"

"And make sure they send the one with the heated snatch. I don't want there to be any more screw-ups." Mr. Parka's agitation was almost comical. He *really* wanted that fucking doll. "I mean, can't you just get on the blower with your supplier and find out what the hold up is?"

"Well, as I said, that's my mother's department."

"Will you tell Maude for me that Ernie is very upset?" He zipped up his parka and crossed his arms. "Say 'Ernie told me to tell you that he is very upset about his Slippery Suzie'. You got that? And then maybe we'll see some action. Okay, point made." He finally gave way at the counter, glancing at me as he passed.

"Hey," he grunted.

"You should try getting a *real* girlfriend, Ern."

"Yeah, and fuck you too, pal." And out the door he went.

I waited until Tara finished writing down *'Ernie very upset about Slippery Sally'*. She had the handwriting of a twelve year-old kid. Big and loopy. When she looked up, she was beet red.

"Tara," I began.

"Oh, hi, Mr. Nightstalk."

I tried to think of the best way to broach it. "Does the word *penis* bother you?" More blood rushed to her face. "*Vagina*? *Nipples*? *Ass*?" She shuddered. "Kiddo, you've *got* to tell your mother that you shouldn't be working in a place like this. You're not suited for it. Tell her you're allergic to latex or something."

"It's no use." She settled onto a tall stool behind the cash register. "She can't find anybody decent to work here. They steal from the till or walk out with merchandise. Or give their friends big discounts. Shit like that."

"Yeah, but I'm guessing dildoes probably don't make them nauseous."

She clapped a hand over her mouth. "I can't help it. It's the rubbery smell. And the big, mushroomy heads." She gagged.

"Easy, girl. Try not to think about it."

She took deep breaths. "Maybe...maybe I'll get used to it. Like Mom. God, she can talk about *anything* with these sickos."

I resented that. "Well...not *all* of them are sickos. But the point is that you need to explain the situation to her. I don't think she understands how difficult this is for you."

She thought about it but shook her head. "She needs me to help out. I have to learn to be more like her. She knows all about this shit. It doesn't embarrass *her*. Fuckin' penis leashes and butt plugs and..." She swallowed hard.

"There's a garbage can behind you." While we waited for her gorge to settle, I reflected on it and had to admit she was right. Maude was absolutely unflappable. She could talk knowledgeably about the most bizarre appliance or sexual act and sound completely business-like the whole time. "Okay, well, I thought I needed to say something. It's your life, kiddo."

"Thanks. I have to desensitize myself, that's all. Get it through my head that I'm a sales girl and it's just, y'know, product." She looked at me. "Um, was there something you wanted or...?"

"Well, " I almost hated to mention it. "Your mom said some movies I ordered might be in." She went over and opened the drawer where the DVDs and VHS tapes were kept.

"Was it a special order? There should be something with your name on it—"

"They were about tit-fucking," I piped up helpfully. "And I think a pair of rubber breasts come with them."

She made a gurgling noise and lunged for the wastebasket.

"Oh, *shit*...sorry, Tara." The sound of her woofing made my stomach churn. I told her I'd come back for the films later and hightailed it out of there before I made things worse.

I felt bad for Tara but also, I admit, a tad let down for my own sake. I'd *really* been looking forward to having a crack at those fake tits.

The good news was my partner had beaten me to work for a change. The bad news was she had company.

Philippe DeBarge was everything I was not: tall, handsome, debonair and (I had reason to suspect) a former lover of Cassandra Zinnea. *That* I would never forgive him for. Besides, he was such a fucking arsehole, with his Hermes ties and designer suits and perfectly coiffed hair and that flowery cologne he applied with a bloody soup ladle.

He reminded me of Pierce Brosnan.

I've never liked Pierce Brosnan.

He wasn't stupid but he wasn't brilliant and witty and wonderful the way an ex-paramour of my partner should have been. He was vain, petty and his ego rivaled that of an Old Testament deity. We'd met on two prior occasions[11] and neither of us had acquitted ourselves well in terms of behavior or basic civility. I saw the sparks that flew whenever they were around each other and it really got to me. Imagining the two of them together and not having to work very hard at it.

And here he was again, in the flesh, sitting in *my* chair, next to *my* woman. He pretended not to notice me. *I* pretended not to notice the pompous prick had his "Order of Dupin" prominently displayed on the lapel of his Euro-trash suit jacket. Fucking show-off.

Then I caught wise to the fact that they were holding hands. I checked again and saw that *he* was the one doing the holding. Her fingers were limp and unresponsive, not giving back any pressure. I eased up a bit. Almost pitied the guy. I knew what it was like to fail to measure up to the somewhat warped standards of Cassandra Zinnea. I knew what it was like to be found wanting.

He leaned close and whispered something in her ear and she gave a little nod while, at the same time, nimbly extracting her hand from his. Nicely done, I thought.

"Ah, at last we are graced by the presence of your, how do you say, *amanuensis*? Is that the correct term?" I had no idea but strongly suspected I was being insulted. And he *still* hadn't gotten out of my chair. I pondered the best way to deal with the situation. Rip off his head and stick it up his ass? Tie his balls in a sheepshank behind his ears?

My partner, reading my mind, tried a diversionary tactic. "Philippe's here on business, Nightstalk. Specifically, that business in St. Andrew's Park." She met my eye...and winked at me. I heard her voice in my head, as clear as a bell: *Yeah, I know he's a blowhard but let's pump him for as much information as we can get.* I wasn't the slightest bit telepathic, of course, but could sort of "think/speak" short sentences on our private wavelength, which she was usually able to decipher: *Okay, but don't expect me to kiss his hairy, puckered arse.* "He's acting on behalf of a certain organization that shall remain nameless—" Otherwise known as the Brethren of Purity, *aka* The Black Brotherhood, *aka* Dickheads United. "—and he's come to, well, I guess you could say he's here to assist our investigation."

---

[11] "Paris, in the Spring (With Dead People)" (*The Casebooks of Zinnea & Nightstalk, Vol. I*); "The Return of the Ripper" (*Casebooks, Vol. II*)

"Call it...an advisory role," he clarified. "Even so, my presence in Ilium must remain a closely kept secret, yes? And that is why I question the necessity of involving your *assistant*," a withering glance in my direction, "in affairs that are beyond his, how do you say, purview." That settled it. I hadn't performed my patented sheepshank maneuver in a long time.

"Nightstalk is my *partner*, Philippe," she responded tersely. "I consider him my equal in every way. You *will* address him with the respect he deserves." You could practically hear the whip crack. DeBarge looked over at me, dipped his head in mock apology.

"No offense intended, Monsieur Night*stick*. It is clear I have underestimated your status." He glanced down. "Ah, I see you've noticed my 'Dupin'. Bestowed only rarely, as I'm sure you know. And yet history will never record my actions or the circumstances under which I so undeservedly obtained it." He brought a finger to his lips. "State secrets are the hardest to keep. And the most dangerous. But this medal is a mere bauble to me. I feel no sense of pride when I recall the accomplishments for which it was rewarded. To me, I am not a hero, only one who acted according to his training and—"

"Yeah, yeah. Word for word from your acceptance speech, I bet." Cassandra stifled a giggle. "Go on, DeBarge, pull the other one, why don't you?"

"The other what? I'm afraid I do not understand, Nightstick. Is that a sexual reference? Are you making a pass at me?"

"In your dreams, you little pimp." I began to open and close my hands, pumping up my arms and shoulders.

"Getting back to the point of Philippe's visit," my partner prompted, hoping to appeal to our professionalism.

"Yeah, why *are* you here, DeBarge? Please do enlighten us, *s'il vous plait*. Before I take that Dupin of yours and—"

Again Cassandra headed me off at the pass. "I keep trying to tell you, Philippe is here to *help* us, Evgeny. We were waiting for you but he's already let slip that the Brethren—sorry, Philippe—are short one deep cover guy. It's not too much of a stretch to deduce that their missing agent and the burned man in the park are one and the same."

"And what leads you to that conclusion?"

"Those readings you took. The energy released that night. I told you that was significant."

"Arturs Esch, the agent in question, was a 5th Degree adept," Philippe DeBarge said. "I knew him well. He was a top-flight operative. One of our best men."

"Not any more," I countered. But I had to admit it added an interesting new wrinkle to the case. "Okay, I'll bite: what's a member of the Black Brotherhood doing getting his ass barbecued on a park bench in our fair city? Seems a bit off the beaten path as far as you boys are concerned."

He nodded. It was a question he'd been expecting. "For some time we have been aware of certain amateur occultists here in Ilium who meet and perform rituals, most of them relatively harmless. Black magic, if you will, but more closely resembling what has been referred to as 'Satanism Lite'. But then we started hearing rumours of a more ominous nature, unsubstantiated yet disturbing. This coven was allegedly recreating certain rites proscribed for centuries. Behaving in a manner that was reckless, irresponsible, perhaps even dangerous." I shook my head in disbelief but he paid me no mind. "Esch was given the task of infiltrating the group and was able to do so with the assistance of certain individuals who shall remain nameless. And then he either erred or was found out...*something* happened because, as you say, he was executed in this most grotesque and abominable manner."

"You're kidding, right?" It was worth a chuckle so I obliged. "You mean the Cabal, don't you? The Baron's group? I got news for you and the Brotherhood--they're just a bunch of pseudo-satanic wackos who are into group sex and circle jerks. Dangerous? Those pussycats? They may sacrifice a goat or two in honour of Samhain or whatever but that's about it. C'mon, partner," I motioned to her, "say something. Explain it to this tool." She was about to but DeBarge cut in again.

"We believe they are more dangerous than you think. In fact, they may be more dangerous than we dare believe."

I made a face. "Oh, come on! We *live* here, all right? If they were a threat or up to no good, don't you think we'd have heard about it by now? They're strictly weekend warlocks, take my word for it."

"Our sources say otherwise."

"They're fucked up society sluts and bored millionaires—"

"Yet their power and influence is growing."

"They're no threat to anybody—"

"That is not correct. They are tampering with powers and principalities they do not fully understand."

"*Boys...*" Cassandra said.

"Yeah, says who?"

"Says *us*, that's who." He smacked his hand on the desk with considerable force. Squared his shoulders and threw out his chest. The Dupin caught the overhead light and glinted like fool's gold. "And who are we? Merely an organization devoted to ensuring mankind achieves its rightful destiny, a sacred duty bestowed upon us many hundreds of years ago." Now he was on his feet, his voice rising with emotion. "We Brethren have our ways, Monsieur Nightstick. Our powers of divination are not perfect but we have assessed the situation and see a clear pattern emerging. Our informants tell us that there are forbidden practices being performed, *blood rituals*, and therefore our mandate is clear."

"But the Baron—"

"--may be inconsequential, as you say, but there are other parties involved whose motivations may not be so, what is the word, *benign*."

"*Boys*."

"Who?"

He looked smug. "Ah, as to that, I'm afraid I'm not at liberty to—"

"Gregory Fischer." We both turned toward her. "A little birdie told me." She shrugged, smiling impishly.

It was a pleasure to watch DeBarge fume. "That information is classified." He pointed a finger at me. "*You* will not divulge what you have just heard to *anyone*."

I was barely listening. "Gregory Fischer. *Wow*. That's quite a catch for the Baron."

"There have been rumours flying around for awhile. Apparently Fischer and his wife are serious occultists. They own an impressive collection of Crowley memorabilia. He has a genuine crush on A.C. Some call it an obsession." She paused, considering. "And if the Fischers are involved, that means Victor Skorzeny is too."

"Skorzeny?" I knew the name, of course. Along with Anton LaVey he was probably the best known Satanist of the past twenty or thirty years. "I thought he was retired. Or dead."

"He's been Gregory Fischer's...I guess you'd call it spiritual advisor for some time." She looked at DeBarge. "You think Fischer and Skorzeny are up to something, something potentially dangerous."

He wouldn't give her a straight answer. "We have *suspicions*," he hedged. "We consider them worthy of further investigation. There are other factors, as well. Certain...anomalies, yes?"

"Like what?" I cracked. "Two-headed calves? Nine-legged spiders? Doughnuts shaped like the Virgin Mary?"

"No, monsieur," he retorted, "I am referring, for instance, to the missing cats."

That shut me up.

Cats were a touchy subject around *After Hours Investigations*.

We'd received our first call about six weeks previously. An old gal had lost her most prized possession, Kym, a gorgeous, spirited calico. It was a slow time for us but not *that* slow. I asked the standard questions, tried to sound sympathetic and forgot about it as soon as I put the phone down.

The next evening there was a memo left on my side of the desk. The Old Man laying down the law: *Investigate all missing cat reports. Top Priority.*

So guess who had to drive all over the city, interviewing distraught pet owners, who were either befuddled old farts or misanthropic paranoids. As an interesting sidebar, it turned out that most of the folks who'd lost cats were either witches or adepts of one kind or another (whether they knew it or not). And the cats involved, without exception, were praised for their intelligence and inquisitiveness.

Cats are special creatures, even an unrepentant animal hater like yours truly has to acknowledge as much. They're the eyes and ears of the night, the best spies you could ask for. Diligent and attentive, curious and inconspicuous. Only now a bunch of them had vanished and try as we might, we hadn't been able to find hide nor hair of them. A few truant tabbies could be chalked up to roadkill, rogue dogs and random misfortune, but the number of felines MIA in such a short period of time pointed to other causes.

What was happening to them? On that point, we were stumped.

The reference to cats took some of the wind out of my sails. Advantage, Philippe. "So...so you're telling us that the Cabal is behind this epidemic of cat-nappings too?" Which, if true, was a pretty serious crime in and of itself. We night folk treat cats with mucho respect. We know they aren't just glorified rat-catchers. They're smart, resourceful and in one particular episode I can think of, an heroic kitty named Festus gave his last life to save Cassandra and I from almost certain annihilation.[12]

"The Breth—the organization I represent finds it worrisome, to say the least, when some of the leading felines in your community start disappearing. Without explanation, their fate as yet undetermined."

---

[12] "Colonel Mustard, in the Library, With a Candlestick" (*The Casebooks of Zinnea & Nightstalk, Vol. II*)

"Yes," my partner agreed, "it's troubling. Clearly these were special cats. And singled out for that reason. Textbook tactics. Eliminate scouts and sentries, depriving your enemy of critical intelligence. And, meanwhile, plan your attack..."

He was nodding in agreement.

"*Attack*? What attack?" Digging away at that bald spot again.

"It's all leading up to something," she declared, ignoring me.

"Undoubtedly," he agreed. They were looking at each other and from their blank expressions I could tell they were communicating telepathically, leaving poor l'il un-Gifted me out of the loop.

I felt myself getting hot under the collar. "Excuse me, the peanut gallery has a few questions. Like, for instance, what the hell are you two talking about?"

He seemed amused by my ignorance. The creep. I was a badly groomed mountain gorilla next to him. I might have been able to turn Philippe DeBarge inside out physically—I'd visualized it often enough—but if it came down to a magickal tussle between two adepts, he'd be going home with my ass in his back pocket. Usually we observed a prickly truce. It kept us from killing each other.

"I shall cooperate as much as I am able," he told us. "My role is to act as a liaison between my organization and the Old Man. However, there are some matters I will not or, I should say, *cannot* discuss." He shrugged. "You must understand there is a limit, certain information or details that cannot be divulged under any circumstances. This is...as it must be. For all of our sakes."

"You people fucking slay me," I retorted. "*You* decide what we need to know and when we need to know it. What makes you so bloody omnipotent? *The Brethren of Purity.* What a crock. Your bunch are about as pure as yellow snow. And I know what sort of help we can expect from you: zilch. *Nada.* As in nada fuckin' thing. We take all the risks and you get the glory."

My partner looked none too pleased but my intended target was fairly vibrating with rage. "*Lies*," he snapped. "Petty slanders. *Bullshit.*" We were making significant eye contact, staring each other down. I began clenching my fists again, inflating my arms and shoulders. Cass, clever girl, called it "going Popeye".

"How'd you like to go home in an urn?" I snarled.

"And how would *you* like to be a capuchin monkee?" he replied. "The ones with the cute, puzzled little faces."

"*Enough already*." She was genuinely pissed. "How about I zap you *both* with a pacifying spell? Make you waltz around the room, singing old sea shanties together. You get the picture?"

"Aw, we didn't mean anything," I muttered, not liking the sound of *that* spell one bit.

But she wasn't taking any more chances. "Philippe, unless you've got anything more to add..." He shrugged. "...then we thank you for dropping by. Now if you'll excuse us, Nightstalk and I need to get down to work."

"I hope you are able to shed some light on the true intentions of this so-called 'Cabal'. My organization would appreciate your efforts and your... cooperation." He looked nettled about something. Maybe I'd spoiled his evening. *Tsk, tsk.*

"Yeah, and in the meantime you and your buddies will sit on your arses while we do the shit work." I laughed bitterly. "Don't worry, we know the score."

Zing. Got him again. "We have our mandate, you have yours," he responded icily. "Sometimes it's difficult to see the big picture from the bottom of the monkey cage, yes? Just do your job, Monsieur Night*stick.* I also suggest you learn some manners. And pray that our paths don't cross again, under less hospitable circumstances." *Oooo, a threat.* Now the prick was kissing her hand. I'd make sure she washed it after he left. In *extra* hot water. You never knew where his lips might have been.

When he was gone, I reclaimed my chair, first ensuring that he hadn't hexed it or, worse yet, changed the settings on me. I expected her to read me the riot act but all she said was: "Nightstalk, we'll need him before this is over."

I smiled, biting my tongue. Sometimes for the sake of maintaining an excellent working relationship you have to know when to quit.

But Philippe DeBarge's visit touched a nerve in both of us and the mood was unsettled for the rest of the night. It reminded us of the fragile, precarious nature of our partnership, the care and discretion required to sustain it.

Honestly, it was a miracle it worked as well as it did.

Tuesday night—surprise, surprise--she beat me to work again.

I could smell her perfume as soon as I opened the office door. I started to call out a greeting...but she'd already come and gone.

She'd been doing some research, by the look of it. Her side of the desk was covered in file folders and *Post It Note*d books. Volumes on subjects relating to demonology, spell-casting, the most recent *Who's Who in*

Modern Witchcraft and a remaindered copy of Gregory Fischer's best-selling autobiography, *Rich Beyond My Wildest Dreams*. But she hadn't found what she was looking for. Deductive reasoning? Perhaps. Or it might have been the note she left:

> *Nightstalk:*
> *Meet me at the Hall of Records around 11:00.*
> *See you there.*
> *C. Z.*

Neil was on duty, which was a nice stroke of luck. Floyd, the other guard, was a boozehound who sometimes passed out in one of the comfy seats in the basement film theatre, dead to the world. Useless if there happened to be a fire, a break-in...or a fellow Shade tapping on the front entrance of the library with his car key, trying to get his attention.

Neil was cool though. I waved at him through the glass and he motioned me around to the back. The staff parking lot was well lit and there was only one vehicle in evidence, a yellow Ford half-ton with more miles on it than a fleet of space shuttles. I assumed it belonged to the man himself.

Neil was holding open the door. "Thought it was you," he called out cheerfully. "C'mon in. I gotta re-jig the alarm within a minute or the security company'll be calling. Don't want the fuckin' cops showing up. A hassle with the pigs is the *last* thing I need."

"Hey," I said, "have some respect for our fine law enforcement professionals. If I'm not mistaken, you are presently in uniform so technically that makes you a pig too."

He shook his head. "I'm not a cop, man. Shit, I'd wear a fuckin' bunny suit as long as it got me a sweet job like this one."

Neil dealt with the security system then led me through the administration area, past the chief librarian's office and into the main part of the building. "Me and Floyd switched tonight. He was gonna try to catch his wife at something. Make her think he was going to work and then double back on her."

"I wouldn't blame her. Fuckin' old rummy."

He laughed. "Aw, Floyd isn't so bad. He's got some cool war stories. You should ask him sometime." He stopped by the escalator. "Well, I guess you know the way. I'll be around if you need me. Probably up by the internet computers, jamming with my buddies. Just gimme a shout."

"You still into that Irwin Allen crap?"

He looked hurt. "It ain't crap, Nightstalk. We're *Voyagers*, man. We love that stuff. There's this on-line chat room and we sit around for hours talking about our favorite episodes of *Land of the Giants* and *Lost in Space*. Those are classic programs, man. They don't make 'em like that any more."

I rolled my eyes. "You call yourself *Voyagers*? As in *Voyage to the Bottom of the Sea*, right? Another classic?" He nodded, grinning sheepishly. "Kee-ripes, Neil, how many of your virtual pen pals still live in their parents' basement?"

He took it in good stride. "No point arguin' with a closed mind. But you should log on to our website some day and have a look around. Check out some of the links."

I grunted, conceding nothing. "I'll come find you when I'm done." He went up the escalator and I made my way past *Large Print Books* and *General Fiction*, then *Business* and *Social Sciences*...

The occult section consisted of four or five shelves next to *Religion & Philosophy*. Like our office collection, it was eclectic: from near death experiences to alien abduction. Jacques Vallee butted heads with Colin Wilson and Elaine Pagels shared uneasy shelf space with Erich Von Daniken.

I took down Montague Summers' *Witchcraft & Black Magic*. It was marked with green tape, a *Reference* book and therefore no one was allowed to borrow it. Plus it was protected by at least a dozen aversion spells. Cassandra thought it very appropriate that a book by Summers, written with his poisonous, witch-hating pen, should serve the purpose it did.

I found page 177, closed my eyes and turned clockwise three times.

As an experiment, I'd once tried it with my eyes open. Didn't work. Tried making only two turns and then opening my eyes. *Bad news.* Don't even want to *think* about where I ended up that time.

Page 177.

Three times.

Eyes closed.

When I opened them, I was in the Hall of Records.

Think library. Think BIG library. Library of Congress. Times a million. Then times that by a *trillion*. And so on. Get the picture?

Hall of Records. As in *Akashic Records*. As in *only* the combined knowledge of the entire universe, stored and preserved in timeless ether, free for the asking.

You can access or retrieve data through a variety of formats. Print definitely *not* preferred (it's unwieldy and takes up too much space). There are viewers and visors and virtual stations, as well as various ports and plugs for those fitted with cranial inputs…

Can't decide? Confused by the sheer scale of the facility? That's all right. There's always Georgie, your ever-helpful guide, infinitely wise, anxious to be of service.

Aware of your presence the moment you arrive, a greeting already forming on his lips—

"Good afternoon, Mr. Nightstalk," said Georgie. Somehow he managed to appear dignified and servile at the same time, a rather neat trick. "It is most agreeable to see you again." If I was casting the part of Georgie, I'd pick someone like Sir John Gielgud. He would fit the bill perfectly, except he's dead and not accepting bookings at the moment.

Georgie had a long, diamond-shaped face, with thick, bushy brows, an over-large nose and deep set, watery eyes. He was tall but his posture was so poor that he never seemed to tower over you. I liked that about him. His actual age was anyone's guess, but his immense faculties were still, for the most part, intact.

"It's afternoon here?" I looked around.

He chuckled. "It's *always* afternoon here, sir. Three o'clock in the afternoon, to be precise. Just after teatime."

I struggled to understand. "And you find…that helps?"

"It does wonders for staff morale, sir." Staff? The only staff I'd ever seen was Georgie or one of his many clones or copies. But there would have to be other employees, wouldn't there? Working behind the scenes.

"Oh. Okay." I never knew how to take Georgie. He had to be *at least* an Eighth Degree but he was also supposed to be serving me, right? To be honest, I never felt completely at ease around him. I mean, one snap of his fingers and I might suddenly find myself the world's only talking parsnip.

"And Miss Zinnea? Is she—"

"Late as usual? Yes, she is, as a matter of fact."

"Ah, but here she comes now." A second later she materialized a short distance away. She turned, spotted us and waved. This particular aisle was wider than the ones adjoining it; there was enough room for Georgie and me to stand side by side. If you looked both ways you could see for *miles* in either direction. Each connecting corridor represented a different area of endeavor, human or otherwise. The more esoteric your research, the deeper you were drawn into the Hall. But then you ran the risk of doing something really stupid like taking a wrong turn and getting *lost*.

Well, never fear, Georgie would find you.

Eventually.

We watched as my partner approached, looking smart in a navy blue, pinstriped outfit that must have set her back a ton. The way she wore it, it was worth every cent.

"Such a lovely woman," Georgie observed.

"She sure is."

"Right on time too," she announced.

"Wrong," I shot back. "You're late. You're always late. No clocks where you were or..."

"Nope. And you know I can't wear watches," she reminded me. "I fry them. It's those nasty spikes in my electro-magnetics—*Fzzzt!*"

Georgie waited for us to finish our playful jousting, then came forward and offered his hand. He also *bowed*, a quick dip of the head. He never bowed to me. "Miss Zinnea."

"Hello, Georgie."

"You look, if I may say, magnificent." Hey, he may have been older than the Sphinx and as chaste as a ninety-year old nun, but one look at her reminded him that he was, after all, a simulacrum of a *man*. Blew some of the accumulated book dust out of his system and got the lubricants flowing again. "How can I help you today?"

"We're seeking information about a coven that may be involved in a case of ritual murder." She waited while he assimilated that. Was it my imagination or did there seem to be a slightly longer pause than usual?

"Can you be more specific?"

"Um, just the most recent scuttlebutt," I improvised. "Anything you have on some of the more high profile members. Names: Baron Frederick von Stahl, Gregory Fischer and, uh, Victor Skorzeny—er, something wrong?"

He had an odd look on his face. He beckoned us closer...then, without warning, seized our elbows, gripping us tightly. There was no time to react, we could only hang on for dear life as he whisked us through the Hall of Records at speeds that would've made Einstein swoon. He seemed to be steering us deeper into the facility, to a quieter, more discreet location.

Just as quickly as it began, our journey ended. We came to an abrupt stop, both of us lurching slightly as we regained our balance. "Uh...is there a problem, Georgie?" I watched him closely. Did he seem...*furtive*?

"I merely wanted to make you aware—" He lowered his voice. "There was another party requesting information along similar lines."

"That party being Philippe Arnaud DeBarge, representing our friends, the Brethren of Purity, am I right?"

He was taken aback. "You surpass yourself, Mr. Nightstalk."

I resisted the urge to stick my tongue out at Cassandra. "And did the aforementioned Monsieur DeBarge order a complete embargo on all relevant material or was he good enough to leave us some scraps?"

"As I told *him*, there really is very little information available. This particular coven is, dare I say, of rather slight repute. Baron von Stahl merits hardly a mention in *Who's Who* and just about anything you wish to know about Mr. Fischer is available in the public domain." Georgie shrugged. "I got the impression that Monsieur DeBarge didn't feel there was any sensitive material to weed out."

He led us into a tributary aisle filled with mouldy parchments and scroll-like cylinders. Sometimes we had to squeeze sideways between the stacks, holding our breath so we wouldn't breathe in thousands of years of dust and decay. Soon I was completely turned around, as lost as a kid in the woods.

Finally he stopped beside a table hemmed in by two ordinary plastic chairs. They had somehow been finessed into a tiny alcove, a space devoted to study and contemplation...or solitary masturbation.

"You've used a light table before, of course." Cassandra nodded and took a seat in one of the chairs. I hated the bloody things. You really had to focus and keep your thoughts on tight beam or else it fucked up the search engine. You ended up with a whole bunch of crap to sift through, most of it totally useless.

As soon as she made the connection, the surface of the table shimmered, awaiting her instructions.

"Please list all current members of the Cabal," she said. Giving it an easy one to start with.

The table blinked and a sexless voice intoned. "Please specify."

"The Cabal. Ilium. Frederick Von Stahl."

"Please restate question."

I let out my breath in frustration. Georgie looked apologetic. "The system has been giving us a bit of trouble of late," he explained. "We've been trying to rectify the situation but, in the meantime, try to be patient."

It took three or four more tries and an impressive display of concentration on her part but we finally got something. Names began to flash onscreen, a rapid fire roster that included both Gregory and Charlotte

Fischer, Victor Skorzeny, Vivien Vickers and Kali Brust. Some names were highlighted in boldface, while others—

The screen hummed loudly and winked off.

"What the fuck's wrong with this thing?" I complained. I scribbled the last of the names in my notebook: Tibor Benes, Joe Duthie and Julian Finchley.

He frowned. "This is most peculiar." He came forward and placed his palm on the table. I heard him mutter something and then he was *gone*. Just like that.

"Shit. Now what?"

We had no way of knowing when he'd return. There were countless patrons making endless demands on his time. What if he *forgot* about us?

While we waited, my partner tried another tack. She went looking for related material and must have found a way in because the screen hummed to life again. This time it offered up a newspaper article on the Baron from our illustrious rag, *The Ilium Observer*, accompanied by a fuzzy picture taken at Davos with a telephoto lens. "Mystery Man Moves in the Highest Circles". The Baron stood between a former Secretary of State and a member of the Kuwaiti royal family.

I'd heard from a hack I knew at the paper that the original version of the piece had packed more of a wallop. The reporter spent more than six months on the Baron's trail and unearthed damning evidence regarding some of his more unsavory activities. The centre piece of the article was the affair that earned him the nickname "The Bandit of Bucharest". It was a post-Cold War scandal involving Romania's largest bank and a top-level cabinet official. Tipped off ahead of time, the Baron flew the coop with over a hundred million dollars siphoned from state coffers only minutes before the *polizei* came knocking.

When the hack turned in his story, twelve tons of shit hit the fan. The article was kept in limbo while libel lawyers were consulted. The lawyers talked to the publisher, who called in the editor and…well, you know how it is. The article was gutted, whittled down to a human interest story, the Baron transformed into a colourful jet-setter with "alleged" shady connections and "purported" friends in high places. Nothing incriminating, no smoking guns. All references to that "Bandit of Bucharest" business and the industrial espionage conducted on behalf of a certain Israeli aerospace firm eliminated—*snip, snip.* The Baron retained his air of mystery and the reporter later lost his job. Typical…

There was also an article from *People*, of all places. A photo spread on Gregory Fischer and his lovely trophy wife. On the slopes at Vail, playing *chemin de fer* at Monte Carlo and snuggling up on a love seat in their living room atop the Leiber Building. When the Revolution finally comes, people like them will be the first against the wall. That is, if I'm around to have any say about it.

Charlotte Roper-Fischer listed her hobbies and interests as "scuba diving, nude sun-bathing and stuff to do with fashion". Her husband was the smartest man she had ever met and when asked for a role model or personal idol, thought hard for a full minute before replying: "Cher."

"Christ, what a bimbo," I snorted.

"Fischer didn't marry her for her brains, dummy," she pointed out.

"That much is obvious."

"Don't be such a simp, Nightstalk. She's merely using the gifts she's been blessed with to obtain a standard of living most of us can only dream about." She sounded almost...wistful? I stared at her. "You wouldn't understand."

"Maybe I do. She's beautiful, you're beautiful. People are always taking you for granted, thinking you can't be both gorgeous *and* smart." She tried to hide her smile. "She'll never get the respect or credit she deserves. She could very well be a totally decent, intelligent person only she's cursed because most of us can't get past the image we have of her as a gold-digging airhead."

She was shaking her head in amazement. "Evvie, Georgie was right, sometimes you really do surpass yourself." She took my hand, gave it a squeeze. "You're not such an old poop after all."

I squeezed back. "But I'll tell you right now you have *nothing* in common with that woman. She really is as dumb as a stick. I saw her being interviewed and Koko the gorilla has a higher I.Q. Her two main interests in life are her hair and shopping. On the other hand, you, my dear, are a fuckin' genius and that is no exaggeration." I think if Georgie hadn't rematerialized at that moment, she would have gotten up and hugged me. Damn him and his relentless competence!

"Please excuse the delay." He glanced at the table, shook his head regretfully. "Not much there, I'm afraid."

My partner sat back in her chair. "Not really, no. You're right, as far as these sort of groups go, they're pretty low-echelon. But I *am* curious about a few points. For instance, according to this," tapping the surface with a well-nibbled fingernail, "a number of the coven members are listed as inactive or, in the case of Paul Briere, missing altogether."

That gave me a start. I hadn't noticed the absence of Briere's name. The master chef was, as far as I knew, one of the Baron's closest confidantes.

Georgie shrugged. "The fault might lie in the system. I'm afraid I cannot vouch for the accuracy of this material. I *am* sorry."

I counted the names in my notebook. "Do there *have* to be thirteen members? Is that mandatory? Because with Briere gone and some of the others listed as inactive or whatever..."

"The figure of thirteen is part of popular folklore but not necessarily set in stone," Georgie stated.

"True." Something else was bothering her. "Did you notice the Baron was one of the members listed as inactive?"

"*What?*" I flipped back to my list.

"I've heard rumblings that there had been changes lately. Fischer and Victor Skorzeny cleaning house. Forcing out some of the old guard."

"The Baron would let them to do that?" Dumbfounded at the notion.

"He may not have been given much of a choice. Victor Skorzeny isn't a man you want to trifle with." She looked at Georgie. "You say your system's been giving you trouble lately?"

"Yes." Georgie's face clouded over. "I hesitate to say this but based on my preliminary investigations, it shows signs of tampering, perhaps even *corruption.*"

We gaped at him. "I...wouldn't have believed that was possible," she ventured.

"Nor would I," he agreed, "but the evidence is persuasive. We have been seeking the source of the infiltration but thus far have had little success. I can only tell you that it appears to be the work of someone of considerable power and sophistication." He was clearly peeved. "Well, I shan't bore you with my speculations."

"Who would want to do something like that? What would be motivating them?"

He nodded. "Those are excellent questions, Mr. Nightstalk. Believe me when I say they are among the many for which we are currently seeking answers." He cleared his throat. "Now if you'll excuse me, I must be about my business. Do you require further assistance or--"

"No," Cassandra replied, "you've given us plenty to think about. Thank you, Georgie."

"My pleasure, Miss Zinnea. And good day to *you*, Mr. Nightstalk."

Before I could answer, he was gone.

The Cabal, under the Baron's direction, consisted of rich, bored kooks who hoped that making a pact with the dark side would grease the way for a merger or help them scratch a sexual itch they'd endured and/or nurtured for many a long year. The majority of the Cabal-leros (Cass loved that one) were people who should have known better, one of them being Vivien Vickers. Yes, *the* Vivien Vickers, beloved siren of the silver screen. She always gave the impression of being a pretty sharp lady. How she ended up associating with a bunch of posers and dilettantes—

"I love Georgie." Cassandra said, temporarily derailing my train of thought. "He makes me feel special. He's so old-fashioned and elegant. A gentleman. Did you see how he kissed my hand as we were leaving?"

I steered the Taurus around two drunks dancing in the middle of the street. One of them flipped me the bird for this act of consideration. "It was very, uh, chivalrous," I allowed, electing not to mention the rather prominent erection the archivist had sported while performing the aforementioned deed.

"That's exactly the right word. *Chivalrous.* I like that in a man. So many guys I know are so...coarse. Present company excluded," she quickly amended. She switched on the overhead light and began to dig through the contents of her purse. "Do you know how Sir Richard Francis Burton refers to a woman's naughty bits?" She held up a paperback. *The Erotic Traveller.*

"Tell me." I was mad at myself. I'd taken Finlayson Drive out of habit, somehow forgetting that much of it was closed off for resurfacing and maintenance, an annual rite of spring. I was about to make my second detour. At that moment, if she offered to give me a tutorial on the finer points of quantum physics, I would've welcomed the distraction.

"'Mound of Venus'." She sighed and settled back in the bucket seat. "*The Mound of Venus.* If I hear it one more time, I'm yours for the taking, Nightstalk, I swear. We'll pull over and for the next hour we'll forget about the case, our careers, the Old Man, everything. What do you say?"

Mound of Venus! Mound of Venus! But only thinking it. Even so, I was afraid to look at her. Afraid of what my face would reveal, even in such lousy light.

"Do you know your ears are glowing?" She giggled. "I'm serious. It's like I'm seeing them in infrared. Their heat signatures. Now they're actually *smoking*—"

"Could we *please* change the subject?" I groaned. I was *this* close to pulling the steering wheel off.

"Don't you think that's a big improvement over 'cooze' or 'snatch' or the various crude euphemisms people employ for such a sacred part of the anatomy?"

"Sacred?"

"Well, men worship it, don't they?" she fired back.

"Certain ones," I allowed. I could tell she was watching me so I kept my eyes straight ahead, approaching the third and, hopefully, last detour.

"Anyone I know?" she teased.

"I thought we were changing the subject." I was sweating, literally on the hot seat. She was toying with me and part of me was enjoying it. Kind of.

"That was your ears, now we're back to the Mound of Venus." She sighed again.

"Y'know, it gets any muggier in here, we're gonna have rain," I bitched, cracking open the window to make my point .

"I was going to read you something..." She started paging through *The Erotic Traveller.*

"Please don't," I begged. "High class porn is wasted on a deviant like me." I glanced over at her and we burst out laughing. We were giddy, stupid, our minds fried from trying to get a handle on this fucked up case, let alone *solving* it. Laughing was a release valve.

It got real quiet afterward. Almost like post-coital letdown. An awkward silence that lingered like a smelly beer fart.

For some reason I started thinking about the many long, dark nights we'd spent together over the past two years. Back at the office or, better yet, on stakeouts. Stuck in a car for hours on end with the most beautiful, intelligent woman I'd ever met. Tough job, huh?

What I remembered most about those nights was that they always seemed to end on an unsatisfactory note, important things left stubbornly unsaid. Both of us fearful, I suppose, of what the repercussions might be if certain words were ever spoken out loud.

Not that we didn't have great conversations. Witness the following exchange, as recorded in my trusty notebook. At the time we were parked down the block from a restaurant where our suspect was enjoying a solitary meal. Needless to say, we were bored out of our minds and so:

Cassandra Zinnea on "The Goddess Within"

ZINNEA: My whole routine? Are you serious?

NIGHTSTALK: Yeah. I'll take it down in my distinctive shorthand. Type it up later.

ZINNEA: But will you be able to read it?

NIGHTSTALK: Just get on with it.

ZINNEA: Well, it may sound really weird and superstitious but I always get up on the same side of the bed. No matter where I am, I get out the right side. Because I know if I go left, it would throw off my whole day. I'd be a wreck. Are you sure you're getting this? Are you doing it this way because I fried your tape recorder last week?

NIGHTSTALK: You didn't have to touch it.

ZINNEA: I brushed it with my hand. Honestly, the way you carried on you would've thought it was a family heirloom or something.

NIGHTSTALK: I'm waiting here.

ZINNEA: The first thing I do every morning is re-align my *chi*. That's my life force. You know I'm very moon-oriented; the fuller it is, the better I feel. Unless I get moonstruck, of course—

NIGHTSTALK: Can you explain that?

ZINNEA: (*Giggling*) Well, you've seen me. When the moon is at its ripest, I sometimes get more, um, more *everything*. Smarter and faster and sexier...and, of course, the reverse is true. As the moon wanes—

NIGHTSTALK: You cry a lot.

ZINNEA: There's more to it than that! I'm vulnerable, at my lowest ebb. Really logey and out of sorts.

NIGHTSTALK: So what do you do to fight it?

ZINNEA: Try to keep my body and spirit in proper alignment. That whole mindfulness thing I've been trying to get you into. It would do wonders for you, believe me.

NIGHTSTALK: Right.

ZINNEA: I do this series of exercises to get everything back into synch. It's basically seven or eight different movements designed to, I don't know, reintegrate everything. I used to do them out on my balcony but the creep across the courtyard started taking pictures so now I use a yoga mat in my living room.

NIGHTSTALK: Could I see a few of them? Just to get the general idea.

ZINNEA: The first one goes...and then you move to...

(*And even though seated in the cramped confines of the Taurus, she proceeds to demonstrate a degree of flexibility that would make the compilers of the Kama Sutra drool.*)

Once I get limbered up you'd be surprised by the positions I can get myself into. Is that enough or--

NIGHTSTALK: Yeah, well, I think I get the point. What comes next?

ZINNEA: I should have mentioned that I always face east when I do my warmup. That's important. I focus on the power of the Earth rolling beneath me, drawing my strength from it. Calling on the Goddess to protect me and make me worthy of being her servant. Well...it's more complicated than that. There's sort of a pantheon of wise women. Selene, Artemis, Hecate: I call upon qualities that are associated with each of them. Maid, mother and crone.

NIGHTSTALK: So these are actual incantations requesting protection against, ah, curses and dark forces and that sort of thing.

ZINNEA: Well, there's that but there's also a whole other spiritual component that you're missing. It's about striving for communion with the infinite. Trying, through prayers and meditation, to achieve the sense of being an extension of the cosmic mind. The all-pervasive female consciousness responsible for...*everything*. She gave birth to the Earth, the Heavens, space, time, eleven dimensions so far and still counting. It wasn't a Big Bang, Nightstalk, it was a Big *Squirt*. Did you just roll your eyes?

NIGHTSTALK: *Rii-iight.* But what about...you also have all sorts of amulets and talismans--

ZINNEA: I'm glad you make the distinction. Most people don't. And again, they aren't just about protection from evil. They represent part of my belief system, who I am and the things most important to me. Love, Eros, wonder, laughter, the pursuit of wisdom, justice—

(Leaning forward to point out an assortment of symbols and stones hanging from her neck or from thin, silver bands on her wrists.)

This is Hyacinth, for healing. And this reddish-brown stone is sarder, for passion. This signifies Mercury, for intelligence. Yggdrasil, the World

Tree. And here's the cosmic egg. You gave me that one.

NIGHTSTALK: For infinity.

ZINNEA: For *forever*. It's my favorite.

NIGHTSTALK: And is that the end of your ritual preparations?

ZINNEA: You're still missing the point, Nightstalk. You shrink from the idea but it's my version of *prayer*. It's when I connect with the higher powers. Get my marching orders. I usually meditate for awhile, clear my mind for the day ahead. Do you have daymares? Aren't they the worst? I don't think nightmares even compare.

NIGHTSTALK: Daytime dreams seem more real, they're harder to shake after you wake up.

ZINNEA: You notice that too? And they're more believable, even when they don't make sense. *Scarier*. So that's part of the purification too. Purging the dreams that refuse to fade away, that might still be skulking around the dark corners of my mind. And then...well, other than taking a shower and popping a multivitamin right after I eat, that's about it. How about you?

NIGHTSTALK: What do you mean?

ZINNEA: C'mon, Nightstalk, don't be coy. Don't you have certain rituals or whatever? Crazy superstitions?

NIGHTSTALK: I crack my knuckles.

ZINNEA: That's an annoying habit, not a ritual.

NIGHTSTALK: At least once a week I like getting into a scrap with two or three seriously *big* guys.

I'd say I'm fairly religious about it. That's how *I* stay mindful, doll.

ZINNEA: In that case, you're talking about a *felony*. You mean to tell me you don't have any crazy beliefs or customs, things you do in the privacy of your apartment? What do you do when you go home in the morning? *(Long pause)* Nightstalk?

NIGHTSTALK: That's personal. I think I've got all I need for now...

Wednesday, May 5th

The night after our trip to the Hall of Records, *After Hours Investigations* received a visitor. In my experience, such occasions rarely boded well. The people who came to see us in person invariably fell into two categories: they were either slightly loopy or out and out nuts. There didn't seem to be any middle ground. Mainly, it was locals, not too many clients willing to risk the drive into mid-town after dark. A silly prejudice; trouble will find you wherever you are, it's only a matter of time.

Dealing with the Renfields was the worst part. Street folk too far gone to know any better, assorted crackpots banging on our door, expecting us to fix their fucked up lives. Someone's been following them or they're secretly millionaires, see, except they've got amnesia and want to hire us to find out who they really are. One guy even tried to *stab* me. Apparently I reminded him of his older brother, Vern.

I preferred it when the Old Man assigned us a case, leaving a typed, unsigned memo on our desk, telling us to look into this or that. Situations ranging from the trivial to the near-lethal, depending on his whims.

The vast majority of the people entering our building through the street door made a sharp right turn into *The Tool Shed* to lay in a fresh supply of lubricants or pick up another batch of cappuccino-flavoured condoms. But around 11:45 someone came in and began a slow, steady advance up the steps. *Clump, clump, clump.*

I saw my partner tense and glance toward the door. "Oh, *drat*. I think I forgot to recharge the warding spell on the front door. I've been meaning to but--"

Clump, clump...

Whoever it was was right outside, although he or she seemed to be having trouble with the whole doorknob concept. "I've been expecting this." Her frown deepened as the scrabbling at the door became more frenzied. She fingered an amulet on her throat and mumbled a mantra of protection. My right hand brushed the pea shooter I kept duct-taped under my side of the desk. A palm-sized Smith & Wesson .38. It didn't come equipped with silver bullets but it would do the job.

"I don't think whatever it is is dangerous," she announced, "it's hardly giving off any life force—"

The door opened…and a few seconds later a dead man shambled in. He wasn't clutching a black bird rolled in newspaper. Then again, he wasn't packing an Uzi either, much to my relief. I left the .38 where it was, for now.

As far the living dead went, he wasn't what you would call a prime specimen. His face was battered and he dragged one leg, which had been badly mangled in some mishap. "Holy Diana, Nightstalk, do you know who that is?" I shook my head. *It's Paul Briere.*"

I did a double take. I'd seen pictures of Chef Paul, even watched a few minutes of his Sunday morning cooking show once when I couldn't find anything else on. Still, I had a hard time associating that guy with the deadhead in front of me. "Are you sure?"

"He must have been wandering around for *hours,*" Cassandra proposed. "Yes, he was lost, circling the block, trying to find the right door. Look at his injuries. I'll bet he can't see out of that eye. Nearly blind, confused…"

"Do you think someone waited too long to re-animate him or whatever?" I couldn't believe how clinical I sounded when confronted by such a macabre scene. Talk about jaded.

She came around the desk but was reluctant to approach the corpse formerly known as Paul Briere. "This a terrible thing. Someone truly evil has done this."

He was facing the wrong way, trying to speak. It came out garbled, verbal mush.

"*Oi!*" I called, snapping my fingers. "We're over here, Paul buddy. *Hey!*" I waved my arms, trying to catch the attention of his good eye.

"Don't, Nightstalk," she implored. "It's not his fault this has been done to him. He's a victim, not a bad guy. Look at him," she said and we watched as he slowly tacked in our direction. "Whoever's doing this is *sick.* I suspect they're using the power they gained from the park killing. This is black arts crap at its worst and I *hate* it."

It took him awhile but he finally got himself facing the right way.

He opened his mouth to deliver his message and promptly vomited a pint or two of fresh maggots and weevils onto the carpet.

She blanched. "Oh, *gross*. I am *not* cleaning that up, Nightstalk. No way. I'll take on the demons of hell, fend off magicians and warlocks and risk eternal damnation for this place, but I will not go *near* freshly puked maggots. That's a *blue* job, partner."

I glared at the offending cadaver. "You asshole. I oughta toss you out the window and see what kind of splash you make. You are fouling our personal space, motherfucker, and—"

"*Be...warned*," he gurgled. "You...are...in...*dangerrrr...*"

"This is *vicious*," Cassandra stated. "It's bad enough they've disturbed the dead, but to torture him like this..." Her lips were tight with anger.

"You are...tampering...you must...stop." More maggots pattered onto the carpet.

"I am going to toss my cookies in a minute," she gulped.

"Oh, for God's sake, woman! You've seen people ripped apart and decapitated before your eyes.[13] A few measly bugs shouldn't bother you." I was pretty brassed off at that point. It wouldn't be the first time I'd had to vacuum up maggots and I knew it wasn't a pleasant duty. "Okay, buster, finish saying whatever it is you have to say and then fuck off and decompose somewhere."

"Let *me* talk to him," she urged. Addressing the ambulatory corpse: "Who are you?" The stiff pivoted awkwardly to face her. "Who speaks through this poor creature?"

His lips moved, curling upward. An attempt at a smile? "You will...stop inquiries...live longer."

"Right. 'Stop inquiries, live longer'. That seems pretty clear to me. Message received. Anything else, douchebag?"

"*Wait*." She stood directly in front of him. "I want to know who this is. Whoever you are, you've been meddling with the Goetia.[14] You'll pay dearly for that."

"Perrrhaps," the cadaver gurgled, with another twitch of those cracked, grey lips, "the Goetia...has been...meddling with me."

---

[13] A few examples: "Medusa's Heir", "The Bride of the Nephew of the Son of Frankenstein", "Someone is Killing the Great Porn Stars of Europe" (*The Casebooks of Zinnea & Nightstalk, Vol. I*); "The Smiling Vivisectionist", "Charlie Was No Angel" (*Casebooks, Vol. II*); "The Affair of the Interesting Accountant" (*Casebooks, Vol. III*).

[14] A grimoire or book of black magic devoted to the invocation and control of spirits

She nodded and came over to stand beside me.

"So is that it?" I asked. "Nothing else you want to add, fuckface?"

He gazed at me, doll-eyed. *"There are some things...worse...than...death."*

Hearing him say that gave me a funny feeling. Was it part of the warning or some surviving fragment of Paul Briere's personality letting us know what hell was *really* like?

He tottered toward the door and I prayed he'd negotiate the stairs all right. I imagined what would happen if he slipped and took a bad fall. He'd come apart at the seams, explode all over the front landing like an over-ripe melon. Maggots are one thing; picking up bits and pieces of burst open dead guys something else. Definitely *not* part of my job description (I'd check the fine print to make sure).

I listened and he managed to make it down okay. Bless his decaying carcass.

"He's on his last legs. Looking for somewhere to curl up and die. For good this time." Her voice husky with emotion.

"R.I.P., motherfucker." Displaying my usual sensitivity.

She moved back to her side of the desk. "I think this visit was most instructive, don't you?"

"Yeah," I concurred, "real educational. I never knew how many different varieties of maggots there are until now." I went downstairs and borrowed Maude's shop vac. Lugged it up to the office and got to work on the bug-splattered carpet while my partner ruminated, chair tipped back, her gaze directed at the ceiling. She was going through the clues, reviewing the evidence, synthesizing every piece of information we had accumulated thus far.

Or maybe it was all just an act; pretending to be deep and thoughtful so she could duck out on the maggot detail.

Blue job, my great auntie's panties.

I finished the vacuuming. Considerably dumped and rinsed the receptacle before returning the machine to Maude, no worse for wear. When I came back, my partner was still in the same position, wearing the exact same expression.

"Okay, resident genius, let's hear what's on your mind."

"Just analyzing things, factoring in some new variables."

"Such as?"

"This tactic, or whatever you want to call it, was meant to impress us but in execution it seemed...clumsy." She paused before continuing. "If the Cabal *was* responsible, their powers are still nascent, not fully formed."

She lapsed into silence again, her mind attacking the case from every conceivable angle, a multiplicity of viewpoints.

My job, on the other hand, was to point out the bleedin' obvious. "But it also tells us these people are serious. Not every garden variety black magician can raise the dead."

She fluffed her hair. It was longer again; curly, with red highlights. "True. However, whoever's behind this is still developing as an adept. They're not invulnerable—at least, not yet."

"On the other hand, I'd say they're showing real promise," I commented.

"Did you hear what he said about the Goetia? He knew the quote."

"Right. And what quote are we referring to?"

"The first time Allan Bennett met Aleister Crowley, he accused him of meddling with the Goetia. Crowley's response was almost word for word what Briere said."

"You said Gregory Fischer was really into Crowley." She nodded. "Great. So he's behind this. Showing off and trying to scare the piss out of us at the same time."

"I'll do what I can to protect us," she promised. "I'll upgrade office defenses, use stronger spells and counter-measures. I'll make it so anything that doesn't have a body temperature of a living, breathing human being can't take more than three steps inside the door without getting zapped."

"Make sure it covers mice. Something's been getting into my junk food stash again."

"You should be cutting down anyway."

"Sure, kid, whatever you say. One last question: can you be sure *any* spell you come up with will work against people who have the power to send zombie-grams? Maybe...maybe this is beyond you." I tried to choose my words carefully but it still came out wrong.

"I know what I'm doing, Nightstalk," she snapped, getting up and going over to the bookshelves. She started hauling down heavy tomes, some of them lacking covers, their bindings warped and split. "If I have to bring out the heavy artillery, I will. Big-time conjuring. Smoking cauldrons, consecrated circles, the whole nine yards. Obviously the situation has changed and we have to take precautions. But I'm dealing with it, *okay?*"

"The Old Man should be helping more," I complained, hoping to deflect her anger elsewhere. "Or your buddy DeBarge. Seems like we're the ones running the risks."

She shook her head. "Philippe has his own problems right now, believe me. As for the Old Man...behind that door," she pointed, "he's working his magic. Sometimes I feel the building humming and I know he's up to something. It's been like that *a lot* lately. In terms of helping us, I think they *both* assume we're capable of taking care of ourselves. And they're right. We're the A-team, aren't we? We've proven ourselves, survived our trial by fire. If there's a problem, we can handle it."

"I'm worried that sometimes people forget we're, y'know, mere mortals. You're good, kid, real good, but even you can't outrun a bullet." I loved that hard-boiled talk.

"The Old Man and Philippe have their priorities, we have ours." She flashed a smile of encouragement my way. "Right now, the first thing we have to do is seal off those stairs to non-human entities. I think I know a nasty aversion spell that I can adapt into..." Paging through a text with thin, brittle pages, covered in fancy lettering.

I don't know why, for some reason I couldn't leave well enough alone. I pretended to be working on my report about the visit from the warmed up remains of Chef Paul, but all the while I was brooding. Trying to figure out what she could possibly see in someone like Philippe DeBarge.

I cleared my throat. "Y'know, come to think of it, it was probably your old boyfriend who tipped off the bad guys about us. Who knows what they have in store for us next. Maybe nail a fucking *cat* to our door." Rubbing salt in that old wound. "Agents of the Black Brotherhood tend to draw attention, often not positive attention, if you get my drift."

"Is there a point to this rather odd digression?" she inquired warily.

"Only that it isn't surprising we're having quasi-dead people dropping by not long after a friendly visit from one of the Brethren." She was no longer immersed in the book in front of her; I had her complete attention. "Our buddy Philippe's movements have likely been monitored since he got here, which means—"

She shook her head, visibly irritated with my reasoning. "Nightstalk, whatever you think of Philippe, the man is a consummate professional. He'd pick up any tail and lose them like *that*." She snapped her fingers and a framed picture of Allan Pinkerton crashed to the floor on the other side of the room. She flinched and shrugged apologetically.

"Watch it," I warned. "Remember what you've been reading."

"Some of it must be rubbing off," she quipped.

"No kidding."

"I know you don't like Philippe, Nightstalk—"

"Change 'don't like' to 'loathe' and 'Philippe' to 'pompous shithead' and you're pretty much spot on."

"*Fine*. Regardless, we're stuck with him. So whatever it is you have against him, I suggest you get over it." She saw my sour puss. "Yes, Evgeny, he and I were very close at one time. Sorry about that. Sorry about my overall lousy taste in men. Is that what you want to hear? Are you happy now?"

I tried to act innocent but that's never been my strong suit. "Hey, I'm sorry if I was out of line or—"

She slammed the book shut, producing an impressive cloud of dust. "No, it's better if we deal with this right now. You despise Philippe, he despises you. I like both of you, but you also make me want to scream. The point is we're all in this together and I expect everyone to act as adults and that *especially* applies to you."

"Sorry as hell to have brought the whole thing up," I said meekly, unsettled by her anger.

"Shut up." She pointed her finger at me and I thought for a second she was going to *zap* me. She was mad enough. "Philippe is a pain but we'll manage. All I ask is that you don't mess things up to the point where we won't have a chance to pry anything decent out of the supercilious bastard."

"Okay. I hear you." Submitting to her utterly, doing everything but baring my backside to her.

"For the record, I *hate* the way he talks down to you, like you're some kind of moron or lackey." Score one for Evgeny Nightstalk. "I also *hate* the way you try to bully him, puffing up and going all Popeye, cracking your knuckles like some kind of Neanderthal thug. Which is exactly the way he perceives you, by the way, so nice going." Going on to the next point. "I *hate* the way he flirts with me when, truthfully, he has no more interest in me than a side of beef." Then she unloaded her big guns. "And I absolutely *hate* the way you assume some kind of proprietary role over me, disapproving of my lovers, *as if you have any right to tell me how to live my life*. We're *partners*, Nightstalk, and that's all we'll ever be so you'd better face it." I lowered my head. It was a worse beating than any I'd absorbed in my many years as a pugilist. I was on the verge of begging for mercy.

"Is it because—I'm only 2nd Degree?" Giving voice to my worst fear.

"That's part of it," she replied. "That's something else you have to deal with. You aren't Gifted and you don't cultivate what few powers you *do* have...but, Nightstalk, your biggest problem has always been *you don't believe*. Being an adept means transcending yourself, your limitations as a creature of flesh and blood. Drawing on the strength of a miraculous, *divine* source." She took pity on me, leaning forward, softening her tone. "Until you give yourself over to that higher power, Evgeny, Philip DeBarge is way out of your league."

"I still don't trust him," I declared obstinately.

"Oh, listen to yourself, Nightstalk! Philippe has devoted his entire life to cultivating his magical abilities. He is absolutely incorruptible. Do you know what the Brethren puts their people through, the training regimen? You don't speak for *five* years. Fourteen hours of instruction and meditation every day, seven days a week. No contact with the outside world. And the most important thing you learn, what's ingrained in your very being, is that the universe is a living entity, informed by a central, conscious, directed *will*. A will to life, a will to *create*. And we're part of it, everything sacred, everything divine. Even us. With all of our flaws and weaknesses..."

"I don't exactly live in denial, you know," I argued, trying to rally. "I've seen things with my own eyes that would drive most ordinary people nuts. I know these powers exist. You don't have to convince me."

"But you don't take it any further. Part of you will never accept anything I've just said. You're like one of those debunkers, willfully blind to the ineffable forces at work in the universe. Conscious energies that can be accessed by true believers. But you rationalize that away. To you, most adepts are some kind of clever sleight-of-hand artists, *illusionists*. 'All mediums are quacks, astrology is crap, religion is crap'. That about sums it up, doesn't it?" She stared across the desk at me, daring me to deny it.

"I—well, maybe. But still—still—" *What?* I was boxed in by her unrelenting logic.

"What do you find so hard to believe? You've seen ghosts and demons, every manner of phenomena...why can't you believe in a god or goddess? *Any* god? And if there's a god, doesn't that mean there's a possibility, even a probability, that there's an *anti*-god, a diametric opposite, the two forces eternally at war with each other? Call it Manichaeism, call it what you will."

"B-but I don't think I've ever denied the existence of these forces you're talking about."

"The higher powers I speak of are, to my mind, as real as this desk." She rapped her knuckles on its scarred surface. "Unseen and ever present. But it's not that way for you. In your heart, you're a skeptic. You see evil everywhere, people getting away with murder...but when things work out right for a change and good triumphs, you don't acknowledge the invisible hands responsible. The grand design that is slowly taking shape over great spans of time."

"You see design but maybe it's chance or plain, old coincidence."

"*There is no such thing as a coincidence.* Everything is connected. At least in the world *I* live in. You're still half in and half out, not sure which way you're going to jump."

"I *want* to believe," I blurted. "And as much as you may hate to hear it right now, you're the one who makes me feel that way. You're someone I really rely on...put these things into perspective for me."

She smiled, relenting. "Thank you. I'm glad you see me in that light. I also know you love me and that you're trying to protect me from...the worst parts of who I am. You're so solid and reassuring. Sometimes I think you're the only thing that keeps me going. I mean that." She ran her fingers along the edges of the dusty book in front of her.

"I'll try to make nice with DeBarge," I vowed. "And I promise I'll work on the rest of it too. Maybe with your help I could take a crack at making at least 3rd Degree. The psychometry would be a bitch, I don't have a sensitive bone in my body."

"But at least you'd be *trying*. Of course I'll help you. It's the least I can do after my little tantrum." She held out her hand. "Pals?"

"Always."

She plunged back into the antique book, occasionally mumbling words or phrases, working on her pronunciation, committing relevant portions to memory.

I decided to put off writing the report on Maggot Man. I needed to be *doing* something.

I informed my partner I was going out to try to rustle up a few leads. Hopped in the Taurus and hit some places I knew. Private clubs and hangouts that never advertised and never closed. Establishments offering an assortment of attractions, as long as you weren't too squeamish and minded your own damn business. I never stayed long. Whispered a word or two in certain ears. Trolling for information. No threats or intimidation. On my best behavior. Not looking to make any new enemies. Almost as an afterthought asking if anybody had run across my old buddy, Glen.

Heard from Glen lately? You know Glen, right?

Sure, everybody knew Glen.

If not by sight, then at least by reputation...

While I was out and about, my partner was exploring other, more rewarding avenues of investigation.

Almost as soon as I'd left the premises, a messenger arrived. Not your garden variety flunky either, some anonymous, blank-faced functionary with the personality of a doorstop.

The Baron, true to form, sent a *ghost*.

Fortunately, Cassandra was well-nigh unflappable when it came to apparitions. She told me she could always tell when a spook was in the vicinity; the fine, little hairs on her arms stood up.

"Who's there?"

Something was flickering, coalescing over by the door, fading in and out like a radio signal from a lost ship. Finally she could make out who it was and smiled to herself. Expedited the ghost's arrival by deactivating her defensive spells, reciting them backward, as custom required.

The ghost fully translated, though the resolution wasn't perfect and you could see through him in places. He seemed confused, looking about in bafflement.

"Hello, Roger. *Roger*? Over here…"

She caught his attention and he smiled in relief when he recognized her. "Ah, excellent. I thought for a moment I had transmitted to the wrong location. That can be most awkward." He gazed at her with an expression of bemused interest. His absent-mindedness was notorious.

"I take it there was something you were supposed to tell me?" she prompted him. "A message…"

"Ah! Yes, of course. Well, it's more of an invitation really."

She nodded. "When and where?"

"Yes, well, ah…it was supposed to be at your convenience." He shrugged. "But you know my employer."

"He really means fifteen minutes."

He seemed grateful for her intuitive grasp of the situation. "There will be a car waiting in front of the building." He hesitated. "Your colleague is not here tonight?"

"He's out."

The apparition, mission accomplished, was losing definition, nearly transparent. "So you will be coming alone? Good. That will please my master all the more."

The Baron was punctual, as usual.

Fifteen minutes and thirty seconds later she was being whisked on her way to Little Bavaria. She'd made two previous visits to the Baron's personal Xanadu, both times in my company.[15] Those encounters had been cordial, despite my best efforts to act up and generally misbehave.

Little Bavaria is supposedly a miniature version of a castle near Munich. It looks like something out of a fairy tale. Tall, rounded turrets and stained glass windows. There's even a moat of stagnant water and a drawbridge that swings down to admit you inside. It sits on a big parcel of expensive real estate in the city's most exclusive suburb, Breed Grove, Ilium's version of Bel Air. Not bad, when you consider the castle and its trimmings were built on the ill-gotten gains of all manner of nefarious schemes. The Baron was, if nothing else, a world-class swindler.

My partner didn't mind playing up to the old lech but I couldn't abide him. I thought that as far as phonies went, he gave Eva Jauch a run for her money.

The Baron liked to come across as a mysterious Count St. Germain figure. Eternally old and all-powerful. That whole "mystery man" routine, what a load of bullshit. He'd drop hints that he had been present at Waterloo or acted as special envoy to various Popes and potentates down through the ages. He knew his history and told a good yarn. Some of the details he threw in to add colour to his stories had a ring of authenticity to them. But I'd be willing to bet my last dollar that if you did some digging, you'd find out the guy was really one Walter S. Mitty, hick son of the best barber in Polk City, Iowa.

It probably wasn't coincidental that the Baron's unearthly messenger didn't show up until after I'd removed myself from the scene. He knew what I thought of him and his Cagliostro routine.

The drawbridge came down with a rattle of thick chains. Once it *thunked* into place, the metallic grey Mercedes coupe continued on into the castle's courtyard.

She was ushered inside, passing across the threshold and through doors twelve feet high, sporting the Baron's ancestral crest (as far as I was ever able to make out, it depicted two badgers fucking on a four poster bed). Roger, appearing slightly more substantial here at home, led the way to the Baron's spacious study. She noticed as she followed him that despite his best efforts at preserving the illusion, Roger's feet weren't *quite* touching the ground.

The walls of the study were crammed floor-to-ceiling with precious first editions, works of arcana from down through the ages. The Baron's

---

[15] "Come, Darkness" (*The Casebooks of Zinnea & Nightstalk, Volume I*); "The Tingler" (*Casebooks, Vol. III*)

collection was legendary. There were volumes on every aspect of the supernatural and occult, many extremely rare (and not a few banned or proscribed by either the Vatican or the Brethren...or both).

Left to her own devices, she browsed, clucking with pleasure when she spotted certain titles. Tugging a leather bound book from its slot, she made herself comfortable in one of the big armchairs placed before the enormous hearth. A fire was burning but the brisk, flickering flames produced no appreciable heat. It was a spectral effect, meant to impress.

The Baron entered and found her deeply engrossed in the book.

"Just a moment," she said, without looking up from her reading, "I'd like to finish this section." He waited but inwardly he was likely fuming. Not a man known for his patience, our Baron. Finally she closed the book, stood and offered her hand. "Baron von Stahl. Frederick. How nice to see you again."

He smiled. "So. You have found something of interest in my collection of *incunabula*."

"Yes. Forgive my earlier impertinence." She held up the book. "I've never seen an actual copy of this. There are some who say it doesn't exist."

He took it from her. "May I?" Turning it over and glancing at the spine. "Hmm. Indeed. But please believe me when I tell you that its reputation far exceeds its actual value as a true artifact of the occult. It is a well-meaning blasphemy, nothing more. Portions of it are rather obvious reworkings of the *Kabbalah*. Which, of course, is where the search for knowledge *truly* begins." He motioned for her to reseat herself and settled into the armchair opposite her. "Don't you agree, my dear? Can you not tell the difference between pale imitation and the presence of...the ineffable?" He was keeping the banter light but she saw his eyes were tired and his posture less stiff and formal than usual.

"Something on your mind, Frederick? You appear..." She tried to be diplomatic. "Troubled."

He straightened. "I confess I am somewhat distracted this evening. Perhaps it is simply that I am overwhelmed by your ethereal beauty—"

"Take your hand off my knee, Baron, or I'll inherit the family jewels, if you get my meaning."

"Of course. Certainly." He sat back in the chair, absorbing the rebuff with good grace. "A token attempt at seduction, my dear. To preserve my reputation, you understand."

"I understand completely. Now tell me what's bothering you."

"Nothing, my dear. Simply a case of being over-tired." His hands trembled. He tried lacing them together on his stomach but they kept jumping around on him. It took a great deal of effort to restrain them. "Shall I pour us some wine? Or perhaps you would prefer something stronger. I am, as always, your servant."

She refused to allow the conversation to veer off-topic. "You know, I have a pretty good sense when someone's lying to me, especially someone I've known for a number of years and whom I consider a friend."

"Cassandra, I assure you—"

"Look, Frederick..." She didn't cut him any slack, I give her credit for that. "I personally don't care if you're nine hundred years old and as wise as Solomon...or the world's greatest grifter. Understand? Fake or fakir, it's all the same to me. You're someone I care about and if I can help you, I will. So spill it: what's on your mind?"

He stared at her, taken aback by her directness. Clearly agitated, he got up and began to pace back and forth before the comfortless fire. "I find myself in a difficult situation. While I would like to reward your astuteness, at the same time I am afraid..." He paused. "Yes, that is exactly right: *I am afraid.*"

She closed her eyes, extending mental feelers. "You're barely holding on," she whispered, surprised at the intensity of what she was picking up. "You're in over your head. You don't know what to do. Things have spun out of control. You're wondering if it's too late to extricate yourself—"

Then, *wham*, powerful shields slammed into place, an insurmountable wall severing all contact between their two minds. He nodded in appreciation. "Impressive. *Very* good. The equivalent of a 5th Degree, I would say. In future, I must remember that and take proper precautions."

"Your screens are leaking. You're trying to hold too much in."

Suddenly he really *did* look nine hundred years old. "Please," he implored, "we must not speak of these things."

He should have known better than that. "Where's Paul Briere, Frederick?" He shuddered, closing his eyes. "Would you like to know? I saw him tonight. What was left of him." She described the encounter.

"*Mein Gott...*"

"All right, Frederick," she said, "I want to know what's going on. You know me and you know you can trust me."

"Yes, my dear. You're quite right, I retain a great deal of respect for your formidable intellect *and* your discretion. You must understand that the only reason I cannot, ah, illuminate you further is out of concern for your safety. Endangering you, dear Cassandra, is one of the few sins I simply will not commit."

She was touched. "But you brought me here tonight. Sent Roger to fetch me—"

He bowed, all stiffness and *faux* Prussian formality again. "Please forgive the inconvenience. It was an error in judgement on my part. I had heard the Old Man was looking into certain matters and I thought...I thought..."

"Thought you'd warn me?" She ventured. After a few seconds, he nodded. "Why risk it? I don't understand. What's your motivation? *Friendship*? Is that it?"

He smiled but, like the fire, it lacked warmth. "We are fellow explorers. Colleagues. Our life paths have taken us in different directions and yet we...I feel a certain..." His head dropped. "Please, you must go now. Good night and fare you well." He turned away.

"I know you. You would never have gone along with what they did to Paul or the killing of a Brethren agent, for that matter." He stopped. "You created the Cabal, they're *your* group. You were into sex magick and admitted to me that starting a coven was a great way to get laid." His shoulders slumped perceptibly. She got up and moved toward him. "Now you stand by and watch *your* creation taken over, usurped by a *nouveau riche* buffoon." She told me later that when she finished, she held her breath, not certain what sort of response her gambit would provoke.

He spoke without turning around. "Five years ago I moved to this inconsequential city and commenced work on what has charmingly been called Little Bavaria. At first, I did not know what drew me to this place but then I began to notice indications of great energies at work here. I had the matter looked into by eminent specialists and they confirmed my suspicions. It may be the proximity to a large body of water or the result of certain important ley lines converging. I have also heard stories that this area was once the site of an ancient Indian burial ground.[16] Possibly it was a place of sacrifice, where fierce savages ritually tortured and killed their prisoners." He turned to face her. "Whatever the truth may be, there *is* something special about Ilium. Something in the air, you might say." He wandered back and reseated himself. "I moved in and gradually attracted a group of like-minded individuals, fellow searchers all. We rejected the quaint notions of Christianity, Judaism and their pale imitators, outdated

---

[16] I checked with this guy I know, Alvin Longbottom, who scoffed at the suggestion. "This whole area used to be one big swamp, dude. They had to fill it in to build your fuckin' city. Only white people have that much time and energy to waste. You think Indians would be dumb enough to put a graveyard in a fuckin' *swamp*?"

concepts of right and wrong. We sought freedom from the tyranny of the status quo and answers to great questions. For some of us, our group became a symbol of hope for a better world."

"But then Gregory Fischer arrived on the scene."

His upper lip curled in contempt. "That *peasant*. He is crude and unlearned and vacuous, as you have so accurately intuited. Enriched by risking other people's money, nothing more than a parasite. A venture capitalist. *Ugh*. Do we really need to speak of these things?"

"Only if he's the one behind what's been going on." He looked uncomfortable at her choice of words so she backed off. "Okay...look. If there's *anything* you can tell me, some way that I might be of service to you—damnit, Freddie, I swear I'll do my best to help. Nothing you say will leave this room."

"Does that include your partner?"

"No," she admitted. "I keep nothing from him and trust him with my soul."

"Then he is not as big a lout as he pretends?"

She laughed. "Like a few others I can name, Nightstalk plays his role to the hilt. Surely you can acknowledge another consummate performer."

He chuckled. "Of course. You are quite right. Your Mr. Nightstalk and I are like two great hams, bent on trying to upstage each other. If you trust him, that is good enough for me." There was an interval of silence as he considered his next words. "But I confess I am torn. I don't know what information can be safely imparted. I feel I must be...reticent, for both our sakes."

"Who are you worried about, Gregory Fischer or Victor Skorzeny?"

He flinched. "No, my dear," he shook his head, his face grave. "Such boldness can have unfortunate, even fatal consequences."

"Why? Can you at least tell me—"

He raised his hands, a quieting gesture. "Certain unnamed individuals have acquired powers far beyond their capacity to control. Somehow they have managed to gain access to depraved and profane texts." His eyes lost focus; a sightless stare. "These same people are using my organization for their own evil ends. We were students, pilgrims of sorts. Enlightened amateurs. We dabbled, to be sure, but we were able to manifest certain tangible effects. That is undeniable. But for some this was not enough. So when...those people you mentioned arrived and began to insinuate themselves into our devoted circle, it created conflict, schism. There were private meetings from which I was excluded. Not only me--Paul and Vivien as well."

"So Vivien isn't part of this either?" He shook his head. "Good for her." She leaned forward and he followed suit, so that their heads were only inches apart. "Now tell me the truth: what do you know about the killing of the Brethren agent? I need to know about Arturs Esch, Frederick."

Baron Friedrich Burkhalter von Stahl answered without hesitation: "I had no part in the death of that poor devil. I did not have prior knowledge but...I doubt I could have stopped it even had I known. I told you, there are circles within circles in our group and I have been marginalized—"

"Marginalized? *You*? It's your coven. Are you and the others going to allow that to happen?"

"What choice do we have?" He threw up his hands. "Do you think we want to end up like Paul? The rest are allied with Fischer and that asshole Skorzeny or else they're deathly afraid of them. Skorzeny gives the impression he's capable of anything. He's the one to watch. Fischer is a mere playboy, him and that shrew of a wife. Capitalist swine. But no one dares question or raise their voice against them. Skorzeny and his goons see to that."

"Who ordered the killing of the Brethren agent? Fischer or--"

He shifted uneasily. "*Please*, Cassandra, must we speak of this?"

"But why risk such a bold move?"

He shook his head. "I cannot say. But I know they will not hesitate to eliminate anyone who gets in their way. *No one is safe.*" His face pale, strained.

"Do you have any intention of forcing the issue, confronting Fischer and Skorzeny? Would there be any point trying to rally support among the others?"

He regarded her with condescension. "I think such things would not only be unwise but distinctly unhealthy as well."

"But you can't just give up and let them get away with it. You must do *something*."

"Fight back? Challenge them to a duel, a black magic showdown at the O.K. Corral?" He shook his head. "I think not."

"I can't believe you're letting them intimidate you."

"As I told you, Skorzeny is a dangerous man. Pure evil. He and Fischer have done their job well. I am isolated, alone. There are meetings and I am not informed, decisions made without consulting me." He clenched his fists and muttered a German epithet.

"What are they up to? Can you at least give me a hint?"

He was emphatic. "No, my dear. Your ignorance is probably the only thing keeping you alive right now. The 'Cabal' you used to know is no longer a harmless group of students and researchers. You have seen evidence of their growing power."

"But what's going on? You tell me to be careful and then you--"

"They have obtained certain items, artifacts that, when wielded by the wrong people, can be very, very dangerous. *But that is only the beginning.*"

The ominousness with which the pronouncement was delivered caused her to draw back from him. "Yet you refuse to do anything about it. I knew you were amoral, Baron, but I never took you for a coward."

He averted his eyes. "As I have already explained, my enemies have taken on powers and abilities that I—" He froze. *"Cassandra..."*

She felt it too. A third presence in the room, as if someone had just entered and was waiting to be greeted and invited to join them for a spot of sherry and after dinner cigar. They looked about, a fruitless reflex. The intruder was not of the physical plane.

The Baron motioned her closer. "You see what it is like," he whispered. "We must speak no more of this."

A chilly breeze pushed past them. The fake fire was sputtering, dying down and then flaring up again. Someone making a point.

"I'll...say good night then." Movement behind her, the temperature around her plummeting. She could see her breath as she retrieved the book from the arm of the chair. "I was sure you'd have a copy of this. Thanks for loaning it to me on such short notice."

He shrugged, playing along. "It is a trifle. As I indicated, there are far more powerful and authentic grimoires available. That said..." His eyes met hers. "One must always exercise caution these days. There are other principalities involving themselves in our petty affairs, entities beyond the comprehension of even an agile mind such as yours."

Roger was waiting outside.

The Baron was shaken but remained in character. "I regret your visit cannot be a longer one. I do enjoy your company. Until we meet again, Miss Cassandra Zinnea."

"Take care, Baron." She surprised him by embracing him, using the opportunity to whisper: "Watch yourself, Freddie. Call if you need help."

When she moved back, she saw that he was having difficulty maintaining his composure. "Whatever comes to pass was meant to be. This much I learned a long time ago." He nodded and she caught on, switching over to telepathic mode: *Now you understand the forces at work. Be careful, my dear, and take all possible precautions.* He brought his heels together and bowed. "*Auf wiedersehen.*" The study door closed behind him.

Roger hovered at her elbow. She followed in his cool wake as he led the way back to the magnificent front doors.

"I hope to see you again soon, ma'am."

"I hope so too, Roger. Good night."

The driver had kept the Mercedes running so it was still warm for the return trip. She felt bad leaving him alone in that spooky, old castle. Wondered how many ghosts were chasing him, how many murders you could fit in a dozen lifetimes. One of the drawbacks of being virtually immortal, the way the sins accumulate, across centuries of villainy, avarice and deceit. The victims who refuse to rest easy, their roaming spirits bent on revenge.

III

"So-called 'luck' in investigation comes from diligent work. Observation without investigation or deduction is of little or no value."

Edward Smith, *A Practical Guide For Private Investigators*
(Paladin Press; 1990)

Friday, May 7th

Well, I may have been only a 2nd Degree but I still knew when I was being followed. Sixth sense or rampant paranoia? Sometimes I wasn't sure. For her part, my partner believed that most of us have at least some inherent extrasensory or supernatural powers, it's just a case of identifying and cultivating them.

Two nights after Cassandra's *tete a tete* with the Baron, I left our building and my spider sense immediately went *ping*. I estimated my tail to be about a hundred yards back and across the street. Now came the decision. Did I stay out in the open where he, she or it was unlikely to confront me or did I take an apparent shortcut down a dark, scary alley, deliberately inviting attack?

Those of you who can't guess the inevitable result of that line of reasoning haven't been paying close attention. But my pursuer refused to be drawn in and after my third fruitless detour into a dingy alley, I felt him withdraw. Sonofabitch wasn't up for a fight. Not that night.

Once I was satisfied he was gone, I made for O'Donnell Park. I was still keyed up. It had been nearly two weeks since I had dented someone's face with my knuckles and that was *way* too long by my standards. If I wasn't careful, I'd lose my edge.

I entered the park, finding it nearly deserted. It was only a block square, a patch of green space not far from the bus terminal. The fountain was working for a change, lit from beneath by blue, yellow and red lights. It created a weird effect, especially at night. The centerpiece of the fountain was a hideous sculpture of Joshua Talon Trainor, the man who founded Ilium in the mid-1700's. It was carved out of some kind of white stone and the artist must have been a fan of the old *Davy Crockett* TV series because Trainor bore an unmistakable resemblance to Fess Parker, coonskin cap and all. Joshua Talon Trainor with his arm extended, pointing the way to what was then little more than marshland, likely the worst spot on Lake Erie to locate a community. Was he a lunatic or a visionary? Legend has it that he liked the terrain because it provided good cover for his bootlegging racket.

I took a seat on a bench beside a metal garbage bin that looked like one of those Daleks from *Doctor Who*. The bench was bolted to cement blocks which were, in turn, bolted to the bedrock beneath. Theft-proofing, taken to ridiculous extremes.

It was a pretty innocent scene: a fine-looking figure of a man in his mid-to-late thirties taking his repose while, two benches away, two gay gentlemen tongue-kissed and fondled each other. Bats flew overhead, gorging on the bugs drawn by the multi-coloured lights of the fountain, a constant whisper of wings just above my line of vision.

The garbage can cleared its throat and I jumped about a foot. "Sorry about that, Nightstalk. You were sitting there so peacefully it seemed a shame to disturb you."

So much for my spider sense. "Glen, you asshole," I hissed, "I nearly crapped myself. What the hell are you doing, skulking around like that?"

"I wasn't skulking," the garbage can corrected me. "I left word to meet me in the park. Well, here I am."

"Right, but—never mind, I guess it doesn't matter."

"Where's your beauteous partner tonight?"

Egads, not another one. "Who knows? Back at the office probably."

"She is a most excellent example of the female species. Truly hot and—"

"Yeah, yeah," I said, "but I'm here and she's not. Hope that don't rain on your parade."

He chuckled. "Sorry, man, didn't mean anything. I know how you feel about her and all."

"You don't know squat," I snarled. "Just talking through your arse, as usual."

"Hey, hey, it's all right, man, no need to get defensive. I see the way you look at her sometimes. Not that I'm spying or anything..."

I glared at the garbage can. "Being invisible gives you certain advantages, pal, but don't abuse them. Not if you know what's good for you."

"She's right, you really are an old poop, you know that, Nightstalk?" The metal barrel vibrated with laughter.

"Funny, I have this sudden, powerful urge to piss in a handy trash receptacle."

"Okay, okay, don't get hot under the collar. *Sheesh.* When you think about it, I'm doing you a favour just by showing up tonight. I heard you were looking for me and I could've ducked you for, like, months. Because you can't find what you can't see, right? Here one minute, gone the next. They don't call me *el hombre invisible* for nothing."

"I need some information—"

"*Huh uh*, no way, man, this isn't that kind of conversation. Tonight I'm not taking requests. Tonight I'm just *telling*." All at once I got this sinking feeling. "I hear you've been asking around about that weird shit that went down in St. Andrew's Park, is that right?"

I managed to keep my seat but just barely. "I never said anything about that! I only said I was looking for you, I didn't say why. *Fuck*."

He snorted. "It's all over the street, dude. The word is out. *Nobody* is to lend aid and assistance to you. The people involved are rumoured to be terminally fucking *evil* and if you mess with them you could end up invited to another wienie roast. Take it from me, this is one job you gotta pass on, man. Seriously."

"And here I was hoping you'd help me find these shitheads. Maybe even I.D. them for us."

The bin wasn't impressed. "I.D. *this*, Nightstalk. I'm telling you, dawg, these are *not* people you want to fuck with. If they suspected I was sniffing around—man, I don't even wanna go there. It's all about self-preservation. I intend to lay low and not do *anything* to get on their bad side. In other words, this info you need? Forget it."

"What's got you so scared, Glen? You're invulnerable, man! You said it yourself, *el hombre invisible*. Shit, you're a fuckin' legend in this city. You're the *Shadow*, you go where you want, places no one else can. That's why you're so valuable to Cass and me. You are the *man*, Glen. At times like this, you're one of the best weapons we've got."

He sounded cautious. "Well...that's true, I guess."

I didn't give him a chance to think about it. "With the cats disappearing, it's like you're the only game in town. We need you now more than ever. And in that sense it's your responsibility to, uh, bear witness and help protect the weak and the vulnerable and—and the pathetic."

"Still..." Doubtfully. "I wouldn't want to end up charbroiled like that other poor fucker."

"Not a chance." I scoffed at the notion. "You can't catch what you can't see. Right?"

"Yeah. That's right." He wasn't quite there yet but I was definitely making progress.

"So...so you see my point?" The two queers were whispering to each other, wondering what sort of freak would carry on an animated conversation with a garbage can. They decided not to take any chances, got up and moved off, watching me until they were a safe distance away. "I mean, just the fact that you showed up tonight means something, don't you think? You were warned off but still you came. *Why?* Why agree to meet me if you're so worried about your personal safety? What's with that?"

He sounded embarrassed, and there was shame and pride mixed in there as well. "Uh, y'know, the loyalty thing, I guess. I didn't want to keep ducking you without explaining why. But now you've got me thinking." Some aluminum cans clinked inside the bin as he shifted. "Some people don't understand the concept of recycling," he complained. "So...as far as the park thing goes..." I waited. "Maybe I *could* do something for you. Sniff around a bit, see what's out there." I danced a victory jig in my head but outwardly showed no reaction. "If things seem like they're about to get hairy, I can always fade like old cigar smoke and we forget the whole thing. Is that workable for you? I know I'm being, like, completely chickenshit but, y'know, those are my terms, take it or leave it."

I nodded, then realized his sight lines probably weren't too good in that thing. If he really *was* in there; sometimes I suspected the bugger of throwing his voice. "It's a deal. No one expects you to endanger yourself, just find out what you can and come back in one piece."

He was still fretting. "Well, that's the thing, isn't it? Not getting caught." His voice dropped. "I hear these people are into some spooky shit, is that right?"

"Uh, could be," I allowed, not wanting to risk scaring him off. "Look, all we're asking is that you keep an ear to the ground. Give us a head's up if we're walking into something. For Cassandra's sake, if nothing else. You wouldn't want *her* to get hurt, would you, Glen?" It was a dirty tactic but I needed him and that was that.

He groaned. "I must be nuts going along with this. You too, man. It's heavy shit, a lot of bad, *bad* ju-ju attached to it."

"In my case, I don't exactly have a choice." I reminded him. "The Old Man gives us an assignment and we do our job. These pussycats are up to something and we have to find out what their game is. That's where you come in. We need to hear about things *before* they happen, dig?"

"Yeah, yeah," the garbage can muttered. "And the thing is I *swore* I wouldn't put myself on the line for you guys again. Fuckin' hell, man, remember what nearly happened to me last time?" [17]

"Getting up in the morning is risky," I countered. "Look around you: this city's dying, pal, and lemme tell you, it's gonna be one ugly fucking death."

"Everyone's really tense lately, have you noticed? People acting jumpy and weird. Dudes getting cut or stomped for no reason. It's nuts. Ask the cops, they'll tell you. It's a zoo out there. Serious karmic misalignment. Can't you feel it?"

I shrugged. "I'm not sensitive that way. I get little twinges sometimes but that's about it. I think Cass would know what you're talking about. She's the Gifted one. Lately she's been extra touchy."

"Is it her period, do you think?"

"How the fuck would I know, Glen?" I seethed at his presumption. "What do I look like, her gynecologist?"

"Hey, man, I'm sorry. Mellow out."

"What a stupid fucking question." I debated giving the receptacle a resounding kick. "Besides, women aren't ruled by their cycles. That's a myth."

---

[17] "The Sinister Dr. Sinistre" (*The Casebooks of Zinnea & Nightstalk, Volume III*)

"My old lady is," he retorted, "and I got the lumps on my head to prove it." We both laughed. "Okay, Nightstalk," he said, "give me a few names and I'll see what I can do." He didn't know Skorzeny but when I mentioned Gregory Fischer, his reaction was immediate. "You're swimming with sharks, you know that, don't you?" For a second, I thought he was going to back out of our deal. "Fuck it, I'll give it a shot. I'll leave a message if anything turns up. Hey, change of subject, but what's the latest on the cat situation? Any news that's fit to repeat?"

I shrugged. "Nah. We're working on it but there's no leads, no *nothing*."

"Too bad. I knew some of them too. One was this huge, grey tom with six toes on both of his front paws. Fucker must have weighed fifteen pounds. Used to hang out behind my building. He was one tough hombre, all right."

I looked at my watch. "I'd better get going. I want to stop by the office again and see what Cassandra's turned up. Glen?"

"Still here, man."

"Sometimes it's hard to tell."

"When I split I always say 'good-bye' or 'catch you later' to let people know I'm booking."

"Do you ever hang around and eavesdrop?"

"Shit, *no!*" He sounded shocked. "Who wants to hear what people have to say once they figure you're gone." The receptacle shuddered. "Fuck that."

"I see your point."

"Sure. Besides, it would be a betrayal of trust, wouldn't it?"

I had to laugh. "But, Glen, you eavesdrop on people all the time. That's part of what you do."

"But never on my *friends*."

"Riiight. Well, stay in touch."

"See you, Nightstalk."

"Watch your shadow, Glen," I warned him playfully, "it's a dead giveaway."

"Thanks for the advice. Say 'hi' to that babelicious partner of yours for me."

"Will do."

"You're a lucky man, Nightstalk."

"That's what everyone keeps telling me."

The phone rang just before one a.m. and things *really* started heating up.

"*After Hours Investigations*. 'Solving the toughest cases while the—'" I looked over when I heard her gasp, saw from her face that it was bad. "Is that you, Frederick? Hang on..." She switched to the speaker and we could hear him breathing. When he spoke, his voice was muffled and some of what he was saying hard to make out.

"Cassandra, please, I implore you..."

"I'm here, Frederick. How can I--"

"Help me, please...please...help me..." He began to sob. "I cannot go on...they are destroying me...I am frightened, so frightened...even poor Roger...*mein Gott*..."

"Frederick, we'll be right over, all right?" I pointed at myself, shaking my head vehemently. She scowled. "Did you hear me? We'll be right there."

"I—perhaps that is not for the best—"

"We're on our way," she retorted and hung up before he could argue the point further.

"Do I *have* to go?" I whined. "Maybe he's just drunk or--"

"Get your coat," she commanded. "I'm not driving up to that creepy mausoleum by myself. He's in trouble and he needs us."

As we donned our coats I voiced what was going through both our minds. "I wonder what the deal is. He sounded really freaked out, didn't he? It's not like the ol' squarehead to lose his cool." I held the door for her.

"He betrayed the Cabal. Now Fischer and Skorzeny are making him pay for it." We hurried down the stairs. "They know he's the one who alerted the Brethren. Once their suspicions were aroused, he knew the Brethren would send an agent to Ilium to check things out." We waved at Tara Dreyfuss through the front window. She sat stoically at the counter while an elderly man sprayed something onto a pair of panties and pressed them to his nose, sniffing the material critically.

Poor kid.

I jogged to keep up with my long-limbed partner. "The *Baron* helping Philippe and his bunch? His mortal enemies? Have I missed something?"

"Don't you always?" she teased.

"Don't push your luck, woman."

She explained on the way to Little Bavaria.

Her theory: the Baron narcs to the Brethren and Arturs Esch is dispatched to investigate the Cabal and find out what they're up to. But somehow Fischer and Skorzeny become wise to the situation and decide to eliminate the threat. Unfortunately for the Baron, the majority of the Cabal are cowed by their new masters, which leaves a shortlist of candidates for the role of Judas.

Once Esch's cover was blown it's possible he gave up everything before being killed. Either way, the Baron was a man marked for death and he'd known as much the night he'd sent Roger to collect her.

"And how exactly are we supposed to help him?" I bullied a small import into letting me slide in front of him and made the off ramp in the nick of time.

"At the very least we can comfort a frightened old man. Is that too much to ask?"

"Maybe we should pound a stake through his heart and put him out of his misery."

"You'd better be nice, Nightstalk."

"I'm *always* nice," I protested.

She didn't say anything for the next five miles. Probably didn't trust herself.

The imposing iron gates that usually barred the drive were wide open. *Not* a good sign. I drove through, accelerating up the lane. I had a bad feeling, warning klaxons going *whoop-whoop-whoop* inside my head.

The castle was lit up like there was a party in progress but we didn't see a living soul anywhere. None of the Baron's bodyguards or personal staff were in evidence. We weren't challenged or waved down as we bumped across the drawbridge and there was no response when we rang the front doorbell.

"Right," I said, "this is where we either do something *really* stupid or else call the cops and let them handle it."

"Watch my back," she said, reaching for the knob.

I rolled my eyes. *Here we go again...*

There was music playing somewhere. Something classical, Bach maybe or—

"Schubert," she supplied helpfully, "'Death and the Maiden'."

I sniffed. "Kee-ripes. What a *stink*." The inside of the Baron's mansion smelled of decomposition and shit. *Fresh* shit. Really rank.

"Definite indications of a psychic attack," she announced. "Stay on your toes, partner."

We found him in the study. The centre of his world. Surrounded and insulated by thousands of depraved tomes, the perfect spot for a last stand.

He had thoughtfully wrapped his face and hands with gauze, but thin, mucilaginous liquid, yellow in colour, was leaking through in places. "Boils!" The Baron roared. "A plague of boils has been visited upon me. An added indignity." He fumbled for a glass, drank deeply. "*Ah.* Good Kentucky bourbon. The best possible use for a revolting vegetable like corn."

I hung back but Cassandra approached him, shocked by his grievous condition. "Did Fischer do this to you?"

"Ach, more likely Skorzeny. They leave the dirty work to him. That is his specialty."

I spoke up. "Where is everybody? Your staff, your--"

"Gone. Flew the coop. Bastards! *Bastards!*" His face was leaking like a sieve. I had to look away.

"Why?" Cassandra asked.

"Scary noises. Things that go bump in the night." He took another drink, slurping eagerly. "They used all the tricks in their arsenal. The walls ran blood, ghostly laughter, pictures falling down, doors slamming, candles levitating across the room..." He shook his head. "I had men I thought I could trust, good, strong men, *begging* to be let go, nearly in tears. *Ach.* I should have been like Howard Hughes and hired Mormons." *Glug, glug.* Banging the glass down. "Look at me!" He thrust his wrapped hands at us. "I have been disfigured and abandoned and they are not done with me yet. First me and then you and then..." He was bawling again. "Forgive me but I have not slept. The pain--"

She knelt beside him. "Is this your punishment? For warning the Brethren?"

He leaned over, his voice cracking. "Something came and *ate* Roger. Do you understand? *It tore him to pieces before my eyes.* A creature conceived in a nightmare. It devoured his essence and I could do *nothing.* The power to create such a thing...unimaginable. Far beyond my amateurish fumblings. I am an old fool..." Bowing his head. "You must go, save yourselves if you can."

"Frederick? *Frederick.*" She spoke sharply to get his attention. "Tell us what you know. Help us help you."

He gazed at her. Raised his hand, almost as if he intended to stroke her face, then lowered it. His regard was tender, doting. "I can see from your thoughts, which you have kindly opened to me, that you know some of it already. I congratulate you on your ingenuity, *liebschen*." Pouring himself to another slug of bourbon, slopping it all over the place.

"I want to know why you betrayed the Cabal to the Brethren. Not just out of resentment toward Fischer, there has to be more to it than that."

"That pretender, that *poseur* stole my people away from me, you understand? Acting like some sort of celebrity and winning them over with his tall tales and big promises. He perverted our ideals, performed secret rites, the blackest of the black arts. These people are dangerous and they must be *stopped*."

"But what's motivating them? Why risk provoking the Brethren by killing their agent?"

His face looked like it was melting. "The Black Brotherhood are of no concern to them. The forces they are bringing in to play dwarf the power of such moribund institutions. Besides, even the so-called Brethren of Purity are not immune to their corrupting influence."

"What do you mean?" she asked excitedly.

"It is worse than you can imagine. They intend to—"

It happened so quickly there was no time to react. A silver letter opener with a decorative hilt (the badgers and four poster again) rose from the desktop and leaped through the air in one swift motion. The slim dagger was moving with considerable speed and force when it penetrated the Baron's left eye, burying itself to the hilt in the soft, living brain behind it. Dead in a heartbeat.

"*Sonofabitch*." I felt like breaking something. "You notice how that always happens to us? We're just on the verge of learning something important, something absolutely crucial to our case and the next thing we hear is '*gak gak*'. It never fails, every fuckin' time—"

"Uh, Nightstalk, I think you'd better..."

"—before you can say 'Jack Shit' the key witness gets fuckin' *offed* right before our eyes, this totally melodramatic and clichéd fuckin'—"

"*Nightstalk!* Would you shut up listen to me?" I broke off my rant. "*Whatever it was that got Frederick is still in here*." We edged toward the center of the room, senses on high alert.

"It might be gone."

"No."

"Why would it hang around once it—"

"What was *that*?" She spun about. "It's *definitely* still here. Something just brushed against me."

Then it swooped past *me*, a moving stream of cool, fetid air. *Bogey.* I got the impression it was spiraling in closer with each circuit, looking for an opening.

"Let's try for the door." I was thoroughly unnerved at that point, ready to bolt like a spooked horse. "I'll go first, see if I can draw its attention and then you make your break."

"No, wait, we should—"

But I was already moving.

The room exploded around us.

Books burst from the shelves and blasted past us at supersonic speeds. Pictures and framed documents detached themselves from the walls and frisbeed about the chamber. We were leaping, ducking, spinning, doing everything we could to survive the furious onslaught. Only I wasn't quite in Cass's league so I got clipped several times, taking a hard wallop on the shoulder from a ten-pound Attic Greek dictionary while trying to avoid being decapitated by a hurtling *Malleus Mallificarum.*

We had to anticipate the trajectories of dozens of lethal missiles at once, dodging between them while trying to make progress toward the door. From the outside it must have sounded like a war was raging within the confines of the study. Thunderous impacts, concussions that rocked that area of the building--

--and then, a few seconds later, Cassandra and I scrambled out, looking a trifle flustered but showing no signs of apparent injury.

"You've still got the moves, Nightstalk," she complimented me, patting my shoulder. I winced and hastily popped it back into place. Fit as a fiddle and ready to take on all comers. Her hair was tousled and two buttons had popped on her blouse. The bogey hadn't so much as laid a glove on her. What a gal.

"Nothing a 2nd Degree can't handle," I replied modestly.

The frustrated bogey was still tossing things around the study, including the Baron's lifeless body by the sound of it. Clearly disgusted with itself. Just to be on the safe side, Cassandra sealed the room with a a binding spell I'd seen her use previously. It would hold...for awhile.

I was anxious to get out of there. "Okay, what now?"

"How do *I* know, Nightstalk." She sounded cross and upset. She'd really liked the old fart and mourned his rather icky passing. I heard her muttering something: "—should have known, set up like a bloody fool."

"Set up how?" Once again, I was two or three steps behind her.

"There won't be any fingerprints on that letter opener, Nightstalk. There *will* be a record of his call to our office. Now here we are and, thanks to my stupidity, we're officially the last two people to see him alive."

"...which makes *us* prime suspects. Holy shit."

"We've got to get out of here." To confirm that point, something heavy smashed against the door behind us. We jogged down the hallway.

"Couldn't we call the cops and take our chances?"

She shook her head and shoved me ahead of her. "It's a frame, Nightstalk. This whole thing. We haven't been here in *months*, savvy?"

"Got it."

"We'll call from a convenience store."

"An anonymous tip—" I wrenched open one of the tall front doors.

"That's right," I heard her say, "we don't want to end up--"

We were two steps outside the door when they hit us with spotlights, cruel and unusual punishment for night people. The glare was dazzling. I grabbed Cass and pushed her behind me. Ready to defend her to the death even if I couldn't see past the end of my bent nose. They cut the lights and I heard footsteps approaching.

My vision was clearing; I could make out two figures. I bared my teeth, started toward them, intending to inflict grievous harm--

"Well, well. Lookie what the cat dragged in."

Someone, it seemed, had already made that call.

Busted.

They put us in separate rooms and left us to stew in our own juices. The bastards knew they didn't have anything they could pin on us and that it was only a matter of time before the Old Man sent Arnie Beddoes or some other fast-talking shyster to spring us.

Detective Wojeck, in particular, was itching to hang a charge of "obstruction of justice" on us. He didn't take kindly to the way we involved ourselves in police business. Never mind the many, many occasions we tackled cases the cops wouldn't touch with a two-foot expandable baton, the real life "X Files" no one ever hears about.

Wojeck was petty and vindictive but Faro was a *bad* cop, plain and simple. Stupid, uninspired, hater of homos and non-caucasians and, oh yeah, especially *Shades*.

After awhile, the walls started closing in on me. The room was small and airless. There was a table and two chairs and, strangely enough, a half-empty box of tissues. Guess there isn't too much even a crazed psychotic can do with a box of kleenex. Choke on it, I suppose.

They hadn't officially arrested us. We were being "detained as material witnesses", to quote Wojeck, who slipped his partner an evil wink as he said it. It wasn't legal but they did it anyway. Locked us up without due process or just cause. Standard operating procedure as far as those boys were concerned.

At least they let me keep my watch...which meant I could check it every few minutes, the time *crawling* by on two broken legs and a shattered pelvis, nothing to do except stare at the bare walls. And pace. And get madder and madder.

Some fun, huh, Nightstalk?

The reception was a bit tinny but it was my girl, indulging in some telepathic teasing. She was six or eight feet away, sounding bright and chipper.

I'll take the rubber hose treatment over this stuff any day, I sent back.

You may still get your chance. Faro really went wild over that "rent a cop" crack you made. That guy's on the take for sure.

I sniggered, unrepentant. *How are they treating you, kid?*

One nice detective sent out for some cappuccino. And I've got donuts and coffee cake and butter tarts...

I groaned.

It's your own fault, Nightstalk. You come across too gruff. It turns people off.

I let that slide. *Any sign of when we're getting out of here?*

I'm afraid our story didn't make a good impression. They still want to know why we didn't call for help from the house, why two law-abiding citizens were in such a hurry to leave the scene of a crime.

We were in a state of shock. The Baron called us but when we got there, the place was ransacked, he was dead, end of story.

That's the gist of what I'm telling them too. Let's make sure we keep our stories straight.

They're lucky that bogey had vacated the scene by the time they went inside.

Leaving no traces it had ever been there, she reminded me.

Which means, I pointed out, *they've got nothing on us and no reason to be holding us. This whole thing is just Wojeck, pulling his prick.*

They have a dead body and two witnesses telling half-truths or outright lies.

Details.

I'm glad you can be so glib, Nightstalk.

No prints, no motive, no crime. Case closed, shweetheart.
The non-verbal equivalent of a sigh. *Faro wants to lean on you. He thinks they can trick you into making inconsistent statements.*

Been doing some mind-reading, have you? You'd need an electron microscope to find anything in Faro's thick skull.

I'm just giving you fair warning, Evvie. They're going to push you hard.

Only I'll have you coaching me, won't I?

We have to be careful. Most importantly, you have to keep your temper. They're thinking a whole lot of nasty thoughts about you, partner.

I'm crying great big crocodile tears in here.

I've never seen you so mad. You ripped their car door right off its hinges--

They didn't have to bust us. We were cooperating, goddamnit!

Don't shout, Nightstalk, it gives me a headache.

Sorry.

You notice they didn't try to put cuffs on you?

Alone in my cubicle, I chuckled. *Smart move on their part. I would've squashed them like bugs.*

Have they been rough on you?

Worse. They're pretending I don't exist. They wanted a statement, I gave them one. I thought Wojeck was gonna blow a gasket. That's when I got dumped in here. Where I currently sit. And sit. *Nothing to read and all the strippers are ugly.*

They gave me a room with a couch and TV. Cable.

Those bastards!

They're just mad about that car door, Nightstalk. After all, how do you go about explaining something like that?

They cut us loose around ten that morning.

It was a deliberate slap in the face, one final fuck-you-very-much from officers Mutt and Jeff. They opened the door and shoved us out into the white, blistering light of a lovely spring morning.

Painful. That doesn't begin to describe it. First the spotlights, now this. My poor eyes felt like steaming piss holes in the snow. We got a reprieve when Cassandra sweet-talked a young cop into loaning me his sunglasses so I could run to the nearest pharmacy and buy us some wraparound jobs that were as ugly as they were functional. When I returned with the shades, I told the kid I owed him one and made a mental note to remember his face. *Click.*

The sunglasses helped but we both had pounding headaches by the time we got to the office. I kept the Underwood under wraps, using a plain, old legal pad to write up a semi-coherent account of our latest escapades, while holding a cold paper towel pressed to my forehead to help me see better. It wasn't pretty but it would have to do.

I couldn't face the sunlight again. Cassandra left me there, on a fold out army cot we kept around for just such emergencies, while she endured a daylight cab ride so she could crash in her own bed.

I tried to sleep but, thanks to the headache, that turned out to be a tall order. At one point I was certain the door to the Old Man's office opened and sensed somebody standing beside me. I was about to pull off the paper towel for a look...but was seized by a sudden reluctance I can't explain to this day. I let my arm fall back to my side and waited a good long while before rising to resoak the towel, passing the door to the inner office on the way to the john, shivering at the thought of what might have emerged.

It was late afternoon and my head felt like a litter of sick puppies had slept in it. The pain was immune to the Tylenol tablets I kept popping at regular intervals. Strong coffee helped, incrementally.

At some point I noticed the memo he'd left:

Z + N:
Please attempt post-mortem contact with Von Stahl.
Invaluable info might be obtained. Apprise with
results. Top priority.

I groaned, wadding up the note and lobbing it toward the wastebasket, narrowly missing the three pointer at the buzzer that would have won the game. The story of my life.

The instructions were unequivocal. There was nothing to interpret, no ambiguity to factor in. It meant another session with the irrepressible Eva Jauch and a creepy conversation with the Baron's restless shade. Have I mentioned how much I hate séances? [18]

Cassandra came in around nine. She looked paler than usual and admitted she was subsisting solely on aspirin and bottled water. And she

---

[18] In at least four other accounts: "The Really BIG Shop of Horrors", "Stairway to Oblivion" (*The Casebooks of Zinnea & Nightstalk, Vol. I*); "The Burglar Who Thought He was Jesus", "Remembering Maria Ouspenskaya" (*Casebooks, Vol. II*). Vigilant readers will, no doubt, discover other examples...

refused to take off her expensive designer shades, even within the relatively dim confines of the office. I sympathized.

I showed her the Old Man's memo and she got on the blower to Eva Jauch. The stars must have been in alignment or business on the slow side because she agreed to see us that night. "Twelve o'clock? Fine, we'll be there. Yes, he'll be coming too." Cassandra glanced over at me and grinned. "I know, but we'll manage somehow." She was laughing as she hung up. "You don't want to know," she told me and, after giving it some thought, I decided she was probably right.

I've never understood why anyone would want to contact the dead. It seems so absurd to me. Once I kick the bucket why in the name of Harry Houdini would I want to hang about, answering questions like "who was supposed to get the silver set, Uncle Sidney, it was me, right?".

"Madame" Eva would counter by saying that some revenants have unfinished business on this plane. They might have died suddenly or violently and are disoriented, stuck in the *qliphoth*, a formless and terrifying void. Or, like her spirit guide, Austin, they could be well-meaning souls who voluntarily stay behind to help the rest of us. In my view, Eva smoked a tad too much of the wacky weed and had mistaken the movie "Ghost" for a documentary.

Nevertheless, there I was, five minutes to midnight, watching Cass greet the old charlatan. "Thank you for seeing us, Eva. We appreciate you making time for us this evening."

Eva led us to the table in her sitting room, indicating where she wanted us seated. "I'm worried about Mr. Short, Dark and Ugly over there. The spirits are easily disturbed and his negative energies might be...counter-productive." She eyed me appraisingly. "Look at that aura: black and sparking with violence and negativity. Whereas you—" turning to Cassandra, "--are a beacon of light. The departed will be drawn to you like moths. Ah, well," she raised her shoulders, "maybe you'll compensate for him."

She lit a dripless red candle and set it in the middle of the table. After turning off the lamps, she had us place our hands flat on the surface so that our pinkie fingers touched the person's on either side of us. My big, scarred mitts and thick, knobby digits looked odd next to their soft, feminine hands.

So far I'd minded my manners and kept my mouth shut. Ever since that blow-up at the office I'd been watching my step. I was determined to stay on Cassandra's good side even if it meant swallowing about five pounds of baloney doled out in heaping spoonfuls by a badly dressed harpy with the personality of a rottweiler. Maybe by absorbing Eva's abuse for the next hour or so, I'd chalk up a few karmic points to my credit. I was definitely in arrears in that department.

I'd sat through a number of seances and was always amazed by the sheer banality of the information the dead passed along. Nothing like "Hey, I got a blowjob from Marilyn Monroe the other day" or "I finally know where they buried Jimmy Hoffa, Morty, and you're never gonna believe it!". No, instead it's that the spirits love us and watch over us and don't want us spending our money unwisely and do I know anybody whose middle initial starts with "C" because they're going to have a slight accident in a week or two, nothing serious but—

I'll say one thing for Eva, she dispensed with the usual histrionics mediums like to employ for effect. She didn't go for all that eye-rolling, speaking in tongues crap, cracking her knees and toes to simulate spirit rapping.

About a minute after we'd placed our hands on the table I saw her stiffen, turning her head as if she'd heard something. "I can feel you, Austin. Are you there? Come closer, don't be afraid. Will you come to us?" And that's when the spooky shit started because I *swear* I could hear the patter of child-sized feet running past us. "Hello, Austin." She inclined her head and spoke as if addressing a child at eye level. "How are you today? We're looking for a friend." She paused, listening. "No, don't be frightened, he's all right. He just *looks* scary." Cassandra applied pressure with her little finger and I took the hint and stayed mum. "Our friend's name is Baron Frederick von Stahl. He is well-known to the spirit world." I saw her nod. "Thank you, Austin." For our benefit: "Austin will find him. He's a good boy."

It sounded like someone running around on the ceiling above us. The flame wavered and flickered and I found myself devoutly hoping it wouldn't go out and leave us in the dark. "Focus on the candle. Let all other thoughts depart. Think of the Baron, how you remember him. Form an image of him in your minds. Concentrate. *Concentrate...*"

The modest ring of light cast by the candle left our faces in deep shadow. It was like we were floating in space. Nothing else was visible, nothing beyond the tiny bubble of light in which we were suspended. I got a sense of great depths around and beneath us. I wondered if I was experiencing some kind of drug flashback--and at that moment a weird current went through our hands, like a circuit had been closed.

"He's coming," Eva said.

Okay, I admit it, I was more than slightly freaked out. Seized by a feeling hard to put into words, a certainty not supported by any physical evidence that *there was something in that room besides us.*

Then, to my left, at the very limit of my vision, I saw movement. A cool breeze blew on the back of my neck. I solemnly swore to myself that not only was this the last séance I would ever attend, but that if anyone ever tried contacting *me* after I had joined the choir invisible, I'd loose the hounds of hell on them.

"Thank you, Austin. Thank you for bringing our friend to see us. Austin found him wandering. He says he hasn't completely accepted that he's passed over. He's angry and confused. Do you still wish to speak to him?"

Cassandra, without hesitation: "Yes."

"Are you there, Baron? I wish to make contact with Baron Frederick von Stahl. Please approach us and be heard. There are friends here who want to talk to you. Please, come forward. Are you there..."

--and will you accept charges for this call, I somehow resisted adding. I think Cassandra picked up on my giddiness because I felt her warning glare even in the near dark. I turned back toward Eva...and found myself face to face with the Baron.

It was the eeriest thing. It wasn't that her appearance physically changed, the bones rearranging themselves, her skull enlarging to take on the proportions of the Baron's massive dome. It was more the way she held herself, the posture and angle of her head just right, her carriage ramrod straight, shoulders squared. I suspected that had the light been better she would have had the sharp, alert gaze and crooked slash of a smile down pat too.

The candlelight seemed to be shrinking, darkness closing in on us.

The pitch and timbre of her voice didn't change much but it was still clearly the Baron who addressed us. It was beyond mimicry, the transformation utterly convincing. "I see you but it's like looking through a mist." She/he squinted at me. "Herr Nightstalk, the distinctive outlines of your body are quite unmistakeable. Ah. And that must be Cassandra." The Baron looked about him. "I don't know this place." At last, he focussed his attention on my partner. "So...this is what it is like to be dead. *Pah!* I have absolutely no sexual desire and no requirements for food or liquor. What sort of afterlife is that?"

"Frederick," Cassandra urged, knowing how tenuous these contacts tended to be, "we were there when you were—when you died, remember?"

"It is...not clear. My memory...or perhaps the past isn't so important on this side."

"But we're still alive and need your help."

He sounded distracted. "I am...indifferent. To think about my former existence requires too much energy and already I feel myself dissipating. Perhaps in the end my essence will merely scatter to the far reaches of the universe. That would be...anticlimactic, don't you think?"

She pursued her point with admirable doggedness. "You were *murdered*. Your soul has not gone on because it requires closure. We can help with that. Once you're free of the ties that hold you here, I'm sure you'll be able to pass on. I guarantee it."

"The worst part is that I am so *alone*. And I am slowly losing myself. Oblivion awaits..."

"You are Baron Frederick von Stahl. You were a pioneer, a respected explorer in the world of the occult. You had many goals and dreams and someone came and took that from you. Took away everything, including your life."

"I don't remember dying. Was it gory and spectacular?"

"I'll say," I muttered.

"You were murdered in cold blood and the people responsible must be brought to account. You know this. Your spirit should be crying out for justice."

"Skorzeny...it was that bastard Skorzeny. He told us he had created an elemental. Performed a working to bring forth an entity to do his bidding. Most of us thought it was nonsense at first." He sighed, a dispirited spirit. "But it turned out we underestimated the cretin. It wasn't all parlour tricks."

"Was it Skorzeny or Fischer who ordered the hit on the Brethren agent?" I blurted out. I knew how these incorporeal types tended to wander off topic.

"Such knowledge is dangerous, Herr Nightstalk. Look where it got me. But I suppose the short answer to your question is: does it matter? Skorzeny and Fischer, they are one and the same. Fischer coaxed him out of retirement. God knows what sewer he found him in. But Skorzeny possesses great power, that is certain. The man is a sorcerer. An adept without a spark of humanity. That makes him very, very dangerous, *liebschen*."

"But why do you think—"

"God, I detest them! They destroyed our group. They are evil and *must be stopped!*" The last few words emerged as a very Baron-like roar.

The table rattled, rose about six inches, then came down with a clatter, knocking over the candle and plunging the room into darkness.

There was movement all around us, formless shapes flowing and swirling in the gloom. I yearned to free my hands, grab my partner and bolt for the door.

"*Who is there?*" the Baron barked.

Something flew past me, too quick to see, and from the air above us came a howl that made my skin crawl. Eva rose from her seat and, without warning, flung herself backward. Cassandra and I seized her hands, clinging to her for dear life. By tradition, only an unbroken circle would preserve our safety. Eva arched her back, her spine bending to an impossible angle while Cassandra and I strained to maintain our grip.

"Nightstalk, I'm *slipping*—"

"Hang on, babe!" I shouted. But I was having a hard time too, Eva's strength superhuman, nearly pulling us over on top of her.

Then, without warning, she collapsed into her chair, head lolling.

"We need a fucking light," I hissed.

"It's hunting him," Eva Jauch moaned. "*Listen...*"

Another piercing cry from a different corner of the room, followed by an impression of something zipping past us, a desperate chase on the periphery of perception. I got a glimpse of a glowing blue-green ball scooting up the wall and through the ceiling. A moment later there was a terrified squawk and the ball reappeared, fleeing for its existence. Something came after it, red-eyed and lightning quick, seizing the ball and pulling it back through the ceiling. From directly overhead there were blood-curdling shrieks, Eva and Cassandra screaming along with it, experiencing the creature's excruciating soul-death, a torrent of psychic pain—

And then silence.

I could hear someone panting. There was a slight whiff of ozone mixed with perfumed incense (sandalwood, I think).

"Lights," Eva croaked. She was slumped over the table, wheezing for breath. Cassandra sprang to her assistance while I turned on the nearest lamp and then went around prying open windows, letting in fresh air. Got Eva a glass of water, straightened the table, cleaned up the candle mess and generally made myself useful.

"Are you all right?" Cassandra asked Eva, who had produced a fat joint from somewhere and was in the process of firing it up.

"Nothing like that has ever happened before," Eva said, her voice quaking. "If there's trouble, an angry or violent spirit, Austin always helps me." She took a long hit off the bomber. "It was *awful*. I hope Austin is okay."

Cassandra sought to reassure her. "I'm sure he's fine."

Eva blew smoke in my direction. "So what do *you* think about all of this? Don't see something like that every day, do you? You need to go somewhere and change your underwear?" My partner coughed, covering her mouth with her hand.

I was still trying to assimilate everything, answered without thinking. "It was quite a show."

"*Show*?" Her eyes narrowed into furious slits. "That was no show, peckerhead."

"I don't think Nightstalk meant—"

"Sure he did." Eva waved the joint at me. "You think it was all an *act*? So how do you explain what happened? You want to search the place for projectors or secret panels, be my guest."

"I didn't mean any offense." Backtracking hastily. "You're right. I *don't* have an explanation. For any of it."

Eva was showing the effects of the weed, blinking up at us lazily. "I told you, lately it's been crazy over there. Everything stirred up. I don't feel welcome any more." She offered me the joint. "Here. You'll be needing this."

I almost hated to ask. "Why do you say that?"

"That thing you saw, that was no projection, boy. It was a *soul-eater*. Lesser demon. Dumb but ferocious. If your enemies have access to creatures like that and are willing to pay the price for using them..." She grimaced.

"I get the picture." I took a half-hearted toke. "By the way, sharing the same body with the Baron, that must have been quite the experience."

"What do you know about it? *Huh*? Let me tell you what it's like when you open yourself up and let one of *them* in." She snatched the joint away from me. "What I do is go back into a deep, far corner of my mind and let them have the rest. We're two separate people inside the same body. And I keep my firewalls up to make sure we stay that way. *Because you can't trust them.* Some of them don't want to give up control and go back. It's dark there and they talk about a fog that covers everything. They can't see very well and there are *creatures* moving through the mist. They pray for help from their gods and no one answers. People like me are a warm place to hide. It gives them the illusion they're still alive."

"But you *help* them," Cassandra said. "You and Austin. You've sent many of them on their way. They aren't damned or abandoned, they're *lost."*

"I won't be going back, not for awhile. It seems alien to me now, hostile." Eva Jauch reached over and took Cassandra's hand. "It will be very dangerous from now on. They were watching and they know someone tried to contact the Baron. They *know* who we are..."

Cassandra ended up giving Eva twice her going rate, referring to the generous bonus as "hazard pay". God knows how I was going to explain it to the Old Man. Just to be on the safe side I got her to write out a receipt so I could partially cover myself on that count.

They hugged at the door. When they parted, Eva had tears in her eyes. She caught me staring at her and cuffed my arm angrily. "You! You should look after her. Believe me, it's gonna get a lot worse, sonny-boy. Bad times ahead. I can feel it. None of us are safe any more." She shooed us out. "That's it for me. I need to unwind. I'm getting to old for this stuff. Think I'll get stoned and watch an old Marx Brothers movie." She stood in the doorway, watching us go. "Be careful. These people have no souls, remember that. They have no souls...and so they have nothing to lose."

This is the way I picture it:

About an hour later, halfway through Animal Crackers, *she feels heat. Strange, because she keeps the thermostat turned down low to save on the gas bill. Her clients, most of them quite elderly, constantly complain about how cold it is.*

At first she thinks she's having a hot flash. She stands up and takes off her robe. Doesn't help. If anything, it seems to be getting hotter.

What the hell? Furnace busted?

She checks. It's set on "Low" but the room temperature is over ninety and rising.

She goes to the kitchen to get a glass of water. Doesn't bother turning on the light, she knows her way in the dark. As she stands at the sink drinking, Eva notices the blue glow. It emanates from the doorway behind her and grows in intensity, changing colour, yellow and then pure white. She turns and--

--only catches a glimpse of it, a glowing ball or disk skipping toward her. She throws up her hands, the flesh on her palms and forearms immediately blistering, peeling away from the sinew and bone. Her hair and nightgown ignite almost simultaneously and when she bares her face to scream, flames leap up and set fire to her tongue.

She collapses against the counter, burning inside and out. Now come the death throes, spasms of agony that propel her from one side of the small kitchen to the other. Her flailing limbs leave sizeable dents in the refrigerator and smash in cupboard doors, an explosion of flour and sugar and rice.

What happens next is beyond horrific. Her internal organs boil and steam issues from her pores, whistling from her ears. Her brain bubbles and liquefies in the hard, brittle bowl of her skull, one final burst of heat energy reducing Eva Jauch to little more than a mound of grey ashes, a human-shaped outline burnt into the kitchen floor...

*Sunday, May 9th*

Cassandra wept when I read her the Old Man's memo. His communications were always terse and unadorned and this one was no exception:

Z + N:
Eva Jauch dead, incinerated.
Investigate.

Some sheets were clipped to the memo. They contained information cribbed from investigators' notes and the preliminary forensics relating to Eva's death. It painted a graphic picture of the scorched kitchen and the state of her body. Cassandra barely made it through that part before breaking down again.

I knew there wasn't much I could say to her. Any attempt to eulogize Eva Jauch would sound hypocritical coming from me. All I could do was go over and hold her, let her press her face into my shoulder and cry herself out.

"You—you remember what the Baron said? About Skorzeny using elementals?" Even in her grief, her mind was hard at work. "He sicced one on her, the *bastard*. Damn him. Damn him to the deepest, darkest ring of Hades and may he roast there for all eternity. Nightstalk, you've got to help me. Promise me this won't go unpunished."

"We'll get them, babe," I agreed readily enough, knowing it might be a tall order but unwilling to sound a cautionary note at such a delicate time. "We'll make 'em pay for Eva and the Baron and Esch too. You got my word on it."

I drove past Eva's but neither of us was of a mind to break in and reconnoiter the place. I was relieved, thinking it might be too much for my partner (and, to be honest, my stomach was a trifle ticklish at the notion as well).

We stopped by the cop shop but the investigating officers (guess who?) refused to come down and talk to us, telling the desk sergeant to eject us from the building, post-haste. So it was back to the office where, not long afterward, Cassandra fielded a call from Philippe. She informed him of the circumstances of Eva's death and he, in turn, offered his sympathy and condolences. He also indicated he would soon be sending information our way but refused to provide details.

"Whoopie," I grumbled after she hung up, "I can hardly wait."

"I want whatever he has. What they did to Eva was unforgivable. An affront against everything I hold sacred. You promised, Nightstalk, you promised you'd help me get those—"

"And I will," I said. "But while we're waiting for Brother Philippe to come through for us, is there anything we can be doing in the meantime?"

She thought about it and nodded. "There is one person we haven't tried yet. He may not be cooperative..."

"Hon," I told her, cracking my knuckles in anticipation, "you leave that to me."

"--so our friend Arturs comes to town and needs a contact, someone that can put him in touch with the Cabal."

"Someone other than the Baron," she added. "He and Victor Skorzeny despised each other so if the Baron appeared to be promoting Esch, Skorzeny would naturally be suspicious of him."

"Enter Winston Gillette." I drummed my fingers on the steering wheel. "I hate this guy. He's *such* a slimebag."

"But he might be a helpful slimebag."

"Maybe I'll get a chance to rough him up a bit." Trying not to sound too hopeful.

"Just stick to our plan. Remember, we're here to get information, not rearrange his face." She reached for her door handle.

"Speak for yourself," I muttered, but I don't think she heard me.

96

Metaphysica: The Occult Bookshoppe
Winston Gillette, Proprietor
Open from whenever to Midnight
Especially Sundays

It was another chilly night, a real nip in the air. The wind was fairly whipping through my thin cotton pants. It's a good thing balls are retractable.

She opened the door and a brittle tinkle from above announced our arrival.

"Interesting chimes," I remarked. They were composed of various miniature bones attached by thin wires to a small, disturbingly child-like skull.

That wasn't the only thing disturbing about *Metaphysica*. Its eccentric proprietor had painted the walls black and nailed an upside-down cross over the front counter. There were speakers placed on top of the bookshelves playing a continuous loop of thunder, an ominous soundtrack for people who liked to dress in dark clothes and play at being *evil*. A faulty fluorescent light even gave the impression of intermittent lightning.

"This is *sooo* tacky," I said, not caring who might be listening.

Winston Gillette wore a black turtleneck and black denim jeans and smoked a cigarette in a long, fake ivory holder. He had a plump, well-groomed black cat draped over one arm. Both regarded us with bored contempt.

"Ah, if it isn't the dynamic duo of the night." He gazed down his long nose at us. "It's been some time since our paths last crossed. That business with the guy who thought he was the anti-Christ. [19] Am I right? Yes, well, that's old news, I suppose. Still, I was helpful in resolving the situation, wasn't I? That should count for something. Isn't that right, Tabitha?" he asked the cat. He bent and set the beast on the floor. It glanced up at him insolently and wandered off. "Foul creature," he called after it with apparent affection. He had plucked his eyebrows into severe V's and his skin was so pale it looked bleached. A real specimen, this guy.

Arturs Esch was the reason we were there and Cassandra wasted little time before inquiring if Gillette had known the gentleman.

---

[19] "A Case of Biblical Proportions" (*The Casebooks of Zinnea & Nightstalk, Vol. III*)

The bookseller was cautious but cooperative. "Sure I knew Artie. Came in here a few times. Not a big buyer, but steady. Nice guy too. Soft spoken and he never bitched about my prices. I liked that."

"You must have been pretty broken up when you heard somebody had flambéd his ass. You say he was a regular of yours—shit, that's money right out of your pocket." I practiced for hours to get that particularly annoying, pissy tone of voice and it usually paid dividends.

"Hey, show a little respect for the dead, Nightstalk," he snapped, dispensing with civility. "And by the way, *fuck you*. I liked Artie, I thought it was a really fucked up way to die. Anything beyond that...well, some stuff is better left unsaid, know what I mean?"

"Why, Mr. Gillette," Cassandra's voice dripped honey, "are you saying there's more to this killing than meets the eye?"

Gillette snickered. "The man was taken to a public park and burned alive. You figure it out."

She locked on to him. "I'd rather have you explain it to me. Tell me what message the death of Mr. Esch was meant to convey. *In your opinion.*"

His grin faltered. "My opinion?"

"Yes, Mr. Gillette. I am asking you as an acknowledged expert on the occult. I am asking you because it's well-known that you're a talent spotter for the Cabal. I'm asking you to tell us what you know about the death of Arturs Esch because if you don't, my partner is going to start dismantling your store from the floorboards up. Do I make myself clear?" He cowered. I caught his eye and gave him a big, toothy smile. I'd even pumped up Popeye-style in advance. For extra effect.

"I, ah, ah..." He scanned the store for customers, standing on tiptoes to see better. "Think I'll close up early tonight." He went to the door, locked it and turned off the lights.

"What about the big sign outside?" I asked.

He waved it off. "I got it hexed up the yin-yang. Besides, fuckin' thing weighs a ton. Who's gonna steal something like that? Come on."

He led us down a short hallway to the back. The door to the alley sported a huge deadbolt, almost medieval in its proportions. He had a room set up as a kitchenette, with a table, two chairs and a microwave oven. Very homey. He sat down and tried, without success, not to look nervous and self-conscious.

"Listen, I know you guys came here looking for information." Gillette showed us his empty hands. "But there's nothing I can tell you. Even if I wanted to talk I can't because, well, let's just say there's certain people I'd rather not fuck with."

"Tell us about Esch, Gillette," I growled.

"I knew him, like I said, but only as a customer—"

"Oh, *please*." Cassandra rolled her eyes. "Should I get Nightstalk to practice his juggling—starting with those six hundred dollar fake crystal balls out there. *Talk*, Winston."

He was practically groveling. "Wait a minute! I'm serious when I say these are dangerous people. I have to be really careful, all right? I mean, I like you guys and everything but, come on…"

"What kind of books did Arturs Esch buy?" My partner, coming at him from another direction, keeping him off-balance.

"Uh…nothing heavy. Stuff on the Rosicrucians, um, the history of Wicca. That sort of thing."

"How long had he been coming by the store?"

"I dunno. Three, four months? That sounds about right."

"Did he seem like a serious student of the occult?"

Gillette made a face. "How can you tell? Look, I get a lot of freaks coming in here, plenty of wannabes. Goths and girls with pierced cunts, fucked up kids looking for the latest thrill. People wanting a copy of the *Satanic Bible* or asking me if I know anybody wants to buy fresh blood. It's fuckin' unreal."

"Would you say that Esch was a freak?" I piped up.

He glanced at me. "Artie? Nope. He seemed pretty straight to me."

"And you liked him."

"Yeah, I guess so. Like I said, he didn't complain—"

"--and so when he seemed to check out you offered to introduce him to—who? Skorzeny? Was he your contact in the Cabal? Or was it someone else?" Cassandra, turning the tables again.

"Hey, wait a minute! You can't pin that on—"

"Oh, yes we can, *Winnie*," I snapped. "And a lot more too. Enough to make you an accessory maybe. How does that suit you?"

He looked sick. "Listen, I sell books and—and candles and fucking ceremonial daggers, that's all I do! Anybody tells you different is a liar!"

"You work part-time for the Cabal," I charged, keeping up the pressure. "Anybody you think shows promise, even if it's only as a thug, you send them to Skorzeny. Don't you? I said, *don't you?*"

He tried to rally, regain some lost ground: "Okay, I don't have to put up with this and I want the two of you out of here *right now*. You're not cops and you're not gonna rough me up so just shove off."

"Esch is dead, Winston." She went over and sat in the chair across from him. Seeking his gaze and holding it. "Esch is dead and *you* introduced him to the Cabal. You brought a traitor into their midst. That makes you suspect in their eyes."

"No," he shook his head vigorously, "it wasn't like that. Esch, he tricked me. I thought he was on the up and up and I just—they asked me and I told them, y'know, as a courtesy that, y'know, as far as I knew he was cool. I told them..." He was jittery, suggestible. And she kept pouring it on:

"But that's not the way *they're* going to see it," Cassandra pointed out. "First they got Esch," she held up a finger, "then they got the Baron," another finger, "and then it was Eva Jauch." She held up a fourth finger and stared at it meaningfully. "Who do you think will be next, Winston?"

He was sweating like those sumo guys I'd seen on TV. "You're just fucking with me. Trying to make me panic and say something stupid." But he was hanging on for dear life, you could tell. "What do you *want* from me?" he demanded.

"Nothing." She reached over and took his hand. "We're trying to *help* you, Winston. They're tying off loose ends. It's only a matter of time before something comes through that wall and—"

"*Through the wall?*" He jerked his hand back. "What are you talking about?"

"Elementals don't run up and ring the front doorbell, *Winnie*," I reminded him, bad cop to the hilt.

"How's your defense system, Winston?" He stared at her. "Do you think it could stop an elemental? That's how they got Eva."

And then it was magic time.

Something crashed to the floor in the darkened store. It sounded like one of the speakers.

"*What the fuck?*" he screeched.

"You locked the door, right, Winston? I watched you do it. So how did they get in?" Something else went bang and I kept at him. "That sure doesn't sound like fuckin' mice, does it?"

"You guys gotta do something!" He looked at us imploringly.

Pow! Pow! Those crystal balls go off like fragmentation grenades when you drop them.

"Tell us what you know," my partner urged him. "How can we help you if we're working in the dark?"

Ka-ching! Ka-ching! Ka-ching! The cash drawer opening and slamming shut and now the overhead lights had come on again, spasmodic flickers lighting up the hallway outside the kitchenette.

"They'll fucking kill me!" he howled.

"Winston," I pointed out as gently as I could, "they're already trying."

After my partner used a bogus incantation to "banish" the bogey besieging his store, Gillette was only too happy to spill his guts. Downright grateful he was.

Mostly what we got was confirmation. Gillette had indeed vouched for Arturs Esch to Skorzeny, part of the vetting process that allowed Esch to insinuate himself into the Cabal.

Gillette had met Victor Skorzeny a few times and wasn't anxious to repeat the experience. "The man is a fucking *monster*," he said with a shudder. "He's like how you picture Count Dracula. I mean the real thing. Tall, bald—Jesus, have you ever *seen* him? His eyes stare right through you."

Winston Gillette, it was clear, was a small time player, a bottom feeder with a bulging credit line. He knew nothing of the Cabal's plans and was privy to none of their deliberations. They used and tolerated him and that was about it.

Cassandra hardly spoke as I drove us back to the office. I wondered aloud if she was feeling guilty for our heavy-handed tactics. "Because it definitely did the job. Making him think Skorzeny sent something after him." She didn't reply immediately. I was well aware that my partner took her Gift very seriously—any misuse of it was strictly against her principles. "Aw, I'll bet there wasn't more than a few hundred bucks worth of damage. The guy sells *junk*."

"It's not that. I'm just a little tired, I guess."

"Does it take a lot out of you?"

"My PK abilities aren't my strongest suit," she reminded me with a yawn. "It doesn't help that the moon is waning right now. I feel kind of drained."

"You did great," I assured her. "Thanks to that show you put on, Gillette sang like the little yellow canary he is."

"Can we stop for a pop or something? My blood sugar feels really low."

There was a convenience store coming up on the left. "Man, what I wouldn't give to be able to move things around with my mind.

Psychokinetic. I love it." I signaled and got ready to make the turn. "The trouble a guy like me could get into with powers like that..."

"Mostly it gives me a headache," she remarked with a grimace. "And right now I've got a doozie."

Recorded Tuesday, May 11, 01:08 hrs.

WG= Winston Gillette   VS= Victor Skorzeny

GILLETTE: Yeah, hi, it's me. Winston, y'know?

SKORZENY: Mr. Gillette. Yes, indeed. I've been meaning to get in touch with you.

WG: Are you sure you haven't already tried? Earlier tonight maybe?

VS: I'm afraid I don't get your meaning. You sound a bit overwrought. Perhaps you should call back another time.

WG: Something busted up my shop tonight, Mr. Skorzeny. Maybe someone sending me a message, I don't know. But I didn't like it and I wouldn't want it to happen again.

VS: I don't like your implication, Winston, and I certainly don't like your tone.

WG: I, ah, I'm not trying to get heavy on you, Mr. Skorzeny. I just want it made clear to you people that I did not in any way endorse a certain person. If there was a security problem, it was on your end. You and your people. I think we both know what I'm talking about.

VS: Indeed. And I appreciate your discretion. One must always be conscious of security these days.

WG: Yeah. Uh, so I guess I'd like some kind of, ah, you know, reassurance. That you don't blame me or--

VS: Let us look at this hypothetically. Person A introduces Person B to Person C. Person B turns out to be, let us be blunt, a complete shit, the worst kind of vermin. Does Person C not have a right to expect Person A to accept at least partial responsibility for any harm done by Person B?

(Pause)

WG: Uh, sorry, you lost me. Who's Person B again? Is that me or Esch?

VS: You are an imbecile, Gillette. As for this most recent business, if you were not culpable then you were certainly negligent. Why I suffer such incompetent, blundering--

WG: Yeah, see, that's why I'm calling. To prove you're wrong and--and that I can still be of use to you. I have some information that I think you might want to hear.

VS: Indeed.

WG: Yeah. Those two snoops Zinnea and Nightstalk came around here tonight, asking all kinds of questions, if you get my meaning.

VS: Go on.

WG: Well, heh heh, like I said, they asked questions but I just sat here and played dumb.

VS: Hmmm...

WG: What?

VS: Can we get to the point, please. What did they want?

WG: Well, they wanted to know about Es—I mean, Mr. A, didn't they? They knew he used to come here and thought I might have recruited him. You know. For the, uh, organization.

VS: And so I take it you're claiming that you were able to withstand their interrogations and steered them in the wrong direction. Away from...the organization. Do I have your assurance on that? Your word written in blood, as it were?

WS: Mr. Skorzeny, I came from a bad, broken home. I've been through the foster family system, did time in juvie and even a short stretch in the pen a few years back. I learned a long time ago to keep my mouth shut and my ass to the wall, you know what I mean?

VS: That's good, Winston, that's very good. I hope I never have reason to doubt your loyalty. I think you'll find that if you cross us, behave in a manner that threatens our sublime order, you will be visited by horrors from your worst nightmares. On that you have my word.

WG: I know, I know.

VS: Do you, Winston, do you really? I have great power at my disposal, power to do wondrous and terrible things.

WG: I get the point, all right?

VS: I'm delighted to hear it.

WG: So there won't be any more...visits, right?

VS: Good night, Winston.

(*Disconnection*)

WG: Yeah, right.

We agreed that we'd take Tuesday night off. What the hell. We were due for a break and needed some time away from the case. The Old Man didn't squawk so I guess he saw some merit to the idea.

Cassandra told me she was going to sleep all day, rising only to eat and perform necessary bodily functions, then sleep all night. And most of Wednesday too.

"What about you, Evvie? Do you have any plans?"

I just smiled.

I struck pay dirt not far from the old docks. A good, old-fashioned bucket of blood, frequented by bikers and cheap whores, with thugs and villains galore. I could tell right off the bat that it was my kind of watering hole. There was an authentic atmosphere of seediness, enhanced by an undercurrent of barely repressed violence. It wouldn't take much to provoke hostilities. Not when working with such a potentially explosive mixture of alcohol and borderline personality types.

The joint didn't even have a name. You went up and banged on a metal door, somebody eyed you through a Judas hole and if they liked the way you looked, you were in. I guess I appeared sufficiently ugly, stupid and dangerous to fit their demographic.

At one time it had been a warehouse. There were about twenty tables and a scattering of chairs, everything mix and match. A door laid across two wooden saw horses acted as a makeshift bar. No wine. No mixed drinks. Hard liquor in styrofoam cups and cold beer kept in galvanized tin tubs filled with ice. A battered pool table, some VLT's, nobody dancing, nobody laughing.

I nodded to some boys I recognized as *Diablos*. Hooked a long-necked Bud from a bartender who looked like an extra from "Easy Rider". The sound system was shitty, the acoustics worse. Was that a Bob Seger song? I spent a minute or so playing "name that tune" before giving up.

Two inelegant gentlemen detached themselves from a group occupying some tables near the back. When they got closer I saw it was Kevin Bryce and Tommy Schultz. Schultz was a neo-Nazi asshole but I liked Kevin and had partied with him on occasion. Schultz rolled his shoulders and cracked his neck. He was nearly as short as I was, his thick, hairy arms thrust through a cut off blue jean jacket. Shaved head. Iron Cross earings. Goatee. *Punk.*

Kevin seemed down in the mouth about something. "Hey, Nightstalk, how ya doin'?"

"Good, Kev, good." I was picking up some odd vibes. Kevin and I had no quarrel between us but it was almost like he was working himself up to something. "How about yourself?"

He shrugged. "No use complaining, right? Life's a fuckin' movie, my friend, and we all got our parts to play, know what I mean?" Kevin was like that. A deep thinker compared to most hog jockeys.

I had already drained the bottle and was motioning for another one. Paid cash. There wasn't going to be time to run up a tab. "That's very philosophical, Kev. One day you should consider answering your true calling and enter the priesthood."

"I might at that," he allowed, "I hear there's plenty of sex." We had a chuckle while Schultz glowered in the background.

I disposed of the second beer in a few long pulls, feeling a slight buzz, nothing more. "I suppose you're here to tell me that my presence isn't welcome in this fine drinking establishment." Kevin dropped his eyes, embarrassed to be the one delegated with the task. "It's a sad thing to be treated as a leper, even among my own kind."

"Outside, asshole," Schultz glowered.

I raised my eyebrows at the display of bad manners. "Why, Tommy, I swear you're trying to hurt my feelings."

"You gotta leave, Nightstalk," Kevin urged. Chairs were scraping, several more uglies rising to their feet and heading in our direction. "You don't want any part of this."

"That's where you're wrong, Kev," I told him. "This is *exactly* what I've been looking for."

To be fair, there were *only* five of them and I'd hardly touched a drop at that point. As they advanced on me, I wasn't exactly quaking in my boots.

"I'm gonna fuck you up, asshole," Schultz growled.

"No, Tommy, you'll do no such thing. You're not good enough or fast enough. Tell you what, though: to show you what a good sport I am, I'm gonna let Kev here have the first go. Just so he can impress his friends. Come on, Kev. Take your best shot. It'll look good on your resumé."

He looked at me gratefully then hit me flush on the side of the jaw. It was a decent punch but I think he might have pulled it because it didn't pack enough wallop to do more than bruise. I took pity on the guy by dropping him with a sweet hook while he was still admiring his handiwork.

Schultz rushed in and tried to throttle me but I broke his hold...and then every one of his fingers. Had him blubbering his eyes out by the time I was done.

Pussycat.

I let him crawl away while I dealt with the others. One of them was one of those martial arts freaks. I could see him setting up for some kind of fancy-ass kick and bottled him before he could get himself planted. Out for the count. I hate those guys.

The other two kept coming, one guy waving a dagger he pulled from his boot, the other brandishing a pool cue.

The cue swished harmlessly over my head. *When will people learn,* I thought, stepping inside and driving my elbow into the bridge of his nose. *You don't swing a pool cue, you use the butt end like a fucking spear.*

I caught buddy by his greasy hair and used him as a human shield while the goober with the knife did his best to carve me a new arse. Unfortunately, he accidentally impaled his pal through the forearm instead. The knife got stuck in the sinew and as they waltzed around trying to free it, I settled the issue by bashing their heads together.

My performance earned a smattering of applause from a drunk woman with what appeared to be a dead sewer rat draped around her neck.

Kev was starting to come around. I helped him back on his pegs and he and I set the bar right again. I let him know there were no hard feelings and he responded with a groggy acknowledgement.

"It was business," he slurred. "We do work for some people and when the word comes down..." He lurched sideways, nearly stepping on my foot. "You sure you're all right?"

"Fine, Kev, fine. That was a helluva shot you gave me. Would've put down a lesser man, I swear. Have another?" Signaling for more beer, the bartender hurrying to comply.

"Thanks, Nightstalk. But, hey, you'd better take off. I'm serious. You got the mark of Cain on you. Watch your back 'cause people are gunning for you."

"People like you," I reminded him. "Independent contractors. Just business, like you say. Nothing personal."

"Sure, Nightstalk. That's right." Grinning woozily, tapping my bottle with his in a spirit of renewed camaraderie.

I leaned in close. "A word of advice, Kevin lad: with me, it's *always* personal."

We drank to it.

IV

"It is an old maxim of mine that when you exclude the impossible, whatever remains, however improbable, must be the truth."

Sherlock Holmes, (in "The Beryl Coronet")

Wednesday, May 12^{*th*}

Fun and games over, it was time to get back to work.

Unfortunately, when we returned to the office Wednesday night we found no messages, no memos and no new leads to follow up. Neither of us was feeling especially sharp, maybe due to the layoff or, in my case, a byproduct of the brawling and boozing I'd engaged in the previous evening. It felt like I'd pulled something in my lower back and my right shoulder was out of sorts. The same one that got dinged in the Baron's library. But it was my *hands* that bothered me most, my knuckles aching from the workout I'd given them, pain that went right to the bone. *Fuck fuck fuck fuck fucking* arthritis.

I gobbled three more ibuprofen, paged listlessly through the case file.

We sat across the desk from each other, both of us in a lowdown dirty funk, and I realized in a flash there was only one course of action.

"*Delfino's*," I said and saw her brighten immediately.

It was *only* the city's best bistro. It meant a jaunt to Little Italy, at least ten blocks away, but it was well worth the trip. And in the spirit of combating global warming, we decided to leave the car and make the trip on foot.

I was already imagining wrapping my lips around my usual triple cappuccino. Maybe complimenting it with a sesame and poppy seed bagel, fresh from the oven. Cass was partial to café au lait, topped with whipped cream and sprinkled with cinnamon. After about three sips our brains would be jump-started and we'd be ready for whatever this case threw at us.

That was the plan.

We hadn't gone far when she stopped or maybe it was more like *froze.* She glanced about warily, sensing something, and whatever it was, she didn't like it. "Nightstalk—"

Suddenly I was all goose pimples, my body tingling. Then I *heard* it, a growling and huffing noise, growing in volume, approaching at good speed.

"Now what do you suppose *that* is?" I wondered.

"I hate to be the bearer of bad news—"

"Aw, *shit,* it's definitely coming this way. Must be locked on to us somehow." I grabbed her arm, pulling her after me. "Hardly anyone out this late, of course. No way to lose ourselves in a crowd. *Fuck!* Nothing to distract it…"

"It wouldn't do any good. Not if it's what I think it is." We turned a corner and picked up our pace. Now we were nearly running. "I lost a scarf," she confessed. "I'm not sure where. Usually I just whip it off and stuff it in a pocket. Maybe I dropped it—"

"—or *maybe* someone took it."

"I noticed it was gone when I went for a walk the other night. It bugged me. I really liked that scarf."

"Great. Marvelous." Truthfully I was surprised and a bit pissed off at her carelessness. When you're dealing with the black arts, the *last* thing you want is for your adversary to get their hands on something personal, an item that has touched you and bears some trace of your essence.

This was *not* good.

There were a series of ghastly whoops from behind us. Too close for comfort.. "Okay," she said, "we have to think of something fast. I'm pretty sure that's a ravenor back there and if it is we're in big trouble. Now, since it's after me—"

"A ravenor, huh?" I was impressed. "I've heard of those buggers. But maybe it's *me* he wants. I lost a pair of gloves awhile back. Left them in a movie theatre." It was a lie but I was trying to head her off before she did something heroic.

We jigged again, sprinting down a side street, most of the shops boarded up, abandoned, real estate posters stuck hopefully in whatever windows hadn't been broken. Flew past a used appliance store and one of those huge, hockey rink-sized storage places where you can rent space by the month. Not a soul around.

"What kind of fucking city is this?" I raged. "Where is everybody?"

"These places are closed, Nightstalk, everyone's gone home. Nobody actually *lives* in mid-town anymore, you know that."

High pitched cackles from behind us, with a bloodthirsty howl thrown in for good measure.

To a normal, everyday citizen of this city, a ravenor would register as a small whirlwind, a spiral of dust and debris created, no doubt, by the tall buildings that channel air currents, creating all kinds of strange effects. But this was no ordinary whirlwind. It could change speed and veer around corners.

If I'd had the time and inclination I might have felt pity for it.

The ravenor is a tormented soul plucked from the *qliphoth*. As a weapon, it can only be wielded at great risk. After it performs its part of the bargain, its controller is well-advised to give the creature its much desired release. The ravenor has but one purpose: assassination. It is tortured, demented, feral, almost completely mindless. A personal article is placed in front of it. The ravenor cannot resist this chance to finally gain everlasting peace. It coils around the article, drawing out a scent, the slightest scintilla of its owner. That's all it needs.

Then it's cast loose into the world to do its grim work. It must not fail. *It will not fail.* Failure means a continuation of its existence along with the inconceivable pain borne by a soul warped and twisted beyond redemption.

Cassandra stopped to pull off her shoes—which reminded me of this crazy notion I'd once entertained. It was hard to focus with those unnerving whoops and snarls not far behind us. I was trying to keep cool and level-headed but I was also aware of two pertinent facts: as far as I knew, ravenor attacks were as rare as dodo sperm and, even more worrying, I couldn't recall hearing of anybody who'd survived one.

The thing that weighed most heavily on my mind was that *Cassandra Zinnea was in danger*. She needed my help and protection. I was her self-appointed knight in tarnished armour, determined not to let her down.

"Gimme your coat," I gasped. I'm good over short distances but if I have to run more than two city blocks my ex-smoker's lungs take their revenge for all the years I abused them.

She shrugged off her coat and handed it over. I waited until we were passing a construction site, then lobbed it on top of a pile of scrap threatening to overflow a metal disposal bin. "*What are you doing?* Nightstalk, that coat was *Versace*. Well, okay, imitation Versace. What you just did was a crime against fashion—"

"Shoes next," I barked. She was muttering under her breath as she handed over her high quality footwear. I hoped it wasn't an impotence curse.

"I *love* those shoes," she pleaded. "Three hundred and fifty bucks. On *VISA*..."

I was a rock. "Then your blouse, your nylons and pretty much everything else while you're at it." Over the next block she stripped right down to her, ah, essentials, high cut panties and a black silk camisole that left very little to the imagination.

"Admit it," she said, wrapping her arms around herself, "on some level you're really enjoying this."

"Hey, babe, I'm just trying to save your skin." Meanwhile trying my best not to ogle her.

We could hear the ruckus behind us as it went for the bait. There were sounds of wood splintering, metallic thumps, gleeful cackles...and a screech of disappointment as it discovered the unoccupied coat.

"We can only keep this up so long," I warned as I threw her shoes down an alley we were passing. She just about started blubbering. "We're running out of clothes."

"*Wait.*" She rubbed her arms. "I'm *freezing*. At least give me your jacket so I don't end up with frostbite." I took it off and handed it over. She looked great in Raider black and silver. We started running again. Not for long, though, I had to keep slowing down to catch my breath. I wasn't in the best shape. "What's your master plan?" she asked when I motioned for yet another break. Wench hadn't even worked up a decent sweat.

"I...want...you...to run." I was hunched over, my hands on my thighs, breathing deep. The view was great. The bomber jacket barely covered her delicious derrière. "Don't—don't keep in a straight line. Try to find somewhere where there's people." I clutched her arm and pulled myself upright. "Get going. Go to *Delfino's*. I'll come and find you." It had pounced on one of the shoes and didn't seem inclined to seek out its mate. Resumed its pursuit, zeroing in on us. I doubted it would allow itself to be fooled again.

"What are you going to do?"

I grinned. "Smart gal like you hasn't figured it out already?"

"If it's what I think, you're out of your mind and—"

"Get going, Cass." I thought of something. "And you might want to roll in any fresh dog shit you find along the way. To help cover your scent."

"What? And wreck your fancy jacket?" She loped away, her long legs covering ground quickly. There was another "*arooo*" that sounded uncomfortably close. "On second thought," she called, "you're right, why take any chances? Besides, I've always been a 'Niners fan." She waved when she reached the corner and disappeared from sight.

So now there was just me and this great scheme of mine against a murderous, spectral predator with an over-sensitive nose and killer overbite. The thing was, I had spotted some possible flaws in my plan and all at once it didn't seem nearly as clever as I'd originally thought. There was an accompanying loss of confidence, a surge of primal fear that threatened to unman me.

I could hear it coming, moving fast.

Fuck this, I thought.

Pointed myself in the opposite direction and started running...

I couldn't catch my wind, subsisting on quick, stabbing gasps. I was seeing spots and my lungs couldn't keep up with demand. Every time I was forced to halt, I'd pull on another article of Cassandra's clothing, take a few seconds to get my bearings and then continue on.

Blouse. Skirt. I decided to dispense with the nylons. Better dead than that.

It was a pretty desperate tactic, I admit, but cross-dressing was the very *least* I would do for Cassandra Zinnea. Love moves mountains and spans mighty gulfs...it can also make a heterosexual male willingly don women's clothing. Strange but true.

"Hey, you." It was an old rummy and I guess I'd disturbed his sleep. He was propped up against the shell of a burned out auto shop. Buddy had about three teeth in his head and the renal system of a thirty-five hundred-year old mummy.

"Relax, pops." I straightened, raising my arms over my head, fighting a wicked stitch.

"What are you doing, boy?"

"Trying to fool a bogey," I replied. Which seemed to satisfy him. I waited, praying the ravenor's legendary single-mindedness would operate in my favor. If he ignored my trail and went after Cassandra, I was fucked. Then I heard it approaching, snuffling and grunting as it skittered along. "Gotcha," I muttered.

And was off again.

I must have been quite the sight, legging it down the street in a knee-length skirt and expensive designer blouse that still carried an enticing blend of aromas unique, as far as I know, to my partner. Meanwhile, the ravenor closed the gap between us, homing in on the scent that I was doing my best to get all over me. More excited yipping and I heard the wino yell something but he was lucky, his stink was wrong so it let him be.

At last I found what I was looking for, sort of, a concrete ramp sloping down to an underground parking garage. The doors were white and sealed tight. The proximity lights clicked on at my approach so the area was bathed in illumination.

I saw the ravenor twirl and bound into the light, veering toward me as soon as I was in sight. It started its final run...but at the last moment it must have realized I was not the intended target because it seemed to hesitate in mid-leap--

That's when I struck, a reflex action, quicker than thought, fastening my hands around something solid near its centre and *squeezing.*

The ravenor went berserk, bucking and slashing at the air but my long arms kept it at bay, holding it away from me so it couldn't inflict serious damage. Applying more and more pressure, my arms and shoulders expanding, and when I finally felt it weakening, I gave it a final, hard *twist...*

"To *hell* with you," I said.

Everything consistent and obeying a fundamental and ancient article of magical lore: in order to do damage on the earthly plane, a bogey must take on physical properties and characteristics. A solid form. Tearing claws and snapping teeth, a throat that howls...and a neck that can be wrung.

The ravenor dissolved in the cool night air, leaking through my fists, dissipating into nothingness. I wish I could record a final, grateful sigh but it wasn't like that. It was just...gone. Up in smoke, leaving an oily residue on my hands. It was sticky and smelled, I discovered, faintly like over-ripe bananas.

I checked at *Delfino*'s, only guess what? She wasn't there. Got some funny looks from Al Ponti, the head waiter, and it wasn't until I was outside that I realized I was still wearing her blouse. Not only that, it was liberally splattered with drying yellow ichor. Ravenor goo. Al must have thought I'd puked on myself. Lucky thing I'd remembered to ditch the skirt...

She was at Bashir's joint, another four blocks away and never mind my *specific* instructions to go to *Delfino*'s. Then again, she knew she could walk into *The Purple Turban* wearing nothing but my Raiders jacket and a smile and nobody would bat an eye. And if anyone took too long a look or, worse, made a crude comment, look out. The Lebanese have some rather quaint— one might even say *medieval*--views on proper decorum around women.

I can imagine what happened when she showed up *sans* most of her clothes. Waiters and patrons alike falling all over each other to lend assistance, tut-tutting over the condition of her bare feet, summoning a basin and towel from the kitchen, Amin insisting on tending to them himself...

Okay, maybe I was exaggerating but not by much. Amin, owner/manager (but only on paper, Bashir Ayoub and the Lebanese mob really called the shots), worshipped the ground she walked on. Collected it in little clay jars and labelled it. As a result, we were always given the royal treatment at the *Turban* and let me tell you, hospitality means something when you're dealing with folks from that part of the world.

The coffee was served strong and scalding hot. Multi-course meals, warm hand towels and discreet, unobtrusive service. Funky music playing constantly in the background, Marcel Khalifeh or the divine Fayrouz. You could order all sorts of spicy appetizers—the prawns were absolutely lethal—and my partner had a mouth-watering assortment spread out in front of her when I walked in the door.

The waiters and customers grouped around her, laughing at her easy banter, spotted me and drifted back to their tables.

I went down on one knee before her. "Milady, your Prince Charming has returned. The beast is vanquished and all is well in your realm once again."

If I expected her to hurl herself into my arms and cover me with grateful kisses, I was sadly mistaken. "Did you bring my clothes with you?"

I slipped into the chair opposite her, shaking my head in regret. "Alas, they did not survive the encounter. Things got...messy. But, please, allow me to describe the terrific struggle that I—"

"You mean I have to go around like this?" she squeaked. "Nightstalk, the zipper on this jacket is broken and it's too short so it doesn't cover *anything*." I raised my shoulders. What could I do? "You bastard," she hissed. "There's more to this than meets the eye. But you *did* save me and for that, if nothing else, thanks." She held out her hand and we shook on it.

"You're welcome."

"How did you do it? You used my clothes, didn't you?"

I gave her a blow-by-blow account, minimizing my role whenever possible, displaying my customary modesty and restraint (*ahem*). At one point, Amin popped in to refill our cups with *black* coffee and then quickly withdrew, respectful of our privacy.

"Not bad," she allowed, once I finished.

"I've heard about those things and wondered if switching clothes would work. I never imagined I'd get to try it out for real."

"Well, I repeat: I'm very, very grateful to you." She took my hand. She'd had to roll up the sleeves of the bomber jacket to accommodate her shorter arms. "You never hesitated, did you? You knew it would come after you and you didn't give it a second thought." She was going mushy on me. It was too much. I got ready to say something stupid to break the mood but she wouldn't let me. "You make me feel safe, you know that? You make me think I have nothing to fear as long as you're by my side."

I squeezed her fingers. "That's good, kid, that's real good. Because it's the truth. I'll always be there for you, no matter what. Don't you forget it."

We switched to tea and took our lives in our hands by ordering a main course of prawns to split between us. We didn't speak of our close call after that. Guys kept sending drinks to our table. When she stood up and made her way to the bathroom, every eye in the place was on her, including mine. Amin offered her a table cloth to preserve her modesty and earned a round of good-natured *boos* for his magnanimous gesture.

I was as enraptured as the rest of them. I'd face a dozen ravenors, back to back, if it meant being able to see her slink about in my scruffy old Raiders jacket. Laughing and flirting and soaking up the attention. Exotic without really trying, valuable beyond measure.

Worth dying for...although I still held out hope it wouldn't come down to that.

Thursday, May 13th

Another night, another memo from the Old Man:

Contact C.I. Glen Feschuk
Report any progress.
Top priority.

"Interesting. Somehow Glen got upgraded from peeping tom to 'confidential informant'." I wadded up the memo. "Won't he be thrilled."

"How *does* one go about finding someone who's invisible?" Cassandra wondered.

"Ah, now that's the trick," I admitted. "Call it a trade secret."

"Well, I'll let you take care of it. In the meantime, I'm going to see Wojeck and Faro. Squeeze them for some information, anything new about Eva. They might be more amenable if—"

"—I'm not with you. Right. Go for it. And, hey, do me a favour and *please* make decent notes so I can use them in my report. It saves time."

She waved her notebook at me. "Already ahead of you." She paused at the door, spoke without turning around: "Evvie, I know you didn't think much of her—"

"Aw, Eva wasn't such a bad old gal," I lied. "Her bark was worse than her bite. And like her or not, nobody deserves to die like that. Find out what you can and we'll meet back here and put everything together. Got it?"

"Got it." She blew me a kiss, opened the door and as she did—

"Hey, kid." She looked back at me. "You be careful out there. Eva was right about one thing: I love you like crazy and I don't want anything happening to you."

"Oh, *Evvie...*"

"Get going," I said, swiveling in my chair until I was facing the desk again. "I'll scout around for Glen. Let's pretend we're a couple of working dicks for a change."

"Okay, you old poop. I'll see you later." I heard the door close and her footsteps on the stairs. But she sent one last thought my way, on our private band: *You're a lovely, lovely man, Evgeny Nightstalk. Whether you like it or not.*

About thirty seconds later the phone rang. Guess who?

"Hey, Glen, I was just thinking about you..."

Another chilly night. I wore the Raiders jacket, which I'd reclaimed from Cassandra, busted zipper and all. There were lots of hidden pockets in the jacket, special adaptations I'd made over the years. I could pack an entire armoury of offensive weaponry in the lining and up the sleeves (and sometimes did). I like to be prepared, as that Marine dude in "Aliens" says, in case of close encounters.

Glen told me to meet him at "the usual place", knowing full well that we'd never met at the same location twice in all the time we'd had dealings with each other. But for longtime city dwellers "the usual place" refers to a local landmark, a pedestrian bridge near the mouth of the Nameless River where people like to go to off themselves. There's a deep ravine below where the current surges as it enters the lake. Sometimes they never find the body.

"Hey, didja hear Lew Archer offed himself?"

"You don't say? Where'd he do it?"

"The usual place..."

It was late so hardly anybody was about. There was a guy on the bench nearest the footbridge. I stood about ten feet behind him, next to another one of those Dalek garbage cans.

"Okay, Glen," I muttered. "You wanted to see me, here I am." The garbage can played it dumb. "No fucking around, I haven't got time for this." Trying to keep my voice low so John Q. Citizen on the bench wouldn't be distracted from pondering the big plunge. "C'mon, man, let's hear it. Did you find out anything about Fischer or Skorzeny?"

"Psst."

I scowled at the bin. "I can hear you, motherfucker, you don't have to—"

"Hey, Nightstalk. Over here, man." The voice wasn't coming from the garbage bin. It seemed to be originating from the guy on the bench. It *sounded* like Glen but I couldn't be sure. I wandered over, alert for a set-up.

"Excuse me. Did you say something?"

"It's me, man. *Glen.*" Then I saw his face and the job they'd done on him. "Nice, huh? Real charming people you got me mixed up with, pal."

"Now hold on a second," I said, genuinely taken aback by his appearance. "Nobody put a gun to your head. I asked you to do a favour for us. It's not my fault that you're looking and feeling like a hundred and sixty pounds of ground chuck right now. Sorry as hell and all that but don't try hanging your bad news around my neck."

We glared at each other. His shiners made him look like an angry panda bear.

"I'm here to deliver a message," he informed me. "I'll make it short and sweet because I wanna go home and crawl into bed for, like, a year."

"I'm listening."

"The first thing I wanna say is that I am hereby announcing my immediate retirement as your resident spy, source, stool pigeon, whatever you wanna call it. I'm hanging 'em up, Nightstalk. You want information, you better start looking elsewhere 'cause I'm done."

If he was serious, it was a major loss. "Glen, shit...what the hell happened, man?'

He shook his head and winced. Any movement caused him considerable pain. Which meant he likely had busted ribs too. Busted ribs are a bitch. "Now here's the second part of my message: the people who did this want you to know that *you're next*. Got that? You and your lady friend. For sticking your noses into other people's business. Old Man or no Old Man, they intend to fuck you up." He used his good arm as a brace to shift positions, moving very, very gingerly.

"But...there's no way they should have been able to—to detect you."

"Oh, that's where you're wrong." His smile came out upside down. "They made it look easy. They played me along, the fuckers. You told me to look into this Skorzeny guy? So I did my thing, drifted around, keeping my ears open and I got lucky, if you wanna call it that. I start hearing about this top secret meeting. I go check it out and it's in this old hangar at Tarkenton Field. This big, bald guy was there and he looked *right at me*, man, and pointed me out to them. They were *waiting* for me, okay? Fucking *expecting* me. From that point on, I was *fucked*. They didn't ask any questions, they didn't wanna know anything, they just went to work. Real pros."

"*Skorzeny*. Shit, now I *am* feeling bad."

"He looks like *Nosferatu*. He didn't fuck around either. He told them where to kick me and how hard and meanwhile he stood there, enjoying himself, watching them do their thing." He reacted to another sharp twinge of pain.

"Got your ribs pretty good?" I ventured.

He nodded. "Sadistic fucker." He used that good arm again--the other was in a sling, resting against his stomach—and slowly eased himself up off the bench. "I pissed blood for, like, thirty-six hours. My girlfriend's been having kittens."

I felt bad, despite what I'd said earlier about not being responsible. "So you, uh, got someone looking after you?"

He nodded. "This great lady I met. It was on a bus, if you can believe it." He managed a grin that was at least half wince. "I was in total invisible mode 'cause I'd snuck on board, right? I was kind of bored and I notice this chick standing there and she's got this nice, big ass." He raised his eyebrows, likely the only movement he could make that was pain-free. "I'm reaching out and I'm about to give that ass a squeeze when she goes 'I see you, y'know'. I was totally blown away. Maybe one in a million people can see me and it turns out *she's* one of them. Talk about fate."

"Can I--is there some way to...make it up to you? Compensate you or whatever? I'll talk to the Old Man." He gave me a look of disgust. "Okay, but I want you to know there's gonna be payback for this. I'm gonna break somebody's fuckin' neck."

He began to hobble away, making for a footpath that led to the parking lot, taking his time. "You hard of hearing, man? You wanna end up like me? Get out of town, while you can. Get the fuck away. 'Cause as far as I know you don't have a girlfriend, Nightstalk. Somebody that can take care of your sorry ass." He wasn't content leaving it at that. "Hell, man, you hardly have any friends at all, do you?"

It was a cheap shot, way below the belt, but I let it go.

I figured I deserved it.

I can reconstruct Cassandra Zinnea's evening based on later conversations and by deciphering scribbled entries in her reporter's notebook.

She cabbed over to police HQ around 10:00 p.m. Asked to see Detectives Wojeck and Faro. This time they didn't give her the bum's rush. Impromptu meeting in the lobby. Neither was forthcoming. They appeared baffled by the circumstances of Eva Jauch's death. Wojeck wanted to know if she knew anything about spontaneous human combustion but when she queried him further, abruptly changed the subject. Faro was his usual thick-headed self. Stubbornly unhelpful, about as sentient as your average, garden variety slug.

They'd sent uniforms door to door, canvassing the neighborhood. A pointless waste of man hours. In the end, the whole thing would undoubtedly fall under the broad category of "death by misadventure". Shuffled, reshuffled and forgotten.

Never mind that a woman had been burned alive, burned to *ashes* while the room around her remained virtually unscathed. It was weird, *uncanny*...no wonder the cops were so tight-lipped and tetchy.

Had they asked, put aside their stupid prejudices and fears and solicited her opinion, Cassandra could have told them a thing or two, got them on the right track at least.

Then again, how would those dimwits have reacted to any allusion to the supernatural and/or paranormal? As it was, they refused her entry to Eva Jauch's lodgings and eventually told her to fuck off in no uncertain terms. She kept trying to win them over, promising to share information with them, cooperate fully...but they just stared at her like a pair of groupers.

As luck would have it, on the way out she met the young cop who had loaned me his sunglasses. He was much more accommodating. Police had responded to a 9-1-1 call. Caller refused to give a name, sounded old and frightened. Likely a client who had popped in for a reading and found what was left of her favorite clairvoyant. They were going through Eva's daybook, checking her appointments. And Wojeck really *was* leaning toward spontaneous combustion as cause of death but those involved had been told to keep their traps shut about it. The young cop ("Dennis Findlater 462-1134") was soon called away on business but let it slip that the first uniforms who arrived on-scene had to take stress leave afterward. Must have been grisly, walking in on something like that.

The two of them exchanged pleasantries and he asked if he could call her some time. They made arrangements to meet after work. For an early breakfast. Or maybe they would rendezvous at a terrific pizza place they both frequented. Extra cheese and hold the salami until later, when they were alone...

Okay, granted, it probably wasn't like that. She described the cop as "innocent, freshly scrubbed" and insisted he wasn't at *all* her type.

She left the station and found herself standing on the corner, wondering why she hadn't thought to call a cab while she was inside.

She never heard him approach, he was just *there*.

"Cassandra, my dear, I was hoping our paths would cross tonight," he oozed.

His car was waiting.

In *my* version of events, they don't kiss.

I could smell him from the bottom of the stairs. That cologne again. *Yecchh.*

I was already in a foul mood because of what had happened to Glen. Losing him as a source, the best we'd ever had. Then, to make matters worse, a trigger-happy hex on the third step nearly cut my feet out from under me. I gingerly skipped over the troublesome stair and continued on my way, alert for any other surprises my partner might have in store for potential intruders.

I opened the door and, it killed me, the sonofabitch was sitting in my chair *again*. Cassandra stifled a giggle—a phony one—in response to some witticism that likely would've been lost on dumb ol' me.

But I remembered my manners and glued on my best fake smile, keeping my lips closed so they couldn't see my gritted teeth. "Philippe."

"Nightstick."

"You know his name," Cassandra admonished him. "I *warned* you, Philippe." Turning to me: "I ran into Monsieur DeBarge outside the police station. By the way..." She tossed me her notebook. "I jotted a few things down. Philippe said he had some important information to pass along so I brought him back here. We've been expecting you."

"Perhaps you would like to tell us where you've been? In the spirit of cooperation, and so on and so forth." He wasn't expecting a straight answer so I obliged him.

"Visiting a sick friend." I nodded at Cass but said nothing. I was alert for any mental probes from his direction. He *was* a 6th Degree, after all.

"How nice that you have a friend." He turned back to Cassandra. "As promised, I have brought you information relating to this affair. Documents and such. Perhaps it will aid your investigation. Accelerate the pace, as it were."

"Philippe isn't too happy with our progress," she put in.

"Is that so?"

"Time is of the essence," he said. "We must redouble our efforts. Cooperation is essential to our success." His expression was grave. "Be forewarned, my friends. I will do what I can for you but do not take advantage of me. That would be...unfortunate." He wasn't bad; for a few seconds he managed to appear genuinely menacing.

"As a sign of good faith, Philippe says the Brethren are prepared to release intelligence to us in a more timely manner. In return, we have to start showing some results. Is that correct?" He nodded and they both waited for the eruption they knew was coming.

But I decided to surprise them. "Well...it's a tough case and we're doing our best. I guess we'll just have to work harder--right, partner?" Presenting them with my best poker face.

He was caught off guard, expecting a far different reaction. "Yes. Indeed. I, too, will do what I can. You must understand, I am at the mercy of my superiors..."

I walked over to the desk. Pointed to a stack of folders. "Is this your top secret stuff?" I picked up a file and began paging through it. "*Hmm.* Some of this comes from wiretaps, I'm guessing highly illegal. Certainly inadmissible. *Tsk, tsk.* Whatever happened to constitutional rights in this country?"

He smiled. "We have considerable resources at our disposal and no small amount of experience when it comes to surveillance and covert operations."

Cassandra was frowning as she perused another dossier. "There's a heck of a lot of stuff missing." She showed me. On some pages only a few words were legible, the rest blacked out.

I snatched the file from her and, I admit it, lost some of my new found self-control. "*This* is cooperation? *This* is trust? Are we on the same side or what?" I shook the folder at him. "Goddamnit, DeBarge, this is bullshit and you know it."

He was glowering. "What would you have me do, Monsieur Nightstalk? I give you what they give me. These are secretive people. Centuries of living in the shadows have made them that way. Their minds are inscrutable but I have come to respect the wisdom of their decisions. Most of the time."

I made a face. "Great."

"I will do what I can," he repeated. He pleaded his case to Cassandra, hoping for a friendlier hearing. "I will press them on your behalf. Believe me, there is still much worthwhile information here, I promise you. You just have to know where to look and to, how do you say, see between the lines, yes? Trust me, my dear."

She practically batted her eyelashes at him. "I *do* trust you. I always have. I know you'll do what you can for us." If they kept it up any longer, I'd have to leave the room.

After he departed, we took a few minutes to get caught up with each other. Her account of the episode at the cop shop made my blood boil. The pricks.

Then it was my turn.

"Did you find Glen?"

"I saw him."

"That was fast. How did you--"

"No, you're not getting it. I *saw* him, Cass. He isn't invisible any more. He's been scared straight. As of now, he's visible to the naked eye and intending to stay that way. Our number one spy has quit the game and I mean for good."

She was taken aback. "What brought this about?"

"Skorzeny. Fucker set him up and then beat the living shit out of him." She sat up, angry and dismayed at what she was hearing. "They must have suspected we'd use him to get at them. Lured him in and did a number on him to make him see the error of his ways."

"But how? *How* could they see him?" she wondered.

"He says one in a million people can."

"Or a *very* highly skilled adept." She mulled that one over. "The Cabal is certainly taking great pains to protect themselves. Security seems to be something of an obsession to them."

"So what are they up to?"

"Exactly." She looked glum. "So Glen is...gone?"

I nodded. "He's not much use to anybody right now. His girlfriend's taking care of him."

"He's going be tough to replace," she mused. "An invisible man, a guy who can go anywhere, a see-through snitch. This is another serious setback." She drummed her fingers on the desk. Her nails were short, bitten to the quick. A sure sign of anxiety.

"By the time this is over *nobody'll* be talking to us," I fretted.

"It's happening already. I called Carl, that scryer I know? He claimed to be booked up until further notice. Same with Louise and Vonda and everyone else I contacted." The drumming increased in tempo.

"First the cats, now this. How are we supposed to find out what's going on?"

"All part of the plan to shut off the flow of information. That is absolutely critical to their diabolical design."

I grunted. "So what does that leave us to go on? Not a helluva lot."

"Tut, tut, Nightstalk," she remonstrated. "What about this material Philippe left us? You never know what nuggets of gold it might yield."

I made a face. "Odds and sods and you know it. Not the stuff we *need* to see, just the junk they can bear to part with." I picked up a folder containing grainy, out-of-focus photographs. Some appeared to have been taken at an airport, night scenes of people walking across the tarmac toward a line of waiting vehicles.

"I'm not so sure," she said suddenly. "It's like pearls in a dungpile, you just have to know where to look. This one is interesting. There aren't that many deletions. It's a transcript of a conversation between Victor Skorzeny and Tibor Benes."

I went over to join her. "Benes. The super jock. Some kind of sprinter or something, wasn't he?"

"A decathlete, Olympic silver medalist. Made a killing with endorsements and sank his money into a sporting goods chain. He still runs in the city marathon, I see him every year. He's a very well-preserved man."

I let that one slide. "So what are they talking about? What's the gist of it?"

"See for yourself."

Recorded April 24th (21:46 Hrs)

VS= Victor Skorzeny   TB= Tibor Benes

BENES: Hello?

SKORZENY: Yes, go ahead.

BENES: I was hoping for an update. The last time
we talked there had been quite a bit of progress
and I wondered--

SKORZENY: I think we can safely say that the last
piece of the puzzle is finally in place. It's
incredible, watching it come together.

BENES: (Inaudible)

VS: What?

TB: Wonderful. Yes.

VS: I am relying on you. Both of you. Together
you will help usher in a new era of human history.
Those who are fearless and cruel will walk with
the gods. The rest will be trodden underfoot.

TB: It's an exciting prospect.

VS: Are you ready to take on such a grave
responsibility?

TB: I am, Master. But I must say that Julian
seems nervous.   I think it's a case of old
superstitions dying hard.

VS: I believe our Julian is a lapsed Catholic.

TB: Lately he's taken to quoting from the *Book of
Revelations*.

VS: Jesus Christ!

TB: I think it's just nerves. Julian is a highly strung individual.

VS: Well, this is certainly an, ah, unexpected development.

TB: He'll be all right. I asked him if he wanted to withdraw but he adamantly refused. ************** (Name blacked out) thinks he's fine. He says Julian can be relied upon to fulfill his part of the assignment.

VS: Yes, but is ************ a reliable judge of character? I wonder.

TB: I don't understand. Is ******** under suspicion?

VS: Never mind. These matters will be dealt with in due course. Just make sure you guys don't fuck up.

TB: We won't, Master. If your recipe is correct, all will go as planned.

VS: This is merely a test run, Tibor, remember that. Make sure you're vigilant for any...anomalies.

TB: Yes, of course. And we've already picked out the site. Everything has been taken into consideration.

VS: Good. That's very good. You've done well, Tibor. The others will be pleased.

TB: It's tremendously exciting to be a part of something of such awesome significance. That's what I keep telling Julian. This isn't the end of the world, it's the beginning of a new and better age.

VS: Precisely. Where it will be survival of the fittest. The strongest and most cruel. Those who understand what Crowley means when he says: "The mighty are righteous for their morals are arbitrary."

TB: When the time comes, Julian will be fine. It's these old myths and misconceptions that get in the way.

VS: How true. Well done, Tibor. Keep our friend in line and soon great things will be in store for all of us.

TB: We're waiting for the final translation of the recipe and then we'll get things underway.

VS: It should be ready in a week, perhaps a bit sooner. It is difficult but we must be patient.

TB: It must be exactly right.

VS: Of course. And it will be. We shall leave it there. Good night, Tibor.

TB: Yes. Good night.

"There are other calls here. Most involve Skorzeny. He's definitely the focus of their attention, not Fischer. Interesting..."

I lowered the stapled sheets I was reading. "I've never even met the bald-headed prick and already I hate him."

"I get the feeling there's something staring me right in the face and I'm not seeing it." More finger drumming. "Clearly there's some kind of conspiracy in the works but what are they up to? This bit about a 'recipe'...what does *that* mean?" I could see she was drifting off into her own private world, her tireless mind going over everything again, looking for anything she might have missed.

My presence was no longer required.

Well, that was fine with me. I had a small mountain of files to go through as well as my nightly report to write up so I had plenty on my plate.

But I found it hard to concentrate. Glen's warning bothered me. I wasn't scared or anything, just...*apprehensive*. I couldn't get his battered face out of my head, imagining what it would do to me if something similar happened to the woman across the desk from me. I must have been radiating ugly, black thoughts. All at once she spoke up, making me jump.

"I want you to know we're not completely helpless. Nor are we without resources and allies we can draw on. You'll see. So stop your worrying." She winked at me. "And if it comes down to just you and me, so be it. Because nobody's beaten us yet, Evgeny Davidovitch. We've had a few draws but we've never, *ever* walked away from a fight. It's not my style and I know for a fact it's not yours either."

I sighed. "So we keep going? No matter what?"

"To the bitter end."

"I was afraid you were going to say that."

"I need to think out loud, if that's all right." It was almost five in the morning. "I'm beginning to see some interesting correlations," she added, "and talking about them will help pull things together for me."

That was fine by me. I'd spent the past few hours bouncing my eyes off dozens of heavily censored pages and welcomed a break. My head was throbbing like a stubbed toe.

"I'm listening." I eased back in my chair, covering a yawn.

"Okay. The Brethren decide to infiltrate someone into the Cabal to find out what they're up to. Their agent, Arturs Esch, makes contact with them through our bookseller friend, Winston Gillette. His credentials check out and he begins to work his way up the ladder. He passes along information to the Brethren but then his cover is blown and he's killed. The Baron dies, then Eva..."

"Right. With you so far." Stretching my arms over my head. "Esch is a spy, the Baron's a traitor but what about Eva? You said yourself she posed no threat to them."

"Yes, but she contacted the Baron on our behalf. They found out about it and cut our best conduit to the spirit realm. Tactically, a sound move."

"I guess. Maybe I'm just having some kind of cognitive meltdown but I still don't see a purpose to any of this. Do you?"

"That remains to be discovered," my partner conceded. "Shall I continue or do you intend to interrupt me with more impertinent questions?"

I rubbed my eyes. "Sorry. Please go on with your summation."

"The Cabal is planning something but we don't know what." She sounded thoughtful. "It must be a matter of great consequence, otherwise the Brethren of Purity wouldn't be involved. Not only that, it's important enough for Victor Skorzeny to bring in *them*." She fanned out three blurry photographs.

"Who are they?"

She pointed at one photo. "Unless I'm very much mistaken, that's David Harriman. The last I heard, he was teaching ancient languages at some college on the Eastern seaboard. I saw him give a lecture once. Very impressive."

"So why should we be interested in him? Some academic guy with elbow patches and an over-sized brain. So what?"

"Well, for one thing that plane he just flew in on is Fischer's corporate jet. See?" Dang, she was right. I'd completely missed the logo on the fuselage. "I should also mention that David Harriman, among other things, is probably the world's foremost expert on the Enochian language."

I searched my memory. "That's, like, a special lingo used by bogeys, isn't it?"

She chuckled. "Not quite, but you're on the right track. It's been utilized in spellcasting and ritual ceremonies for hundreds of years. As for its origins and actual age, we can only speculate."

"What about these other two hombres?"

"It's hard to tell but I'd swear that this one," fingering a second snapshot, "even though you can only see his profile, is Simon Margate."

I whistled. "Simon the Magus? Are you sure? Jeez, I didn't think he ever left Europe. What's he doing out here in the boonies?"

"That's what worries me. Margate is a world class sorcerer. If they're consulting people like him and David Harriman…"

"And this third guy?"

"I don't know," she replied. "He keeps his face covered. But he must be important because there's at least five separate shots of him. I think it's safe to deduce he's an expert on matters relating to the occult or some associated field." She put the picture with the others. "Curiouser and curiouser," she murmured.

"And what about us? What part do we play in this? Aren't we getting a bit out of our league if we're up against serious ass mages like Simon Margate? And where's Philippe and the Brethren while this is going down? Just standing by, doing *nothing*."

She glared at me. "I think we're getting off topic. No matter what you think of the Brethren we are, after all, on the same side." I rolled my eyes.

"The Brethren have their own agenda, there's no disputing that. We may question their motives at times but they *are* the good guys."

"Oh, brother," was all I could say to that.

"I just wish I had more to go on. These dribs and drabs we're getting aren't enough. There's a bigger picture we're not seeing yet. The connections. It's getting clearer, coming into focus, but we're not quite there..."

"What's crystal clear to *me* is that this stuff here," I waved at the disorder of files and paper, "doesn't add up to a hill of horseshit. I've been staring at it all night and the only thing I've gotten out of it is a headache the size of Rushmore. You talk about connections, *what* connections? I'd like to *connect* with your buddy Philippe..." I made a fist and shook it.

"I'll admit this case is frustrating but it does have its attractions too."

"Zombies vomiting maggots, blood-thirsty ravenors, that kind of thing?"

"Nightstalk." It was late and her sense of humour was nonexistent. "*Think* about it. The Brethren have been practically dormant for decades, their power waning. Suddenly, something happens here in Ilium that triggers alarms in Brussels and provokes this flurry of activity. Eva talked about how much turmoil there is on other side. What has so things stirred up? What's going on? This is almost unprecedented. As a matter of fact, I can think of only one other instance in recent history when something even remotely...when there was..." She stopped speaking and appeared to have stopped breathing as well.

"*What*? What is it?"

"My God, Nightstalk," she whispered, "I don't know how I missed it. Yes, when you examine it from a certain perspective, it fits, all the pieces fit!" Her eyes were flashing, it was an absolute peak moment and she was in her glory. The tumblers had fallen into place. The victory was her's.

"So," I urged, "what is it? What's the big discovery?"

"It's only a hypothesis at this point," she said, trying to contain her excitement. "I have to check a few things out, do some research..." She bolted from her chair, gathered up some of the files and swept toward the door.

"Hey, hey, wait a minute!" I jumped up, moving to intercept her. She frowned, clearly impatient to be on her way. "You can't leave me like that!" I protested. "You have this massive breakthrough and then take off without clueing me in? Don't I even get a *hint*?"

She considered briefly. "Think late Forties. A whole series of strange, unexplained phenomena. Mount Rainier. Lights in the sky..."

I mulled it over. "Nope. Still drawing a blank."

"Let's just say that some of the odd occurrences from around that time—and there were a lot of them—were the direct result of magickal workings conducted by minions of the greatest occult figure of the past century. The Brethren had to step in back then too, in a big way."

"I'm still not following you."

"I'll fill you in tonight, I promise." She pointed at the clock. Outside the sky would be tinged with pink and orange, an ominous pre-dawn glow. "Back to your coffin, Count."

"I *hate* when you do this. You like to draw things out and build the suspense. Ah, what the hell." I stepped out of the way and motioned for her to pass.

She kissed the top of my head on the way by. "See you tonight. Sleep well, my dear. *Ta*."

Sleep.

Yeah, right.

Even a good wank didn't take my mind off the case (not for long anyway). The hints she dropped were on constant rotation in my head. I spent *hours* trying to come up with a plausible solution...but always ended up with a random scattering of puzzle pieces that refused to fit into any sensible configuration. Maddening.

I suppose I could have gotten changed, wandered over to the nearest library and *Google*d around on one of their public internet terminals. But that meant venturing out into the daylight, which appealed to me not at all.

Burn out my eye sockets just to satisfy my stupid curiosity? Don't be ridiculous. Sooner or later I was bound to drop off and--

That night I showed up at the office looking like a crack freak in the midst of a major bender. Bloodshot eyes, shaking hands; I was as jumpy as a pogo stick. And of course she was *late*, even later than usual. I was reduced to making coffee, catching up on the filing, re-alphabetizing the books. Anything to piss some time away.

Finally, around eleven, she came floating in, dressed to the nines in this Wilma Flintstone wraparound number that hung on her with no visible means of support other than the curves and swells of her body. Her hair was different again, short and spiky. Brunette. I guess my eyes must have bugged out because she burst into laughter.

"Sorry, it was a late supper. I thought I finally had cause to celebrate."

"I've been waiting all day to hear about it," I responded neutrally. "By the way, who was the lucky fella?"

"Just an old friend. There was no hanky-panky, honest."

I didn't believe her.

She was flushed, radiating this brassy, sexy confidence and I blurted out my suspicion before I had time to stop myself: "You weren't sharing this great epiphany or whatever with Brother Philippe by any chance, were you?"

She stiffened. "No, as a matter of fact, I wasn't. You wouldn't know her. *Her*, Nightstalk. As if that's any of your business."

Yikes. I watched as she plunked her purse down on the desk and tugged off her earrings. "I, uh, did the filing and, uh, y'know, kind of straightened up a bit."

"That's nice." She dropped into her chair and dug her fingers through her new 'do.

"Listen, partner, if I was out of line—"

"Skip it. We have more important things to deal with." Disposing of my attempted apology like a wadded up tissue.

"Er, yeah, that's right. So tell me about it. This morning you were saying—"

"I underestimated Fischer and Skorzeny," she began. "The scope of their ambition. I never thought they'd have the nerve to attempt such a thing. The Crowley connection is the key that unlocks it all. The Fischers revere the Great Beast—remember I told you they were collectors, real aficionados? But now I see it's more than that. Having some of A.C.'s old robes and signed first editions of his books wasn't enough. They want to out-do the Master."

"Which means..." I prompted.

"*The Babalon Working.* Ring any bells?" She was surprised when I shook my head. "I was sure you'd have it put together by now." I shrugged. "Well, it *is* a very interesting tale," she teased. Now we were back on familiar ground.

"I'm *waiting.* I've been waiting all bloody day."

"Been on pins and needles, have you? Shall I keep you in suspense a little longer?"

"You're a bigger ham than Miss Piggy, you know that?"

"Frankly, I resent the comparison. She has fat thighs. That vein is bulging in your forehead again, by the way."

"That's because I'm about to *strangle* you unless you get on with it."

"Okay," she conceded, "I'll try to make a long story reasonably short. The so-called 'Babalon Working' is a ritual ceremony, a particularly potent and scary one. It was last attempted in southern California during the late-

1940s by a guy named John Whiteside Parsons. Aleister Crowley was especially fond of Parsons and seemed to be grooming him for bigger and better things. You see, Parsons wasn't your ordinary, run of the mill occult kook."

"No?"

"Absolutely not. The man was a *bona fide* genius, a rocket scientist no less, one of the guiding lights at what later became the Jet Propulsion Laboratory. There's even a crater on the far side of the moon named after him. His superiors weren't aware of his avid interest in the occult, nor did they know about his personal life, which was pretty screwed up and disaster prone. In his loneliness and despair he turned to black magic, in particular, a series of rituals that he hoped would produce an elemental creature who would be his spirit guide, familiar and lover all in one. Together they would conceive what amounted to a cosmic anti-Christ who would hasten in the Age of Horus and--"

"You're kidding. Please tell me you're kidding."

"Wait, there's more." Clearly enjoying herself. "He wasn't acting alone, he also had the assistance of a friend and fellow adept, none other than L. Ron Hubbard."

"Good grief! I can't imagine a sharp cookie like Elron going along with such bullshit."

"Well, he did eventually end up running off with Parsons' wife and a good chunk of his money."

"Now *that* sounds like Elron."

"But not before Parsons and Hubbard collaborated on a series of workings that climaxed with the two of them heading out into the Mojave Desert and...well, after that no one's really sure. But *something* must have happened because the people staying with Parsons began noticing all kinds of bizarre manifestations. Apparitions, voices in the walls, cold spots--"

"Wait a minute," I held up a hand, "you're saying these guys make up some kind of spell and conjure something out of—"

"They *didn't* make it up. Parsons could read and write Enochian, and they also used Crowley's Abra-Melin spells from the early part of the 20th century, adapting them for their own use."

"This Babalon thingee—this is the first time I've ever heard of it."

"Summoning spells have existed, in various forms, for hundreds of years. In the sixteenth century Paracelsus described a rite that allowed him to contact what he believed to be angels. It's possible a similar working was used by John Dee in his ritual magic. Crowley often bragged that he had a copy of a powerful spell handwritten by Dee that purportedly could summon Satan himself. "

I grimaced. "Wonderful. So this Parsons guy and Elron fuck around out in the desert and manage to raise a demon? Could they actually do that?"

"These rituals are highly dangerous. One commentator referred to such workings as tearing an alchemical hole in the fabric of creation and inviting the spawn of hell inside for an orgy."

"Oh, great," I groaned. "Sounds like a whole lotta fun. Getting fist-fucked by Yog-Sothoth. *Yippee.*"

Her expression was grave. "We're talking about forces beyond our comprehension. These beings have no concept of anything like a conscience. Monsters, in every sense of the word. Crowley and Parsons were unbelievably irresponsible for tampering with the integrity of our dimension for their own selfish ends. They tried to open doors sealed for our own good without any idea of what might be waiting on the other side."

"Yeah, but did they really do it?" I argued. "I mean, where's the hard evidence? These guys were amateurs, the whole thing should've been a complete bust. What makes you think it wasn't?"

"For one thing, Hubbard was never the same afterward. Some trace his mental deterioration to that jaunt in the desert with Parsons. And what about those incidents Parsons' housemates reported?"

"And then afterward, Elron vamooses with his wife and dough?"

"Correct," she confirmed. "That's when things started falling apart for Parsons. His security clearance was revoked, which meant he couldn't be involved in any high level research. He began to behave so erratically that even Crowley disowned him."

"He sounds like a terminal fuckup."

She nodded. "He came to a horrible, ghastly end. Blown up in his home laboratory, supposedly while handling volatile chemicals. Stuff he'd worked with his entire life."

"But accidents *do* happen," I interjected. "He's a bit dopey, maybe hungover, adds the wrong ingredient—BOOM. Buddy ends up buried in a shoebox."

"He lived for at least an hour after the fire, conscious much of the time." She shuddered. "It's one of the worst deaths I can imagine. There were rumours floating around that he was immolated while attempting to create a homunculus."

"Mess with the dark forces, that's what you get."

She crossed her arms. "As I see it, there are two possibilities: either Parsons succeeded and opened a door...or else he failed and was insane, deluded, whatever."

I raised a hand. "I vote for option number two."

"So would I...except for the rest of it."

"Rest of it?"

"*Think*, Nightstalk. 1946-47. What does that mean to you?"

"Um, let's see. Truman is president, probably a great year for the Yankees, uh, Berlin Airlift—"

"--*and* the Mount Rainier UFO sightings, followed by a flood of reports of strange phenomena from around the world. Dozens of eyewitnesses. Then there's the alleged crash of an alien spacecraft near Roswell, New Mexico—"

"UFO's are involved?" I shook my head. "This case keeps getting stranger and--"

"They *weren't* UFO's, Nightstalk. The real story here is not a government coverup of the existence of aliens. The Babalon Working, had it been completely successful, would have been far worse for humankind than an invasion from outer space. Summoning rituals are meant to release creatures from other *dimensions*, Evgeny. Exiled or cast out from our universe who knows how long ago and plotting their return ever since. If they break through it would mean, quite literally, hell on Earth and I kid you not. Human sacrifice, great multitudes enslaved, a cruel and bloody era that would make the Aztecs blush. Pretty much the end of civilization as we know it."

There was a loud *clang* and rattle as a pin dropped somewhere in the office. Then: "That's completely nuts. I don't buy it."

She shook her head impatiently. "The UFO cover-up was just a cover-up for the *real* cover-up. As soon as the Brethren became aware of the portal Parsons and Hubbard created, they rushed people to the scene and threw a blanket of secrecy over everything. Then they had to deal with anything that had already made it through. They destroyed one near Roswell, New Mexico in August, 1947. That was no crashed saucer, it was an extra-dimensional being. What's left after the occult equivalent of a firefight."

"Was there just the one or—"

She clucked approvingly. "You're really on the ball, aren't you? The answer is *no one is sure*. There are people, credible people, who insist some of the entities escaped the net and made it to urban centres where they blended in, eventually acquiring human identities."

"—or splashed down in more remote places and became sasquatches and abominable snowmen," I suggested playfully.

She glared. "You're reaching, Nightstalk."

"Look, this stuff is news to me and, sorry, babe, it sounds pretty far-fetched."

She bent and retrieved some books from her bag. "I made some notes. Or you can ring up Professor Fuchs and ask him about it. He'll confirm what I'm telling you."

"Yeah. Right. Don't get me wrong, Cass, I like the perfessor, he's a funny guy, but not somebody I put a whole lotta faith in. So if he's your expert witness or whatever—"

"*Listen to me.*" Recapping her argument: "Parsons and Hubbard perform the Working. Fact: not long afterward there's a flurry of UFO sightings and other strange goings on. Which, in turn, causes the Brethren to get involved in a big way. They were doing their job, Nightstalk. Following their credo. *Ordo ab Chao.* 'Order out of chaos', right? Safeguarding humankind, always vigilant, swift to respond to danger."

I sat back, locking my fingers behind my neck. "Some of this, of course, might be the result of sheer coincidence. Babalon and the UFO's. Just a matter of timing."

"I don't—"

"—believe in coincidences," I finished, "yeah, so you've said."

"The facts fit," she insisted stubbornly.

"But how does all that jibe with what's going on here in Ilium?"

"Isn't it obvious?"

I scowled. "Obvious? No, it's not fucking *obvious.* If it was *obvious* I'd know what the fuck you're talking about, wouldn't I?"

"Fischer and Skorzeny intend to perform their own version of the Babalon Working."

"*What?* Says who?"

"Remember the report--it's in here somewhere." Poking at the pile. "It describes the break-in at the Felderhof Museum in Zurich."

I thought about it. "Nope."

"That particular museum happens to specialize in occult artifacts. It contains a number of historically significant documents, including the original *Book of Enoch*, as well as spellbooks and manuscripts attributed to John Dee and his scryer Edward Kelley. One of the grimoires contained a version of a ritual very similar to the Babalon Working."

"And this was the stuff that was stolen?"

"*Yes.* Not only that, several weeks later a number of documents allegedly authored by Paracelsus himself were taken from a private collection kept in a sealed, high security vault in Paris. It was literally an impossible crime. Yet somehow the perpetrators managed it."

"This Pericles or whatever, he was some kinda crackpot scientist, right? I've heard you mention him before..."

"Nightstalk!" She was outraged. "Paracelsus was much, *much* more than that. He was a bold and original thinker, perhaps one of the finest minds of all time."

"You said that about Madame Blavatsky too."

Her eyes narrowed. "Let's not start *that* argument again." Sage advice; it had nearly caused a nasty and potentially fatal rift in our relationship.

"Sorry." I hastily changed the subject: "Let's stick to the, uh, matter at hand. These occult documents are stolen or spirited away and they-- what? Describe how to open portals into other dimensions and let Cthulhu loose, that sort of thing? Sorry, kid, but you're boggling my mind here."

She nodded. "Okay. Then let's hear *your* explanation."

Ah. *Well.* She had me there. I could keep on saying "screwy coincidence" until I was blue in the face but eventually that would run afoul of the complete confidence I placed in my partner's judgement, intelligence and deductive abilities.

"—*and* last but not least." She plucked some sheets of paper out of a file folder and waved them at me. "Remember the transcript where Skorzeny is talking to Tibor Benes about a 'recipe'? It must be a working! They're translating and patching together their own summoning ritual. Skorzeny tells him that the last piece of the puzzle is in place...and that conversation was recorded within *days* of the theft of the Paracelsus material in Paris."

Coincidence?

"Skorzeny is sending Benes and Julian Finchley on some sort of replay of Parsons' trip into the desert. They're incorporating the various texts they've stolen, looking for the right combination. Remember: wording and pronunciation, proper ritual preparation, all of that is *crucial* to a successful working. I've done some reading and discovered the standard Parsons text, which you can find on-line, is incomplete. Much of the Dee and Paracelsus material is fragmentary as well. The Cabal are assembling the pieces, helped by people like Simon Margate and David Harriman, trying to recreate the original *ur*-spell. Once they have a complete translation, they'll give it to Finchley and Benes and then they'll...*holy Diana*, that conversation was recorded *ages* ago. Who knows what progress they've made by now."

I was still processing everything. "So *if* these fuckwits open a door and let these things in, what does that gain them, other than getting a whole bunch of people slaughtered?"

"They believe these entities will somehow be beholden to them and will reward them for their help." She held up a hand. "I know, it's completely crazy. If they're *lucky* the Old Ones will kill them outright." She leaned forward, rested her elbows on the desk, her chin on her hands. "So what do you say? Still having a hard time buying it? Is it too much?"

"I'm...adapting. I guess I can accept it as a working premise or whatever." She looked relieved. "You make a strong case. It's clear the Cabal is up to *something*. That's good enough for me."

"And now we know what we're up against. Skorzeny and Fischer— they want to become Nietzschean gods. And when the stakes are that high, it means they'll do *anything* to get what they want."

"I hear you."

Drumming her fingers again, musing out loud. "We have to assume that Philippe has a tail on Benes and Finchley. Let's hope they don't lose them."

"Your old boyfriend could have saved us a lot of time if he'd given us the lowdown right from the start."

"He couldn't. The Brethren wouldn't let him. But he knew me well enough to know I'd read between the lines, like he said."

"Maybe. I still have my suspicions. I mean, let's be honest, if push comes to shove, whose interests would he put first, ours' or the Brethren's? *Because it's not the same thing, Cass.* What's good for the Brethren may get *us* killed."

"That's your view but I don't agree."

Stalemate.

We spent some time going through our weird library, pulling anything that seemed remotely relevant. I read through some sections of Lawrence Sutin's biography of Crowley, then got sidetracked by a book that contained "indisputable evidence" the Earth is hollow and inhabited by a vanguard of alien colonists—

"There isn't much, I admit," Cassandra said, clearly frustrated. "I suspect the Brethren have gone to great effort to suppress or distort the facts. It's not the kind of knowledge you want getting around."

"You mentioned the perfessor. Maybe we should call him up." I was half-joking, just tossing out the idea as I settled in front of the Underwood.

If I hurried, I'd be able to summarize everything for the Old Man and make it home while it was still dark.

My partner looked conflicted. Professor Edwin Fuchs had been helpful in a number of our most perplexing cases [20] and was an expert of some repute when it came to the paranormal. On the other hand, Fuchs was so absolutely *besotted* with her that she felt uncomfortable spending more than a few minutes in his company. He fawned over her to the extent that you were embarrassed for the poor guy.

Edwin Fuchs was, even by academic standards, an odd duck. I suppose he was brilliant in his way and, as I said, highly regarded within the field of psychical research. Unfortunately, the administration did not share his enthusiasm for bogeys. He was chronically under-funded, largely ignored, shunned at faculty teas. As a result, he became even *more* insular and socially awkward, earning a name for himself as the university's resident crank. It was only tenure that saved him from an attic room and a steady diet of sardines and day old bread, washed down with cheap port.

To be honest, he had the wrong temperament to be a spook chaser. Ghosts, he once admitted to me, scared the living daylights out of him. So he stuck to the theoretical end of things, dividing his time between the classroom and laboratory, lecturing and grading papers while, simultaneously, trying to come up with methods for analyzing and quantifying a genuine paranormal event.

He moonlighted as an inventor, building all manner of devices and contraptions, a number of which we'd field-tested for him. Some of them turned out to be useful, whereas others...well, let's just say they didn't always work as advertised.

Even with his very limited and largely secondhand exposure to occult phenomena, Fuchs' hair had turned completely white and he spoke with a slight tremor. He was easily distracted, often appearing befuddled or, if you didn't know him better, nutty as a fruitcake.

She sighed. "Are you sure it's necessary?"

"Sure I'm sure," I told her. "If nothing else, it'll make the poor fucker's day."

---

[20] "Hold That Ghost!", "The Secret of the Old Mill" (*The Casebooks of Zinnea & Nightstalk, Vol. I*); "Let's Scare Nightstalk to Death", "Dancing With Mr. D" (*Casebooks, Vol. II*), etc.

Saturday, May 15th

She insisted I make the call. Fuchs sounded pathetically eager to see us—that it was a weekend bothered him not at all. Like us, he kept odd hours.

"Ah! Ms. Zinnea!" As soon as he caught sight of my partner, Fuchs sprang up from his desk, inadvertently snagging his toe on something and crashing into a half-dead potted plant. He lurched forward and grabbed her hand, pumping it vigorously, then bent to kiss it but ended up poking himself in the eye with his own thumb. She reclaimed her hand as quickly as she could, backing up until she was standing beside me. "Ms. Zinnea, Mr. Nightstalk, this is *such* a great pleasure. It seems like ages since the last time we met. That business involving the unfortunate Mr. Talbot, the chap who believed himself to be a werewolf..." [21]

"I still have the scars on my ass to remind me," I remarked ruefully.

He barely noticed me. "How have you been keeping, my dear? I must say, you look ravishing tonight. A face Rubens would delight in." He sucked in his breath as he examined her from head to toe. "Exquisite."

"Nice to see you too, perfessor," I said.

He sidled around his desk, his trailing hand knocking his metal nameplate into the garbage can. When he bent to retrieve it, he cracked his forehead on the edge of his desk and Cassandra took the opportunity to glare at me. "And so—so what brings you by this time?" Still groggy from the bump, he jostled his desk, spilling coffee all over the book he'd been reading. "Yes, indeed, to what do I owe the pleasure of your company— and it is a pleasure—this evening?" He brightened. "Another case, I hope. Mysteries within mysteries and all that. The enigma of the human heart. Have I told you, Ms. Zinnea, how much I admire your methods? The quickness of your mind, the way you--"

"Riiiight," I broke in. "Yeah, perfessor, as a matter of fact we *are* working on something and Cassandra thought you might be just the man to help us." I avoided looking at her. "I can't go into details for reasons of confidentiality, you understand, but we have some general questions, stuff that's right up your alley." He nodded, having heard the spiel before. "It'll take a few minutes and then we'll let you get back to work." Cassandra had toned down the colour of her hair and pulled it back into a severe bun. She'd also taken care to wear the longest skirt she owned and a plain, white blouse that buttoned to her throat. The way he was looking at her, she

---

[21] "Full Moon Fever" (*The Casebooks of Zinnea & Nightstalk, Vol. III*)

might as well have been wearing a thong and a couple of strategically placed pasties. "Hello? Perfessor?"

"I'm listening, Mr. Nightstalk. You command my complete attention. Do you by any chance colour your hair? It's such an intriguing hue…the way it catches the light." He wasn't talking to me. I don't think.

There were several plastic models on his desk: the Mummy, the Frankenstein monster and Wolfman, held together by Testor glue, inexpertly painted. On the wall behind his desk, a movie poster for "The Exorcist". There were others: "Near Dark", "The Entity" and, incongruously, "The Sound of Music" over top his file cabinets. I figured the prof's emotional age to be somewhere around twelve and a half.

"*The Babalon Working*," I said.

That did the trick.

He turned from Cassandra. "What did you say?"

"The Babalon Working. 1940's. Jack Parsons and Elron out in the desert, calling on the spirits—"

"Yes, yes," he responded sharply, "I know the story. But how is that relevant to your present investigation?"

"Okay, you've heard of it," I went on, deflecting the question for the time being. "Professionally speaking, can you confirm the, uh, details of the story?"

"Confirm--?" He gawked at me. "Mr. Nightstalk, you are referring to matters far beyond the conception of ordinary human beings. A whole other level of reality. I've been trying for nearly twenty years and I can tell you that it's difficult, if not impossible, to subject occult phenomena to hard and fast science. It simply doesn't work that way."

I grunted with satisfaction. "In other words, it could be a load of hooey."

His face reddened. "*Mr. Nightstalk.* I would hardly call one of the most significant occult events of the 20th century a 'load of hooey'. Parsons and Hubbard were attempting to smash down the walls between dimensions, unleashing God knows what. I would hardly characterize *that* as 'hooey'."

"Excuse me, Professor Fuchs," Cassandra said. "Sometimes my partner can be a trifle rough around the edges. What he's trying to say is that we would be gratified to hear what you know about the Working."

Which corresponded pretty closely to her account. He added a few intriguing details, however: "Parsons was a true black magician. He *loathed* Christianity and was drawn to the nature and reality of evil. So much so that even Crowley despaired for him, especially since he relied on the financial support that Parsons doled out. Crowley was infuriated by what he saw as Parsons' and Hubbard's amateurish attempts to raise an elemental. He knew full well what the consequences might be. 'Bab-El', after all, literally translates as 'Gate of God'."

"Parsons was a fool," Cassandra said.

"But a genius. We can't forget that. He believed that through his efforts he was going to accomplish something extraordinary. He was deadly serious, I assure you."

"But did he succeed?" I pressed.

He shrugged. "The accounts differ. But...something happened that changed his life and eventually destroyed it."

"I agree with you, Dr. Fuchs, but my partner isn't so sure."

"How sad." His eyes were roaming the contours of her body again. She could feel the weight of his gaze and shifted self-consciously. "How can he deny the existence of the wondrous and fantastic when he is blessed with your presence on a daily—"

"Right, well, thanks, perfessor." Wrapping things up while Cassandra peeled his eyes off the front of her blouse. "You've certainly given us a lot to think about and—and all that."

"Any time, Mr. Nightstalk," he said, moving to escort us out. "My door is always open to you, day or night." He cleared his throat apologetically. "Ah, I hesitate to say this but tonight was not the first time I've encountered the Babalon Working in recent days." We paused, waiting for the rest of it. "I take the bus to work and last week when it pulled up at my stop I saw those exact words spray-painted on the side. It's such an obscure term...it certainly caught my attention. And now here you are, asking about it. Most curious."

Coincidence?

"You were right to mention it, doc. Thanks."

He waved us on our way. "Not at all. Now if you'll excuse me, I have to finish up some prep work. I'm giving a workshop on how to safely operate an *Ouija* board." He sighed. "I do hope this year's crop of students can at least *spell...*"

When we got to the car, Cassandra asked me to cover for her. She'd heard about a new club that was opening downtown, very hard core, very *chic*, very Cassandra Zinnea. Called, believe it or not, *Baudelaire's Withered Cock*. And did I mind dropping her off...

"Dressed like that?" I indicated her school marm-ish attire.

"Actually, I brought along a change of clothes..." Whatever it was fit in her purse. It wasn't a very big purse.

The dive was in North Ilium, miles out of my way. She didn't bother asking me to accompany her inside. She knew I wouldn't fit in with the crowd. And, anyway, I would only cramp her style.

I took the long way back, using the opportunity to indulge in a well-earned (I thought) bout of self-pity. Found a golden oldies station, turned up Blondie's "Heart of Glass". It was the absolute perfect song for how I was feeling.

Had nothing else to do so I went back to the office. Parked the car. Got out.

I guess I was preoccupied.

Preoccupied and *stupid*.

I didn't notice her until she was close, maybe ten feet away. The lady in question was, to say the least, *stunning*. Not too tall, not too short, knee high boots, fishnet stockings and silver microskirt. They certainly did their homework. We passed, almost rubbing shoulders. I stared at her, she looked at me—

Wham!

It was like I was flash-frozen in liquid nitrogen, teetering on my feet, stiff as a plank. I tell you, being blasted is worse than getting zapped with a Taser (and I speak from personal experience). Complete paralysis, total loss of voluntary muscle control. It's lucky I didn't piss myself, most people do. My blonde bombshell stopped and backtracked until she was even with me. Looked into my eyes, the only part of my body that was still functioning.

"It's called an *enamorata* hex," she informed me, peeling off the wig. *Fucking Kali Brust*. "One of my own design. A hundred per cent effective. *Gotcha*." Acting bloody pleased with herself, the little witch.

A black Mercedes pulled up and a guy with the shoulders of a chronic steroid abuser pried himself out. Almost cartoon-like in his proportions. "We'll take it from here, Ms. Brust." He and his partner, a coloured guy with a serious chip on his shoulder, weren't too gentle about it as they wedged me into the backseat of the car. I was still mad at myself for getting blasted like a dope so I sort of exaggerated my condition to make their job that much harder.

For some reason I've always had a strong resistance when it comes to most spells and hexes of a non-lethal nature. I like to think it's some kind of special facility I possess, rare and under-appreciated. Rather than merely a thick head.

We were about three blocks from the office when my curiosity got the better of me. "Hey, what's the story here, guys?" I asked.

I guess I surprised them because the car swerved and the big lug in the passenger seat smacked his head smartly on the side window. "Fuck!" The driver squawked. "Shit! This asshole s'posed to be *out*."

His buddy yanked out a piece and waved it around. "You pull that shit again and I'll blow your fuckin' head off," he warned. "Nearly gave me a concussion, ya fuckin' mook." He pointed the gun at me. "And *you*. Don't fuck with us or you're dead, you got that? I'll paint you all over the backseat."

"You cleanin' it then," his partner grumbled.

"Shut up, Donnie."

"Fuck you, bwana. You think I never seen a firearm before, boy? Never had one stuck in my face? Shee-it, come down to my neighbourhood some time. I'll show you some *serious* artillery."

"Hey, you two pussycats," I spoke up, "sorry to interrupt the love-in, but where are you taking me?

"Never mind, wise guy," the gunsel retorted. "You'll see soon enough."

My arms were free, I could have reached out, snatched that popgun from him and stuck it up his nose in the time it took him to blink. My legs were tingling. It wouldn't be long.

"Don't get lost this time," the human growth hormone chided.

"Yo, suck this," Donnie replied, never missing a beat.

I was curious to learn who was behind this. Laying side bets on where they were taking me. So instead of pulling them into the backseat with me for some close quarters battering, I decided to sit back and bide my time.

They took me to a place uptown, an office tower sheathed in blue glass and about as warm and personable as a 25-story block of ice.

We pulled up at the stroke of midnight and I *walked* into the building. That freaked my handlers out. They'd thought they were going to have to wheel me inside strapped to a trolley like Hannibal Lector.

The guard at the front desk scrutinized us closely before buzzing us in. Not a rent-a-cop. Marine Corps tattoo on his forearm and a look on his face that said "born to kill".

We took the elevator right to the top.

There was more muscle once we got there. Wall to wall thugs. They weren't taking any chances.

I was led down a corridor and into a boardroom. A long, polished table stretched almost to the door and a chair was waiting for me. I took a seat, surrounded by tall shelves of leatherbound law books. The room smelled of old cigar smoke and expensive cologne. I was supposed to be either impressed or intimidated (depending on the purpose of my visit).

There were three men sitting at the far end of the table but only one of them counted. He was older than the others and reminded me of Terence Stamp. That same air of distinguished menace. Something about him told me I shouldn't take my eyes off him, not for a second. The other two looked to be just out of law school, sharp-eyed ferrets, of no more consequence than the wallpaper.

"Mr. Nightstalk," the older man said. He didn't rise or offer his hand. "Welcome to the offices of Trotz, Hass and Rache. I am Herman Rache, senior partner, and these are two of my associates." Not bothering to introduce them by name. "I thought it was time you and I had a little chat." The two ferrets bobbed their heads, showing small, pointy teeth. The door opened behind me. "Ah, Gregory," Herman Rache called. "Good. We've only just begun."

Gregory Fischer moved past me and sat with the others. He looked like he did in pictures and on TV: trim, tanned, and slick.

Herman Rache laid it out for me. He couldn't have been nicer about it. "Mr. Nightstalk, my firm has been retained by Mr. Fischer to represent him in situations where certain groups or individuals may not have his best interests at heart. Frankly, Mr. Fischer is concerned that your present investigation may lead to embarrassing revelations or disclosures of a personal nature that go far beyond the pall of the public's right to know." He smiled without smiling. "We act as his agents, empowered to do what we must to protect his good name. Prepared to employ whatever means are necessary to achieve that outcome. Do you understand?"

"You sound like a lawyer, Rache." I said. "If someone's threatening me, I prefer they do it man to man."

The ferrets hissed but he gestured with his hand and they subsided into silence. "Mr. Nightstalk..." *Something flickered across Rache's face.* It's like when they splice a single frame of a naked woman in the middle of a film. It registers subliminally, below the level of conscious thought. I can't describe it any better than that. Just a quick, fleeting glimpse, but it definitely got my attention.

"Ours is a rather small firm, our clientele correspondingly small...and select," Rache continued, unperturbed. "Despite our modest inclinations, we have gained a reputation for diligence and professionalism second to none. We have protected the vital interests of presidents and foreign potentates. We never fail to provide premium service, whatever our clients require. Our very *exclusive* clients." A nod to Gregory Fischer. Who still hadn't spoken or reacted to what was being said on his behalf.

"If you don't cease your harassment of Mr. Fischer," one of the ferrets spoke up, "we'll kill you."

"Slowly," added the other.

"Roast your balls and feed them to you."

"And what about Ms. Zinnea?" Rache asked placidly.

"Cut off her tits and rip out her eyes—"

"Fuck her and make him watch—"

"Fuck her with *his* cock—"

Rache cleared his throat and their jaws snapped shut with a simultaneous *snick*. "So you see, Mr. Nightstalk, you have some formidable foes arrayed against you. Your situation looks quite desperate." He paused. If he was waiting for a cute comeback, I was going to have to disappoint him. At that moment I wasn't feeling too plucky. He seemed pleased by my reticence. "I hope I've made myself clear."

That was my cue. I was supposed to nod, letting him know I understood. I nodded.

"Excellent. Gregory, do you have anything to add?"

Fischer seemed taken aback by the question. He glanced at Rache, then at me. "You're messing around in my business, gumshoe, and I don't like it." He grinned, turning to the others. "Wow, that sounded like something out of one of those old movies." He stopped smiling when he realized they weren't reacting. "Seriously, ah, Mr. Nightstalk, I've got some big things planned in the next while and I don't want anyone—"

"You mean the Babalon Working, don't you?" Not daring to look at Herman Rache. "We know all about it."

The billionaire blanched. "I'm afraid that I, uh, I must decline to answer that, uh, particular—ah—Herman?" He finished plaintively.

"*Mr. Nightstalk.*" His voice drew my gaze to him. Herman Rache's expression was forbidding. "I'll tolerate such impudence only once and *only* because you are a representative of the Old Man. Don't push your luck, son." His eyes blazed. "You are not here to ask questions or fish for information. You are here to *listen.*"

"And I *have* listened, Rache." I pushed back from the table. It was important, mandatory in fact, that I walk out of there with my dignity and moxie still intact. "I've listened, I've heard and now I'm leaving. If any of those pussycats in the hallway try to stop me..." I began to inflate. Fischer gaped at me, clearly unnerved, but the others weren't impressed.

"Please spare us this ridiculous spectacle, Mr. Nightstalk," Rache commanded. "In any event, if you won't see reason, perhaps Ms. Zinnea will be more...amenable."

"You lay one fucking finger on her, Rache—"

The ferrets growled and seemed ready to go for my throat but Rache had no further need of me. "That is all. You are free to leave whenever you wish."

"I always was," I shot back.

I blew them kisses on the way out.

In truth, I was shit scared.

Home was halfway across the city but I walked the entire distance, so immersed in my thoughts I barely noticed my surroundings. When I got back to the apartment I sat in the dark with the TV off, feeling stupid and useless and *small*. Started drinking and that never helps.

Rache was right, the odds didn't look good. After all, the bad guys could summon demons, raise the dead and conjure up killer elementals to do their bidding. What did *we* have going for us? Our arsenal looked mighty puny in comparison.

There was something about Rache. He scared me far more than either Fischer or Skorzeny. That moment when he gave me a peek behind his flesh mask. I couldn't recall anything specific but whatever I'd seen or *thought* I'd seen really put the whammy into me. I experienced a bone-gnawing fear I hadn't felt since childhood.

Before I knew it, it was noon and I still hadn't slept. I couldn't get Rache and the ferrets out of my head and was tormented by mental images of my partner brutalized and mutilated before my eyes.

I won't let it happen, I vowed. I'll keep her safe, no matter what the cost or consequences might be.

Even if that means sacrificing your life, dying in her place?

Yes.

And your soul? Would you offer that up in exchange as well?

Again, my response was immediate and emphatic: *yes.*

It was my last waking thought.

BOOK II

May - June

"To achieve the essence of real externality, whether of time or space or dimension, one must forget that such things as organic life, good and evil, love and hate, and all such local attributes of a negligible and temporary race called mankind, have any existence at all. Only the human scenes and characters must have human qualities. *These* must be handled with unsparing *realism*, (not catch-penny *romanticism*) but when we cross the line to the boundless and hideous unknown—the shadow-haunted *Outside*—we must remember to leave our humanity and terrestrialism at the threshold."

Howard Phillips Lovecraft
(from a letter to Farnsworth Wright; 1928)

"…what is unknown is always more attractive than what is known; hope and imagination are the only consolations for the disappointments and sorrows of experience."

Italo Calvino, *Six Memos for the Next Millenium*

I

"I have taken the Oath of the Abyss and entered my rightful city of Chorazin..."

John Whiteside Parsons (*The Book of the Anti-Christ*)

I dream of Chorazin.

The city on the edge of forever.

It's not real, *I tell myself, gazing about the desolate landscape,* it's an illusion, something produced, written, conceived and created by my haunted subconscious. *Oddly enough, however, this knowledge brings no comfort, no sense of relief.*

Because real or not, I am all alone in the scariest place in the universe.

I know *things, though the source of my information isn't clear. Not memories, nothing so concrete. I'm aware, for instance, that Chorazin is old beyond measuring and cursed for all time. It's not purgatory, not hell...at least there you know where you stand, your status and eventual fate. Whereas here, you exist in a kind of perpetual netherworld, a ghost inhabiting a familiar body, retaining vague recollections of another life, dim reminders of colour and light and hope.*

The city is surrounded on every side by the Desert of Set, with its infamous "singing sands". That soft, eerie, flute-like sound is the product of the wind moving through hollow, meatless bones, exhalations from the parched throat of the wasteland. Sooner or later everyone consigned to Chorazin succumbs to the irresistible lure of the song and wanders out to seek its source in the endless dunes and dips. Lost. Consumed. Their bones joining the chorus and taking up a tune uncountable eons in the making.

I've arrived at night.

It's always *night in Chorazin.*

I find myself in the middle of a broad, cracked avenue and realize with a jolt I'm not far from the Temple of Sheol. I begin to tremble, imagining the vast, earthen pit, bodies shuddering and bucking in the flames, the screams drowned out by—

Oh, no.

I can hear them, the tum-tum-tum *of the tophim drums. The high priests believe only fire can purge us of our sins. Those selected for martyrdom don't see it that way. Often they resist, wishing to decline the honour, screaming torrents of abuse until they are forcibly subdued. The children are valued for their docility, usually remaining calm and cooperative right up until—*

I run, run as fast as I can but in my panic I get turned around and somehow end up back at the Temple, skidding to a halt before its corroded steps. The tall pillars of its portico are still intact, though the front doors hang crookedly askew, like broken teeth. The statues in the courtyard, most at least twenty feet tall, depict an alien menagerie: hawk-headed creatures and multi-limbed monstrosities equipped with twenty-four sets of eyes and some pretty impressive sexual equipment.

There's a grating sound from overhead and dust comes sifting down. The gargoyles, their features nearly obliterated, scoured by the ages, swivel and incline their heads, beads of red light igniting in their eyes.

I'm running again, waiting for those gargoyles to unlimber their stone wings and take to the air after me. I hear thunder, a bass rumble I can feel in my feet. A cold rain begins to fall, drenching me in seconds. I think to myself, fuck, if this is a dream, I wish I'd wake up because I'm freezing; *my sodden clothes clinging to me, scraping and chafing my skin, adding to my misery.*

Then it starts to get misty, probably due to the humidity. The mist soon develops into a fog thick enough to cut with a chainsaw. I'm forced to use the Tower to guide me. It hovers above the gray haze, a slim spire of black rock, by far the tallest structure still standing, looming over everything. It is my final destination--another certainty that is beyond mere knowing. I'm supposed to find my way there and climb the fifteen hundred steps to the top. What I'll discover once I reach the summit is unclear but something tells me it's not likely to be pleasant.

It won't be an easy journey. The ruins are scattered and extensive, an obstacle course or, more precisely, a maze. *A direct route to the Tower is impossible...and navigating the ruins means encountering some of the assorted nasties inhabiting this godforsaken city. I can hear them snuffling and growling on every side. I pluck up a hefty rock and right after that nearly trip over a short length of wood that has petrified with age. It makes an excellent club.*

Now that I'm sufficiently well-armed, I set out for the Tower. I take three steps forward—

--and glimpse something in the fog. At first I can only make out that it's significantly bigger than me and has two legs. It springs at me without warning and I glimpse a bulbous, ridged head and eager, snapping beak. My reflexes take over and I bring the club up, instinctively moving to meet the attack—

But the confrontation ended up being postponed 'til a later date. My bladder was feeling the effects of the six-pack I'd guzzled just prior to crashing and I barely made it to the john in time, closing the door out of consideration to Tree.

Interesting dream, I thought, relieving myself of those tasty beverages with a good, long slash. By the time I finished, washed up and crawled back on to the couch, to tell you the truth I had just about forgotten it.

Hey, in my line of work, you get used to having weird dreams.

You might say they go with the territory.

Sunday, May 16th

"Is something bothering you, Nightstalk?"

I was hunched over the Underwood, re-reading the section of my report describing my visit to the offices of Rache, Hass & Trotz. It was...incomplete. So far I hadn't gotten around to mentioning the subliminal flash, the moment when I glanced over at Herman Rache and saw...ah, that was the trouble. What *exactly* had I seen?

I'd been sitting there for a good stretch of time, trying to figure out how to put it into words but nothing was coming to me. Dead air and static.

"Nightstalk?"

"I've been counting," I groused, "and that's the third time you've asked me that question since I got here."

"Ye-es...and that's the third time you've avoided answering it." She grinned as something occurred to her. "You're not mad about letting Kali Brust zap you like that, are you?"

"I didn't *let* her zap me," I corrected her. "I just didn't recognize the little slut in that get-up she was wearing."

"Well, it's been awhile since you two crossed paths[22]," she teased. "Don't be too hard on yourself."

"I *told* you, nothing's the matter. Lemme be, woman." I should have known better than that. She leaned back in her chair, closed her eyes and

---

[22] *See*: "The Shadow *Doesn't* Know" (*The Casebooks of Zinnea & Nightstalk, Vol. II*)

right away I could feel her trying to pick her way past my mental defenses. "Cut it out."

"There's something you're holding back," she stated, opening her eyes and giving me a searching look. "They got to you and I want to know how they did it. You've been staring at that typewriter for the past fifteen minutes. Out with it."

"You're being a pain in the ass, you know that?"

"*Tell* me, Nightstalk."

I gave up. "I saw something." She waited. "Something...happened to Rache's face." I let out my breath in frustration. "It's hard to explain. I looked at him and...it was like the mask came away for just—less than a second, and I saw his *real* face, the one he hides and never shows to the world. It was..." Again, I found myself stuck. Lacking the words to describe—

"Keep going," she urged. "Don't analyze it, just let it come. Go back to that moment and say what you're feeling."

"It was just a glimpse but...even that was almost too much. This flash of absolute *hate*. So much hate and...and also this incredible emptiness, a void, like space, endless and *black*..." I opened my eyes. My armpits were soaked and my guts felt liquid and cramped.

She smiled encouragingly. "You're doing fine, Evvie."

"You know me. I don't get spooked. Bring on your living dead and talking corpses and villains of all shapes and sizes. But Rache...he really did a number on me. I've never been in the presence of someone who made me feel like that and...I didn't like it." My hands were balled into tight, painful fists.

"He showed you what he really is."

"And that is?"

"You know. You just won't say it."

I nodded reluctantly. "He's one of those things Parsons and Hubbard let in back in '47, isn't he? One of the ones that got away."

"Rache was smart, he went undercover and managed to assimilate. Over the years he's built up his influence but never to the extent that he draws attention to himself. Working behind the scenes, attracting and cultivating powerful friends. And, in the meantime, should the opportunity come along to help more of his kind escape from exile, he's only too happy to oblige."

"So he's working with the Cabal to bring back his pals. And then what? They reward him with Malta or something?"

"I wouldn't try to fathom his motivations. His thoughts are alien and unknowable, beyond our comprehension." She paused, looked over at me. "But that's not all, is it? There's something else you're keeping back. C'mon, Nightstalk, out with it."

I tried to look confused, a feat I usually managed quite easily. When that didn't work, I went into full defensive mode. "I don't understand. I just told you how much it bothered me when Rache—"

"Besides that. Sure, he gave you the ya-ya's for minute. You were *still* able to stand up to him. You were down, Nightstalk, but you weren't out." Softening me up with praise. "I think it was incredible what you did. But, afterwards, when you really thought about it..." I couldn't duck those eyes. "It was what they threatened to do to *me*, the thoughts that put in your head, *that's* what really lowered the boom on you."

My throat closed. I tried to say something but couldn't muster a peep. No false denials, lies, rationalizations, just a silence that accused, convicted and condemned. Guilty as charged.

"Now you listen to me," she said sternly. "We can't show them any weakness or vulnerability or they'll exploit it, use it against us. There's too much at stake. Our role is clear. We're the good guys. We get to save the world. And if one or both of us have to be sacrificed in the process, well—"

"If it comes to that, it should be me," I croaked. "I'll...protect you, keep you safe."

She got up, came over and crouched beside me, as earnest as I'd ever seen her. "You *can't*, Evgeny. That's one of the rules of the game and you know it. We can look out for one another but in the end who knows what's going to happen? And when it comes right down to it, I'm no more special than--"

"You *are*," I insisted. "You're special. You don't realize how you...you don't—you can't—"

"*Oh, Evvie...*" She hugged me and it took a monumental amount of self-restraint not to blubber and drool onto her blouse (rayon or silk, by the feel of it, soft and very sheer, almost insubstantial). She smelled heavenly. I felt myself growing stronger, a surge of positive energy that worked like a shot of B-12. It took me a minute to identify the source.

"Knock it off," I said, thrusting her away. "You shouldn't be wasting your energy like that."

The transfusion left her drained but still cocky. "It worked though, didn't it?"

"Maybe," I allowed. Then it was my turn to make with the stern gaze. "I think it's time we started taking extra precautions. For one thing, you should cut back on your social life, at least for awhile. Stay home, no more gallivanting about. Take up knitting or something."

"Oh, you'd love that, wouldn't you?" She regarded me with amusement. "Good luck enforcing your curfew, Officer Nightstalk. But if you want to tag along and be my chaperone," chuckling evilly, "you're more than welcome."

"And *you'd* love *that*."

"So, we're clear." Standing, hands on hips, her best *Supergirl* pose. "We're in this to the end."

"I'll be keeping my eye on you."

"I feel safer already." She moved toward her side of the desk.

"You said something about getting us some help. So far we're the ones who've been carrying the load."

"Funny you should mention that," she replied. "Tomorrow I'm taking you to meet someone. We'll have to get there fairly early. Seven-thirty? Eight? I don't think the club keeps late hours."

"Club? What kind of club? It's not one of your weird hangouts, is it?"

But she wouldn't tell me any more.

Keeping me in suspense again.

Vixen.

The brass plaque screwed to the door at eye level read *The Diogenes Club*. That sounded familiar but I couldn't put my finger on it. The club was located above a smokeshop and newsstand on Willeford Drive. It had its own entrance and mailbox. A good location in a decent neighborhood, a nicely kept park across the street, not a rockhound or crack whore in sight.

The smokeshop didn't look like much but it was a whole other world at the top of the stairs. The second floor had been remodelled to give it the appearance of an English drawing room, circa 1880. Wood panelling, high-backed armchairs, polar bear skin rugs, the works. Not even a token attempt to observe the city's strict smoking bylaws—the air was purple with pipe and cigar smoke.

We found ourselves closely scrutinized by the eight or ten men present. One of them seemed to be the official greeter. He had thin, greying hair but looked trim and fit and had an official bearing. Ex-military, I guessed, watching him approach. Waited for confirmation.

"Ms. Zinnea! It's been awhile since your last visit. You've brought a guest, I see. You'll have to sign him in, of course."

Cassandra Zinnea, my Cass, a member of such a starchy, whitebread—

"How are you, George? Keeping everybody in line, I hope?" She did the honours while he gushed away.

"Fine, thank you for asking. As for our membership, for the most part they're quite well-behaved, as you know."

"George Simmons, meet Evgeny Nightstalk."

"A pleasure, sir." He had a good, firm handshake. Back to her: "I think you'll find that not much has changed around here." He lowered his voice. "You should come by more often, my dear. This old place could use a bit of excitement. It can be somewhat *stodgy* at times."

"That's okay, I like it that way."

"Kind of you to say so. Oh, by any chance are you free next Wednesday? We've got a chap from the Surête dropping by to brief us on the latest advances in forensics."

"I'll see if I'm available."

"One moment please." Someone was beckoning to him from an armchair in the corner. "I have to see what Alec wants." He hurried off.

"Who is that guy? He looks familiar."

"George Simmons," she repeated. "He was our chief of police until about five years ago."

"Sure! Now I recognize him." So much for my powers of deduction. "And he's the maitre d' here?"

"I wouldn't call him that if I were you." She took in her surroundings with an appreciative eye. "Wonderful, isn't it? The ambience, the smoke...I love coming here."

"What is this place? You've got an ex-cop as a doorman—"

"*The Diogenes Club*, Nightstalk. Its membership is made up of former police officers, detectives and other law enforcement professionals who live in the area. Just about everybody is represented, from the CIA to the Royal Canadian Mounted Police."

"So what do they do, besides kill themselves with second hand smoke?" Simmons was wrapping things up with Alec, chuckling gamely at some witticism, clearly anxious to be on his way.

"They meet and talk shop. Consult with police forces around the world on cases they're having trouble with. The Club's assistance is unofficial. They're not looking for publicity or glory. Sometimes ex-policemen can do things their working colleagues can't."

"And *you're* a member? That seems so—so--"

"Honourary, actually. They approached me right after we helped Governor Staub with his little problem." [23]

I remembered it well. I'd risked death on three different occasions, took a bullet meant for the old crook *and* helped uncover the guy in his inner circle who was behind it all. "Funny how they invited you and not..."

She was rescued by the return of George Simmons. "That Alec, what a rascal. He'd like to buy you a drink, Ms. Zinnea. And your companion as well, of course."

"Maybe later." Taking him into her confidence. "This is...sort of an official matter. I need to see Mr. Holmes, if he's available."

Wait a minute! *Holmes*? Diogenes Club? It *couldn't* be...

Simmons was nodding. "Yes, of course. You'll find him in the library, as usual. He's become quite a fixture here." I detected a flash of annoyance. "I must say, the man seems to take pleasure in trying the patience of fellow members. He receives special dispensation because of his—ah—unique circumstances but *really*."

"He's worth the trouble," she reassured him.

"I'm beginning to wonder," he replied. "But if you insist, come along. And if you think the air out here is thick, wait until you get a whiff of the noxious stuff *he* smokes. You can smell it through the entire building." Lowering his voice again. "I've had members confide to me they're certain it's cannabis--although he, of course, swears high and low it's some obscure Turkish blend." He led the way toward the back and we trailed after him.

"The guy's name is *Holmes*?" Keeping my voice low. "You gotta be kidding me. *He's* one of the people supposedly helping us?"

"Just wait," was my partner's enigmatic reply.

To be fair, he didn't wear a deerstalker or smoke an enormous meerschaum pipe. That would have been overdoing it.

He was poring over some papers spread out on the table in front of him and I did a double take when I saw what looked like a water pipe off to one side, within easy reach. One sniff told me that George was on the right track. Primo hydroponic skunk. Less habit-forming than cocaine, perhaps, but just as potent and mind-altering. Turkish blend, my eye.

He was perfect, exactly how you imagine a master sleuth should look: the Basil Rathbone profile, the piercing eyes of Jeremy Brett. It was *eerie*.

---

[23] "A Capitol Crime" (*The Casebooks of Zinnea & Nightstalk, Vol. II*)

But the overall effect was diminished somewhat by the fact that the poor guy couldn't have been more than four and a half feet tall.

"My dear Ms. Zinnea," he cried, bouncing off a regular-sized chair and hustling over to greet her. He wasn't a midget exactly; more like a miniature human being. It was like he'd fallen victim of some kind of diabolical shrinking device wielded by Dr. Moriarty.

"Mr. Holmes," she greeted him warmly, taking his small hand in hers.

I was having a hard time keeping a straight face. All the same, being a short man myself, I felt an immediate affinity for his predicament. Facing down an arch-criminal when you're the size of your average nine-year old requires a delicate touch...not to mention balls of steel.

"Mr. Sherlock Holmes, may I present my colleague, Evgeny Nightstalk."

Holmes coolly shook my hand. His appraisal was swift and thorough. "A pleasure, sir." He didn't release me from his grip, making a big deal of examining my hand, clucking at the state of my bent fingers. "Ah, I can see at once that you are a hunt and peck typist. I also note that you use an old, manual typewriter that requires significant force on the keys. That explains the extra wear. You are a pugilist and win more fights than you lose. However, I also detect the early onset of arthritis so you may have to curtail such activities in the near future. You spend most of your time indoors, out of the sun...in that sense you are an ideal companion for Ms. Zinnea. You are a loner, a misanthrope and a romantic. I also observe that you seem to be a chronic masturbator—"

I snatched my hand back. "Why you sawed-off—"

He stood his ground, smiling up at me, his expression devoid of malice. "My apologies, Mr. Nightstalk. It's been some time since I've had visitors. Please excuse my uncouth humour." My partner was coughing into her fist to hide her giggles.

"I'll let it go this time, *Mister* Holmes," I said, making it sound as sarcastic as possible.

His smile faltered. "Point taken, sir. I shall overlook your dearth of humour if you'll overlook my...affectation." We declared it a draw. "Nonetheless, for the sake of simplicity and because I refuse to answer to any other name, Sherlock Holmes it is."

"Fine with me."

He backtracked to the table, resumed his seat. "As in the case of my illustrious namesake, I place myself at the disposal of those who require the services of a first rate investigator. I'd like to think that my counsel has been invaluable to any number of national and international police organizations. I have not done Holmes' legacy any lasting damage, I assure you." George Simmons cleared his throat but Holmes ignored him. "I *deplore* injustice. The name Sherlock Holmes has long been associated with crime-fighting. I intend to carry on that tradition, within my limitations and to the best of my abilities. I shall do so to the end of my days, regardless of the ridicule and contempt of others."

"I'll leave you then," Simmons said, closing the door behind him.

"Mr. Holmes," Cassandra, trying to patch things over, "my partner, besides being the biggest oaf in the room, is also the finest man I've ever met. Loyal and fearless, a courageous and steadfast companion. Very much like someone else we both know."

I didn't know whether to kiss her or slap her upside the head but Holmes appeared mollified by her remarks. "Very well then. Mr. Nightstalk, if you can put up with my eccentricities, I shall pledge myself to assist you in whatever manner I can. Is that an equitable arrangement, sir?" I nodded. "Excellent. I assume you're here on official business so let us tarry no longer." He rubbed his hands together. "No doubt time is of the essence so please apprise me of everything that has transpired thus far and we'll take it from there."

Conan Doyle's Holmes frequently expressed a dim view of supernatural goings-on. His rational, ordered mind and legendary intellect left little room for the uncanny. In that sense he was completely at odds with his far more gullible creator.

But the diminutive detective's face remained impassive as Cassandra summarized the case thus far. The whole thing sounded pretty far-fetched as I listened to her lay it out for him, totally off the wall, and I wondered how he'd react once he'd heard her through to the end. She left out nothing: our trip to the Hall of Records, the encounter with the ravenor...she even mentioned Rache's subliminal spook show.

That was one of the few occasions he interrupted her, directing a question at me over steepled fingers. "I require further clarification on this point. You saw *something*? Can you be more specific? I have an absolutely *Proustian* obsession for details."

I made a helpless gesture. "I tried to explain to Cass but...it's hard to pin down."

"Did you sense age? Great age?"

"Yeah, that was part of it."

"Hunger? Fury? Unquenchable greed? Hate. *Pride*, I'll wager. Yes...obscene, overweening pride and unmitigated contempt for lesser creatures such as yourself."

I was knocked for a loop. "Yeah. *Yeah.* That's exactly right. *Cripes,* Holmes—"

But he had already returned his attention to Cassandra. "Pray, continue."

When she finished, the silence stretched and the minutes ticked by and that itch on my ass kept getting worse and worse. My eyes roamed about restlessly. The library was long and narrow and poorly ventilated. Books, binders and periodicals filled the shelves and stacks of file boxes took up most of the remaining floor space.

"Uh, Sherlock," I finally ventured, "are you deducing right now?"

"Quiet, Nightstalk," Cassandra hissed.

But my gambit did the trick. He reached over and picked up the water pipe; its reservoir was topped up with weed. "That's all right, Ms. Zinnea. Your colleague is clearly a man of action, impatient when it comes to idlers and buffoons." He blew out a plume of smoke that hung in the air like a big, grey thought balloon.

Simmons opened the door and stuck his head inside. Sniffed audibly and glared at Holmes. "If this place gets raided, I'm going to *throttle* you," he vowed. Holmes merely smiled and Simmons shut the door behind him.

"They'll never throw me out," he confided. "I give the place a certain...cachet. What's a *Diogenes Club* without a Holmes?"

"As I recall," I pointed out, "it was his brother Mycroft who was a member. Holmes never struck me as much of a joiner."

The pint-sized sleuth regarded me with amusement. "Piffle. Do you want to hear my views or not? You...*purist.*"

"Please, Mr. Holmes," Cassandra begged, directing a kick at my shins that would have crippled me had it connected.

"This 'Cabal'. They are the key. We know the identities of the principal and supporting players but...I sense a central guiding intelligence at the heart of this bizarre affair. Is it Skorzeny? Fischer? Rache?"

She nodded. "I've been thinking along the same lines. I would say Rache is a strong possibility—"

"That is mere supposition. You have names but you don't have *the name.* The identity of your main antagonist. A dangerous situation, methinks."

"What about Mrs. Fischer?" I joked. "Maybe she's your criminal mastermind."

"The Barbie doll? Former beauty queen and trophy wife?" Holmes scoffed at the suggestion. "I read about her sometimes in the society pages. I am simply *mad* about newspapers. I read at least six a day. It helps me keep in touch with what's going on out there. No, not the Barbie doll. I have my own view but, again, it's nothing more than guesswork on my part."

"We welcome any advice you might have for us."

He didn't need much prodding. "I would suggest that you consider contacting some of the members of this group. Your efforts might turn up a weak link or a disaffected individual willing to talk."

Cassandra nodded, her relief evident. He hadn't called the whole thing preposterous or intimated that we were both off our rockers. "Thank you, Mr. Holmes. That's an excellent suggestion. Is there anything else that comes to mind?"

"Yes. Regarding Herman Rache." *Puff, puff.* "I think it would be advisable to give him a wide berth. I have no reason to doubt he is every bit as formidable as his reputation suggests. I've only dealt with him through intermediaries but regard him with no small amount of respect."

"But do you really think he's…one of those things? Some kind of extra-dimensional being or whatever?"

He hesitated before answering. "You saw it with your own eyes, Mr. Nightstalk. Clearly, you are still experiencing the after-effects of that encounter. The supernatural and related matters are not, I confess, subjects of great interest to me. Still, I have a very high regard for my colleague," a nod to Cassandra, "and as far as I have been able to discern, her conclusions *are* congruent with the facts. Speaking confidentially, I can tell you that I have been involved in a number of cases of late that would seem to be related, directly or indirectly, to this one. I was consulted with regards to the robbery of the Felderhof. The John Dee archive. This has all the earmarks of a conspiracy global in scope and yet somehow centred here in Ilium. I must ponder this further." His eyes were glassy, unfocussed.

Cassandra put her hand on my arm. "We should go. Mr. Holmes, it's been a pleasure, as always."

He slid off the chair and stood, somewhat unsteadily, beside the work table. "Not at all, my dear. Ah, would you have any objection to my discussing this case with some of the other members? Many are acknowledged experts in their fields and eager to lend their advice and assistance to a good cause."

She nodded assent. "Feel free, Mr. Holmes."

He looked thoughtful. "I shall use discretion. No need to mention the, ah, more unconventional aspects."

"Hey," I put in, "we need all the help we can get."

He fluttered his hand as if it was a matter of small consequence to him. Arrogant little prick. "Please keep me updated as to any future developments. I shall endeavor to find out what I can and will inform you once I've turned up anything of substance."

I couldn't resist one final jab. "So...you'll be putting on some clever disguise and hitting the streets for clues, will you?"

He seemed crestfallen and Cassandra looked like she was about to kick me again. "Alas, Mr. Nightstalk, due to certain quirks in my brain chemistry, of late I have found myself unable to venture beyond this building. I suppose you could call it a rather extreme case of agoraphobia. I haven't been outside these few rooms in more than nine months. The members are good enough to allow me the use of the facilities and my needs are fairly simple."

I almost hooted with laughter. The master detective, mastered by his own phobia. A great mind beaten by *itself.* Then I felt an onrush of pity, combined with a healthy dose of shame. "Sorry. Didn't realize...*mumble mumble...*"

"Quite all right, old boy," he commented. "What I have come to realize is that there are other ways of gathering information in this day and age. One does not have to visit a crime scene when it is described in minute detail in the newspapers and on CNN. The volume of data available on the internet is nothing less than astonishing. And when I find myself in circumstances when I need someone to stake out a location or find a missing person, I do have certain, ah, human resources at my disposal."

"You mean the Baker Street Irregulars?" I asked. "Street urchins who do your bidding?"

"Not as many as I would like," he admitted. "Maintaining a steady, dependable pool of agents is next to impossible. Expensive too--sadly, a shilling a day and a guinea bonus no longer suffices." He shrugged. "Still, I would not hesitate to use them, should the need arise. Do you have a card?" I gave him one. "Here is mine." A plain, white rectangle, ordinary card stock: *Sherlock Holmes, Consulting Detective* and a phone number, presumably the Club's. "Very well. I shall do what I can for you."

"Thank you, Mr. Holmes."

"Yeah," I grunted, "I feel better already. Or maybe it's just that stuff you're smoking. That rare Turkish blend George was telling us about."

"Ah, yes. Exquisite shag." Was there a twinkle in his eye as he reached for the pipe? *Puff, puff.* "Very potent stuff. Much stronger than kif, which I had a chance to sample once in North Africa. All in the line of duty, of course."

I was getting a terrific buzz from breathing in that fine ganja. The air was ripe with it. I allowed Cassandra to steer me toward the door, leaving the Great Detective to his solitary speculations...

We waved to George Simmons as we passed through the sitting room. On the way down the stairs, I asked the obvious question. "Where's Watson? If there's a Sherlock Holmes, there's gotta be a Watson."

"There was," she said from several steps below me, "but she died."

"Murdered?"

"Cancer. That's when he became Holmes. After he lost his wife, he lost his zest for living. Becoming Holmes was his way of coping with the grief." She opened the door at the bottom and I followed her out. The proprietor of the smoke shop was locking up for the night and greeted us cordially. Cassandra made his day by smiling at him.

"So who is he *really*?"

"His name is or *was* Edward Hanson and he used to be the city manager here in Ilium. Brilliant man. And something of an enthusiast for detective literature."

I had to scuttle to keep up with her long legs. "Slow down, will ya? So how did he become a member of such an exclusive club? He was never a cop or—"

"He owns the building," she replied. "After his wife died, he took early retirement. He used his severance package to buy it." We had just about reached the car. "He lets the Club use the space virtually rent free. That's why he isn't worried about them evicting him."

I unlocked her door and trotted around to the other side. Got in and started the Taurus. "Where to? Back to the office or--"

A voice came from the backseat: "How about dropping me off first?" A second later, Winston Gillette's head popped into view.

"*Jee-zus*, Gillette—"

He raised his hands. "Sorry about that, man. Gave you quite a jolt, huh?" He snickered. "Wow, Nightstalk, I gotta tell you, I disabled your security hexes in no time. Very second rate and sloppy, if you don't mind my saying so. You don't even have a fucking *club*."

"I'm gonna club you in a minute, *Winston*," I snapped.

"What are you doing here?" Cassandra asked him.

"Hiding out, lady. Drive and I'll explain. Just hurry up and get going, will you?" I pulled out and we started away.

"Why did you have to get in the car? Why not wait for us outside?"

He peered through the back window, twitchy with nervous energy. "I have to keep out of sight. Certain people have it in for me, thanks to you two."

"Have you been following us?"

"For awhile, yeah. Stay in this area, I don't wanna get too far from my car."

I made a right turn. "Shouldn't you be at work?"

"Well, that's just it." The face in the mirror was pale and anxious. "My store burned down tonight and, uh--" My partner gasped and twisted around in her seat.

"Burned down?"

"*Don't look at me!*" he bleated. "Act like there's nobody back here." She obeyed and we listened to him muttering to himself, his monologue occasionally loud enough for me to make out. "Fucker said I was in the clear...didn't *do* anything...fucking Skorzeny and his lousy...what am I gonna do...fucked any way you look at it..."

"Winston," Cassandra spoke up, "why did you come to us?"

"—kill my ass...end up like some—"

"Are you gonna keep babbling away like a fool or are you gonna say something that makes sense?" Hoping my sharp, no bullshit tone would get his attention. "'Cause otherwise I'm sick of listening to you."

"I...had my fortune read. I go to this one woman--Sonya Krydor, do you know her?"

"I hear she's good," Cassandra said.

"She is. I'll give you her number," he offered. "She isn't taking on any new clients but if you use me for a reference—"

"Could we get on with it, you two?" I barked.

"She told me the cards were bad, *very* bad. Almost the worst she'd ever seen. I had to change my routine, go on a holiday for awhile. And don't delay, do it right away. It really freaked me out 'cause I've been thinking the same thing. Getting away, going some place to unwind. Circle this block here. And keep your eyes peeled."

"What's the matter, Gillette? Your past catching up with you? Instant karma gonna get you?"

"Ha ha, Nightstalk. At least I have the brains to know when to get hell out of Dodge. " He ducked as a car passed, lighting up the interior. "Tonight, I didn't even bother opening. I parked in the alley and went inside to grab a few things. As I was putting stuff in the trunk, something bounced off the hood and went through the back window of the store. *Right through the fucking bars.* The next second: *poosh!* Flames everywhere. I only got a glimpse of it, looked sort of star-shaped, left a burn mark on my hood—"

"Elemental," Cassandra observed. "They used one on Eva too. Except yours missed or malfunctioned--"

"Malfunctioned, *fuck*. My store is a total write-off, lady. That thing was not natural, it was intended for me and that is why I am fucking *leaving*. There's my car, pull over here." I slowed to a stop. "Listen, you guys, things have gotten really, really weird and fucked up. If they're coming after me, you'll be next. Count on it."

"Thanks for the warning, shithead. Where should we send the 'thank you' card? Timbuktu?"

"Be nice." She placed a restraining hand on my arm. "Winston's trying to help."

"That's right," he affirmed. "I came to warn you at, like, great personal risk."

"Why?" I asked. "Since when did you become such a good Samaritan?" I watched him in the mirror, saw the way he was gazing at her and got my answer. Like the songs says, he was just another victim of love.

"Turns out you were right all along. You warned me and I didn't listen and look where it got me. So now I'm repaying the favour. Let's just say Skorzeny knows what you're up to and he's gonna fuckin' kill you. That's it. I did my part. Now I'm getting out."

I turned around and gave him the bad news. "You ain't going anywhere."

"*What*?" His face registered shock and bewilderment.

"I dunno. Maybe we're not done with you yet. Maybe there's something else you can tell us, something useful. Think about it, *Winnie*."

"*If you don't let me out of this fuckin' car, I'll—*"

I thumbed a button and the door locks snapped down.

"Sorry, Winston," Cassandra said. "I'm afraid if you want out, you'll have to make it past us first. I don't like his chances, how about you, partner?"

"Definitely not," I said, fixing him with a menacing leer. "I'd yank his fucking head off in a heartbeat." He shrank from my villainous gaze. His lips trembled and he seemed close to tears.

"Time to tell all," Cassandra advised him. "Nightstalk's in one of his moods. In another minute, I won't be able to hold him back."

Poor bastard never had a chance.

"Look at it this way," I told him, "they've already tried to kill you twice. What have you got to lose?"

We watched him drive away. Didn't say anything for awhile.

"I feel...wretched," she offered. "Threatening and harassing the poor guy like that."

"Yeah," I said, "what we did was truly rotten. Then again, fuck him." "Nightstalk, he was the equivalent of an errand boy. We ganged up on him and for what?"

"Hey, we learned stuff. He seemed pretty sure Skorzeny's the one calling the shots. Hadn't even *heard* of Rache. That says something."

"Hmm. Maybe."

"Well, it makes sense, doesn't it? The Fischers provide the dough and in return Skorzeny supplies Armageddon in 3-D with Dolby/THX sound." She frowned. "What?"

"It's just that Skorzeny, despite his fearsome reputation, has always been more image than substance to me. I know he *looks* scary and he's undoubtedly capable of a lot of things, not excluding murder."

"*But...*"

"I read his book, *Satanic Majesty*, and it seemed, I don't know, *tame*. His so-called knowledge of the occult is superficial and derivative. He worships Crowley but doesn't *begin* to grasp the complexity and depth of Crowley's vision. To me, he doesn't fit the role of criminal mastermind. Maybe I'm underestimating him but I don't think so."

"What about Rache? I can't see him playing second fiddle to anybody. I bet *he's* our man."

"I don't know. Possibly. But Holmes is right: *we have to be certain*. A lot may depend on it." She sounded grumpy and frustrated and what I said next didn't improve her disposition.

"What about Philippe? How much of this are you planning to share with *him*? If you ask me, I think it's pretty suspicious the way he's kept us in the dark all along."

"He had his reasons," she insisted. "I get a sense that he's conflicted. He wants to do more for us but—"

"Maybe 'conflicted' isn't the right word," I suggested. "Maybe he's been holding out on us for more selfish motives."

"Go on," she said. "Go ahead and say it. You think he's been compromised." She closed her eyes, concentrating. "You really *don't* trust him, do you? You half-suspect he's working for the Cabal. *Hmm.* Interesting theory."

"Look, I don't mean to be the one who constantly—"

"You might be right." I couldn't believe what I was hearing. "At this point we can't rule out the possibility. But our essential strategy doesn't change. We get as much from him as we can and, meanwhile, do our best to hide our suspicions from him."

I took my right hand off the steering wheel, held it up: "I, for one, promise to treat him with my usual hostility and contempt."

"Fine. You do that." Her tone was frosty.

We didn't talk much the rest of the way.

As we were getting out, she looked across the roof at me. "I suggest you save your hostility for our *real* enemies. Until I have reason to believe otherwise, Philippe is still my friend."

"Okay. *Fine.* I take back everything I said. Philippe's a sweetheart of a guy and a credit to whatever species he belongs to." It was too dark to gauge her reaction.

After we'd walked awhile, she slipped an arm through mine. "I've been bagging at you a lot lately, haven't I? Forgive me?"

"Ah, hell, it's my own fault. I've been doing plenty to get on your nerves."

"No more than usual." We laughed. "I feel...on edge. Jumpy. I'm taking it out on you and I shouldn't."

"Got a bad case of the heebie-jeebies?"

I felt her shiver. "Maybe. I'm not sure. But I'm beginning to wonder if I'm experiencing some kind of psychic attack. The sense of oppression, the almost paralyzing fear...those are strong indications of a bane at work. I've been taking counter-measures--ritual baths, extra prayers and meditations. Dion Fortune has a couple of good chapters on psychic defense, I'll have to see if I can find them when we get upstairs..."

At that point we passed *The Tool Shed* and were rewarded with a tiny dose of normality. Tara Dreyfuss was on duty. The store was empty and she was bored, leaning on the counter and pretending to poke a cucumber-sized vibrator up her nose. When we rapped on the window, she jumped, nearly driving it into her brain. Now *that* would've been a death by misadventure.

Cassandra paused at the foot of the steps, spoke without turning around. "I've got a bad feeling tonight, Nightstalk. I need you to talk me down. Will you do that for me?" She sounded genuinely lost. It scared me.

"Sure, kid," I said gently, "no problem. Hey, don't we always come through in the end? You said it yourself, we're at our best when our backs are against the wall and everything's on the line. I believe that, I really do."

She nodded. "So...it's going to be all right?"

"You bet. You got my word on it."

"Thanks," she said, starting up the stairs, "I just needed to hear you say it."

The following evening, within minutes of our arrival, a guy from a 24-hour courier service showed up. I signed on one of those electronic hand pads and he passed me a 9 X 12 manila envelope. Transaction complete, he left without uttering a word. My kind of guy.

I glanced at the envelope and handed it to Cass. "It'll be for you, naturally. I never get mail. It's like I don't *exist*."

"I told you," she said as she slit it open, "it's your attitude. The hostility thing. It tends to intimidate people." She pulled out a sheaf of papers. "You should learn to cultivate relationships, be more open and forthcoming."

"Not in my neighborhood. People shoot you for smiling funny."

She was about to respond when something seized her complete attention. She scanned the next few pages, zipping through them. Finally, she looked up, somber as a hanging judge. "It's all here," she said. "Confirmation of everything."

"Is that from Brother Philippe?"

She checked but there was no cover note. "It must be."

"Never mind. What does it say?"

"It's better if you read it." Holding out the sheets to me. "And you should prepare yourself because some of it's going to blow your mind..."

Transcript of telephone conversation—May 16th, 13:22 Hrs.

VS= Victor Skorzeny   TB= Tibor Benes

SKORZENY: Yes? Who is—

BENES: Skorzeny! Skorzeny! It's unbelievable, it's (*Inaudible*).

VS: Tibor! We've been waiting for—

TB: —everything is just so (*Inaudible*). Oh, God! God!

VS: --(*Inaudible*) fool, what have you and that idiot Finchley been up to?

TB: Up to? *(Nervous laughter)* Skorzeny, my God...

VS: Tibor, listen, you must tell me. What happened? Did you—was the experiment successful?

TB: (*Muffled, inaudible*)

VS: Tibor?

TB: Fuck, fuck, if you'd seen it. It—it's—

VS: Were you successful?

TB: (*Nervous laughter*) What do you mean? Do you mean is Finchley dead? Yes, I suppose in that sense we were successful. You pompous fucking—

VS: Dead? How? Tibor, you must—

TB: We fucked up, all right? Or I should say Finchley fucked up. The idiot. I should have known he'd pull something. But I thought it would be all right, I really did.

VS: Is this line secure? Should we be talking about—

TB: I saw it, Skorzeny! I watched him die. It was awful. It just reached out and took him. Tore him to pieces right there in front of me. I still don't understand how--damnit, the circle should have held. But he—he—

VS: Come and see me about this personally. Don't say any more.

TB: --should have quit, postponed it or whatever once I realized what he'd done.

VS: What did he do?

TB: He was scared, I caught him smoking a joint--

VS: What? The fool! I warned you both--

TB: He was terrified. He couldn't go through with it otherwise. I caught him and I—I didn't (*Inaudible*) I thought it would be all right, don't you see? A minor infraction.

VS: Disaster. An utter disaster.

TB: You weren't there, you bastard! You and your bunch made sure you stayed safe. We were the guinea pigs...your sacrificial lambs. It's your fault as much as anybody's.

VS: You said something got him.

TB: It was horrible. After it grabbed Julian, I just fucking ran. Got lost in the woods. I've been wandering ever since, scared shitless and... (*Inaudible*) No food, drinking from puddles. And the whole time I could feel it following me. I kept moving but it was always there—

VS: What? What's after you? Damnit, man, where are you?

TB: (*Inaudible*) What? What did you say?

VS: Where—

TB: (*Whispering*) I think it's here.

VS: What?

TB: It followed me out of the woods. Skorzeny! Skorzeny!

168

VS: It's all in your imagination. You're in
shock, man.

TB: I've got to get out of here!

VS: Tell me where you are. I'll send someone.

TB: In—in a gas station. A truck stop. I haven't
slept, I think I'm losing my mind.

VS: It's all right, Tibor. I'll send someone and—

TB: I see it! It found me! It's—

(*SOUND: struggle, screams*)

VS: Tibor? What's happening?

Disconnect.

VS: Tibor? Tibor?

    "Oh, my," was the best I could manage after finishing.
    "You can see from the date—this conversation was recorded the afternoon of the 16th. *The 16th*. Too much time has elapsed." She looked careworn, fretful. "Who knows what's happened since then…"

    He has reached the outskirts of the city.
    There have been annoying but necessary delays as he accustoms himself to all things human. An accelerated process of learning: how to walk and talk, eat, sit down and excrete waste in a socially acceptable manner. Although he has better command of the body, a firmer hand on the controls, he still draws funny looks, especially when forced to communicate orally. The speech mechanism in the throat confounds him. As a result, his voice comes out sounding gutteral and unpleasant to human ears.
    He calls himself Aiwass, *a nonsense name he's used before. Over the centuries, he has assumed many different designations.* Aiwass. Gargat. Singilla. *Names aren't really that important where he comes from. His function or job description is roughly equivalent to "Opener of the Way" or "Cosmic Keymaster", something along those lines. A facilitator, of sorts.*

"Tibor Benes" is no more. Tibor Benes has ceased to be. Extinguished. But not before every scrap of worthwhile information was ruthlessly extracted, absorbed, digested, the detritus cast into the interminable void along with Benes' mutilated soul.

Aiwass is frustrated with the demands imposed by a flesh and blood existence. Vital signs have to be maintained within a very narrow set of parameters or else the host body ceased functioning. This requires constant supervision, a drain on Aiwass's energy and patience.

Aiwass quickly comes to loathe being human. Ridiculous species, poorly designed, laughably fragile. Longing to rid himself of his uncomfortable disguise and take on his true form.

Such a strange place, this world. Disorienting, bright, loud, baffling. His newly acquired senses are overloading, assailed from all sides by billboards and talk radio and commercials and diesel exhaust; classic rock and homicidal motorists, friendly waitresses, lonely truckers on speed and inane chatter. These people never shut up. A broadband of clamour and din. How do they bear it and not go mad?

The sun is sheer torment, especially for sensory organs long attuned to the cold and dark. Sunglasses barely help. The headaches are quite excruciating...

Aiwass senses the woman's fear and frowns. He has done nothing to threaten her or put her on guard. So why does she recoil from him? It's the voice, partly. Facial expressions are another work in progress and mastering anything resembling a smile has proven well nigh impossible.

She's worried that he's going to try something. Make her pull over and take her clothes off. Indecently assault her.

Aiwass concentrates on getting the words right. "You...need not fear...on that account."

She glances at him, her eyes big and stupid.

She doesn't ask where they're going, just drives. Petrified into submission. He tells her when to turn, always certain of the direction and route. He seems to be taking her right into the heart of the city.

"You do not know my identity or purpose. Destroying you would be excessive and...unnecessary."

"Thank you."

"You still doubt me?"

"How did you know that? Can you read my mind?"

"Your fears are easily detected."

"Mister, I am scared. I never stop for people and I'll never figure out what made me pull over for you."

170

"I wished it," Aiwass answers, *"your will obeyed."* Making it simple enough for even her to understand.

"But why me?"

An approximation of a shrug. "I required a—" Almost saying *'conveyance'. "—a ride. Your arrival was…timely."*

"That's it? Just stupid coincidence?"

"Yes. Your automobile is a mode of transportation. I needed, your vehicle was provided. All is as it should be.

He sees her body vibrating subtly and recognizes the tremor as another byproduct of her fear. *"I just want to live."*

So far Aiwass has killed four, no, five humans. Finchley, Benes and, shortly afterward, an unlucky truck driver who happened along, wanting to use the phone. Then there was the young couple at the rest stop who resisted when he tried to take their camper van. An error in judgement on his part. Even with vestigial memories from Benes, he can't grasp the mechanics of driving. It's all the attention he has to devote to maintaining this wretched physical shell. Aping and impersonating human ways. He tries but there are frequent lapses: slurred words, outbursts of maniacal laughter, followed by a string of explosive farts.

This woman has served her purpose well. Her name is Shirley Dahl and she is a thirty-four year old graphic designer, a single mother with two children. She doesn't know it yet but she is taking Aiwass to a location in the city Benes' memories have provided. At which point she'll either be released unharmed…or her throat will be deftly cut and her body dumped in a convenient back alley.

Aiwass hasn't made up his mind which it will be.

Time is of the essence. There are plans to prepare, schemes to set in motion. He doesn't want his compatriots getting the impression he's been dawdling while they languish in eternal exile. Neglecting his duties and responsibilities. They wouldn't like that.

Even immortals can grow impatient.

And angry.

Very, very angry.

Victor Skorzeny buzzes him up right away. He barely has time to crack open his door before the person he thinks is Tibor Benes barges past him without so much as a sideways glance. Skorzeny starts to protest, then gets a whiff of his guest. Benes stinks, an accumulation of aromas sharp enough to make Skorzeny's stomach lurch. Best to keep this interview short and dismiss the oaf as quickly as possible.

"Where have you been?" Skorzeny swiftly works himself into a rage as he follows his guest into the living room of the spacious condominium the Fischers have provided for him. One of the fringe benefits of being a guru to a member of the Fortune 500. *"It's been more than a day since you called." He turns on Benes, his expression wrathful. "Fool! You are an utter imbecile and--"*

"Alone?" Aiwass growls.

"What?" Skorzeny is taken aback by his voice.

"Are...we...alone?"

Skorzeny waves at the living room, his irritation evident. "Who else would be here? Stop talking nonsense, Tibor, and explain yourself."

But no reply is forthcoming. The notorious occultist feels ill at ease, maybe even a little bit spooked. In truth, Victor Skorzeny is no great adept—certainly not when compared to the likes of Rache—but it is obvious to him that something is different about Benes. He fairly crackles with energy, burning with a weird inner fire. Shit, look at him, he's practically glowing.

"I was, er, catching up on my reading. Enjoying a quiet evening at home. Tibor," approaching tentatively, "what happened to you? Your voice when you called from downstairs and just now..." Aiwass moves about the room, scrutinizing the bookshelves, picking up various objets d'art *and knick-knacks. The aromatic candles are intriguing, as well. "On the phone you indicated, rather indiscreetly, that Finchley had been killed. What went wrong?"*

"He was unclean," not-really-Benes snaps. "He died."

Skorzeny's anxiety ratchets up another notch. "Your voice—what's wrong with your voice, man?"

Benes turns, offering him a bent grin. "You were the one who sent them. You are responsible."

"I—I don't think that's true. The others were in agreement—"

"With my assistance, you will complete the ritual and restore the Old Ones. That is your wish, is it not?" Skorzeny nods vigourously. "And so we will try again. Do it right this time."

"Well, the Summoning—it should have worked." Skorzeny, pleading his case. "It's true, what we put together was a pastiche of sorts but our experts, Margate and the others, assured us—"

"I will assist," Aiwass/Benes repeats. "There were mistakes. Pronunciation. Enochian language is difficult. You offered inferior blood. And then there was the unclean fool. Finchley." Spitting out the name. "I will make it right. We must prepare proper sacrifices."

Skorzeny is startled. "Sacrifices? You mean more cats or—"

"I will show you how it is done." Aiwass announces, shedding all pretense, his eyes blazing in their sockets. "There is no room for error. Blood is the currency. Nothing else suffices."

Skorzeny gapes at the entity in wonder, terror, awe. "They did it. They really—"

"Only partially. Their Call was flawed, incomplete. I am Aiwass, Opener of the Way. There will be no further mistakes. You agree to this?"

"Yes, my Lord, yes!" Skorzeny, on his knees now, clutching Benes' hand. "I—I offer myself to you. Do with me what you will."

"That is just as well," Aiwass says. "This vessel displeases me." The body of Benes slumps to the floor, jointless, vacated. Skorzeny is suddenly wrenched upright, dragged to his feet, lifted, suspended in mid-air. Then, with one cruel tug, his personality and soul are ripped from his body, his essence gobbled up, the extraneous bits tumbling piecemeal into absolute nothingness...

"They did it," my partner announced somberly. "The crazy bastards actually did it." She was pale and her fingers commenced drumming as she unconsciously sought an outlet for her rising anxiety. "Holy Diana, queen of the night. Those *maniacs*..."

The way she said it, the look on her face, you would have thought it was the end of the world.

Wednesday, May 19th

Another brief, pointed memo from the inner office was waiting for me when I got in.

> *"Expect visit from P. DeBarge.*
> *Suspect he is withholding information.*
> *Query him re: the enclosed."*

The note was clipped to some sheets containing material that could only have come from a high-ranking source within the Brethren of Purity. The Old Man had really outdone himself this time. I sat down and started reading...

"What's that, Nightstalk?" Cassandra Zinnea asked, once she'd hung up her coat and kicked off her shoes. She preferred to go barefoot in the office. I didn't mind. She had *amazing* feet. "You're practically *devouring* it."

"Oh, you know, the usual crap from the Old Man. He, uh, dug up a few things. Nothing important, really. Just stuff Philippe has been keeping from us. Well," I amended, trying to be fair, "maybe he was operating under orders from his asshole bosses in Brussels."

"What sort of *stuff* are we talking about?" She was guarded but curious.

"Transcripts of phone intercepts, surveillance reports, all of it *very* recent. We're in here too. The Brethren have definitely been keeping tabs on what we've been up to." She snatched the file away from me and began to page through it. "Once again, the Black Brotherhood have proven to be as slippery and scummy as ever. And though it pains me to do so, I draw your attention to the highly incriminating material on Philippe--"

But she'd already found it and shushed me. Her brow furrowed as she zipped through the relevant pages. "These are reports of Philippe meeting with various members of the Cabal. Allan Mayhew. Vivien Vickers." She looked over at me. "The question being, what was he up to, searching for more information, grooming another informant—"

"—or, not to repeat myself, maybe he's been working for the Cabal all along." It would likely piss her off but it had to be said. "That would fit too."

She found something that amused her. "This operative reports that Philippe met with Vivien Vickers on at least three different occasions. Wining and dining her, holding her hand. The last time he took her back to his hotel room and they spent the night together." She chuckled. "Nice to see he hasn't lost his touch."

"There's probably a transcript of them fucking, if you're interested."

Her face went rigid. "That sounds more like *your* type of reading."

"Look," I said, trying to put things right again, "could be there's a perfectly reasonable explanation for this. But you have to look at it from my point of view, someone who maybe doesn't know Philippe as well as you do. He looks dirty to me. Maybe I'm wrong but we owe it to ourselves to make sure, one way or the other."

"He wouldn't sell out the Brethren," she insisted. "It's not in his character."

"Then why all the games? He comes to us for help, strings us along and now we find out he's been secretly meeting with these people, doing shit behind our backs. That doesn't piss you off?"

She shrugged. "Being sneaky, devious and underhanded is part of his training. That doesn't mean he's joined the other side."

"Are you sure you're not letting personal feelings interfere with your judgement?"

"Oh, please..."

"Think about it," I insisted. "You're always going on about how he's a 6th degree and all that. Well, maybe *he's* the one behind everything: calling up bogies, stealing priceless documents out of high security vaults. And what about what Georgie said about someone tampering with the Records. DeBarge could do that, couldn't he? He has the ability, right? *If* he's somehow been turned, *if* he's two-timing the Brethren. Maybe he got turned down for a promotion or the Cabal made him an offer he couldn't refuse. I don't know. I'm just throwing it out there as a possibility."

She picked up a pen and began to doodle. Thinking it over. "I guess...people can change. The Philippe I knew was arrogant, opinionated and self-righteous but he truly believed in what he was doing. Ruthlessly professional and almost blindly obedient. The men in his family have served the Brethren for generations. I can't believe he'd--"

There was a thump and a Gallic curse from the stairs.

"I think we're about to get a chance to ask him," I remarked.

"Maybe we should let it go for now."

"The Old Man says brace him and I agree." I rose as the doorknob turned. "It's time to find out where the fucker really stands."

Philippe limped in and, kneeling down, raised his pantleg, exposing a thin gash about midway up his shin.

My partner was contrite. "Sorry about that. I've been upgrading our security again. That particular hex is a tricky one."

"And ingenious bit of spellwork, my dear," he complimented her. "I missed it completely. I fear I have seriously barked my shin. Mr. Nightstalk, do you mind—" I considerately stepped aside and let him have my chair and then thought *Doh!* Sonofabitch did it again! He dabbed at the cut with a tissue Cassandra gave him. "Normally I am much more conscientious and would not have been caught off guard."

"Ah, well, you've had a lot on your mind, haven't you?" I commiserated. "Like meeting on the sly with the Cabal, that sort of thing. And how about that Vivien Vickers! *Va-va-va-voom,* baby! Hey, I've always wondered, Phil: is she a *real* blonde, know what I mean? Or are you too much of a gentleman to divulge trade secrets?"

He sagged in the chair. Regarded us forlornly. "Ah, I see the cat, as they say, is out of the bag. May I examine the evidence against me?" Cassandra passed him the incriminating material. He flipped through it, grimacing at various points. "These documents," he looked up, "are highly confidential. Withheld from you by order of the Megas Dux himself. It was he who instructed me to seek out and contact certain members of the Cabal. It was deemed necessary to acquire a new source, someone to replace the late Baron. The seduction of Vivien Vickers was, I confess, undertaken at my own initiative. *Bah!*" He tossed the sheets away in disgust. "I have been thoroughly and professionally fucked."

"So *you* say."

He nodded. "Ah. And now in your eyes I am untrustworthy. *Tainted.*" He pursed his lips. "This despite the fact that it was I, at great personal risk, who sent you the transcript that confirmed your suspicions regarding the Babalon Working. Still...I am not unsympathetic to your dilemma." He rolled down his pantleg. "I find myself at an impasse, my friends. I no longer know who, if anyone, I can trust. It is clear there is a traitor in the highest reaches of my order. So where and to whom do I turn? *'Quis custodiet ipsos custodes'*,[24] eh, Cassandra?" She nodded sadly.

Whatever. "So what happens now?" I queried the room in general. "We don't trust you, you don't trust the Brethren --"

"There are things that must be said. But not here." He stood. "My car is downstairs. Let us take a drive, the three of us. In these circumstances, one never knows who might be eavesdropping. Are you, as they say, game?"

"If it means you telling the truth for once then, yeah, I'm game."

"Yes, Mr. Nightstalk, that is precisely what I mean." He hobbled toward the door. "At least, as much of the truth as you are capable of comprehending..."

Prick.

Philippe's car, a roomy Crown Victoria, was waiting outside. Werner was double-parked but that wasn't a problem. His master had the Vic tricked out in all the latest spookery and self-defense hexes. Any parking nazi or beat cop who happened along might spot a violation but would be overcome with a strange reluctance to approach the vehicle. Their anxiety

---

[24] "Who watches the watchers?" (or something like that)

would grow the closer they got. Those bold or foolish enough to forge on would then encounter Werner, an experience they weren't likely to forget. The boy made an impression on you.

Werner uncoiled himself from the driver's seat, a difficult task for someone who stretched the tape to about six-nine. He strode around to the passenger side and wrenched open the door for us. He eyed me like a tiger shark with lockjaw as we ducked inside the idling vehicle. Werner was one of the few guys I would hesitate before taking on. He had fists the size of toaster ovens and a noggin that looked as solid as the nose cone of a Minuteman missile.

Once you took in his imposing size, the first thing you observed about our man Werner was that his lips had been sewn shut and his ears removed. What was even scarier was that Cassandra told me he had to do the bob-and-tuck job *himself*, part of the bizarre initiation rites for the elite fellowship of bodyguards he belonged to. Cripes, and I thought the Yakuza were tough.

"How does he eat?"

She raised her shoulders. "Who knows? Nobody has the nerve to ask. Maybe intravenously or through a tube in his stomach."

"Yechhh..."

I'd regarded Werner with an extra measure of respect ever since.

Our host seemed to have forgotten about his scraped shin. He sat with his face averted, not speaking even after Werner got us underway. It was cozy in the backseat and I enjoyed being in such close proximity to my partner. I was glad it was dark so she couldn't see just how *much* I was enjoying it.

"Indulge yourself, Werner, random pattern." The big man nodded. I noticed he kept glancing at the side and rear mirrors, more alert than I'd ever seen him.

"Does this thing have a bar?" I asked. "You got a bottle stashed away in here somewhere?"

"Alcohol and stimulants cloud the mind and blunt the senses," Philippe replied automatically, still facing out the window.

"Are you all right?" Cassandra rested a hand on his arm.

"I...thank you for asking. These are trying times. I...I'm finding it difficult...to...to..."

I decided to cut to the chase. "So, Philippe, buddy," I said jovially, reaching across her to give him a friendly slap on the knee, "what's new and groovy with the Brethren? Anything we should know about?"

He turned toward me, his face anguished. "Please, Monsieur Nightstalk, you must not make light of these things. A guild, a brotherhood dating back *centuries,* is self-destructing before my eyes. It was a rival faction who provided you with that damning evidence. They wish to discredit me as part of their plan to undermine and compromise our sacred order. I believe this treacherous scheme is being orchestrated by a small group of powerful adepts and that these men are under the sway of the darkest, most inhumane masters." He glowered at me. "I am Philippe Arnaud Debarge and I am proud of my family name, two hundred years of service—" He hitched in his breath. "You would not understand..."

"Take your time, Philippe," Cassandra told him. She stepped on my foot, *hard.*

"Thank you, my dear. If you will give me a moment to collect myself..." He closed his eyes and appeared to slip into a light, meditative state for two or three minutes.

While we waited, I stared at the back of Werner's neck and tried to figure out how I'd take him. I caught him watching me in the mirror, this look in his eyes that said *Don't even think about it, pussycat.*

Finally Philippe propped himself up straighter in his seat. "I am violating the strictest code of secrecy by telling you these things. The penalties for this offense, as dictated by time-honoured tradition, are harsh...and unequivocal." His face was set and determined. "But there are things that must be made known to you and I was wrong for not informing you sooner. The fault is mine but now I wish to make amends."

The origins of the Brethren of Purity are murky, to say the least[25]— and, of course, a super-secret guild of Gifted men (females need not apply), trained and indoctrinated almost from birth to watch over the deepest, darkest secrets of humankind aren't anxious to draw attention to themselves.

The short version: the common wisdom is that they are an off-shoot of the Knights Templar, a scrappy bunch that received Papal fiat to protect Christian pilgrims as they made their way to the Holy Land.

But these good and virtuous knights weren't content serving as glorified bodyguards. The mayor of Jerusalem put them up near the former

---

[25] An unofficial biography of the order, *Keepers of the Secrets*, by Ted Fielding (Marginalia Press; Peoria; 1992), does exist, although it is currently (likely permanently) out of print. It should also be noted that Dion Fortune warned of the existence of "psychic police" in one of her books, and might have paid for the indiscretion with her life, sickening and dying at the relatively tender age of 55.

site of Solomon's Temple and during their off hours, when they weren't acting as muscle for a steady stream of supplicants and suckers, the Templars dug a few holes, poked around and, it is alleged, made some kind of important discovery. Are we talking about the Ark of the Covenant, maybe even the Holy Grail? Who knows? But they definitely found *something* because in a very short span of time their power and influence increased to a remarkable degree. There has been speculation that the Templars unearthed a treasure trove of early Christian manuscripts containing certain texts that challenged the authority and legitimacy of the Papacy. That would make quite the bargaining chip.

The real story will likely never be known. But there is ample evidence that the Templars enjoyed a special status and despite being a modest order, sworn to poverty, their coffers swelled appreciably. Some scholars insist the Templars didn't confine themselves to Christian texts, they also snapped up translations dealing with the *Kabbalah* and alchemy as well as volumes of a more esoteric or, shall we say, *infernal* nature. The booty they accumulated was ferried back to Europe and stashed in remote monasteries and strongholds in France and Scotland.

The Templars' wealth and influence inevitably attracted powerful enemies who worked tirelessly to bring about their downfall. Eventually they were denounced by the Pope and abandoned by their royal patrons. Many of them were burned as heretics and demon-worshippers.

Their treasure was divvied up among various potentates; the material judged most dangerous placed in the care of a *new* order, the Brethren of Purity. They were, it was said, the *crème de la crème*, holy knights of the highest character: steadfast, devoted and absolutely incorruptible.

The Brethren were understandably wary of meeting the same fate as their Templar cousins. They chose a more discreet role in the affairs of the world. Eventually, by the mid-1800's, they had severed most of their ties to the Mother Church. Rome, in the process of modernizing and paying lip service to the Age of Enlightenment, was only too happy to see the back of them.

Secrecy and a fanatical devotion to duty are hallmarks of the Black Brotherhood. The words *Brethren of Purity* are never to be uttered, an *omerta* more savagely enforced than anything the Sicilians ever devised. They work behind the scenes: diplomats and scholars, scientists and "special consultants". Protecting our species from its own stupidity and recklessness. Always on the job. Certain knowledge is forbidden, proscribed under penalty of death. Those who seek to upset the natural order, transgress against the security of our dimension, are punished. Terminated, with extreme prejudice.

Only now, just when we needed them most, the fuckers were tearing themselves apart from the inside out...

Philippe stared straight ahead. Perplexed. Conflicted. "This is difficult for me. But what choice do I have? The organization I have devoted my life to has been infiltrated and I am betrayed."

"Surely the Cabal doesn't have the resources to mount an operation against the Brethren." Cassandra, beating me to the punch. "What you're talking about is a conspiracy that would require years, perhaps even *decades* to reach fruition. But the timing is interesting. The Brethren rendered ineffective while a major working is in the offing. Still thinking coincidence, Evgeny?"

"I see what you're saying."

"There is no such thing as a coincidence, Monsieur Nightstalk."

"If I hear that one more time..."

"It is true," he insisted, "there are causal links, interconnections so subtle they are virtually undetectable. But they are always there. Devious yet invisible hands at work. Information has been leaked, investigations sabotaged. As a result, the Brethren's influence has been greatly curtailed. Do you know that my best contact at Interpol no longer takes my calls? We once had excellent working relations with the world's greatest security and intelligence-gathering organizations. The CIA, NSA, MI6, Mossad, all of them. Now, thanks to a series of blunders and indiscretions, we are being cut out of the chain. Some of our former allies now refer to us as 'spook chasers', 'superstitious Old Europe types'. My god, how did we come to this?" He pounded his fist on the door panel. Werner glanced back in concern. "But there are still some of us who forge on. We recognized the threat the Cabal represented. We lobbied our superiors and managed to plant an agent in their very bosom."

"The same agent who was ultimately murdered because he was exposed or ratted out by someone he trusted. Someone like *you* maybe."

"Ah, Monsieur Nightstalk." His tone lightly mocking. "Even now, you have no faith in me."

"Nightstalk thinks you've been working for the Cabal all along. Isn't that right, Evvie?" Blind-sided by the woman I love.

"Maybe I do," I muttered rebelliously. "I still haven't heard anything that convinces me otherwise."

He shrugged. "To be fair, it is not a far-fetched supposition. Especially once you came to believe I was keeping information from you. The meetings with Vivien and the others; very incriminating. I commend the Old Man for his resourcefulness but I am certain those documents were deliberately given to him to cast doubt on my veracity."

I shook my head in mock sympathy. "Makes you wonder who your friends are, don't it?"

Before he could reply, Cassandra interceded. "And while we waste time suspecting and accusing each other, the Cabal moves ahead with its plans." She sounded worried and that worried me.

"There is no question, time is running short, *mon amis*. You've seen the transcript, yes? Julian Finchley and Tibor Benes attempting the so-called Babalon Working."

"We read it," Cassandra nodded. "Finchley gets killed and something attacks Benes as well. Anything new on that front?"

Philippe nodded. "Benes is *alive*. He was observed entering Skorzeny's residence but no one has seen him since. Skorzeny comes and goes but Benes has yet to resurface. My operatives report Skorzeny has been meeting privately with some of his colleagues. Rache, a few others. He has a new scrambler on his phone, very state of the art, so our ability to eavesdrop is currently...limited. Pity."

"Is that all? There's something else, isn't there?" She was turned toward him, my presence all but forgotten.

Philippe nodded. "There were a number of unexplained deaths near a park north of the city. A truck driver as well as a young couple. I've heard reports that the condition of the bodies was...unusual."

"That's where they did the Working." Her mind clicking away. "This thing gets out, kills Finchley and those other people...but for some reason lets Benes go? That doesn't make any sense. Unless—"

"You astonish me, my dear," Philippe was impressed. "You have arrived at the same conclusion we did but in a fraction of the time. Truly remarkable."

"Well, that must make me seriously retarded because I don't get it. *What* conclusion? What's this about Benes?" I demanded irritably.

"You might say that Tibor Benes is no longer himself." My partner noted my obvious confusion. "Something has taken control of him and he's acting as its host."

"Why only one of them? Isn't the point to throw open the door and let *all* these fuckers in for a big, cosmic gangbang?"

"Ah, but remember what Benes said, Monsieur Nightstalk. They violated the strict conditions that must be observed for a working to be successful. A summoning spell is very complex and precise. Proper preparation is *essential*. If so much as a single element is incorrect or missing," snapping his fingers, "the ritual fails and woe to the unfortunate magus responsible for that failure."

"Finchley smoked a joint," Cassandra reminded me. "Broke a fast intended to amplify their powers by purifying their minds, bodies and spirits. Which meant the summoning was only partially successful. Next time..."

"And there *will* be a next time, rest assured. They will keep trying and as long as the Brethren are divided, impotent, no one will act to prevent them and one day..." He took a deep breath before continuing. "These people, Skorzeny and the others, are committing a crime against their *species*, their treachery unprecedented in human history."

"I can't believe those idiots believe they'll somehow be able to *control* their friends from Dimension X. How stupid can you get?"

He nodded. "It is part of the conceit deliberately built into the Working. It gives the mage a false sense of security, reassuring him that *he* will be master once the portal is opened. It promises limitless power but it is a *lie*. A lie that has fooled the likes of Crowley and Parsons and many others down through the ages."

"If they succeed and these things break through into our world, then what?" I saw them glance at each other uneasily. "Cass thinks they'll either breed us for food or crush us like ugly, pink bugs. What sort of hell on earth are we talking about?"

"That is anyone's guess, I'm afraid." He leaned forward so he could see me. "But ponder this, if you will: whatever world these beings create will be a reflection of their cruel and terrible natures. They are voracious, brutal beyond imagining. Once they secure dominion over us they will undoubtedly turn on each other. It is the way of their kind. Each wishes to reign supreme. There will be many wars and great destruction. They will annihilate one another. And the rest of us in the bargain."

Great. "But you guys have dealt with this before, right? Back in '47? So there's, like, a contingency plan, something to prevent this shit from happening...why aren't you nodding?"

His response was beleaguered. "Our enemies have shown great cunning and foresight. The Brethren are divided, ineffectual and I...am isolated. I have a few agents still loyal to me, running down leads, doing surveillance, but this is not sufficient. Your help will, of course, be invaluable. Particularly now that you are fully apprised of the situation. As for our prospects—"

"We have other resources as well," my partner confided. I thought of our pal Sherlock Holmes and the love-struck Edwin Fuchs. Were they the best we could do? I was starting to think Winston Gillette had the right idea and now would be a good time to fuck off to some remote cabin in the woods with a good-looking hooker, a bag of pot seed and a thirty-year supply of stag films. But when the world is coming to an end, Armageddon raining a shit storm from the sky, *where do you run*?

The weather had warmed up so the car windows were partway open. Philippe started to say something but at that moment there was a sound like bacon frying on a red hot skillet. Werner took both hands off the wheel and clutched his head. He twisted around and I saw something that looked like a blue, glowing starfish attached to the left side of his face. It stretched from the bridge of his nose almost down to his Adam's apple and was still wriggling about, trying to secure a better grip. Amazingly, Werner's long-sealed mouth burst open on one side and he moaned, spitting blood and shredded bits of his upper and lower lips.

"*Out! Both of you!*" Philippe shouted.

I shoved open the door on my side and prepared to bail. "Werner," I hollered, "slow down!" And even with that thing eating its way through his face, Werner instantly obeyed, throwing us forward in our seats.

"Go, my friends," Philippe commanded urgently. "They have come for me—" Something flung itself at his window and tried to squirm through the opening. Another one of those starfish beasties, moving like a giant spider—"*Va! Allez! Go! GO!*"

I grabbed Cassandra and we tumbled out of the vehicle. As we got to our feet, Werner looked back at us and I nearly puked. He had managed to pry the bogey off but it had taken most of that side of his face with it. "Go, Werner—*Aauuugh!*" Again, Werner's instincts and training kicked in and they careered away, leaving us there, a spot not far from the industrial area, if my nose wasn't deceiving me.

The car hurtled off into the night.

Cassandra and I looked at each other as if to say *what next*?

"C'mon, partner," I finally said, "we're a long way from home. Let's see if we can find a ride." Not exactly words of comfort, I know.

But I made amends by letting her cry on my shoulder in the taxi all the way back to our building. Held her hand and whispered comforting lies, kissing her chastely and surrounding her with brotherly arms.

Moping about the office, waiting for something else to happen didn't suit our mindset so we adjourned to the nearest pub to consider our options.

Once we got to *The Blind Owl* and were served our drinks, it was time to put our cards on the table. From where I was sitting, things didn't look too good and I wasn't one to beat around the bush.

"So...I guess we can rule out the Brethren making like the cavalry and arriving in the nick of time." She was sipping a lime and soda while I demolished a pitcher of some Canadian brew they kept on tap. Good stuff. I treated every gulp like it was my last. Which, considering our situation, probably wasn't a bad idea. "Still," I continued, "it was decent of Philippe to break his vow or whatever and clue us in to what's going on. Even if we already knew most of it."

"Don't pretend to like him all of a sudden," she said, her tone peevish.

I raised my hands. "Hey, it doesn't matter what I think about ol' Philippe at this point. Clearly, he can't help us and even if he manages to get away from those things, he's alone, no backup, no *nothing*. Are you sure you don't wanna order something stronger?"

She shook her head. "I think you're being too pessimistic. Maybe it's not as bad as you think."

I was amazed. "Really? Have I mis-stated the facts? Please correct me if I'm wrong but am I not being reasonably accurate when I say, with some measure of confidence, that we don't have a snowball's chance in hell?" I drained the rest of the beer in my mug and used the pitcher to top it up again.

"At least I'm going to face whatever happens with a clear head."

"So am I," I countered. "This stuff's like rocket fuel to me, babe." I toasted her and guzzled a significant portion of the brew. "Damn, that's good." I smacked my lips happily.

"You're a barbarian, Nightstalk," she said, but with obvious affection.

I raised my mug again. "It's us against the world, kiddo. Let's eat, drink and make merry while we can. For tomorrow—" It wasn't funny any more. "Well, who knows." After a few moments she touched her glass to mine.

"'Us against the world'?" she echoed. "What else is new?" We toasted each other's good health and drank deep.

After a decent interval, I returned to the matter at hand. "What's our next move?"

"We have to find out what our adversaries are up to," she replied. "When they're going to attempt the next working. Right now, we're operating completely in the dark. We *need* information."

"How do we manage that?" I poured the rest of the pitcher into my glass. "Seems to me that since the Cabal put out the word, our sources have dried up and that includes your white magic crowd. We can't so much as get our palms read in this town. Even the cats..." I didn't say it.

"Maybe you should slow down a bit," she suggested. "Yes, the cats would come in handy right about now. Their disappearance was the first clue that something was amiss, we just didn't realize it at the time."

"There are no such things as coincidences," I recited, right on cue.

"I'm glad I've finally converted you. Now, to answer your earlier question about what we're going to do, let's just say I have a couple of ideas on that front. You'll be happy to know that one of them allows you to fulfill a lifelong fantasy."

I had an inkling of what she meant. "Really? D'you think you could arrange it? *Nah*, why would she agree to see somebody like me?"

"We'll name drop. Mention Philippe, threaten her with public exposure if we have to. She'll see you, even if it's only out of curiosity. She was the Baron's ally and might be willing to spill the beans, especially," grinning, "to her number one fan."

I chuckled. "What about those other ideas you mentioned? When do I hear *them*?"

"They're still in the theoretical phase." Playing it coy. "Nothing to get excited about. Yet."

"Just don't try to fly solo on me. We're a team and don't forget it."

"You're drunk."

"Am not."

"And argumentative."

"Am not."

She slipped on her coat, retrieved her purse. "I'm off."

I was instantly suspicious. "Where? I told you I wanted us to stick together--"

"Relax, Nightstalk. You sound like an old lady." She looked down at me. "You've got your sources, I've got mine. Most of the people I'll be talking to wouldn't appreciate your humour. See you tomorrow. By then you should have an appointment with your dream girl. Try not to drool and ruin the company's good name."

"No promises," I belched. "I've wanted that woman since I was a boy. She made me into the man I am today." I winked. "And that's sayin' something." We both cracked up. "Yes, indeed," I eyed her lecherously, "I've always had excellent taste in women."

"Ha ha. Save it for your starlet." She surprised me by bending down and kissing me on the cheek. "For luck," she told me. "And lay off the beer."

Before I had a chance to say anything, she was making for the door. Striding away on those impossibly long legs of hers, as beautiful a sight as you will ever see.

I thought about ordering another pitcher but found I'd lost my taste for it. Settled up our tab and left.

I drove around awhile, saw no one, accomplished nothing.

Caught myself yawning, decided to call it a night. Turned in well before dawn, falling asleep quickly and deeply. Didn't notice I'd dropped off, seemed like I'd just closed my eyes and all of a sudden I found myself back in the dream--

I hear harsh breathing, catch a glimpse of it charging again.

Somehow it has gotten behind me and I barely have time to react, spinning and sidestepping, but not quickly enough because I feel its abrasive hide scour my ribs right to the bone. I howl and clamp my arms around its neck, wrenching backward with tremendous force, practically cheek to jowl with the lizard-thing, close enough to hear a decisive crack. *The creature goes limp and voids its bowels down my pant legs.*

Nice....

This battle has been a costly one, two fingers missing from my right hand, bitten right down to the knuckles. I should be bleeding like a bastard but I'm not. There's just this throbbing sensation where my fingers used to be. My left side is an open sore from my nipple to my hipbone. Conversely, it hurts like bejesus. *Feels like I've been scalded, the slightest movement aggravating the peeled flesh.*

But at least I'm in sight of the base of the Tower. I trot toward it as fast as a couple of broken toes, a twisted knee and sprained ankle will allow. Chorazin has turned out to be no fun at all.

Now that I've achieved my first objective, I find myself more wary than ever. I'm as tense as a spring, waiting for a rush from my blindside, one last monstrosity to contend with.

Or maybe—I cast a worried glance upward—the attack will come from above, one of those flying gargoyle things swooping down, gathering me up and bearing me away.

But to my surprise, I reach the base of the Tower unchallenged.

There're no guards waiting, no hooded figure blocking my way until I answer a seemingly insoluble riddle. Of course, there's still the matter of the fifteen hundred steps I must climb and then once I get to the top—

Hmm, yes, well, that's where it gets tricky. I know many things about this place but as to what's waiting for me up there on the summit, I am completely in the dark.

I begin the ascent, making slow progress. My ankle, in particular, gives me a bitch of a time. I pause, thinking: this is nuts, I should stop and rest awhile. *I'm in the process of easing myself down on to the cool stone steps when, from somewhere above me, I hear Cassandra Zinnea screaming...*

II

"So hell has regulations to enact?
Good, for with law a man may make a pact,
Then why not with you gentlemen of hell?"

Johann Wolfgang von Goethe; *Faust, Part I*
(Trans. by Philip Wayne; Penguin Books, 1987)

Thursday, May 20th

I had to hand it to my partner, she was resourceful *and* she worked fast. When I arrived at the office that evening there were two phone messages from Marcia Stegner, personal assistant to Vivien Vickers. I had butterflies the size of fruitbats as I dialed the number.

"Yes, this is Marcia Stegner. Are you Mr. Nightstalk?"

"Uh, yes, I am. Is, uh, Vivien there?"

"Ms. Vickers is here, Mr. Nightstalk, and she's very anxious to speak to you."

That threw me for a loop. I hunted around the desktop for something to fiddle with. Settled for tying knots in a large metal paper clip. "I guess, uh, that would be all right. Sure. When, uh, would be, uh, convenient to, uh—"

Mercifully, Marcia Stegner didn't wait for me to stutter and stumble my way to the finish line. "How about tonight? I can give you the address and leave your name at the gate. They'll let you in."

"Tonight?"

"If that's all right." My hand shook as I wrote down her directions. "Vivien will look forward to seeing you. Shall we say an hour or so?"

Done.

I hate gated communities.

Even if I was a kazillionaire and could afford to live in one, I wouldn't. People say they like the extra security but *I* say if you want to feel safe, get a fucking dog or install deadbolts on your doors. Or buy a gun. At least that way you get to retain your independence. It would drive me crazy stopping every day, going and coming, to show some rent-a-cop my pass. How much actual "security" did that guard represent? When push came to shove, would he put his life on the line for a bunch of filthy rich assholes who drove past him every day, barely acknowledging his existence?

And was it really a question of security or do people of a certain class want to separate themselves from the rest of us? An elitist thing. I've lived in Ilium for years and I've noticed a growing divide between rich and poor, with the number of people in between shrinking fast. Middle class? What's that? The middle class are as extinct as passenger pigeons. Someone should put them on the *Endangered Species* list.

West Point Hills had a gate. A big wall around it too. The "Hills" are a few klicks northwest of the city. I wouldn't really call them "hills", they're more like *mounds*, modest elevations that, admittedly, offer a lovely view of the city and ol' Erie. The slope was barely noticeable as I steered the Taurus on to what I thought was the right off-ramp. I had been to West Point twice previously[26] and felt as out of place there as a skunk at a garden party.

The kid at the gate checked my name and asked for photo I.D. but that didn't satisfy him either. Something about my face, I guess. He ended up calling the house to confirm my appointment. Once Marcia vouched for me, he hit the electronic gate release and waved me through. I waved back, smiling and thinking to myself *you over-efficient buttfuck asshole...*

I drove slowly, ogling the mansions people had erected in celebration of their own success. There were some real monstrosities, proving that rich

---

[26] "The Affair of the Choking Doberman" (*The Casebooks of Zinnea & Nightstalk, Vol. II*) and, most recently, to investigate the bizarre circumstances of Horace Dalrymple, the bogus amnesiac, in "The Man With No Clue" (*Casebooks, Vol. III*).

people have no more common sense or good taste than us poor folk. But everything was kept neat and tidy, each blade of grass regulation length, every square foot landscaped.

I didn't see anyone out walking. I didn't see anyone *period.*

Vivien Vickers' house was reached by an S-shaped driveway cut through a wood of pine, birch and poplar. It created a natural setting despite its close proximity to a city of a million plus people. The screen siren's residence was far less ostentatious, at least outwardly, compared to its neighbors. It resembled an over-sized cabin, rustic and uncomplicated. Its most impressive feature was the wide, spacious deck that extended out over a steep ravine.

She'd recently divorced husband #4 (a real estate tycoon from Phoenix) and professed to be "single and intending to stay that way" (this according to *Entertainment Weekly*). In the article she didn't sound bitter or resentful about getting out of the acting game. She did complain about the constant wear and tear of living in the limelight.

"I always swore that when I retired from pictures I'd come back to where I spent the best years of my life," she told the *EW* reporter in what was touted as an "exclusive" interview.

I thought she was jumping the gun. Admittedly she was in her mid-50's but she still looked fucking *great.* Maybe the makeup had to be applied a bit more carefully and the lights placed just right, but she could still put a rocket in your pocket when she turned on the vamp.

In one of her last (and weakest) movies, "Seducing Mrs. Henderson", she played the sexually alluring next-door neighbor of sixteen year old heart throb Justin Delveccio. During their steamy encounters--that always ended up getting comically interrupted--she *smoldered,* irresistible in a midriff-baring shirt and cut-off shorts that accentuated those incredible gams of hers. I loved the final scene and watched it over and over. The kid finally gets her naked (the blankets discreetly draped) and has his golden opportunity to screw her...but he doesn't because she's on the verge of passing out, too tipsy to know who she's making love to. You never see so much as a nipple, just an enticing V of cleavage, the curve of her supple ass as he takes one last, longing look before closing the bedroom door behind him.

Now here I was, pulling up in my rustbucket Taurus, popping by for a bit of a chinwag with my old pal Vivien Vickers, queen of my wet dreams, closet Satanist...and maybe, just maybe, someone who could put us *inside* the Cabal. *If* she was amenable and inclined to help...

I parked my car behind a late-model Jag and a Mercedes big enough to transport a platoon of storm troopers. Walked past a roomy, three-door garage. One of the heavy doors had been left rolled open; I could see expensive mountain bikes, a pair of matching surfboards, a stair climber and a top of the line *Nautilus* workout station.

A woman, petite, early forties, leaned out the front door. The outside light was on so I got a good look at her. She was fit, attractive, clad in jeans and a t-shirt with that famous shot of Che Guevera silkscreened on the front. "I love the house," I called, "but those big windows must be hell to keep clean."

"You ain't whistling Dixie, bub. You're Mr. Nightstalk, is that right?" I walked up the steps. After we shook hands, my palm came away damp. And soapy. She laughed. "Sorry about that. I've been doing dishes. C'mon in." I followed her inside. "We're pretty informal around here. There's a gardener who comes by a couple of times a week during the summer to do battle with our mortal foes, crabgrass and dandelions. A cleaning woman pops in every Friday to get the places we miss. Everything else to do with the day-to-day running of the place we try to handle ourselves." We went through the living room and into the kitchen. That part of the house faced east, toward a glitter of lights that was Ilium. Beyond that was Erie, represented by a pool of darkness that reached to the horizon. The view at sunrise must have been spectacular. If you were into sunrises.

"You're Ms. Stegner, I presume."

She glanced at me as she went to the sink. "Oh, yes, sorry. Marcia Stegner, Viv's alter ego or personal manager or *bete noir* or chief bitch or whatever you want to call me. To the people who know and love me, it's plain old Marcia from Peace River country, Alberta."

"So you're her manager—"

"*Personal* manager. She also has a business manager and publicity manager and so on and so forth. But we'll be streamlining operations soon. I'll be taking on a larger portion of the duties and responsibilities. It's a relationship, a partnership really, based on the mutual trust and respect we've developed over the past--"

"*Slave!*" Someone bellowed from the deck. "We need more daiquiris out here!"

She looked at me and we burst out laughing. "Impeccable timing, as always."

"Was that Ms. Vickers? I think I recognize those dulcet tones."

"She's having a few people over tonight. You can go out and join them whenever you're ready."

"I need to speak with her about a...personal matter."

"She understands. She's also aware that you have friends in common. She's anxious to talk to you about that and a number of other things. But, in the meantime, she's got some shmoozing to do. Some of these people might be willing to sink capital into a production company we're putting together." She held up tightly crossed fingers. "Tonight we're laying the groundwork. An informal barbeque and a few drinks with film legend Vivien Vickers. It was my idea. Some one-on-one contact with Viv, building the whole intimacy and trust thing and then we hit 'em up for the loot."

"Are you a bit coked up?" I ventured to ask.

"Shit," she giggled, "does it show? I thought it would loosen me up. Is it too much?"

"You're okay. But you're acting a touch speedy. You should take a minute, chill out, maybe smoke a joint. That is, if you've got any on hand."

"We do. And...I might."

I took a deep breath. "Well, I guess I should go and meet the lady herself. Bask in the glow of her fame and glamour."

"Ooooo, she'd *hate* that," Marcia predicted. "You're better off wiping your ass with one of those fancy Amish quilts she collects." She covered her mouth. "Did I really say that? Maybe you're right about the joint."

"Go for it. Listen, before I go and maybe make a fool out of myself..." I paused. "How *do* I treat her? She's this big star but she's retired, right? Dropped out and all that. On the other hand, how do you behave in front of a legend?"

"Do what I do," she advised, drying her hands. "Treat her like a classy older broad. Don't try to bullshit her and for God's sake don't *ever* try to upstage her or step on her lines. Be a good straight man and if you can't do that, shut up and laugh at her stories and you'll be fine. Anything else?"

"Do I bow?"

"Only if you want her to give you a good, swift kick in the butt." She pointed. "It's through those doors. And next time you come in, to use the john or whatever, bring in more of those fucking dishes."

"I'm scared to death right now," I admitted.

"Her bark is worse than her bite. Now *scoot*."

I opened the screen door and stepped out on to the deck. It was a gorgeous night, the air more refreshing back here in the hills, filled with scents unfamiliar to a city slicker like me. I thought she'd picked the most beautiful spot possible for her house. There was some ambient light pollution from Ilium but you could still see the stars, even make out constellations.

Supper was over and the barbeque shut down. *Dang.* So Vivien Vickers, two-time Academy Award nominee, wouldn't be serving me a burger on a bun and asking if I wanted relish or mustard on it. A number of people were sitting on wooden deck furniture or in canvas director's chairs.

And there she was, by God, in mid-anecdote about a gay leading man with a voracious sexual appetite and a young intern who got trapped in an elevator with him—

"Yes? And you are?" Addressing me in a familiar voice, regarding me with eyes I knew so well.

I couldn't think of anything to say. Stood there like an idiot, trying to come up with something, *anything* to fill that yawning silence. Then I remembered "The High Price of Murder", a *noir*ish thriller she did with Willem Defoe and Sean Young. "I'm the private dick."

Her eyes lit up: "Who sent you?"

"The prince of darkness. Who do you think, lady?"

"He wants you to take me back, is that right? Well, I won't go back. Not without a fight. I've got three quarters of a million dollars in a suitcase and I'm offering you half to forget you ever saw me."

"Is that all?"

"What else do you want?" Her eyes flashed just like they did in the movie; it was uncanny.

"You have a nice face."

"You weren't looking at my face." The killer punch line. I read somewhere she improvised it right on the set.

Our audience burst into applause, a bald-headed guy leaping to his feet in excitement. "I remember that scene! Wonderful! Wonderful!"

"Evgeny Nightstalk, ma'am." I held out my hand and she gave it a business-like squeeze.

"We'll talk later," she murmured. "But for now, join the party." Then, for the benefit of the others: "To be honest, you're a little on the short side but your glove size reassures me." Everyone laughed, including me. "You're a good sport, Mr. Nightstalk. Meet the gang. This is Art Forzani and his wife Rita. That's Albert Tomczak and Sheree Siedler...Adam Philpott..." From their watches and personal jewelry and the cars out front, I figured this to be a pretty well-off bunch. Turned out Tomczak owned a chain of steak houses and Forzani was a retired investment banker and Sheree Siedler the daughter and heiress of a drugstore magnate...

"I'm sorry, Mr. *Nightstalk*, is it?" Rita Forzani sized me up. "I didn't catch your line of work."

"My line of work..."

"Exactly what is it that you do?"

"Er...security consultant," I fudged.

"Really? Private security? Are you a bodyguard?"

"Sort of. I'm more involved on the technical side of things these days. Ever since I took a bullet down in Ecuador." Rubbing my shoulder for dramatic effect. "It's classified so I can't really go into it."

Vivien looked away, hiding a smile, but I could tell Mrs. Forzani was impressed. "Sounds fascinating. Maybe you could use Mr. Nightstalk's experiences in one of your future projects, Vivien."

"You never know. What do you say, Evgeny? Would you like to be one of my...projects?" She handed me a wine glass, making sure our fingers touched.

I was flummoxed. "Well, um, that would depend on the fine print."

"Come on, be honest. Wouldn't you give up your soul for me?" Angling her face, using those eyes. No sorcery, no spells, but bewitching just the same.

I hoped no one could tell I was blushing. "Let me put it this way, Ms. Vickers." To buy time I slurped some of her plonk. I wouldn't know a chardonnay from a bucket of cold piss but it tasted okay to me. "Under the right circumstances, I can't imagine how *anyone* could resist you. But my soul? That comes with a mighty hefty price tag attached."

I excused myself, went over and took a seat next to Adam Philpott.

After that, I tried to fade into the background, watching as she very expertly put the screws to them. She wanted to make *serious* movies for *serious* movie-goers. Romantic comedies, mysteries, maybe even tasteful erotica. Films for adults rather than comic book adaptations and endless sequels. She promised to come out of retirement, as well as rope in some of her high profile buddies. She didn't drop any names but she didn't have to. We knew who she meant. Or thought we did.

Her pitch was solid and when she finished, her listeners responded enthusiastically. I didn't see any checkbooks come out and most of the dollars and cents talk was pretty vague. This was a getting acquainted session. A first date. The seduction would proceed in stages until (it was hoped) there would be a consummation satisfactory to the various parties involved.

I made myself useful by ferrying plates and glasses to the kitchen and filling drink orders. Automatically assuming my natural station in the great pecking order of life.

Around 12:30, after a subtle signal from her boss, Marcia started closing things down, reminding Vivien that she had a busy day ahead of her. The guests took the hint, rising and going inside to collect their coats and purses. I remained on the patio while they said good night to everyone, perfect hostesses to the end. Vivien extricated herself as swiftly as possible and rejoined me, fixing herself a *real* drink this time, a stiff vodka martini. Then she seated herself about eight feet away, so that we were facing each other. I watched as she made short work of her martini; was she nervous too?

I think she was waiting for me to initiate conversation but I wasn't exactly holding up my end of the bargain. My tongue was snarled in a Gordian knot, my brain on temporary hiatus. *Say something, make small talk.* I couldn't. Worried it would come out sounding stupid or sycophantic...or weird. We could hear Marcia inside, trying to get rid of the Forzanis. Clearly, they were the most star-struck of the lot.

I couldn't take my eyes off her. It was hard getting used to being that close to *the* Vivien Vickers. I mean, she was *right there*. I could go over and touch her (if I had the nerve). Who could you compare her too? Meg Ryan? Too cute and perky. Kathleen Turner? Closer, and they both had dynamite voices. Not beautiful in the classic sense but something eye-grabbing about her, a sensual quality with a hint of playfulness that made you fall for her that much harder. I realized that the special lenses and key lights only accentuated her natural attributes. Some people are *born* to be movie stars and she was one of them.

"I like the way you look at me." I jumped. "A bit lustfully but mostly it's sweet and romantic. You have a boyish quality to you, Mr. Nightstalk, no matter how rough around the edges you may be." Marcia Stegner came outside and joined us on the deck. "Is that it?"

"Yes, m'lady."

Vivien yawned. "Nice people. I think we made some excellent progress."

"Oh, definitely. They were still talking about it as they were going out the door." She produced a cigarette and lit up while her employer looked on enviously.

"That's pure evil of you, Marcia. You know I'll be tempted. Go smoke it somewhere else."

She looked hurt. "Wait. I'll put it out. I'll sit over here and you won't even—"

"*No*. Mr. Nightstalk and I prefer to have this conversation alone. In private."

"But—"

"This doesn't concern you, dearie, so make yourself scarce." Marcia was finding it hard to believe she was being dismissed. She left in a huff, trailing cigarette smoke and wounded feelings. "She'll get over it," Vivien said. "She still hasn't learned the fine line between where her responsibilities leave off and my personal life begins." She pointed at me. "And you're a liar, by the way. Admit it, buster, you'd sell your soul for an hour in the sack with me."

I hung my head in mock shame. "It's true. And something tells me it's a deal I wouldn't regret."

"*That* I guarantee. And I've got some ex-husbands who'll testify on my behalf, plus a few others besides. Used 'em up and cast 'em aside."

Which segued nicely into another long silence, my mind working like mad to come up with something worthwhile to contribute to the conversation.

Once again, a line from one of her movies came to my rescue: "'Honey,'" I recited from memory, "there's no place far enough and no mountain tall enough to keep me from finding you—'"

She joined in and we finished it together. "'—and then I'd do whatever it took to win you or buy you or steal you...and bring you back to where you really belong'." She beamed at me, her face glowing even in the meager, subdued light cast by the Chinese lanterns strung around the deck. "Oh, Mr. Nightstalk, you *are* a romantic devil."

"I loved that film," I confessed. "It was a bit corny but you were great."

"Yes, you're right. I *was*." I got the point. "The guy in that picture, Milt, really does sacrifice everything for her, doesn't he? Looks for her to the ends of the earth and when he finds her, she's nothing but a scraggly, fucked up junkie--"

"But he still loves her," I reminded her. "He refuses to give up on the soul that might somehow still live on inside her, no matter what she's seen and done."

"I get the feeling you're that sort of guy too." She leaned back and looked up at a sky full of stars. "Lately I've been thinking quite a bit about souls..."

"Yeah? Anyone's in particular? Artie Esch's maybe?

The air seemed cooler and the night just that much darker. She sat up, suddenly attentive. "Have you heard from Philippe lately?"

"Not for a while," I lied. It killed me that she'd actually let the guy boink her. "I'm aware that he, um, met with you a couple of times and that you and the Baron both had concerns about the direction Skorzeny was taking the group."

When she spoke, her voice was flat and lifeless. "He told you that?"

I nodded. "We talked to the Baron too. I know Philippe was trying to recruit you to serve as an informant. After the Baron was killed, he needed someone else inside the Cabal, feeding him information. Those meetings you had--"

"—were personal. And none of your damn business." Eying me coldly. "Have you been *spying* on us, Mr. Nightstalk? Is that how you get your thrills?"

"You've definitely been under surveillance but not by me."

She made a face. "Wonderful. Everyone spying and eavesdropping on everybody else. It makes it hard to know who to trust, doesn't it?" I didn't have an answer and she didn't expect one. "Yes, I met with Philippe. He pushed me hard to cooperate but I wasn't in a position to help. In the back of my mind there was always this little voice telling me it's not a good idea to get on the wrong side of...certain people."

"I understand."

"I doubt it. It's complicated." She finished her drink. "Where is Philippe now?"

"I don't know."

"Is he dead?"

I hesitated. "He could well be. I don't know that either."

"God help us." She buried her face in her hands. It seemed very real to me, completely unrehearsed. "Ah, Mr. Nightstalk," she sobbed. "What have I gotten myself into?"

I waited for her to pull herself together. It didn't take long. She wasn't the weak-kneed type; I liked that. While she dabbed her eyes and blew her nose, I enjoyed the clear, beautiful night and the two million-dollar view.

"How much do you know?" she asked at last. Cassandra and I had talked it over and agreed that I was not to mention anything to do with the Babalon Working—it might spook her--and, instead, try to focus on Skorzeny. I kept it short and sweet, giving her the bare bones synopsis without providing needless details that might trip me up later on. When I finished, she sagged back in her chair, desolate. "So Philippe is out of the picture, the Baron and Artie Esch dead and the rest of us left to fend for ourselves." She turned her face away, angry and shaken. "I must say, Mr. Nightstalk, if you drove all the way up here just to tell me that, I wish you'd saved yourself the trip."

"I know how you feel."

"Hopeless. It's completely hopeless."

"I don't disagree. But I think Philippe had the right idea. We need someone on the inside who can tell us what Skorzeny's up to and maybe prevent--"

"*Uh uh*, Mr. Nightstalk. Not a chance. You see, I'm out. I quit. I don't want anything more to do with those people. It's different from when I joined. Victor and Gregory have total control and no matter what they do, no one raises a word of protest. They're terrified of what will happen to them. I've...*seen* things. Freaky, spooky things. And for that reason, even if I *were* still a member I wouldn't help you. Ask one of the others. Benes, the human steroid, what a fucking moron. Finchley—*Finchley*, that quivering bowl of jelly. If Skorzeny so much as coughs, he craps his pants. Kali Brust, our resident nympho. Trust me, you don't want to know what they use her for. Those are the type of people you're dealing with. I'm on the outside, have been for months." She looked at me beseechingly. "There were things that happened that I had no part in. Decisions made without a quorum, without any discussion. But nobody says a word. Everyone's so scared. *Because you never know what might come after you.*"

"What about Esch? The Baron? Where's the justice if--"

"*I had nothing to do with that.*" Her voice was shrill. "I didn't know, I swear it. I'm no adept, for Chrissakes! I'm an actress with sagging tits and an ass heading south faster than a flock of migrating geese, all right?" She was pretty convincing. I wanted to believe her. "I'm all alone out here. That's why I can't give them any reason to come after me. These are very powerful people we're talking about, Mr. Nightstalk. Powerful and scary beyond belief and it ain't a good idea to piss them off."

"Okay," I conceded. "I see your point. You're don't wanna do anything that's going to risk this big deal you're putting together, your big comeback—"

She was outraged. "That's bullshit and you know it!"

"Isn't that why you got involved with the Cabal? To make contacts for this production company of yours? Or am I simplifying things?" I guess I was trying to rattle her, shake something loose.

"You bastard." She looked away. "But...I suppose you're right in a way. I've felt...useless ever since I left L.A. I'm a very driven person and coming back here, hanging around the house all day...it's *boring*, Mr. Nightstalk, and I can't stand being bored. I was into some heavy occult shit on the Coast for awhile but sort of drifted away from it. The Baron got me interested again. The Cabal—until the Fischers came on board—was pretty tame compared to some of the fucked up stuff I got into in my 20's." Marcia was lurking at the screen door, getting an earful. Vivien sensed her too. "Marcia, quit listening at the keyhole and bring me one of those cigarettes."

"No, Viv," Marcia whined. "You're right, I shouldn't have shown them to you."

"Bring them out here, girl."

Marcia dragged her feet and protested but in the end she complied. "You'll hate yourself later," she predicted.

Vivien lit up and waved her away. "Be gone, missy. And this time no eavesdropping or I'll take away your company car." She pointed at me. "As for you—"

I raised my right hand. "I see nothing. Temporarily struck blind. Not a word about your foul habit shall cross my lips."

"Under penalty of death." She took a long drag. "It helps me when I'm stressed. I keep a spare pack in my sock drawer. Marcia doesn't know about those."

"Yes, she does," her assistant called from inside.

"I'm warning you..."

"Okay, okay." The glass door slid shut with a petulant *snick*. I didn't think it was any of my business to mention the open kitchen window.

"Been under a lot of stress lately, have you?"

"It's getting cool again, isn't it? And it was so nice there for awhile. They say it might rain."

"If you're worried about me talking, spilling my guts to the wrong people, don't be. One of the things I'm known for is my absolute discretion."

"How long have you been in love with me? Tell the truth." She was deliberately throwing a monkey wrench into the conversation and we both knew it.

"I don't know." I did a mental calculation. "More years than I would care to say, for both our sakes. Let me put it this way: on the wall directly behind my couch I have a full-size, pristine poster of 'Five Million Miles To Venus'."

She looked wistful. "None of that is stuffing either, mister, no retouching with Photoshop or any of that crap." Chuckling. "But that was...a long time ago. Nowadays I get calls to guest star on soaps as somebody's long lost mother." She wrinkled her perfect, turned up nose. I read somewhere that Susan Sarandon once said she would kill for a nose like Vivien Vickers'.

"So you chose retirement rather than suffer the indignity."

She winced. "You make me sound like a prima donna when you put it that way but...that's basically what happened. It wasn't that I was sick of making movies, being a star, even a fading one. There's something special about a film set, the intimacy you get when you bring together a group of artists and creative individuals. The atmosphere is incredibly stimulating and exciting. Magic, in a way."

"Why leave that world then? And why come to *Ilium* of all places? What's with that?"

"Haven't you heard? I'm originally from Trent, just a few miles south of here. Born and raised there. Ilium is practically a second home to me. I can't tell you how many fish I've pulled out of that oily, toxic lake down there."

"I hear there's something special about the ley lines or whatever in this region."

She smirked. "Maybe, but it sounds like bullshit to me. I came back here because I know the area *and* it's far enough from New York and L.A. to escape their fucked up karmas. But, like I said, that got old pretty quick and then I met the Baron through Winston Gillette—he ran a local bookstore here in town until it burned down a few days ago." She stubbed out her cigarette. She'd hardly touched it. "I know what you're doing, Mr. Nightstalk. I've done interrogation scenes before. You're trying to develop trust and empathy between us. But then I weigh that against Victor Skorzeny and what he represents and, I'm sorry, you don't measure up." She leaned forward, wrapping her arms around her knees. "You won't get any cooperation from the others either. Witcover, Mayhew--"

"What about Rache, where does he fit in?" She looked puzzled. "Herman Rache. You don't know him?"

"Isn't he a lawyer or something? I think I've heard of him."

"So you haven't run across him?"

She shook her head. "Skorzeny's the one to watch out for, believe me."

"What about Gregory Fischer?"

She snorted. "Mr. Moneybags? Fucker's as rich as Croesus and not shy about showing it. Moving our meetings to his fucking tower, building a special room, having everything *catered*. Frankly, I think we were getting tired of the Baron's puny sex magick. Sitting around and playing the occult equivalent of spin the bottle. Some of us wanted action and Victor was only too happy to oblige."

"Tell me more about Skorzeny." She eyed me nervously. "You say he's the one who really scares you."

She hesitated. "He overwhelms you. Very dramatic, the way he sweeps in and takes control. He likes to shout and bluster and get in your face. A natural bully and terrifying when you get on his wrong side. I'd stay away from him if I were you. You're a tough nut, Mr. Nightstalk, but compared to him..." She left it hanging but I got the message.

"Is he the one that's been pushing the Babalon Working?" I took a chance, went for broke.

She didn't answer right away. Fished the butt out of the ashtray and relit it. Jittery, no question. She looked over at me and I saw fear but something else too. This dame was tough—she didn't *like* being afraid. "Well, well, so you know about that too. You're very good. All along you've been playing dumb." Her hand trembled as she raised the cigarette to her lips. "Fischer's crazy about Crowley. And Victor pretends to be the world's foremost expert on old Aleister. I think that's what brought them together in the first place. They—both of them--believe in this whole idea that the human race needs to evolve, take that next step. It's all about will, *thelema*. We must assume god-like powers to go along with the great advances mankind has achieved through its animal cleverness. That's something Victor said, almost word for word."

"Bringing back those ancient gods is gonna do that? They're deluding themselves."

She shrugged. "Crowley said: 'As a god goes, I go'. That about sums up what they're after. The Old Gods, once they come, will make their allies masters of the Earth. After all, that still leaves the rest of the universe for them to lord over. Why should they begrudge one small, backwater planet to the people who freed them from eternal confinement?"

"That's nuts! And the others bought it? Why?"

"They showed them *miracles*, Mr. Nightstalk. At meetings they...manifested things. Objects flying around, disembodied voices...it was fucking creepy and it scared the living shit out of me. There have been some nights here when I've felt something behind me or heard it walking around in another part of the house."

"You're sure it's not—"

"No, Mr. Nightstalk." Shaking her head vehemently. "No. These people have access to unnatural power and they're not afraid to use it.

Skorzeny claims he's raised an elemental that he controls and manipulates. Ready to do his bidding."

"Meaning no one is safe from him."

"Exactly. So keep your mouth shut and go along for the ride. And that's exactly what we did. Even the Baron and I, for all our plotting and scheming. We were afraid and we did *nothing*. Complicit in our cowardice."

A feeling of gloom descended, settling over us like a cold, wet blanket. "The Baron, at great personal risk, alerted the Brethren," I pointed out. "You talked to Philippe. That was gutsy. At least give yourself credit for that."

"All it did was get Frederick killed. As for me...meeting Philippe was foolish. Pointless. I'm fed up, Mr. Nightstalk. I want *out*. I thought maybe Philippe had sent you. That was going to be my message to him: thanks, but no thanks. Like my daddy used to say, it's time to hunker down and wait for the storm to blow over. And that's just what I'm going to do."

"You could run."

"I've thought about it. I have friends all over the world. There's a gorgeous chalet in Liechtenstein or, how about this, a treehouse in a rain forest. A hundred feet off the ground with all the amenities of home, including satellite TV, hot and cold running water and bananas growing right outside my bedroom window. I went there with Andy, my second husband. Where's Marcia when I need her? I want another smoke." A disapproving cluck from the kitchen window. "Fuck you, Marcia."

"Language," her personal manager chided. "If you want to pry another cigarette from my yellowing grasp, you'd better be nice to me."

"Do you want something else to drink, Mr. Nightstalk?"

"I'll pass. I've got to drive back to town."

"Very responsible of you." She poured the dregs from two different wine bottles into her glass. "Since I live here, the same rules don't apply." Marcia clucked again but it had no effect on her strong-willed employer.

"Anyway, wine isn't really my drink of choice."

"I noticed. You nursed that one glass all night. You could have asked for something else."

"I, uh, didn't want to distract you from your sales pitch. I enjoyed watching you."

"You haven't stopped looking at me since you got here, d'you know that?" Turning it up a notch, staring at me over her glass, making heavy duty eye contact.

"That...doesn't surprise me."

"Tell the truth: would you like to fuck me?"

An exclamation from the window. "Okay, kiddo, I think it's time we packed it in for the night."

"Stay out of this, Marsh," Vivien Vickers commanded. "Well, Mr. Nightstalk, I'm yours if you want me. Just say the word."

I felt uncomfortable. I knew it wasn't a serious pass but there was something behind it, a need I felt I had to address. "I think it's the best, most fantastic offer I've ever had. I'm...deeply honoured."

She got up and *walked* toward me and, man, it was something to see. She stood in front of me—she wasn't that tall, so when I got to my feet we were just about nose to nose.

"This isn't funny, Viv. I'm coming out there." Scuttling footsteps.

"What do you think, Mr. Nightstalk? Does the old girl still have it?"

I looked at the face I'd kissed hundreds, maybe thousands of times, the eyes I'd stared into rapturously for hours on end. "I think if we made love, it would be the one spell I'd never, ever be able to break. I'd be yours, body and soul. And that's no lie."

She smiled, brought her hand up and touched the side of my face. "Oh, Mr. Nightstalk, that's the nicest rejection I've ever gotten." I heard Marcia sigh with relief and retreat, muttering under her breath. "There's someone else, isn't there? And you're utterly smitten with her."

My face reddening. "I would have to say that's true."

"Does she know?"

"We don't...well, we try not acknowledge it. She's—my partner."

She made a sympathetic sound. "One of *those* relationships. It must be tough on both of you." A cagey smile. "Is she stunning? I guess she'd have to be."

"She is. She is that," I agreed.

"But you loved me *first*," she reminded me, "and those are the ones you never forget."

She walked me out to my car, which I thought was swell of her. I still wasn't past the star-struck stage and couldn't think of anything sensible to say as we stood beside the Taurus, wishing each other good night. Turned out she was a Shade too and didn't usually hit the sack 'til after 4:00 a.m.

I was trying figure out a way to tell her—what? How seeing her all those years ago had stirred something inside me, made me sit up and start taking notice of the many fascinating differences between boys and girls (and *vive la différence!*). Instead, I spouted some mealy-mouthed bullshit, mumbling my thanks as I groped for the door handle behind me. She put her hand on my arm.

"Mr. Nightstalk," she said, "please kiss me goodnight. The way you want to. The way you've always dreamed of kissing me." Marcia Stegner was likely skulking in the bushes somewhere nearby but I didn't care. I gathered her against me, she wrapped her arms around my neck and it got pretty torrid for the next minute or so. We didn't hold anything back, going at it with our mouths and tongues, grinding against each other, oblivious to the rest of the world.

When we eased off to catch our breath, I saw stars. Fireworks, roman candles, the whole works. A real light show.

Neither of us was in a hurry to break our clinch and spoil the mood. "Thank you," I breathed. "*Wow.* That was incredible. Now I know what Nick Nolte meant in 'September Rain' when he says: 'Every time I look at you I feel like nothing else matters'. It's true. I couldn't put it any better than that."

She smiled. "You're a sweet, darling man, Evgeny. Is it okay if I call you that?"

"Sure. But, honestly? To most people, it's 'Nightstalk'. Don't ask me why, that's just the way it is."

"I'll try to remember. And don't call me 'Ms. Vickers' or 'ma'am' again or I'll rip your nuts off, *comprendé*?"

"Well, since we're practically engaged anyway..."

She giggled and finally detached herself from me. "I might be on the lookout for husband number five so you'd better watch yourself, pal."

"I'm not in the same league as those other guys."

"You're a world-class kisser, kid, and that helps overcome a lot of social barriers." She waved to Marcia, who promptly ducked out of sight. "I'm going to have to lay down the law to that girl."

"She's looking out for you."

"Do you have a business card, some way I can reach you?" I dug one out of my wallet and gave it to her. My sweaty fingers made the ink smudge. "If you see Philippe, tell him—well, tell him to be careful." In a pig's eye, I thought, but nodded and said I would. I opened the car door and stuck a leg inside. "Nightstalk." The light spilling from the car's interior cast long, crooked shadows. "I keep telling myself this is all a bunch of medieval mumbo-jumbo and there's nothing to worry about. That's what I want to believe."

"I used to think that way too," I acknowledged.

"But you don't any more?"

"No. I don't."

"Good night." She started walking toward the front door.

"Good night, Vivien," I called. "Look after yourself."

She gave a sort of over the shoulder wave but didn't look back.

Coming down from the Hills I kept replaying everything in my head, trying to permanently preserve the choicest impressions of my night with Vivien Vickers. I hadn't taken a camera or tape recorder or made any notes. I would have to reconstruct the conversation from scratch when I wrote my report.

I was only half-paying attention to my driving, reliving that parting kiss. I nearly ran two red lights. Bad news when you're behind nearly two tons of Detroit steel. *Calm down, boy. Keep your mind on the traffic or you'll end up chewing on some citizen's rear bumper...*

It was nearly three when I got back to the office and 4:30 by the time I was finally satisfied with the state of my report and stuck it under the Old Man's door.

There was no sign of my partner and no phone messages either. Freelancing again, damn her. Keeping everyone, including me, in the dark. *Grrr.*

When I got home I fixed myself a good, stiff scotch, plugged in a movie and tried to unwind.

Except I found I couldn't focus. The girls did their best to keep me entertained--willing mouths, straining breasts and glistening vulvas--but I couldn't get into it. Opened a beer to chase the scotch and sparked a joint. Northern Lite, good Canadian bud. I needed it. I was so damn *restless*. I ended up pacing past Tree once too often and she lunged out, taking a not-so-playful nip at me. I decided for the sake of my personal safety to find a different patch of carpet to wear out.

Bored with porn, I switched to cable. Flipped around and came in about halfway through "The Big Sleep". Robert Mitchum redeeming an otherwise spineless remake of the Howard Hawks classic (they even shot it in London, for fuck's sake!). His Marlowe world-weary, cynical, hangdog. An older, seamier version of J.J. Gittes. Both have seen the worst aspects of human nature, endured betrayal and lost their faith. True *noir* heroes: bitter, sentimental, tragic. You just *know* neither of those guys is going to end up with the Girl.

The combination of reefer and booze finally took their toll. I lost track of the plot, which can happen with Chandler even if you're *not* pasted. That Canadian ganja has a powerful kick to it. I lolled back on the couch, nearly comatose. Mitchum, I recalled, was busted for pot possession in the 1940's and it nearly wrecked his career...

Onscreen, Mitchum/Marlowe regarded me with disgust. "Hey, are you paying attention out there?" His voice was faint (I had the sound turned down). He cupped his hands over his mouth. "Are you listening to me, boy?"

"Fuck off," I muttered. "You're only, like, fourteen inches tall."

"You're all messed up. kid. Take a look at yourself. So wasted you hardly know who you are. It's pathetic, man."

I yawned. "You, sir, are a dead actor in a fictitious role in a second rate movie made thirty fuckin' years ago, all right? You got zero credibility with me."

"Look at me, watch the way I am in this turkey. I play Marlowe *strong*. When someone hits him, he hits back. He doesn't play it safe, he *acts*."

I raised my head. My vision was blurry, like someone had snuck in and rubbed vaseline on my eyeballs. "Is there a point to this or are you just flapping your gums?"

"You gotta do the same. Your side's been taking some big shots. It's time to start doin' somethin' about it. Scare 'em a little. Let 'em know who they're dealing with."

"No problem." I grinned. "Which one you want whacked. Skorzeny? You got it. Rache? Just say the fucking word."

He grimaced as he lit up a cancer stick. Unfiltered. "It doesn't matter *who* you hit, dope, the point is givin' the other side something to think about. You savvy? You've been taking it on the chin too long. They're fuckin' with you, man, and you're letting them! Rache and that crowd made with the threats and you sat there like a big, fat dunce." He exhaled a cloud of smoke. "You wanna be a tough guy, you gotta act like one."

"I stared him down, asshole," I slurred. "You weren't there so you don't know shit."

"It's time to let your fists do the talking."

"Not right now. I'm too stoned."

"Just as long as you take care of business. Now if you'll excuse me, these hombres wanna have a word with me, doncha boys?" He nailed one goon with a looping left hook and soon punches were flying and it was right around then, I think, that I passed out...

--ankle completely buggered at that point, swollen, unreliable, barely able to take any weight. And I'm only halfway up the Tower, my progress

maddeningly slow. Every time I think about taking a breather, I hear those screams again, echoing inside my head. Grit my teeth, lurch and hop up five more steps...ten...

Seems like I've been climbing for hours but there's no end in sight. It's taking forever to reach the top of this stupid, motherfucking black spike and in the meantime they could be...they might be...

I don't want to think about it.

Keep moving, no stopping. Cursing myself, cursing them, crazy with pain and fury and fear as I hobble up that endless stairway, vowing retribution with each agonized step I take.

I woke mid-afternoon, still retaining a clear memory of the dream, including a phantom ache in my right ankle. I had a slight hangover too, nothing serious. Splashed cold water on my face and had a nip of the hair of the dog. Mr. James Beam and ice.

The hangover was a minor nuisance but the dream really bugged me. There was no pay-off, no resolution. And on top of everything else I was *still* jumpy. Just like before. A low-level anxiety that I couldn't trace to any obvious point of origin and couldn't shake no matter how hard I tried.

The daylight hours dragged past. It was like watching tennis. In slow motion.

I gave serious consideration to donning sunglasses and heading in to the office early in case there had been any developments. Unfortunately, it was one of those clear, lovely spring days; I nearly burned out my retinas when I peeled back the tin foil on the bathroom window to check. If there had been a decent overcast, I might have chanced it.

Around seven I judged it dark enough, bolting the apartment, shades firmly in place. I made a beeline for midtown, keeping an eye out for cops. By luck and some quasi-legal maneuvers I hoped wouldn't be caught by nosy traffic cameras, I made it in good time. The steep canyons created by Ilium's modest skyscrapers provided welcome shade, a perpetual semi-darkness. I removed my sunglasses and set them on the seat beside me.

I waved to Tara who was using her finger to demonstrate how to fit a cock ring to one attentive customer while talking nonchalantly on the phone to another. *Not bad.* Maybe the kid had a future in the sex industry after all. I bounded up the stairs, deftly avoiding that feral third step.

The phone was buzzing. Our private line. Cassandra wasn't in yet so for once I'd have to do the honours. I crossed the floor and answered. "Yes, sir. Nightstalk here."

I always thought the Old Man sounded like Gregory Peck. Clipped, stern, authoritative. Like an old time sea captain. "Mr. Nightstalk, I'm afraid I have some rather disturbing news to pass along. It appears Ms. Zinnea has been snatched up and spirited off to parts unknown." I sagged into my chair. "I thought you'd like to hear this in person as opposed to an impersonal memo."

"Yes, sir," I replied automatically. "Thank you, sir."

"This situation is simply unacceptable, as I'm sure you agree. Ms. Zinnea is one of our own and I need not impress upon you the importance of finding and retrieving her. I have every available resource devoted to that task and I know I can count on your participation, as well."

"Yes, sir. Absolutely. As you say, completely unacceptable."

"Are you all right, Mr. Nightstalk?" That sort of pierced the fog. "I get the feeling you haven't fully grasped the situation."

"No, sir. I mean, yes, sir." I paused, thought about what I was trying to say. "It's just that...since last night I've sort of had a premonition something was wrong. I just didn't know *what*."

"Indeed. Well, regardless, it is important that we move with alacrity to ensure her safe return."

"Do I have *carte blanche* on this one, sir? Can I use whatever means are necessary up to and including—"

"Do what you have to." His voice possessed an extra dimension, a depth and resonance that made the receiver vibrate in my hand. "Bring her home safely and punish those responsible. Good evening, Mr. Nightstalk. Oh, and do keep those progress reports coming. I find them *most* stimulating reading."

I hung up.

"Okay," and I actually said it out loud, "the main thing is not to get strung out about this. I gotta stay calm and think rationally."

Which one of those cocksuckers has her? That fuckhead Rache? I'll kill him, I'll rip his fuckin' throat out. Ditto the ferrets. Skorzeny? I'll save him for last. Go bowling with his big, bald head, elemental or no elemental. Fuck him. Fuck them all...

The anxiety, the restlessness I'd been experiencing: had she been trying to send me a message, a distress signal transmitted on our private channel?

What were they doing to her? Where was she? How was I supposed to find her? None of the street snitches would talk to me and—and--

Things were coming at me too fast, there was too much to assimilate. I needed to take a step back, get some perspective before my pent-up emotions broke loose and I did something completely stupid and irresponsible.

But I kept imagining what indignities they might be inflicting on her at that very moment. It was totally fucking with my higher brain functions. I couldn't *think*, let alone come up with a plan or formulate any ideas.

I needed help.

Someone with a sharp mind, a person not swayed by emotion, who reasoned with clarity and logic. Unfortunately, I could only think of one potential candidate who fit the bill.

And he, of course, was as crazy as a shithouse rat.

George Simmons came forward to greet me, looking past my shoulder, anticipating the arrival of my partner. "She's gone, George," I kept my voice low, "missing. And I need *his* help to find her."

Simmons nodded, his face reflecting the gravity of the situation. "He's in the library. Stinking up the place, as usual."

I trailed after him. "I hope this guy's the real deal. Otherwise I'm not sure what I'm gonna do."

"Whatever else you may think of Holmes, Mr. Nightstalk," Simmons remarked, "I assure you his intellect is genuine and formidable. If he bends his mind to a task, his assistance can be the difference between success and failure."

"I hope so, George, because right now I feel like I'm grasping at straws."

We left it at that.

Sherlock Holmes didn't waste any time. "I see from your demeanor that matters have taken a turn for the worse. It is as I feared. You are facing a very determined and dangerous foe. Your partner--"

"They took her."

"Yes, Mr. Nightstalk, that much is obvious. But there is one notion you must disabuse yourself of this instant: she was not abducted. In all likelihood, she *allowed* herself to be captured."

I was dumbstruck. "That's insane! And, besides, how do you know that? She wouldn't have—"

"As a strategy, I admit it is somewhat unorthodox but I must applaud its sheer audacity. Think about it: what better way to ascertain your enemy's aims than by becoming their prisoner? Who knows what sort of information might be divulged under such circumstances?"

"I dunno, Holmes, it sounds pretty fuckin' reckless to me." I caught myself scratching my bald spot again. It was a hard habit to break.

"I know your partner to be highly intelligent and blessed with superb deductive and intuitive faculties. Do you think her enemies could easily trick her into falling into their clutches?"

"But they could be hurting her, torturing her." It nearly killed me saying it.

He frowned. "Yes, that is one possible drawback to the scheme. But it is a risk I am certain she was cognizant of, unless I am very much underestimating her."

It was a nutty tactic and yet on some level it made sense. Fobbing me off on Vivien Vickers, knowing I'd jump at the chance to rub shoulders (or anything else) with my all-time dream wank. And while I was up in the Hills, making with the goo-goo eyes, she was alone, conspicuously alone. A tempting target.

The *wench*.

Damn her and her freelancing! I sure as hell hoped she knew what she was doing.

But now what? Did she have a backup plan for extricating herself once she'd learned all she could? Was there something *I* should be doing?

Christ on a rusty bicycle.

Holmes sounded a note of optimism. "Fear not, sir. If my assumptions are correct, her captors will not act precipitously. They know who her employer is and have no wish to incur his displeasure." Steepling his fingers. "I suspect she is giving the impression of cooperating while offering nothing of any real value. Simultaneously, she is watching, listening, taking in as much as she can."

"But is she counting on *me* to get her out? In which case, I need to know where she is and I need to know *yesterday*." I started pacing, trying to burn off energy.

He was sympathetic. "I'll notify my people. Someone *must* have seen something. After all, she's quite a familiar figure in our fraternity of the night."

"If you don't mind, Mr. Holmes," I said, trying not to offend him, "I'd rather not put all my eggs in one basket." He looked puzzled. "I mean," I added, "can't you think of someone else who might give me a lead, someone I haven't thought of?"

He was doing the finger-steepling thing again. "Finding a missing person is usually the result of an inordinate amount of legwork combined with good luck, Mr. Nightstalk. One must learn to cultivate patience—"

"*Please*, Mr. Holmes. Give me a name, a number, a tip on a horse. *Anything*. I need something to do before I start popping people."

He eyed me nervously, suddenly tuned in to the potential for violence. "Well, ah, in a previous conversation Ms. Zinnea mentioned a 'Hall of Records'. I'm certain that with virtually infinite resources at his disposal, a diligent detective such as yourself should be able to unearth something of value, don't you think?"

I nodded. "I can try. But there are all sorts of rules and they're pretty strict about releasing information that might affect future history. It's kind of complicated.[27] Maybe I can convince Georgie to grease the wheels or whatever. Anyway, it's worth a shot, right?"

"In the meantime, I shall be pursuing my own leads. Give me twenty-four hours. Any longer than that--"

"They'll know we're looking for her and they can't hide her for long. They'll have to either release her or..."

"I'm glad you understand," Holmes said. "Let us hope that through our combined efforts we can bring about a satisfactory conclusion to this affair."

"Right. Thanks, Mr. Holmes."

"Good hunting, Mr. Nightstalk."

I ran into a serious roadblock at the Hall of Records. The ever-helpful, ever-dependable Georgie was in a less than cooperative frame of mind.

"Let me see if I understand you correctly, Mr. Nightstalk. You're asking me to locate a *person* rather than a specific piece of information."

I could see where he was heading and had already concocted a line of argument I hoped would sway him. "Yes, but *technically* the location of a person is a form of information, isn't it? Just another piece of data."

"Miss Zinnea is lost. Missing."

"That—that is correct." I was momentarily distracted when something lime green and jelly-like *oozed* past us and flowed down the aisle, muttering to itself about Spinoza. "And—and it's imperative that we find her quickly. Her life may depend on it. Not just her life...maybe everyone's. It's sort of hard to explain but I'm asking you, no, I'm *begging* you, man, *help me find her*." My voice sounded shaky. At that point I was skating pretty close to the edge.

---

[27] These prohibitions are outlined in more detail in "Tomorrow is the Day Before Yesterday" (*The Casebooks of Zinnea & Nightstalk, Vol. I*)

He gazed at me in mild surprise. "But as I've already explained, this facility is temporarily off-line until we discover the source of the contagion affecting the operating system. Access is strictly restricted. I'm afraid I can be of little service to you." He hesitated. "Might I hazard an observation? You are obviously overwrought. Quite naturally you are concerned about the well-being of your partner."

"Buster," I said, all the built up stress and anger sending me into "Popeye" mode, my shoulders and biceps swelling, a surge of hormones prepping me for violence, "you have no idea."

"*Please*, Mr. Nightstalk," he said reprovingly, "you must restrain yourself."

"Restrain myself?" My laughter echoed for miles. "Right now my partner is gone. *Gone.* Trust me, restraint is the *last* fucking thing on my mind."

"Perhaps I'm being facile but have you tried consulting the authorities?"

"Damnit, Georgie—"

"Please, sir, I *implore* you to keep your voice down."

"I'm about *this* close to snapping, old man." I was maybe a third bigger than my normal size, my Raiders jacket bulging at the seams. My heart racing to meet the demands of all that newly grown muscle, a couple of pints of adrenaline surging through my system like high octane fuel. "I'm tired of getting the runaround. I asked you a question and I want an answer."

"Yes, well, I can see you're certainly, ah, very anxious as to the whereabouts of your—"

I got nose to chest with him, crowding him against the overflowing shelves. "I'm looking for an address, anything in the Records. A building, an abandoned warehouse, maybe a property owned by Fischer or one of his subsidiaries. Do some cross-referencing, see if any likely hits come up. I'm not asking you to change the future, I just want a *clue*."

Georgie shook his head. "That information is readily available from public records, your city's land titles office, for instance, or—"

"*I don't have time for this, Georgie.*" Gritting my teeth. Thanks to that hormonal spike, I was in a murderous frame of mind and his throat was tantalizingly close.

Clearly he was anxious to help but constrained by the very real limits of his job description. "We keep a file on Miss Zinnea, constantly updating it. Perhaps something in there might prove--"

"Oh, come off it, Georgie, you know I can't use those fucking light tables. Especially now, my head is spinning like a top."

"There *are* other formats available." He closed his eyes, concentrating. Snapped his fingers and a file folder appeared in his hand. He gently but firmly guided me over to the nearest study carrel, ignoring my loud complaints.

"I don't wanna look through her press clippings, man." The folder was as thick as a small town telephone book and about as interesting. Had I the time or inclination I could have plowed through a university paper in which she proposed a new version of J.B. Rhine's "Zener" cards (whatever the fuck they were). There were college transcripts, copies of poems she'd written for some student-run publication (I'd read a few, they were quite good, reminiscent of what's-his-name[28]). Some newspaper articles that mentioned her in connection with a number of high profile investigations (I noticed with a twinge that my name never appeared anywhere), as well as other odds and ends...

I slapped the file shut and glared up at Georgie. "I told you there was nothing." I shoved the dossier at him—

--something slipped out and fluttered to the floor.

It was a business card, one I didn't recognize or recall seeing inside:

The Moirae Sewing Circle
112-A Erebus Crescent

I held up the card. "Ever hear of this place?"

He scarcely glanced at it. Seemed...I don't know. Overly noncommittal. *Evasive*. Had no idea how long it had been in the file or how it had gotten there but I was certainly welcome to copy the relevant information. The card itself, unfortunately, couldn't leave the premises. Regulations, etc.

I got the feeling I had used up whatever currency I had with him. Pushed him to the limits of his capabilities. I regretted getting heavy with him. I genuinely liked the guy.

In my defense, I point out that I was preoccupied with saving my partner. Nothing else mattered. If successfully retrieving her meant stomping and fucking over my twin brother, so be it.

---

[28] William Blake (1757-1827)

Still, I made a mental note to make it up to him at some future date. Not because he was an 8th Degree and as powerful as God, but because he was a gentle man who deserved far better from the likes of me.

Thanks to the time dilation or whatever you call it, I exited the Hall of Records only a few seconds after I'd gone in. Even though it was almost eight-thirty, I decided to check out that sewing circle. I figured I didn't have anything to lose.

The address I'd copied from the card put the place somewhere uptown, an older, working class district. Poles and Slavs, mainly, with some Dutch and Scandinavians thrown in for variety. Onion-shaped churches and the best sausage in town. Twenty minutes later I pulled up in front of an ailing four-plex just off John Carter Way. There was a broken awning over the front window and ugly rust stains on the siding. The roof was in rough shape too; apparently the sewing business hadn't been very lucrative lately.

It was past closing time, so I wasn't too sure if anyone would be there or what sort of reception I should expect. Another cool night and I told myself that was the reason I had goosebumps the size of strawberries as I reached out and pressed the bell.

A stout woman in her early sixties answered my summons. A nice, normal-looking lady, that was my first impression. Wearing a frumpy, shapeless dress with a fringed shawl draped over her shoulders. She smiled at me through the screen door. "Yes? Can I help you, dear?"

"I know it's after hours or whatever but…I found your card and I don't really understand how or why, but I think maybe you can help me. You see, I'm looking for a friend and maybe you know her or have some idea where I can find her…"

It sounded distinctly nutty to me but the woman didn't seem alarmed or taken aback. "Chilly tonight. Why don't you come in?" She held the door open and moved aside to let me enter. She was quite hefty and I had to squeeze past her. Each of her bosoms was the size of my head. "We were just about to close for the day. But Addie said someone was coming so we waited for you."

There were two other elderly women in the living room. They looked ancient, with sharp, bird-like profiles. Each was engrossed in some kind of craft work. The oldest, a sweet little granny who had to be over eighty, caught my eye and *winked* at me. She was crocheting something with odd, stylized lettering on it that reminded me of runes. My hostess took a seat in a comfortable green armchair and began knitting at a furious pace, sparks flying off the tips of her needles as she added to the huge sheet of wool already piled up before her. The old doll on her left was regarding a single strand of thread with careful consideration before raising a small set of scissors and cutting it. Her hair was pure white and so thin you could see her pink scalp in places. When she looked up, she had the saddest eyes I had ever seen.

They didn't seem overly concerned about having a stranger in their living room. The big gal with the knitting smiled encouragingly, beckoning me forward. "Come on, don't be shy. We won't bite you." She addressed the others. "This gentleman says he's looking for a friend."

"Hot in here, isn't it?" It was the frisky old doll with the crocheting. "If you wanna take your shirt off, that's all right with us." The others cackled along with her and I felt myself shrink six inches.

"I—I'm trying to find Cassandra Zinnea. Have any of you seen her recently? Has she been here? I found your card, uh, with some of her things." Glancing at each of them, watching their faces.

The frisky one waved me over. "I'm Addie. I know you," she stated, "who you are. Know all about you. I like your spirit. Always looking for trouble. Tempting fate, hmmm?" She grinned. "Maybe you'll tempt us once too often and then—"

"Snip, snip," the one with the scissors finished for her, snicking the set she was holding for dramatic effect. "And that's all she wrote."

"Right. Okay, listen up, everyone." I must have sounded pretty stressed because they peered at me attentively. "I think you all know who I'm talking about. Cassandra Zinnea. Our star player, all right? The whole franchise. Without her, we, us, the good guys, we're *fucked*. Plain and simple. They kill her and it's game over. So if any of you old broads has the slightest fucking idea what I'm talking about, speak up now. That's— that's all I have to say."

Addie leaned forward and touched my arm; her fingers were big and tough, like cured leather. "I'll help you, dear."

"I'm not sure that's wise, sister," her chubby sis fretted. "It seems a bit... irregular." Her scissor-wielding colleague seemed inclined to agree. If they weren't careful, I'd smother the two of them with one of the flowery, over-stuffed cushions they had lying around.

"Oh, Chloe, why not? It's been *ages* since we had fun with one of them." She peeked at me over her bifocals. "Make your request in the form of a question, young man."

"*Where is Cassandra Zinnea?*"

Addie's crocheting needles responded immediately, the hooked ends dipping and looping so fast, they were a blur. It quickly became apparent she was creating a *map*. I detected the outlines of a city and recognized Ilium. More details soon emerged; as I bent over her handiwork, I saw, threaded through it, a crosshatching of silvery streets and avenues...and a tiny but distinct red X marking a spot—

I straightened, impulsively giving her a kiss on her soft, plump cheek on the way up. "Kid, you just became my adopted grandmother. I'll send you flowers on Mother's Day and call you every Christmas, I swear."

I headed for the door and Chloe hauled herself to her feet, trailing after me. She seemed worried. "We're not supposed to help people like that. I'm afraid this will turn out badly."

"You let me worry about that, granny, " I told her. Pausing on the front step. "Hey, just curious, but how often did my partner come by this place?"

"Your partner?"

"You know...Cassandra."

"I don't think I know her. Is she an older lady?"

I let it go. "Hmm...well, never mind." Rubbing my chin. Stubbly. Overdue for a shave. "Wonder how your card got in there with that other stuff..."

"Be careful dear," Chloe called after me. She was definitely bugged about something. "What Addie did...it might cause...instability...paradigm shift...possible—"

But I was in a hurry and didn't catch the rest of it.

The area was familiar to me. It was in the same neck of the woods as an adult video store I sometimes frequented for its excellent selection of girl-on-girl stuff. So I knew the territory, I knew the objective. What I *didn't* have was a plan.

I tell a lie. My "plan" was, basically, storm the place, rescue Cass from the bad guys and, oh, yeah, kick the living shit out of anyone who got in my way. It was working out the smaller details that was bogging me down.

I stopped by the office first, chafing at the delay while recognizing its necessity. I dug out the card Holmes had given me and called the Diogenes Club. George Simmons answered but within moments Holmes was on the line. The master detective took the news of the existence of such things as the Moirae sisters and their sewing circle with nary a comment. He said he'd dispatch some Irregulars to assist me, provided any were sober and ambulatory. He made no promises. As we talked, I sketched out a rough map of where Cassandra was being held, scribbled a few details on the bottom and slid it under the Old Man's door.

Then it was time to get it on.

Pounding down the stairs and thinking to myself: *this is more like it.* There was a maiden to rescue, a good chance some level of violence would be required *and* I was in a lousy mood. So anxious to be on my way, I almost failed to notice that my mysterious tail was back. A tingly feeling on a dime-sized patch of skin on my neck gave him away.

Fuck it, whoever it was was welcome to tag along. By that point I was beyond caring, merely making a mental note that if and when things heated up, to watch my back.

I circled the block in question, my trusty nose sussing out the target building right away. The place used to be a pharmacy, I'd been inside once or twice, buying smokes or what have you. Not a great area for a *drug* store, it was always getting held up or broken into and the owner, a kindly Korean gentleman with the work ethic of a plough horse, threw in the towel after getting stabbed and shot once too often.

There were iron shutters over the windows and a chain and padlock secured the front doors. No lights inside. I parked, got out and crept down the alley--

Bingo. Signs of life: a bare bulb, clean and new, freshly installed above a sturdy, metal door. Its yellow, diffuse light shining down on a blue Chevy van, backed to within five feet of the building.

I pondered the alternatives. Part of me was all for crashing through that door and letting the chips fall where they may. A wiser voice counseled restraint. There were no screams coming from inside, nothing to indicate the need for hasty or ill-considered action. The second voice had kind of a poofy quality to it but it *was* persuasive.

I ambled around to the front to have another sniff there and discovered a couple of kids skulking near the corner. They had skateboards under their arms and were still pumped from "bumper-shining" rides on buses and cars from halfway across town. I asked if they were "friends of Mr. Holmes" and their faces lit up like Christmas trees.

"That Holmes guy is way cool," the kid with the bleached yellow mohawk confided, his tone reverent. He introduced himself as Ratfuck and his friend as Shit. "And I mean the original Shit. He's the first. He's been Shit for, like, *forever.*"

I took his word for it.

Shit had what looked like a giant bolt through his nose. He was tattooed, pierced and branded and had the body odour of an incontinent rhino. But at least he didn't talk much. His buddy, however, more than made up for him. "Are you, like, on a case? Is that why you wanted us, man?" Ratfuck was speeding on something and couldn't a) shut up or b) keep still. Some part of the guy was constantly in motion: mouth, hands, head, feet. Completely spastic.

What the hell. Truth to be told, I didn't require them for their brains or social skills.

We wandered down the block while I formulated a strategy. Ratfuck, to my intense annoyance, kept up a running monologue of *non sequiturs*. Within no time I learned they had just been booted out of their "squat", that they were "binners" (people who scrounged through garbage for anything worth selling or recycling) but not "panners" (panhandlers) and that both of them were into "urban exploration".

"It's fuckin' rad, man, you should come and try it sometime. I've been in sewers and old factories and warehouses, not to mention on top of, like, just about every fuckin' building you can name."

"Sounds like trespassing to me," I said. "Nobody invited you or gave you permission to be there. You're lucky someone doesn't shoot your ass."

"No, man, it's way cool," Ratfuck hastened to assure me. "Because, like, to me 'n my buds, there's no such thing as private property, right? Property is theft. We *all* own the earth, man. You can't just draw a line and say, like, this part is mine and that's yours. Mother Earth will not be *subdivided*." Shit nodding in mute agreement.

What a pair of dolts.

Somehow I managed to steer the subject back to the matter at hand. I told them what I had in mind and, to their credit, they quickly grasped the essence of my plan and, I must say, carried out their assignment to near perfection.

We took up stations near the rear entrance. I gave them the signal and they went completely *apeshit* on the van. It was almost comical because within a matter of seconds they inflicted some serious fucking damage. They ripped off the side mirrors and kicked big dents in the doors and fenders, all the while howling like maniacs.

I heard someone yank the deadbolt from inside.

"Go!" I urged from my hiding spot. The Irregulars took off as the door was flung open and three goons came boiling out. They took one look at the van and tore after Ratfuck and Shit, who were making for the end of the alley, setting a world record pace by the look of it. I wasn't worried on their account. I figured the goons didn't stand a chance against such fleet-footed, street smart prey.

In the midst of the ruckus I slipped inside and found myself in a short hallway. If I kept going, it would open up into what used to be the main retail area. But there were doors leading to what were presumably storerooms and office space so I checked them first. I dug out the fetish I'd brought with me from *After Hours* and went from door to door, holding it up to each of them. When I got to the last one, the fetish started vibrating in my hand.

Gotcha.

I heard voices from outside. The chase was over, the winded pursuers returning to their posts. The door in front of me was locked but I kept twisting the knob with increasing pressure until something inside the mechanism broke and I pushed it open.

The room was small, stuffy and windowless. My partner was sitting on a foldout cot, appearing tired and drawn but otherwise no worse for wear. She smiled at me, then turned to the man standing a short distance away. "See? I told you he'd come."

Victor Skorzeny scowled at me. "You are…Nightstalk."

"That's right," I said, heading toward him, intending to grab the front of his high-collared cape and shake him until he was spitting teeth, "otherwise known as your worst fucking nightmare."

"Nightstalk, wait—"

"Save it. Your rescue team is here and it's time to—" At the point where my hand should have made contact with solid flesh, it didn't. I stared in amazement as my fingers passed through him. "What the fuck…"

Skorzeny gazed down at me contemptuously. The projection was perfect, I saw every pore on his bald head, could practically smell him. "You are a fool."

There wasn't time to figure it out; the bully boys were at the back door. "Ready, partner?" I asked, pumping up in anticipation.

She sighed. "I suppose so." She glanced at Victor Skorzeny and shrugged. "Sorry about this. Nightstalk is about to cause a lot of unnecessary mayhem, I think."

"Oh," I said, flashing a fiendish smile, "I think you can count on it."

The warlock was fading away, losing definition. "Remember my words…and heed them."

I wasn't listening. The lads were coming down the hallway, grumbling and swearing. "There's no other way out of here. Front door's padlocked. Which means we gotta go through them."

"I don't suppose you'd consider--"

"*No.* Stay right behind me."

"Try not to hurt them too much," she begged.

"This is your final warning," Skorzeny said, only the blurred, indistinct outline of his body still visible.

"Oh, blow it out your ass, ya fuckin' twat."

Then things started happening in a hurry—

As far as fights go, it wasn't exactly the "Thrilla in Manilla". Lots of yelling and screaming and cursing, a bit of the old wham-bam and maybe a spot or two of blood. There were no weapons involved, so nobody got killed or permanently fucked up.

Truthfully, those lads might've had bazookas or a fucking M-1 Abrams tank for all I cared. Mr. Mitchum was right: it was payback time. The fact that Cass showed no apparent ill-effects from her ordeal made me hold back, but only a little.

I flung myself at those poor, unsuspecting bastards like some kind of stone crazy berserker. I gave this primal scream, a *howl* of pure bloodlust that was so unnerving one of them, a blonde guy in a *Dead Kennedys* t-shirt, fainted from sheer terror before I laid a finger on him. The others tried to flee but got tangled up in the narrow hallway and then I was on them.

I used my fists like flesh pistons, driving them backward, shouting and screeching and falling all over each other. And bleeding. And pissing themselves. It reminded me of the two weeks I once spent working on the floor of a slaughterhouse just outside Kansas City. Don't ask.

But I didn't whup anybody *too* badly or stomp them once they were down. In that sense I thought I displayed real, uh, waddayacallit, *restraint*.

After I had dispatched the last of them with a rather brutal version of a Glaswegian handshake that left me sprinkled with blood, we regrouped beside the van. I was panting and grinning from ear to ear.

Cassandra, on the other hand, looked like she'd just witnessed the equivalent of My Lai. "I'm *appalled*. That was simply the most over-the-top, unnecessary, excessive display of violence I have ever seen. It was too much, Nightstalk."

"It tells them to stop fucking with us."

"Or take us more seriously and rub us out."

"Spoil sport."

She wouldn't lose the frown. "*Honestly*, Nightstalk, they were just about to release me. They delivered their message and put on their little show and I was being let go as a good will gesture to the Old Man. I take it he's been raising a stink."

"He gave me a free hand, told me to do what was necessary to get you back. Unmuzzled the ol' pitbull." I couldn't get that goofy grin off my face. "And so the whole point of this entire exercise was—what?"

"To get the Old Man's attention. It's not us they're worried about, it's *him*. He's the wild card in the deck and they don't like it."

"Clearly these people don't know who they're dealing with. That kidnapping shit just pissed him off. If they were trying to keep him from taking sides, they went about it the wrong way, I'll tell you that."

She was about to answer when we heard a groan from the doorway behind us. "Let's continue this in the car."

I trotted along beside her. "Did they treat you all right? Lots of threats but nothing...nothing physical, right?"

She bumped me with her shoulder, knocking me off stride. "I'm tired, Nightstalk. I haven't slept in nearly two days. They gave me that stupid cot but it was too short. My feet dangled over and I couldn't get comfortable." She yawned. "This turned out to be a bit of a bust. I was hoping for more information, some hint of what they're up to. As it turned out it was hardly worth the--um, ah--" She winced, realizing her mistake.

"*Aha*!" I yelped. "So you admit it! You *allowed* yourself to get caught, just like Holmes suspected. You deliberately put yourself in danger. Goddamnit, you *promised* you wouldn't fly solo and then went ahead and did it anyway."

She put her hand on my arm. "Nightstalk—"

I shook it off. "And that shit with Vivien Vickers. Using her as a distraction. That was low, Cass."

She stopped. Stood there with her head down. So fucking contrite. "I'm *sorry*. Sorry I had to trick you. Sorry for going it alone. Won't happen again, I swear."

"I've heard *that* before."

She gave me a playful shove. "But it did give you a chance to come and save me, right? Don't tell me you didn't *love* roaring in there and kicking butt." She had me there and we both knew it.

We got to the Taurus. "Where to now?"

"They seemed obsessed with the Old Man. Kept asking about him. First Rache, the creep, and then right before you showed up, Skorzeny materialized. Same story. They're worried about him, trying to figure out what part he's going to play in all this."

"That's something I'd like to know too." I started the car. "One of these days we gotta break into that office of his." She regarded me with alarm. "To find out who he really is," I went on. "We've talked about this before. Because we really don't know anything about him, right? How he gets his information or why he seems so fucking omnipotent at times. He could be a supercomputer for all we know or—"

"—maybe he's another one who managed to escape the net in '47." I was poleaxed by the idea. "It's just a possibility," she added, "but it would explain the Cabal's interest in him."

"But wouldn't that make him...*evil*?"

"I keep telling you, morality is an out-moded concept to these beings."

"Did you pick up any clues from Rache and Skorzeny? Did they give anything away?"

She chuckled. "Mostly it was just bluster. Rache...I see what you mean about him. *Nasty*. I thought he was the main attraction but then, about half an hour ago, I see this flickering out of the corner of my eye. Then, *poof*, there's Skorzeny. Maybe the best case of bilocation projection I've ever seen. I get queasy just *thinking* about how much power that represents."

"So they threaten you and pump you for information about the Old Man. Anything else?"

"Well..."

"*What*?" I was about to put the car into gear but changed my mind. "Listen, maybe you'd better tell me about it..."

She'd been expecting them to try something and made it easy for them by hitting all the hot spots, starting with Ilium's one and only Nazi punk gay bar, *When in Roehm*. After striking out there, she cabbed over to *Baudelaire's Withered Cock*, where they first made contact.

I could picture her, dancing like a dervish, smoking hookahs of potent hashish and swilling real absinthe, sugar-coated poison that scrambled the senses and fuelled electric dreams. Every so often popping counter-agents, philtres of her own devising, to stay clear-headed.

She caught the attention of a gorgeous blonde guy, eyes of sapphire blue and the shoulders of Arnie Schwartzenegger's big brother. How could she resist when he steered her toward the door, telling her he knew of another place, *very* underground. There was likely some enthusiastic groping and necking in the taxi (mercifully, she left that part out).

This new dive didn't even have a name. He referred to it as Cabaret X and said it would blow her mind. It was situated in a third floor loft of a condemned building, accessible via a rickety fire escape. Most of the inner walls had been bashed out, creating a decent-sized space that was throbbing with electronica.

The loft was jam-packed, air thick with illegal smoke and free-ranging pheromones. A strobe light pulsed in time to a percussion-heavy dance track, everyone laughing and seemingly having a great time—

--*freezeframe, the revellers caught in mid-gesture, forming a sentence they would never complete. The people around her began losing colour and focus, fading away.*

She told me there were accounts from medieval times of whole castles, appearing as solid and three dimensional as the real thing, constructed out of sand and fog by enterprising wizards. The effect so authentic that many were taken in by the illusion, which included banners and music and scores of men and women who waved merrily at hapless passersby, beckoning them closer...

Her mind was seized in a vice-like grip, her defenses swiftly overwhelmed. Truthfully, she put up only token resistance. All part of her "plan".

Someone hurried forward to steady her before she keeled over. Her blonde hunk. Who smiled apologetically, slung her over his awesome shoulders and carried her down the fire escape just as easy as pie. A blue van was waiting at the bottom. Into the back she went; someone threw a blanket or sleeping bag over her before they sped off. She took the opportunity to eavesdrop on their unshielded thoughts, snooping for any relevant tidbits. They drove for at least half an hour and by the time they got to the pharmacy she had pretty much picked them clean. Interestingly enough, the blonde dude still had designs on fucking her.

Her kidnappers were employees of a private security firm hired by Rache & Co. Low-level thugs with no clue of the bigger picture. Worker drones. They were supposed to bring her to a particular location and hold her until further notice. That was it.

Her captors banged on the back door of the pharmacy for five minutes before someone inside heard them and opened up. They'd been watching a wrestling match on a tiny portable TV. What a bunch of fuckups.

They stuck her in a room with some bottled water, a cot and a clock radio with a busted antenna. If she had to use the bathroom, someone escorted her to one down the hall. The building was humming with magical energy, she sensed damping spells and defensive screens. So even if she *had* been sending for help, a psychic SOS, it would've been bounced right back.

They kept her waiting all that night and most of the following day. Finally, just after supper—"canned tomato soup, yecchh!"--Rache came in and went to work on her like the sleek, smooth cobra he was. He never mentioned the Babalon Working or Gregory Fischer's name. Totally focussed on the Old Man. She fed him morsels and kept her guard up the entire time. At last he smiled, gave a bit of a bow and left. After that, another long, boring interval before it was Skorzeny's turn to do his thing.

"I told you before, I've never been that impressed with Victor," she remarked. "I thought he was a complete poser and phony. But to manage a projection of that sophistication and maintaining it for as long as he did…it's nothing less than remarkable."

There was something different about Skorzeny, she sensed it from the moment he fully materialized. He radiated power and dark energy as he stalked about the room. But he was also acting in a bizarre manner, lurching, visibly struggling to retain his balance, his movements and gestures jerky, unnatural. His eyes bulged for no reason and his speech patterns were erratic.

"It was weird. The worst impersonation of a human being I've ever seen."

"So you think something's taken him over, like Benes."

"He as much confirmed it himself. As a matter of fact, it was one of the first things we talked about."

"Go on…"

"We will…not be dissuaded," Victor Skorzeny stated. He was pacing vigorously and sometimes misjudged the dimensions of the room, walking through a wall and popping back out again. "Your employer would be wise to…join us. These are…exciting times. We would compensate most generously. You will…ask him to consider."

"I'll do that. But couldn't you have just written him a letter?"

He glowered at her. "I do not understand. You will explain."

She leaned forward on the tippy cot. "You want to know what I think?" He nodded, resuming his circuit of the room. "Well," she went on, "I think you're an ancient being, a supernatural entity that's masquerading as a second-rate black magician. I believe you have taken over the body of Victor Skorzeny and assumed his identity. Do you have a name? A designation? Something you call yourself?"

The Skorzeny-thing smiled, sort of, showing his understanding. "For now, I refer to myself as Aiwass. This will suffice."

"Aiwass? Why have you come here, Aiwass?" The expression on the being's face was one of utter bewilderment. "What is your function or purpose?"

"Ah." Comprehension. "I am the Opener. The one who comes before. I cannot adequately explain. Your words are...insufficient. Your mind could not grasp."

That nettled her. "You'd be surprised what my mind can grasp. Look, I don't know if you're aware of this, but the Brethren of Purity know all about your plot to bring the others back from exile. If you think they're about to let you—"

"The Brethren are not relevant," Aiwass said. "You are not relevant. As to your employer...he must play no role in what is to come. His cooperation will be... appreciated. This is the message you are to convey. And tell him...some of my colleagues do not share my patience. He would be wise not to...provoke them further."

"I don't think that's going to—"

"And now a demonstration." He extended his right hand and a fluttering pennant of flame sprang from his fingertips. Fire flowed up his sleeve and soon his whole arm was burning, the blaze spreading across his chest and back and then to his face, his features enveloped and consumed. "I am Aiwass. Behold! Look upon me in wonder and dread." Lips of flame, eyes that sparked and popped within a burning skull. "You will not prevent me from my task. *And let it be known that I will destroy all who oppose me.*"

She held out her hands to the car's air vents and I saw they were shaking. Not just from the cold. I shifted into gear and got us underway. "As if the bilocation wasn't impressive enough," she muttered.

"Was that it?"

"Pretty much. Once he made his point he changed back and—well, that's right when you came busting in and started beating people up."

"Your gratitude is duly noted and appreciated."

"You *did* kind of overdo it, don't you think?"

"Says you." I sulked until we were within a few blocks of the office.

"Oh," she finally spoke up, "I forgot to mention. Skorz...I mean Aiwass implied—more than implied, really—that I should consider switching sides. Join the winning team. Just thought you'd want to know."

"You're kidding. They didn't offer *me* any—" She stifled a giggle. "Okay, smart ass, so what was the deal? How did he pitch it to you?"

"He didn't get specific. I imagine it was the usual thing: eternal life and ageless beauty, getting to lord it over you lesser mortals."

"Sounds good to me."

"But before I got a chance to take him up on it, you came smashing in and provoked that hellacious, one-sided brawl—not to mention scaring my blonde bombshell into a coma. Shame on you."

"Did you try to read this Aiwass?"

"Of course. Couldn't do it—didn't even come *close*. The guy had shielding like you wouldn't believe."

"You couldn't get *anything*?"

"It was like hitting a wall. Serious power, Nightstalk."

"So first Rache and then Skorzeny. What about Gregory Fischer, where was he when this was going down? Again, you have to ask: is he just a figurehead?"

"I know, it's a good question. But any way you look at it, Aiwass is the key to the whole thing. He called himself the 'Opener of the Way' so I guess his role is pretty clear. Next time he'll make sure they get the Summoning right. Next time..." She didn't have to finish, we both knew what she meant.

"I'm still pissed they offered to cut you in and not me. Fuckers."

"They know you're incorruptible. Whereas my weaknesses are legion."

"I'll take that as a compliment."

"It *was* a compliment. And I also compliment you on your detective work. I'm dying to hear how you found me."

I parked just down the street from our building. Someone was peeking in the window of *The Tool Shed,* either casing the joint or ogling the displayed wares. Crotchless panties. Tasty lotions and gels. A vibrator the size of a thermos bottle.

"Now *that* is an interesting story," I admitted. "I have to give credit where credit is due. Holmes gave me the idea of talking to Georgie and Georgie helped me find the old ladies." I turned off the car and she scooted around on the seat to face me. "You know who I mean, those queer old ducks in that sewing circle. The Moirae sisters..."

She made a sound like "oh".

"Their card fell out of the file Georgie keeps on you. He acted kind of off-handed when I showed it to him but I think he meant for me to find it. Maybe even planted it." A cab sped past and I saw her face. "What's wrong?"

"Nothing," she said, patting my arm. "You did what you thought was right."

I felt my guts drop into my shoes. "Oh, *shit*. Goddamnit, Cassandra, I was worried. Fuckin' frantic is more like it. Imagining what they were doing to you. It really messed with my head. So if I've fucked up somehow, I wanna know."

"It's *fine,*" she insisted. "Though I suppose I should warn you, in case you feel the need to consult those particular ladies again...*hmmm,* how can I put this? There are usually *consequences.*"

"What do you mean?" I gripped the wheel, imagining I was strangling that hag Addie. "They knit a mean afghan, I'll tell you that. I asked if they knew where you were and one of them crochets me a fucking *map.* Like *that.* Who are they and--wait a minute. Aw, shit," I groaned, "Chloe said something just as I was leaving. Something about 'messing with the paradigm', I can't remember the exact--"

"What she probably meant was that they interceded and...they shouldn't be doing that. Because when they do, eventually the time comes when they have to put things back in balance. You weren't supposed to find me. Or maybe you were. We'll never know. It's pretty tricky territory, metaphysically speaking. But from now on, we have to be extra, *extra* careful. They need to set things right again...we just don't know *when.*"

I felt sick. "So I may have saved you *this* time but because I did, something rotten has to happen to even things out? Is that it?" I closed my eyes and began to thump my forehead on the steering wheel.

Dummy. Dummy. Dummy...

"Will you forget about it?" She slid over and put her arm around me. "Nothing has changed. None of us knows what's going to happen when we walk outside or go to the corner store for a loaf of bread. It's all in the hands of the divine Mother or Creator or Fate or whatever you want to call it."

"But you said they were planning on releasing you anyway." She nodded reluctantly. "That means I wasted my shot with the old ladies for nothing. It should only be used as a last ditch resort but I panicked and blew it."

"You did your best. And you did it for *me.*"

"Still. I feel ripped off."

She pulled back. "*You* feel ripped off? What about me? I'm the one whose fate is dangling by a thread, you blockhead! Now c'mon, let's go inside so I can find out what other disasters, natural or otherwise, have occurred in my absence. And if there's nothing else, I'm going home and crawling into bed with my cat Esther and sleeping 'til suppertime tomorrow. If that's all right with you." She opened her door, paused. "Are you coming? Your report on tonight's activities should make for interesting reading. Let's see, it'll have to be at least five pages long and since you are the world's slowest thirty-six year old, two-fingered typist, you're in for quite the workout."

By the time we reached the top of the stairs, she'd rattled off four or five one-liners, several double entendres, two or three bad puns and *almost* made me forget what I'd done.

But once we were inside there was no time for anything. We read the note, looked at each other and were on our way again in a matter of seconds:

> *Norm Daplume*
> *Intensive Care Unit*
> *City Hospital*
> *Hurry*

Werner cut quite the figure on the ward.

He stood out like a bashed thumb compared to the others present: an old man who jumped every time someone came in, a woman and her two young children and a couple of aspiring gangstas who were awaiting word on their gutshot buddy.

Now *this* guy was a warrior. Half his face was missing, bandaged and taped over, his hands a mess, swaddled in gauze, but he simply fucking *refused* to leave his post.

Cassandra talked to him—well, it was more like he opened his mind and let her sift through it for the information she needed. It didn't look good. "Philippe is badly hurt and not expected to live. One of those things attached itself to his chest and abdomen and did a lot of damage before Werner could get it off. Werner didn't know who to trust. He was afraid of taking him to a hospital so he—he tried nursing him but Philippe's injuries were too severe so Werner brought him here under an assumed name. He contacted the Old Man, on Philippe's instructions, but besides us no one else knows." Werner nodded his agreement. At some point he'd restitched his lips; the skin around his mouth still looked raw and sore.

I gave her hand a squeeze. "I'm sorry, doll."

We had to put on gowns, masks and paper slippers. The whole works. He was being kept in a sterile environment because of the severity of his burns. Philippe was one of four patients in the room, each of them carefully monitored, each of them with only a tenuous hold on life.

The injuries inflicted on his body were extensive. A harried doctor had filled us in outside and it made me sick to think about it. The creature had burned its way through his stomach and intestinal wall and literally *boiled* his innards. He was a goner and it was probably a good thing because as well as taking his guts, the bogey also fried his sexual equipment. Cooked it right down to a blackened nub. Poor fucker.

Werner had pried it off him with his bare hands, fucking them up badly in the process. The big bastard tried to cope with the situation as best he could but Philippe's condition was too critical. A hospital, while risky, was the only possible option.

He loomed behind us as we stood at Philippe's bedside. The ward was quiet, hushed, the only sounds subdued murmurs and the suck and hiss of life-support machinery. I found myself trying not to stand too close; just *thinking* about what was under those wrappings made my stomach do backflips.

Cassandra wasn't nearly so squeamish. She bent over him, softly speaking his name. His face was white-pale, filmed with sweat, but otherwise unmarked by the attack. The damage confined solely to his midsection and crotch.

I had to hand it to the guy. The doctor told us that he was refusing all medication. He had been apprised of the situation, knew the straits he was in, but declined to let them dull or reduce his pain. He had also informed his huge, silent subordinate that he was to physically prevent any extraordinary attempts at resuscitation.

Philippe DeBarge must have had awesome powers of mental control because he stayed lucid and uncomplaining to the very end. He winced occasionally but that was the only sign of discomfort I saw him display.

"I don't have long," he said. His voice was weak, barely audible. "I feel I must impress upon you...the gravity of the situation. It is worse than I feared. I can trust no one...not even my own Brothers. Make no attempt to contact them...expect no further assistance. I am truly sorry."

"Great," I muttered.

"Nightstalk?" He shifted his head slightly.

"Present and accounted for."

"I wish to speak to you. Come closer, please." Cassandra made room for me. "Closer..." I got to within kissing distance of the bugger. "Protect her. She is beautiful and perfect in a way that...a brute like you cannot hope to...understand." I seethed. "But you love her and your loyalty is...above reproach. I salute you." I saw his hand flopping weakly on his chest and understood, clasping it firmly in my own. "You must...take the ring off my finger. The silver one..."

"Philippe, no—" Cassandra sounded apprehensive.

"*Attendez*, my dear. Say nothing. I can't tell...do you have it, Nightstalk?"

"I got it."

"It is yours now. Put it on. *Quickly*," he gasped. His system had reached its limit, the pain almost overwhelming him.

I did as I was told. Cursing my thick, crooked fingers. "It'll only fit on my pinkie," I told him.

"That will suffice." His eyes were bright with inexpressible agony...and something else. Nobility, I guess you'd call it. "I hereby convey upon you a sacred honour. As a member of our fellowship, you are a keeper of forbidden or proscribed knowledge, protector of all that is good in mankind...and...worth preserving..."

"Hey, wait a minute..." I felt weird, like I was trapped inside some kind of energy field; every hair on my body went *toiinng!*

"Use it well, my friend. My...*brother*." His gaze drifted toward the ceiling. "*Non sum dignus*[29]," he whispered. His grip on my hand tightened. His eyes widened and he drew in a short breath. "Ah..."

I waited a few moments, then slipped my hand from his, reached over and closed his eyes.

III

"Let my servants be few and secret, they shall rule the many and the known."

Aleister Crowley

And so, thanks to Philippe Arnaud Debarge, I found myself duly deputized as one of the Brethren of Purity, with all the privileges and obligations that went along with it. Including an over-sized watchdog

---

[29] According to Cassandra: "I am not worthy."

named Werner. He signaled that he would serve as our driver and I didn't have the heart or, frankly, the guts to tell him the position was already taken.

He handled the Taurus well despite the condition of his hands. My partner and I sat in the back seat, not saying much at first. Werner stared straight ahead and kept his own counsel. Cassandra had wept at Philippe's bedside and stayed with him while Werner and I made arrangements for his body. Now she was slumped against the door on her side, limp with grief and exhaustion. I knew she had to be played out, the past few days had been rough on her. She probably needed time to--

"I don't think you fully grasp what just happened." Our gigantic chauffeur had his seat jacked all the way back so she had her long legs stretched across my lap. "You are now the equivalent of a 6th Degree adept without the slightest training or inkling of what that means or the responsibility it entails." She shook her head. "He must have been out of his mind."

"You don't think I can deal with it?" I kept fiddling with the ring on my right pinkie. Turning it around and around. "Or maybe *you* have a problem with the fact that I now have powers and abilities superior to yours'. Is that it?"

Werner snorted.

"I agree," she replied, "he is, isn't he? It's maddening sometimes. *Stop playing with that.*" She slapped my hand. "You have no idea what that ring is capable of, *that's* what I'm trying to tell you. *And* you lack the years of training and discipline it takes to properly use it. Philippe knew that and yet—"

"—and yet he gave me it to me anyway. Maybe he saw something in me that you don't."

She sighed. "You're going to be impossible about this, aren't you?"

"Meaning?"

"Meaning the *smart* thing to do would be to put it away and give it back to the Brethren once this is all over. That's my advice."

I remembered the look in his eyes when he gave me my commission. That surge of energy I'd experienced. "I—I'm going to keep it, at least for now. It might come in handy, you never know." My head felt clear and razor sharp, my thought processes speeded up. Keeping the ring was a good idea, I was certain of it.

"Just promise me you won't use it without proper supervision," she begged, realizing the fight was lost. "I'll help you as much as I can. We'll *practice.*"

"Hmmm. Sounds boring." I cackled mischievously. "I wanna turn somebody into a frog!"

"*Nightstalk...*"

It was late, time to call it a night. Werner dropped off Cassandra first, then me. He indicated that he would keep the Taurus for the time being. Whenever I needed a ride, regardless of the hour, I was to call him. He gave me his card:

Werner

"Simply the best."

935-2136

He wanted to make sure he stayed involved. He had scores to settle and I guess as long as he had my car he figured that made him part of the team. I watched him drive away and couldn't help wondering whether or not he would live to regret that decision.

Or, for that matter, if any of us would.

Sunday, May 23rd

After a long and fruitless night at the office, I was ready to kill someone. Cassandra kept bugging me about the ring, trying to convince me it was dangerous, I should put it away...*blah blah blah*. There were no new memos, no one called and my partner spent most of the time pouting, her nose stuck in books. My report to the Old Man, when I finished it, read like an exercise in futility. Now I couldn't wait to close the door to my apartment, spark up a joint and watch two nubile lesbians pleasure each other with edible oils and heaping gobs of whipped cream.

"Excuse me? Mr. Nightstalk?" Francine Appleby clutched her frilly purple housedress to her throat. She'd been waiting God knows how long. The old doll was the best lookout a guy could hope for. She never slept and was senile and paranoid to boot. Which meant she wasn't too quick to report the odd habits of her neighbors to the police or the building's super since, as far as she was concerned, they were part of the "Jew-Japo" conspiracy secretly controlling human affairs. She'd be only too happy to explain her theories *in detail* should you wish to know more.

I paused. "How are you this evening, ma'am?"

"I just wanted to tell you," motioning me closer while keeping the security chain fastened. "I heard some strange noises from your room earlier on."

Great. *Now* what? "Could you tell what it was?" I asked. "How long ago are we talking about?"

"About two hours, maybe a bit more. I heard some men go sneaking by, trying to be quiet as mice. But you can't fool old granny." She snickered. "I'd say they were professionals too. Had no trouble getting in. I had a beau who was a cat burglar. Quickest hands you ever saw, with a lock or a brassiere."

"How many, could you tell?" I looked down the hall, gearing up for some serious butt-kicking.

"I would say at least three or four. But that was before."

"Before?" I stared at her. "Before *what*?"

"Before something in there ate them," she said simply, closing the door against further inquiries.

"Goddamnit, Tree!" I raged. "Can't you at least clean up after yourself?"

I was referring to the unattached arm draped over the end of the couch, the leg in the corner, strips and flaps of flesh and shredded clothing everywhere. And blood. *Lots* of blood. Pints of it pooling along the baseboards and liberally splashed on every wall. It was like walking around inside a blender. If I was seeking the source of the carnage, I didn't have far to look. There was a size thirteen work boot protruding from Tree's mouth, which abruptly tumbled to the floor. She appeared *gorged.*

"I'm going for a walk," I told the predatory plant. "Soon it's going to be light so I can't stay out long. I am *not* a happy camper right now. If you want to improve my mood, you'd better have all *this,*" waving at the gore, "squared away by the time I get back." Tree belched rebelliously and shook her leaves.

"Okay," I backed off, mindful of her tricky temperament, "maybe I'm out of line here, coming on too heavy. You're right, I should be more grateful that you took care of these assholes for me." I let that sink in. She straightened and ruffled up again. "But unfortunately I also have to deal with the real world right outside my door. I can't have blood leaking through to the apartment below or—or have somebody calling the cops because they're hearing people getting their heads bitten off down the hall. Sooner or later that shit catches up with you." When I got to the door I turned around, taking one last look at the mess. *Cripes.* "See what you can do and I--I'll be back later."

I walked to a cafe three blocks away. It came fully equipped with greasy food, plastic menus and a surly waitress in a pink fortrel uniform.

There was lemon meringue pie congealing under a glass dome on the counter, mints and toothpicks by the cash register and free refills of the rancid coffee.

Snagged a two-day old newspaper somebody left behind and slid into a booth. Ordered chamomile tea and hoped no one I knew spotted me sipping the stuff. It would blow my reputation to hell and back. Sports didn't interest me so I chucked that part of the paper aside. Ditto the personal ads and financial section. I checked out what movies were playing and the TV listings, scanned the comics as I went to work on my tea.

Nothing in the headlines caught my eye—current events bore me—but there was something on page 5, the name "Fischer" prominently mentioned:

DEVELOPER ANNOUNCES UPCOMING PARTY

Billionaire developer Gregory Fischer and his socialite wife, Charlotte Roper-Fischer, will be hosting a celebrity-studded gathering, set for Saturday, June 5th. The gala event will be held in the Fischer's luxurious quarters on the 66th floor of the Leiber Building. Attendance is strictly by invitation only and the guestlist is sure to include some very prominent names—

Now what was *this* all about?
I wondered if my partner had caught wind of this upcoming bash. Somehow, I suspected she had...

Later that same night:
It felt like there was gravel behind my eyelids and I was muddle-brained and more than a little pissed off at the world in general.

Sitting in front of the Underwood, staring at a blank sheet of paper and imagining wiping my ass with it. Just so it wouldn't look so white and pristine. Suddenly I felt a burst of inspiration, lunged forward and began furiously typing:

I'm too fucking tired to thinkkkkkkkkkkkkkk

I hadn't had a whole lot of sleep lately and it was starting to show. And it was pretty hard catching any shut-eye when I had to listen to Tree burp and fart as she digested the remains of the raiding party. I had to give her credit, she'd done a fair to middling job of cleaning up after herself. I ended up scrubbing down the walls and throwing out the area rug in the living room but, what the hell, it was an ugly rug. Still, the smell of her swamp gas was pretty hard to take. Really noxious. I was surprised no one called to complain. I had some pretty tolerant neighbours in that building.

I finally got tired of hitting the *k* key, ripped out the sheet, balled it up and tossed it in the general direction of the wastebasket.

Cassandra spied on me while pretending to read a book on spellcasting. "Am I allowed to speak to you yet?" I grunted in acquiescence. "Well, thank you very much." She put the book down and sat forward on her chair. "I know you're not in the best of moods right now—"

"It's that fucking plant you gave me," I complained. I filled her in on what had transpired since leaving work that morning, the horror show I had walked into at home. "Thanks to her gastrointestinal system, I haven't slept a wink. I'm seriously thinking about giving her back to you."

"Never mind that Tree saved your life," she retorted. "I hope you showed proper gratitude. That particular breed can be touchy. It's not a Venus flytrap, you know. You get her mad, make her feel unwanted and she's liable to come after *you* some night."

"Typical woman," I muttered.

"*What?*"

"Nothing. Besides, I *did* thank her. I'm not that dumb. I have to sleep in the same room as her." I drained the last of the coffee in my mug. "Usually we get along pretty well. She gets her daily dose of hamburger and doesn't bag at me or remind me to change my underwear."

"These are details I don't need to hear, partner."

I saw what she meant. "Usually I remember."

"Sure you do."

"Can we change the subject? Is there something on your mind or d'you get your kicks taking the piss out of my personal hygiene?"

"Holy Diana, Nightstalk, you are *such* a bitch tonight."

"I need sleep. My body *craves* sleep. Last night I dearly wanted to lay my head down and zonk out for eight solid hours. Instead, I come home and your man-eating plant has decided to have a smorgasbord. It was fucking *gruesome.*"

"Why are you so sleep-deprived?"

"I dunno. Different things. Stress maybe, too much coffee—who knows?" I mumbled something as I lined up another sheet in the Underwood.

"*What?* What did you say?" The woman never missed a thing.

"I've been...having these weird dreams. Well, this one dream in particular."

"Let's hear it."

"But it's so stupid..."

"*Now*, Nightstalk."

So I told her about Chorazin and the creatures and my hazardous journey to the Black Tower. Lately, I'd been retaining more of the dream after I woke up, especially my growing dread as I approached the summit.

"A Black Tower, you say..." I nodded. "How many steps?"

"Fifteen hundred. I don't know how I know that but I do. It seems like I've been climbing for *weeks* already. I keep thinking I'm nearly at the top but there's always more steps."

"Am I there?"

"You're there somewhere. I feel your presence but I don't know where you are. I'm climbing and I'm tired, dog tired, I wanna rest--but then I hear screaming."

"Do you know who it is?"

"It *sounds* like you."

She nodded. "What you're experiencing, my friend, is a form of psychic attack. You need to do something to cleanse your apartment of the occult energies being used against you."

"And this...Chorazin. Have you ever heard of it?"

"There are numerous references to that name in various historical records. Jesus curses the city of Chorazin in the *Book of Matthew* and M.R. James alludes to a 'Black Pilgrimmage' to Chorazin in one of his short stories. If I'm not mistaken, our old pal Jack Parsons claimed to have paid a visit there as well."

"Does this dream mean anything, am I supposed to be doing something or—"

"It's hard to say. Have you tried lucid dreaming, controlling what's happening, manipulating events to your advantage?"

"I don't think it would work even if I tried. Not in this place."

"Does it frighten you?"

I shrugged. "It's kind of freaky but at the same time..."

"You're curious to see what's at the top of that tower, aren't you?"

"Maybe," I admitted.

"Because if you want it to stop, there are things you can do, stuff that will ward off bad energies. You can leave fresh garlic around and bathe in salt water and I've got some prayers and incantations that might—"

"It's not a big deal. At least at this point. I think I can handle it." I shrugged. "I mean, it's just a dream, right? How bad can it get?" Yawning and rubbing my eyes. "*Shit.* Hey, I betcha Werner's probably got the car outside. Waddaya say we get out of here? Go for a drive somewhere. Head down by the lake and take in the view."

"Why, Nightstalk, you romantic devil."

"Whatever. I gotta do something to clear my head." I grabbed my coat. "C'mon, doll. Let's take a break."

"You realize we're playing hooky on company time. The Old Man wouldn't be pleased if he found out."

"If we're caught, we'll blame Werner. After all," I couldn't resist, "he can't talk so it's not like he can rat us out or anything."

"Nightstalk, you are so *bad...*"

"So...do we have anything planned for tonight?" I asked.

"*Shhhh.* In a minute. I'm enjoying this."

I was too, to be honest. We were standing on the broad upper deck of a cement lookout spot that afforded a pretty decent view of Erie. There were several such structures spaced along this part of the lakefront. A sidewalk path connected them. It was a popular spot for sight-seers and lovers, young and old. Unfortunately it also drew a variety of low-lifes. You had to be careful.

We were posed before a waist-high wall. I was directly behind her, my arms around her and clasped about her mid-section. She was leaning most of her weight against me. Her hair, longer again, was in my face. It smelled wonderful. She stretched contentedly, then reached back and curled one arm around my neck. We looked very cozy and intimate.

"Whatever will Werner think?" I mumbled.

"Werner is a complete professional. He averts his eyes from this kind of behavior."

"I take it we're stuck with him for the foreseeable future."

"He's a good man to have in our corner, don't you think? Especially with those creeps coming by your place like that. He gives us extra security."

"Don't trust me to protect you?"

She gave me a cross look. "Of course I do. I merely meant—and as you yourself have stated—we need all the help we can get." Her fingernails scrubbed the short, bristly hair on the back of my head. At that moment, I was as happy as a prize pig.

"He's half-crippled, Cass. Not even muscle at this point, just meat. And cooked meat at that."

She dropped her arm to her side. "He stayed with Philippe to the very end. You can't *buy* that kind of loyalty and devotion. And now he's transferred it to us." Resting her hands on mine. "Don't always look for the cloud instead of the silver lining," she pleaded and I laughed.

"I always thought Werner might be the one guy who'd give me trouble in a fight."

She was happy to be distracted. "Why? What makes him so special? Besides the fact that he's as big and solid as your average oak tree."

"Well, there's that. But I was thinking about, y'know, what he did to himself. Sewing his lips shut and the ear thing. Shows he's not afraid of pain. If you're fighting somebody who isn't bothered by pain, you're in trouble."

"Tell me more." She settled back, enjoying herself.

I was surprised by the sudden, inexplicable interest in blood sport but decided to indulge her. "Sometimes in a scrap, no matter how good you are, you get hit. That's a fact. The guy gets in a lucky shot or maybe he's a genuinely good fighter and *nails* you. What do you do when that happens?"

"What?" She sounded intrigued.

"You react, you counterpunch, you don't let the guy know he's hurt you, maybe even stunned you. The pain, the shock of getting hit, rather than scare you or make you want to quit, should intensify the experience, make it sharper and more real. Sometimes when I'm really going at it, it's like I'm in a movie, totally outside myself, watching the whole thing happening."

"Very interesting. But I'm still curious about one thing: *why* do you fight?"

At first, I wasn't sure I'd heard right. "*Why?* Because...because a good scrap puts you back in touch with yourself. External bullshit goes out the window when you're one-on-one with a guy who knows how to use his fists. And feet. You gotta watch out for fuckers who are into that kick-boxing shit."

"Yes, but I've seen you in situations where it might have been possible to talk your way out of trouble and instead you deliberately provoked a confrontation. Which makes me wonder if what you just said is simply a rationale for beating people up."

I tightened my hold, giving her tummy a playful squeeze. She went "*hup*" and slapped my hand in reproof. "So *that's* it. I'm nothing more than a common thug to you. I had no idea you had such a low opinion of me."

"That's not true," she protested. "I am merely reporting what I've noticed with my keen powers of detection and intuition."

"That I'm a bully? That I enjoy the sight of blood and inflicting pain? I suppose next you'll be telling me that my capacity for violence is a direct result of my short stature. The fact that I'm, shall we say, vertically challenged and therefore must overcompensate by imposing myself physically on those around me."

"Not bad, Nightstalk," she complimented me. "*Now* who's the mind-reader?"

"Never mind. The point is, all of that is bullshit. Most of the time I fight because I *have* to. That's the honest to God truth, Cass."

"No," she disagreed. "And it's not because you're short, either. It's because you're frustrated so you take it out on your enemies with your fists." That piqued my interest. "Basically, you're a romantic. You want to rescue the maiden, defeat the bad guys and make the world safe for Girl Guides and little old ladies." Turning toward me, her voice forlorn: "But nowadays Girl Guides get caught peddling drugs and the maiden turns out to be some kind of deviant who...." She raised her arms and dropped them.

"You make me sound like an idjit," I said.

"No. Not at *all*. You're a very moral and decent man. You have your warrior code, your strict set of rules you live by and for that you're to be saluted. It's the rest of us that are screwed up."

"You wouldn't think that if you saw my porn collection."

"That's irrelevant. You're a good person and you should be happier. Part of the reason you're unhappy is *me*. What I'm not...can't be." Circling *that* touchy subject again.

"Right now I'm happy," I insisted. "It may last an hour or maybe only another minute or two...but I'll take what I can get." I felt her trembling and then she was sobbing, really breaking down, and there was nothing I could say or do, so I just held her.

"Oh, Nightstalk," she gasped, "if I died right now, right this second—"

"No." I tightened my grip again. "Don't say that. Don't *ever* say that. I told you, I won't let that happen. *Never*." Which only made her cry harder. I certainly had a way with the ladies. "I hope you're finished," I said, once the worst appeared to be over, "because I'm half-drowned back here."

"I'm only feeling sorry for myself. It's Philippe and all of this crap we have to deal with, evil creatures and dark conspiracies. For a second I couldn't face it. But I feel better now. My bosom buddy pulled me through." She patted my hand, signaling she was ready and I opened my arms, releasing her. She drew in a deep breath and then turned to face me. "Once more into the breech, dear friend?"

"Wouldn't miss it for the world," I declared. "I'm dying to hear what you have in mind. What our next move is."

"Well, by now I'm sure you've heard of the Fischers' big party—"

"Goddamnit, I knew it!"

"It's obvious, Nightstalk. Previous attempts at the Working have failed because the words were mistranslated or in the wrong sequence *and* because certain formalities weren't observed."

"Such as?"

She flung her arms wide. "Sacrifice, for instance. These are ancient, hungry gods. Offerings must be made to appease their awful appetites. Which are quite considerable after eons of floating around in the eternal void."

"But I don't see what this fancy-shmancy party has to do with—oh." My mouth fell open. "No. They *wouldn't*."

"There aren't that many virgins around any more so they have to use something else. The *crème de la crème* will be there. Imagine that. Have you been reading about it? They're having it at the Fischer's, opening up the whole floor to dignitaries and VIP's from near and far. It's perfect for what they have in mind."

"So *that's* their plan? Open a portal and use the rich and famous as *hors d'oeuvres* for bogeys from another dimension? That seems a bit...extreme. Parsons and Elron went out to the desert—"

"Who says the Working has to be performed in a remote locale? They've got Aiwass now, he knows how it's done. Once you have the correct text and follow the right procedure, you could do it in the middle of Grand Central Station."

"It's fucking *monstrous*. To invite these people to what they think is the bash of the century and they end up having some prehistoric god play jumprope with their intestines. That's fucking cold, kiddo."

"I agree."

"Anyone who attends this party is signing their own death warrant."

"Exactly."

I waited a beat. "So do we have our tickets?"

"Delivered to our door by special courier this very night." Shrugging apologetically. "You were late getting in and then you were so grouchy I didn't want to bring it up."

"Good grief. They really believe in tying up loose ends, don't they?"

She got that stubborn look on her face. "Letting us in so easily is a tactical mistake on their part. We wanted to be there anyway."

"We did?"

"Nightstalk," she reminded me, "you know I love a party..."

There were sounds from behind us. Werner was grunting, his cell phone pressed to one of his ear holes. He waved and we hurried over. Cass scanned his thoughts for the relevant details. "It seems our building is on fire," she reported.

"Wonderful," I quipped. "One minute they're inviting us to their shindig and the next they burn our office down. Talk about sending mixed messages." I got in front with Werner and Cassandra climbed into the back. No need for seatbelts, not with Werner at the controls. The big lug had the reflexes and instincts of a Formula One driver.

"Skorz—er, Aiwass mentioned that some of the others were losing patience with the Old Man so there might be a different faction at work here. Rache, maybe." She drummed her fingers on a moulded plastic armrest; it sounded like rain.

"I hope the Old Man got out all right."

"I'm still not convinced he's in there half the time."

"*Now* who's being paranoid?"

When we got to the block our building was on, we found our forward progress impeded by emergency vehicles. There were two fire trucks, paramedics, an ambulance and three cop cars. We parked and proceeded on foot, getting as close as they would let us.

It didn't look that bad to me. *The Tool Shed*'s big front window had been smashed so the fire crew could pump water in. In fact, most of the damage seemed water-related. Tara Dreyfuss was standing off by herself, looking despondent. When she spotted us, she ran over and threw herself into Cassandra's arms. Once we established she was unhurt, we discovered the young woman had a very strange story to tell.

"I was thinking about closing up early—mom's out of town so I've been here pretty much all day. I went over to the window and sort of peeked out." She glanced at us beseechingly. "This is where it gets really fucked up, all right? Because I'm looking down the street and I see this— this *thing* coming toward me. It's kind of skipping and jumping along and at first I thought it was a bag or some garbage being blown by the wind but it kept coming." She took a breath before continuing. Cassandra put a reassuring arm around her shoulders.

"What did you—" I started to ask.

"Wait, let me finish," she begged. "I'm standing there and this thing gives a jump and sails *right through the window*. I duck, thinking there's gonna be glass everywhere but *no*. It goes through without breaking anything. Don't ask me how. That's the part I'm scared to tell the cops. I turn around and this thing, it's like this silvery-blue pie plate, and it's zipping around the store and everything it touches catches fire. So I'm chasing after it, trying to stomp out the fires and I follow it right up to the counter. Then it, like, doubles back and comes zooming *right at me*." Her eyes widened as she remembered. "And I didn't have time to think, I grabbed the first thing I could lay my hands on—which turns out to be a dildo, this huge, black shlong thing an old perv was looking at earlier." She giggled nervously. "Stupid, huh? But I tell you, that thing saved my life. 'Cause I used it like a freakin' bat and I knocked that suckah out through the window—*pow!*"

"And the window didn't break?" Cassandra inquired.

"No. It went right through, just like before. As soon as it landed outside it sort of went *poof*, like a firework going off. There was nothing left except a smudge mark. By then the fire was going pretty good, so I dialed 9-1-1, grabbed the cashbox and booked it on out of there."

"What an amazing story," Cassandra said, hugging the girl.

"Yeah, way to go, kid," I concurred.

"You believe me, right? Even about the crazy stuff?" We nodded and she sagged in relief.

"Was there much damage?" I asked.

"The fire trucks got here pretty fast," she reported. "Lucky thing we're insured. The water was the worst part. Fuck, those guys went *crazy* with the water. That's when the front window got smashed in. Hey, either of you got a smoke?" We didn't. "Shit. I could use one right now."

"You should go home and get some rest," Cassandra advised.

"Nah. Those asshole fire investigators wanna talk to me some more. I don't wanna tell them anything that might affect the insurance or whatever."

"That's probably a good plan," I agreed. "Sometimes honesty *isn't* the best policy."

"No kidding," she snorted. "Especially with my mother. She'd *kill* me if I cost her the store. She lives for the place. You know what she told me the other day?" She looked sick. "She said, and I quote: 'Cocks are our bread and butter'." She shivered. "*God*. I'm worried she's gonna put that on business cards and start handing them out."

I thought it was kind of catchy and almost said so. Saw the way they were staring at me and realized it probably wouldn't go down well.

Monday, May 24th

The following night it was back to work as usual and never mind that the entire building *reeked* of smoke, even with the windows and downstairs entrance propped open. The door to the Old Man's office remained firmly closed, though a fireman I talked to assured me that when he and his crew checked upstairs, they found the door ajar, no one home, the room completely devoid of furnishings, the walls bare...

We'd only been back at work an hour before my partner had had enough. According to her interpretation of the Occupational Health and Safety Act, we were in an unsafe work environment and therefore entitled to take frequent trips outside to refresh ourselves. As we stood in front of our building, I got that funny feeling again.

"Hey, doll," I suggested amiably, "how about taking a walk with me?" She caught on and fell in step beside me. We started up the street...meanwhile, my radar was scoping out the situation, trying to zero in on our shadow.

"It's strange," she said softly, "there's someone back there but he's hardly registering. Either heavily shielded or—"

"Are you thinking non-human? Some kind of bogey—" She stopped. Watching. Waiting. "What is it? Another ravenor?"

"I don't think so." She never took her eyes off the corner. "This isn't anything unnatural."

"Then what—" I saw her stiffen and squinted in the direction she was gazing. "It's a...*cat*?"

"Not just any cat, I think." How she came to that conclusion was beyond me. "And if I'm not mistaken he's got something to tell us." He trotted toward us, a black and white kitty, fairly skinny, and as he got nearer I saw that he'd been in a close scrape recently. Most of one ear was gone and the fur on parts of his body was gouged and matted, big patches of it missing. He stopped about ten feet away. Sat down. Looking away from us but still giving the impression he was on guard for any sudden movement.

He meowed. Only it sounded more like *ma-ror*. There was an unsettling quality to his cry. This was not a happy kitty.

Cassandra turned to me. "Something's wrong. We have to play this very, very carefully." Keeping her head down, she answered the cat. A fairly lengthy response, not the traditional greeting I'd heard her use on other occasions. It seemed more formal and low-key but, then again, I never learned to speak the lingo.

The cat hissed and got to its feet, tail twitching. Cass told me once that when dealing with cats it was important to watch their tails and especially their ears. Kitty released another wounded cry, then sat back on his haunches and commenced panting. Weird behavior, even for a cat. "He wants to tell us something," she said. "I'm not to interrupt. You can see for yourself how distressed he is and—" The cat yowled again. "He's about to begin. I'll do my best to translate…"

"*Humans,*" the cat spat. "How I despise you! Tooth and claw, I wish you were small and scuttled! I alone can speak of these matters, I alone survive to tell the tale of the holocaust. How they used their evil magic to rob the night of its brightest eyes and sharpest teeth. *Phhssst!* How they lured us into their snares and traps with spells and bewitchments. And we were rendered as docile and stupid as dogs, spirited away in the dead of night. *Hssssssst!* Then they stopped and the doors were thrown open…"

The cat paused. While we waited for it to continue, I fidgeted. "Keep still," she warned. "Remember what I said about body language."

I tried to emulate her posture, eyes cast down, hands at my sides.

"It was a building outside the city. They had prepared it well ahead of time. We were kept in cages, behind wire. How many? I cannot say. Even kittens and they were the most pitiful. We were given no food, no water and each day our numbers increased. Some were dragged out and taken away. We never knew what happened to them but imagined the worst. The men took pleasure in abusing us, clubbing and burning us. They made sport of it. How long it took us to die. *Phsssst!*

Many lost their minds, almost all lost hope. The filth made it difficult since we are, by nature, fastidious creatures. Captivity does cruel things. Hunger ruled our wits. The kittens were small and weak. I did not take part but I did not stop them.

Along with some others I tried every means to escape. The wire resisted us. Day by day, more of us died of hunger, dehydration, hopelessness. Finally, no more brothers and sisters were brought to that terrible place. The men left, closing and locking the doors behind them. Our cries grew more desperate, screams and howls I shall never forget.

It was the rat that saved me. I saw the foul thing and followed it, dragging myself along until I discovered the hole it had made. So anxious to get at all that succulent cat flesh. The hole was small but I had starved many days and was scrawny enough to squeeze through, though it cost me dearly, as you can see. I alone escaped. Truly it can be said: *I live but I am not alive.*"

The cat stuck out its back leg and began to lick it aggressively. I took the opportunity to tug on my partner's sleeve. "Does he know who these guys were working for? Ask him—"

She wasn't listening. Too outraged and infuriated. "Those *bastards.* It was Skorzeny, had to be. Not wanting to take any chances, eliminating any potential security risk. How many cats have we lost? The *monster.* No wonder this poor animal is so distraught. I've never felt such hate radiating from a living creature."

"Yeah, he's definitely pissed," I allowed.

The cat again: "I know some of your language, human. I see the words your body speaks. I came to tell this one," meaning Cassandra, " our story. *You* are not known to us. Remember this well: once I tolerated humans. Like others of my kind, I lived with them, served them when it suited me, went soft at their touch. I was known to my human caregivers as Taco but now I am *Gnasher.* I shall hate humans *forever* for what they have done. I will bite their reaching hands and shun their vile company. I say this and no more. I want nothing to do with your species. I piss in your flowerbeds and soil the graves of your ancestors."

With that, he got to his feet and scampered down the street.

"He's nuts," I commented. "A fucking head case."

"Can you blame him?" She looked fit to murder someone. "Cats are proud animals. This is a terrible, unforgivable sin that has been committed. It might have far-reaching repercussions."

"You think a lot of cats are going to feel the same way as ol' Gnasher once they hear his story?"

She shrugged. "He's very damaged. But…I sensed great power and determination. Who knows what he might accomplish with time and a few devoted followers."

Something to ponder as we made our way back to our stinky office.

Tuesday, May 25ʰ

It was less than two weeks until the Fischers' big bash. The city's rich and blameless were gearing up for the great society event of the year. There were plenty of long faces when the guest list was leaked to, who else, Joe Duthie. He broke the story in his column and the howls of outrage could be heard from one end of Ilium to the other.

The social and entertainment pages were buzzing. Two hundred people partying it up on the 66th floor of the Leiber Building, Ilium's tallest residential building. The roster included the mayor and movers and shakers from the local and national scene. Supposedly, two ex-Presidents were flying in for cameo appearances.

There was no end of speculation floating about. The Rolling Stones had been tapped to play a special "unplugged" set. Sirs Elton John and Paul McCartney would take turns at a grand piano, regaling the crowd with their inoffensive pop lite. Then someone floated the rumour that *Wham!* was going to be reunited. Many column inches were expended on that newsworthy item.

"If *Wham!* reunites," I grumbled, "then the Cabal will have really and truly succeeded in restoring the dark gods." Even with two floor fans going at full blast the office still stank of smoke and damp. We couldn't keep loose papers on our desk *and* we had to worry about moulds and various toxic fungi from Yuggoth growing in the walls. That shit can *kill* you.

"*Really*, Nightstalk," Cassandra clucked, "your gift for hyperbole--"

"I'm *serious*. I hate the fuckers. For the good of mankind we should cut off Andrew Ridgeley's hands and fucking *castrate* George Michael."

She shook her head, returning her attention to the newspaper in front of her, its corners weighted down with books. "According to Joe Duthie, the Fischers are setting the social pecking order in the city for the next five years. I'd be willing to wager there are people who would literally *kill* to be there."

"They're welcome to my ticket," I offered. "Anybody who shows up is basically a sacrificial lamb for vicious, inhuman motherfuckers with a taste for fresh blood. Yep, sounds like fun, all right."

"Don't worry, big boy," she consoled me, "I'll make sure the nasty old dark gods don't hurt you." I grinned. "Oh, I've been meaning to ask..." She paused. "Er, don't take this wrong but, um, this is supposed to be a *formal* affair and that means—"

"I have a suit."

"Wonderful. Is it double-breasted or just reversible and waterproof?" She smiled prettily so I wouldn't be tempted to reach over and snap her skinny neck.

"It's...my father's, actually," I said, hoping to play on her sympathies. No such luck. Instead she wrinkled up her nose like she'd just had an up close encounter with the bathroom facilities at Woodstock.

"Your *father's*? C'mon, Nightstalk, why not splurge and wear something more...stylish?"

"You'll like it," I insisted. "It's kind of Edwardian. Nah, that's not the right word. You know what it reminds me of? The sort of thing John Steed from *The Avengers* wears. Dapper, y'know? The only thing missing is the bowler hat."

"Spare me that, at least," she quipped.

"It's *fine*." No way was I going to tell her that the only reason I'd dragged my Da's duds out of storage was that I was as broke as a dropped piggy bank.

"If you say so." She sounded doubtful.

"I suppose you'll be wearing some Calvin Klein outfit that'll put the rest of us to shame. So I guess it doesn't really matter *what* I wear, does it?"

She laughed. "Oh, Nightstalk. *Calvin Klein*. You're the best, you know that?"

I pretended my little joke had been deliberate. "Well, whatever. I'm sure you'll look very *chic*. What does one wear to a slaughterhouse anyhow?"

"Nothing white," she'd advised, "it shows the blood. I'd go for earth tones. Navy or black would be okay too."

"You have a twisted sense of humour, you know that?"

"Do you have a cummerbund?"

"Sash from my bathrobe will do."

"Tie?"

"Wide and loud, the way I like 'em."

"Maybe we should arrive separately," she proposed.

"I'll be sure to check my cowboy hat and spurs at the door." She lowered her face to the rustling newspaper and pretended to weep. "Listen you," I said sharply, "my wardrobe isn't the problem."

"You're right." She raised her head. "What are we going to do about your *hair*?"

"Fun-ny," I retorted. "I meant our immediate plans. Got anything in mind?"

She sat up. "Well...to start with, I suggest we take Holmes' advice and have a chat with some of the other Cabal-erros. Find out if any of them are having second thoughts. You never know."

"From what the Baron and Vivien said we're likely pissing in the wind. *Hmm*. Which ones?"

"How many are left?" She counted on her fingers. "There's Joe Duthie, Allan Mayhew, Ronald Witcover and Kali Brust."

I scowled. "You'll have to deal with *her*. I can't abide that—that—"

"Are you kidding?" She laughed. "I wouldn't leave you two alone together for a minute. You'd either kill each other or end up making out on the floor." I didn't entirely disagree. There was some kind of strange, perverse chemistry between that little hellcat and me. "First things first though."

"Which means?"

"I just heard your stomach rumbling. Must be time for a junk food run. Either that or there's a tiger under the desk."

I laughed. "It's your own fault, shweetheart. You bring out the animal in me."

"Remind me to have you fitted for a muzzle..."

Ever since I'd slipped on Philippe's Brethren ring I'd felt like a better, stronger man. It was a gradual but steady transformation. I found my focus sharpening and that heightening of the senses I'd noticed was no trick of the imagination.

And there were other changes, less tangible, flickers of intuition, intimations of things to come...

I knew the cops were waiting for us before we reached the bottom of the stairs. I pointed them out to Cassandra just as Faro hailed us. I could feel their frustration as we approached, their disdain for us...and their fear. I noticed they'd been assigned a real beater from the car pool but didn't think it would be politic of me to mention it.

"Evening, boys," I called. Cassandra hung back but I went over and stuck my head through the driver's side window. "How goes the hunt for the mad firebug?"

It was their latest brilliant theory: a serial arsonist was on the loose, responsible for a number of recent blazes, including the attack on our building as well as the fire that destroyed Gillette's establishment. They weren't ruling out some kind of connection to the killing of Eva Jauch either (especially since it would tie things up so nicely).

Faro recoiled from my close proximity. "Get your ugly face outta my car, Nightstalk."

Wojeck patted his shoulder. "*Easy*, Stan. Nightstalk's just being friendly. There's something he wants to tell us, right, Nightstalk? Maybe you even got an explanation for some of the excessively bizarre and fucked up shit that's been going down lately. You wanna tell us about it?"

"Like I always say," Faro's smile was about as authentic as the Piltdown Man's jawbone, "if you wanna know about freaks, ask a freak."

"There *is* one small item of information you might be interested in," I conceded. They looked suspicious but also pathetically eager. "That crazed arsonist? There isn't one. See, what's *really* happening is that an evil warlock is using his powers to create these bogeys that can pass through walls and doors and burn you right down to your component atoms. Y'know, like what happened to Eva Jauch."

"*Christ*, Nightstalk," Faro said, realization dawning in his eyes, "I always thought you were stupid but I never knew you were *nuts*."

"Come on, Evgeny," Cassandra urged. "These boys have work to do."

"Yeah, Nightstalk, bugger off and let *real* detectives handle this." Wojeck's sneer was Elvis-like in its proportions.

I pretended to be hurt. "I'm trying to help you guys out. I mean, usually I let you chase your own tails but just this once I thought I'd take pity and—"

"Fuck *you*, asshole," Faro spat. "Fuck you and your Shade friends. You only come out at night, right? Like a bunch of fuckin' animals."

I sighed. Ravenors? Elementals? I might as well have been talking about the man in the moon. An invasion from another dimension? Right up there with the Tooth Fairy and Santa Claus as far as they were concerned. "You know, you boys shouldn't be trying so hard to rile me." I gave the door an experimental tug. "These shitbuckets sure come apart easy, don't they?"

Wojeck turned three different shades of purple and Faro swore as he put the car into gear. "You hear anything, you call *us* first," he warned.

"What, like a billionaire is throwing a huge bash just so he can sacrifice his guests to the savage pagan gods he worships? Stuff like that?" They stared at me as if I was drooling and had a hunchback. Faro shot me the finger as they pulled away.

"You shouldn't bait them, y'know. One of these days they might believe you and then you're *really* in trouble."

"Never in hell. Those boys aren't that smart."

She shook her head. "It's scary. The quality of law enforcement officers has definitely gone downhill in the past few years."

"What do you expect? They've started recruiting at zoos, fer Chrissake."

"You're exaggerating."

"It's the truth!" We set out for the convenience store, neither of us in a hurry. "They started with monkeys but they turned out to be too smart and tried to unionize, see, so then they tried sloths..." I chattered away at her for awhile but stopped when I realized she'd lapsed into brooding. I knew her mind was preoccupied with the upcoming party. She'd been scrutinizing the problem from every conceivable angle. She even paid a visit to Fischer's building and sweet-talked a maintenance guy into giving her a tour. The 66th floor was off limits, natch, access aggressively denied by the Fischers' private security pigs. Still, she came away with a good idea of the layout and didn't much like it.

"If anything happens, the elevators won't be able to handle all the guests," she'd reported upon her return. "And I suspect they'll likely be disabled anyway, to prevent anyone from escaping. The stairwells can easily be sealed off as well. There you are, seven hundred feet above the ground, all hell breaking loose and there's no way down."

"People will be panicking, tearing each other apart," I predicted.

She closed her eyes. "Yes, of course. *Of course.* People fighting each other, desperate and crazed to get away. What perfect conditions for the Working. It'll act like a beacon…"

The enormity of our task was weighing heavily on her mind. She'd been busting her ass day and night, poring over crumbling volumes of occult lore, looking for something, *anything* she could use to delay or sabotage the Summoning. She was also hunting up protective spells, wearing her eyes out in half a dozen different languages. She drove herself hard and wouldn't let up, even after I bugged her about it. The notion that Skorzeny and Fischer might actually succeed horrified and galvanized her. She would do whatever was necessary to prevent their victory.

"Partner," I said, as the convenience store hove into sight, "we're gonna be just fine. With a champ like you, our side can't fail."

She looked over at me, startled by my perceptiveness. Then she nodded. "It's the ring, isn't it? You're picking up my thoughts. That's a good sign."

"Or it could be that we've been around each other so long I know you like the back of my hand."

"What else do your new-found abilities tell you?"

"Oh, nothing much. Just that we're screwed, doomed, hopelessly outnumbered…and that the store isn't going to have Cheezies and I'm going to have to settle for fucking Cheetos again." I sped up so I could get the door for her.

It turned out I was right about the Cheezies. *Goddamnit.*

I hoped for both our sakes that the rest of my prediction wouldn't turn out to be nearly as accurate.

Thursday, May 27th

"Evening, Joe."

It was after nine, the dining room mostly empty. A godawful strings version of Bob Marley's "Get Up, Stand Up" was playing in the background. A waiter laid out a new table setting by the window, checking each piece of cutlery critically for water stains.

Duthie had finished dinner and had just unlimbered a battered laptop, presumably to work on his next column. The paper gave him a regular slot and left the subject matter up to him. Anything that was on his mind as long as it offended at least half his readers. He also had a weekly radio show, "Dukin' It Out With Duthie". His guest list was wide and varied, no shrinking violets need apply. He'd reduced more than a few politicians to jabbering wrecks, ridiculing reformers, denouncing incumbents, savaging candidates on both sides of the political spectrum.

"You're a hard man to reach—didn't you get my messages?"

The smoking bylaws were in effect but that didn't prevent him from chewing an unlit stogie. He removed it, pointing the wet end at me. "Sorry, kid, your face ain't familiar. Do I know you?"

"We've never met but you might say we move in the same circles."

"Oh, yeah?" He squinted at me. "What circles? You a hack too?"

I pointed at the empty chair. "Mind if I sit down?"

"Nah, I'm runnin' late as it is." He wasn't known for his good manners and not about to make an exception for me. "I gotta come up with eight hundred words of pure wisdom before I turn in. So unless you got some kinda hot tip you wanna pass along—"

"Hot tip?" I took a seat anyway. "Sure, Joe, I got one for you. See, there's this local coven, real wacko types, and--get this—they plan to punch a portal into another dimension and unleash Cthulhu. Isn't that fucking *wild*?" He stared at me. "You want names? How about Victor Skorzeny? Gregory Fischer? You should be writing this down, Joe. This is good shit. Maybe get you a Pulitzer, you play your cards right."

He re-inserted the stogie. "Nightstalk, right?"

I smiled. "At your service."

"You got nerve, kid, I'll give you that. Not much in the brains department though."

The waiter wandered over and gave me the eye. "Any problems here, Mr. Duthie?"

"No, Maurice, everything's fine. But you can bring me another shot of brandy, if you got a minute. The good stuff, huh? Since the paper's footing the bill."

"Sure thing. I'll be right back."

Nobody asked if I wanted anything. Fine by me. Thanks to Cassandra's new purification regime, I couldn't drink or partake of any stimulant stronger than iced tea. All part of preparing ourselves for the coming battle.

"Joe Duthie," I said. "Voice of the people. How many asses have you put in the hotseat over the years? How many poor fuckers have you made *squirm*?" He didn't react. "And how many people know about your, ah, somewhat unorthodox religious views? I wonder what your fans would say if someone spilled the beans about *that*."

"So this is a shakedown, is it?"

"What do you think?"

He looked down at the laptop, pressed a few buttons and closed the lid. "All right, so you're not a blackmailer. What do you want then?"

"I dunno. How about an explanation?" He raised his eyebrows. "You know who I am, who I work for. And you also know we intend to stop you, no matter what it takes."

He leaned forward, his gaze direct, serious. "Why?"

The question caught me by surprise. "Why *what*?"

"Why stop us?" I gaped at him. "Mr. Nightstalk, hear me out. I shouldn't even be talking to you. If certain people found out—well, I don't have to tell you, the consequences could be pretty fucking dire. For me and especially for *you*. So let me say my piece and then we'll let bygones be bygones. You go your way, I go mine."

"Sure. But I don't know about that bygones stuff."

He smiled. Plucked out the cigar and examined it with longing. "Shit, I wish I could light this up. Fucking anti-smoking Nazis." Setting it aside. "I wanna tell you a story, kid. Every bit of it is true too; whatever else you may think of me, you know Joe Duthie's a straight shooter." I nodded, giving him that. "Fifteen years ago, I went to Panama, sent by my paper to cover Operation Just Cause. Remember that? The good guys went in to liberate the heroic people of Panama from that dope-dealing, money-laundering sonofabitch Manuel Noriega. Twenty thousand American troops did the job—probably could've managed it with a busload of Boy Scouts but never mind. Even then we were into the whole 'shock and awe' thing. We rode in our white horse, stopped evil in its tracks and accomplished our mission with a minimum loss of life. Right?"

"If you say so." I was humouring him, wishing he'd get to the point. Maurice set a snifter in front of him and backed off to a neutral corner.

"The official story is six hundred dead Panamanians. The *real* story is no one knows how many people ended up killed. See, old Manny was smart, he had a military compound set up in one of the most densely populated areas of the city. Southern Command troops took it out with helicopter gunships and assault teams and, lemme tell ya, there was nothing surgical about it." He swirled the brandy around, admiring its colour in the light of the candle. "I got one of the locals, a cab driver, to slip me in there. The *Chorillo*, they called it. Thousands of people crammed into slum tenements, hovels. Whole blocks were leveled by rockets and tanks or strafed by choppers and then, afterward, fires broke out and most of it burned to the ground.

I snuck in there and you could *smell* death, who knows how many bodies under the rubble. And then I come around this half-destroyed building and run smack into one of those Special Forces guys. No markings on his uniform, no visible rank or unit insignia. But he was some kind of hotshit officer. Wouldn't answer my questions, just gave me this look and I knew—I *knew* that if I stayed there another thirty seconds I was a dead man. Not long after that they sent in bulldozers and flattened everything. Any bodies they found were dumped into mass graves. Hundreds. Maybe thousands. And no one cared. Not the so-called free press, least of all the new leaders of Panama. Fucking Endara." He took a hit from the sifter. "I never filed any copy, just got the fuck out. Took stress leave and after that I never wanted to cover serious news again. From then on I became the mouth that roared, the man with an opinion on anything and everything, except what *really* matters. And that's fine with me."

I'd been listening with growing impatience. "So that's it? You stepped in some shit down there, find out the good guys aren't good guys after all and for *that* you'd wipe out the human race? Give me a fucking break."

He shook his head, impatient and irritated. "No. *No.* You're missing the point." Leaning forward. "I saw the face of evil, Mr. Nightstalk. Real evil. It wasn't just that Special Forces fucker. It was the face of our society, of our so-called civilized world. *Panama.* Fuck, that was *nothing.* A blip on the radar. A skirmish nobody even remembers any more. I know my history: in the grand scheme of things, Operation Just Cause amounts to a hill of mouse shit."

"Sorry, Joe, you lost me."

"It doesn't matter." He took a sip of brandy. "The point, at least for me, is that having *any* faith in our species is stupid. Because we have nothing to recommend us. History is filled with mass graves and monsters. Anything that replaces us will be an improvement."

"So mankind is depraved and evil and beyond redemption," I summed up.

"*Yes.*" His eyes flashed and I saw rage there and despair, too deeply rooted to reach. "It's time to bring the fire down and cleanse this planet of our contagion. And, no, Mr. Nightstalk, you *won't* stop us. And if you try," he tipped his head back and emptied the snifter, "we'll kill you. You...and anyone else who's foolish enough to help you. Now, if you'll excuse me, I've got a column to finish."

Friday, May 28th

Cassandra fared no better when she finally ran the elusive Kali Brust to ground.

It was a sleazy joint, even by Cass's standards, dubbed *The DMZ*. You went through a door, down a corridor lined with leaking sandbags and then a guy in combat fatigues wanded you for hidden weapons. There was another pseudo-soldier off the side, cradling an automatic rifle, on the lookout for trouble.

The crowd was hardcore, the music industrial/techno. The military motif predominated. Blowups of Vietnam War-era footage and Matthew Brady's Civil War photos adorned the walls. Waiters sporting bandoliers and cartridge belts made the rounds in black, lace-up combat boots, polished to a high gloss. If you wanted privacy, there were booths upstairs where the saw-toothed guitars and thumping bass were somewhat muted. That's where Cass found her quarry and made her pitch.

At that point Kali was at the tail end of a three day methamphetamine binge and not in the best of moods.

"Listen, bitch," she snarled at Cassandra, "you'd better back the fuck off, all right?" Her boy toys were within easy reach, a couple of blonde cuties with surfer tans and about fifteen working neurons between them. "I know the score. Anybody talks to you ends up wormfood." She grabbed the nearest surfer dude and proceeded to tickle his tonsils with her long, agile tongue. If she was trying to shock Cassandra, she'd have to do better than that.

You had to wonder what Kali's parents, two high-powered corporate lawyers, would have made of the scene. By all accounts they'd given up on their wayward daughter years ago, providing her with a decent stipend to live on as long as she didn't publicly embarrass them or dishonour the family name[30].

"I'm not trying to put you in harm's way, Kali," Cassandra explained patiently. "I just want to make sure that you know what you're getting yourself into. Skorzeny is using you and the rest of the Cabal to—"

Kali brayed with laughter. "*Using* me? Fuck that! I *want* to be used. I *need* to be used. Fuckin' sex magick—shit, that's nothing. Getting screwed by old goats like the Baron, that's fuckin' boring, all right? Victor, he's taking us *wayyy* beyond that. If you were smart, you'd come along for the ride too."

"But don't you see? He's doesn't care what the consequences are."

"Neither do I!" Someone knocked on the door. A waiter, face striped with green and black camo paint, leaned inside and Kali waved for another round of margaritas. "Here," she flipped a platinum credit card at him. "Throw on a big tip and charge it to daddy." The waiter withdrew and Cassandra tried to renew her argument.

But Kali wasn't paying any attention. One of the surfer dudes was kneading her tits and she appeared to be masturbating both of them below the level of the table. And all the while she was looking at Cassandra with this twisted grin on her face, her brain sizzling, over-loaded with chemicals.

Cassandra, realizing it was hopeless, prepared to leave.

"Hey," Kali said, "you see Nightstalk, tell him I said 'hi', okay?" She grinned. "No hard feelings about me zapping him, I hope." The surfer dudes were shuddering, close to climax but then she pulled her hands away. When they protested, she just laughed. "Pleasure and pain, boys," she told them, "it's all part of the great game of life."

Wise words, especially coming from someone so hopelessly fucked up...

Friday, May 28th

...neither Duthie nor Brust was willing to lend assistance to our investigation. We have also been actively seeking two other members of the Cabal although our prospects, admittedly, aren't good in either instance. City councillor Ronald Witcover is a close associate of Fischer's, the point man for the scheme/swindle to redevelop the harbour and dockland area. Local businessman Allan Mayhew

---

[30] Note: "Kali Brust" is *not* her real name.

has, it seems, gone into hiding. His downtown
office is guarded round the clock. Our calls are
not returned, so we have no way of confirming his
present whereabouts or—

I quit typing as soon as Cassandra got through to someone at City Hall.
"Could I speak to councillor Witcover, please?" I shook my head in
admiration as I listened to her go into her little old lady act. "Yes, I realize
that but this is one of his constituents and I need to talk to him. Well,
wasn't there a council meeting tonight? I know, dear, but this is an
emergency." Cripes, she was convincing. She sounded at least ninety years
old. "I voted for Mr. Witcover and he's the only one who can help me.
Yes. Oh, thank you, dear. Thank you so much. Yes, I'll hold." She
glanced over at me, giving a thumbs up.

"I still say we should've gotten Werner to go over there and just *snatch*
the guy."

"What? Right in front of City Hall? Even for Werner that would've
been a—" She made a shushing gesture. "Councillor Witcover? Yes, just
a moment." She switched to speaker phone and assumed her regular voice.
"You're a hard man to find, councillor."

"Well, we've been very busy around here, as I'm sure you understand.
How can I help you, ma'am?"

"We need to see you. It's of critical importance that you meet with
us."

"*We*? I'm sorry, I thought *you* were the one who—"

"It's about what you and your buddy Gregory Fischer are up to,
Witcover," I cut in. Cassandra frowned but my patience was stretched
anorexically thin at that point.

"Who *is* this?"

"We know all about the Babalon Working and we know all about *you*.
So waddaya say, Ron? Let's talk turkey."

"You're those…the detectives, right? Zinnea and—and—"

"Right the first time," I said, doubly annoyed because he didn't
remember my name. "We're tired of chasing after your ass. Give us a time
and place and we'll be there."

"I'm afraid I don't know what you mean," he retorted. "I was led to
believe this call was from a constituent. Since it appears I have been
misled—"

"Why have you been hiding, Mr. Witcover?" Cassandra asked, taking a
gentler tack. "You haven't been by your house and you've taken a leave of

absence from your job. Nobody seems to know where you are or what's going on."

"Please," he said, his voice faint, "I shouldn't be talking to you. My God, if they found out—"

"We wanna meet, in person," I broke in. "This phone business is bullshit."

"No," he said quickly. "And don't bother looking for me either. I'm leaving right away and you're right about one thing, I won't be going home or—or anywhere else you'll find me."

"Ron," she tried again, "you're making a big mistake, all of you. You've got to help us stop Skorzeny before—"

"*No!*" he howled. "Don't even say his name! I can't help you. They'll kill me, don't you understand? Don't call again, please! *Leave me alone!*"

Click.

Buzz.

"Well, fuck me with a baseball bat," I commented. "Y'know, I, for one, am sick of getting the runaround."

She raised her eyebrows. "You have something in mind?"

I looked at my watch. "I say we stop pussyfooting about. Witcover's flown the coop so let's move on to Plan B."

"I take it you're referring to Allan Mayhew?"

"He's gone to ground and turned his building into a fortress. He's in there somewhere, holed up like the fuckin' rat he is."

"You want to pay him a visit, is that it?" I could tell the idea held some appeal to her.

"Why the fuck not? If nothing else, I'll get to punch a few people out."

"Let's hope it doesn't come to that."

"Let's hope it *does*. At least it'll help spice up my reports. Jesus, they've made for dull reading lately."

"I suppose we should at least *try* to see him. What's the worst they can do? Throw us out?" She pointed at me. "But when we get there *please* let me do the talking. No need to provoke anyone if we don't have to."

"Sure, doll," I assured her, "whatever you say." She regarded me suspiciously but I just shrugged it off.

Hey, as far as I was concerned, it was a no brainer.

Talking's never been my strong suit anyhow.

Various confidential sources (no names, please!) provided most of the details contained in the following reconstruction. In some cases, specific

*exchanges or utterances are extrapolations or inventions of yours truly but
I stand by the overall accuracy of this account:*

At roughly the same time that Cassandra and I were having the
preceding conversation, a package was delivered *via* courier to the
corporate headquarters of Mayhew Enterprises.

It was left with the smiling, unfailingly courteous ladies at reception
(all of them black belts, incidentally, and as mean as komodo dragons). It
was late for a delivery but due to the scope and diversity of Mayhew's
various business interests, packages arrived pretty much 24/7 so nobody
thought much about it. The parcel underwent standard security screening.
It was scanned and X-rayed...and that's when the true gravity of the
situation was revealed.

You can imagine the reaction of the techie on duty when he glanced at
the screen and saw that the box in question appeared to contain...a human
skull. Looking right at him from his colour monitor.

He reached for his phone and put in a call to Ed Dealey, Mayhew's
chief of security. After concluding his brief report, the techie hung up, took
a deep breath and keeled over in a dead faint.

Ten minutes later, Dealey, looking a tad green around the gills,
gingerly bore the package up to the top floor. That such a hard case as
Dealey was squeamish about the contents of the box spoke volumes. Ed
Dealey had seen and done many things in his years of loyal service to his
boss and even prior to that. It took a lot to get his goat.

The elevator door opened and he nodded to Nathan and Teddie. Good
lads. Thugs and bully-boys of the first order. Lethal with gun, knife or
bare hands. Their steroid-enhanced bulk blocked the hallway, he just about
had to turn sideways to get past them. Dealey knocked once and entered
Allan Mayhew's private office.

Everything in Mayhew's personal domain was *big*: the enormous
mahogany desk, the chairs...even the over-sized paintings and limited
edition prints mounted around the room. His tastes leaned toward Poussin
and Goya--Aristotle O'Leary's influence—but his collection also included
an original Giger I would have swapped my entire porn collection for. Tall,
burgundy-coloured drapes that had once adorned a castle on the Rhine
covered windows capable of stopping anything short of an artillery round.

Allan Mayhew himself was a man of modest dimensions, only an inch
or two taller than me. Unlike yours truly, however, he had yet to come to
terms with his below average stature. He often wore ineffectual lifts and
favoured suits with wide, padded shoulders and tapered waists. Imagine a
miniature version of Jimmy Caan and you'd be on the right track.

The cardboard box that Ed Dealey placed before his boss was perfectly square and could have contained anything from a small bread box to a sizable quantity of TNT.

In actuality, it held the severed head of the aforementioned Aristotle O'Leary, Mayhew's longtime crony, spiritual advisor, *consigliere*, guru, and the closest thing he had to a true friend.

Dealey broke the news as gently as he could. Mayhew, characteristically, asked to see the sickening trophy. With shaking hands, Dealey reached in and withdrew the disconnected head. Despite his rising nausea, he was able to point out certain aspects that he thought needed to be brought to his employer's attention.

The horror and anguish on O'Leary's ashen face distorted his features almost to the point where he was unrecognizable. And then Dealey showed Mayhew *why*.

The head hadn't been severed cleanly with an ax or blade. It had been sawed or possibly *chewed* off. Mayhew groped for his throne-like chair and collapsed into it. Dealey had never seen him like this before. Deflated. Disheartened. Beaten.

"This is bad, Ed," he said at last. "The absolute, the most..." He couldn't find words that were adequate, the shock rendering him momentarily speechless.

"Yes, sir," Ed Dealey agreed. "I've ordered extra security precautions, called in more people on top of the ones we've already—"

"Aristotle saw it coming, you know." Mayhew had tears his eyes. Probably for the first time since childhood. "He warned me something was up, that Skorzeny was going to—that he--he—oh, *fuck*." He covered his face with his hands.

"I think it's safe to assume, sir," Dealey hoisted Aristotle by his hair and put him back into the box, handling the skull with as much delicacy as he could, "that you have been officially warned."

Mayhew's head snapped up. "Oh, is that a fact, Ed? Is that your *expert* opinion?"

His security chief winced. "Sorry, sir."

"Because that man," pointing at the box, "was the *best*, you understand? He made me what I am. I never made a single move in my entire career without checking with Ari first. He was the guy, the one fuckin' guy I could trust, no matter what. Without him..." He had small hands and he squeezed them into small, tight fists. "I *told* him. I warned him to watch his back, didn't I, Ed? People knew who he was, what he meant to me. Fuck, they knew where he *lived*. The man was fearless. He knew the price he'd pay for crossing Skorzeny.   That dirty fucking *bastard*."

"Yes, sir," Dealey concurred.

"Ari told me the last time I saw him he was having dreams. Bad dreams. He thought he was under some kind of astral attack." Brushing the box with his fingertips. "I should have protected him better. Once he spoke up, started questioning Victor, it was only a matter of time before..." Mayhew hitched in his breath, his emotions dangerously close to the surface.

At that moment Dealey's people called from the lobby, informing him that two private dicks had shown up and wanted to talk to the boss.

He cursed. Said he'd be right down. He left Mayhew alone with the head. It seemed like the right thing to do. As he opened the door, he heard Allan Mayhew whisper something, presumably to the remains of his murdered friend. Just a short sentence, nothing Dealey could make out.

He wasn't sure, but it sounded like an apology.

Meanwhile, the two of us loitered in the fancy foyer, taking note of the over-abundance of security goons hanging about. We were, of course, completely unaware of the events transpiring upstairs.

Marching in and loftily requesting an audience with Allan Mayhew, one of the most powerful and notorious men in the Great Lakes region, showed a certain amount of desperation on our part. After all, this was not a man known for his kindness and generosity of spirit. Hey, you don't make it that high up the food chain by being a sweetheart of a guy, at least not in my experience.

Cassandra was nervous as she eyed the hired muscle but I wasn't impressed. They were strictly beefcake, as far as I could tell. Calendar boys. *Pussycats.*

For my part, I was surprised how open they were about it. This wasn't a titty bar or the back room of some private club where everybody had a name that sounded like a pasta dish. It was the corporate head office of Mayhew Enterprises, a multi-million dollar conglomerate (or was that syndicate?).

Allan Mayhew was another true Shade, hardly ever seen in the light of day. Judging from the marble in the foyer, the art on the walls (no nudes, unfortunately) and the level of activity even at such a late hour, he was doing quite well for himself despite that apparent handicap. He had his stubby fingers in just about everything: real estate, car dealerships, fast food franchises, mini-malls...you name it.

The front lobby looked like something out of "2001: A Space Odyssey". Very modern and high tech. Climate controlled, air filtered, everything bright and shiny and *clean*. You probably had to provide a DNA sample to take a dump.

Everyone appeared jumpy, the mood tense. We drew a lot of funny looks. After about ten minutes, Ed Dealey showed up. He looked sweaty, out of sorts. We weren't expecting any special treatment from him. He was an ex-cop, cashiered for sticky fingers, a hard-ass and an old pro at the security game. Fat but not soft.

He led us into a small room just off the lobby and got right down to business. For the record: what the hell did we want? He seemed distracted and sometimes asked questions twice. Or maybe he was being cagey, trying to catch us out.

He wasn't inclined to take us up to see his boss. Apparently the CEO of Mayhew Enterprises had too much on his plate to waste valuable time on a couple of two-bit gumshoes.

I'm paraphrasing. He used a lot more "f" words than that.

But Dealey was no match for Cassandra.

She went right after him. She began by mentioning the presence of the goons—what was up with that? The place looked like it was under siege. Had there been any threats made? Did this have anything to do with the bad luck that had befallen the Baron, Winston Gillette and Paul Briere? Making with the eye contact, working her wiles.

Dealey was sweating buckets by the time she was through with him. Wordlessly, he beckoned for us to follow him out of the room, leading us to a bank of elevators. Pulling out a keyring, he inserted a metal tab into a slot on the control panel inside the car and pressed a button. We were going right to the top.

I raised an eyebrow at Cass: *your doing?*

I admit nothing.

You are a woman of many talents. Telepathy, assorted spells and enchantments, psychokinetics--

Not to mention crossword puzzles, charades, chess and fellatio--

We both snorted and Dealey snapped his head around, giving us a dirty look. "What's so fuckin' funny?" he demanded.

"Nothin'," I replied, "just the dry air in this place."

I could tell he didn't believe me.

We waited outside while he went in to brief Mayhew on this latest development. I figured they'd take the opportunity to hash over the best way to kill us and dispose of our bodies. Allan Mayhew was no Vito

Corleone but I was under no illusions. He'd have us chopped up into gourmet dog food in a heartbeat if he believed we posed a threat to his bottom line.

A true capitalist in every sense.

I amused myself by goading the two gorillas blocking the door. I questioned their intelligence, their manhood and their sexual preferences. Cassandra cleared her throat in warning but I was having too much fun to take any notice. The gorillas glanced at each other, trying to decide who would jump me first. It was right about then that Dealey stuck his head out and waved us inside. I wiggled my fingers "toodle-oo" to my new playmates and sauntered after my partner.

The cardboard box was still sitting on the desk, though pushed off to one side, the flaps discreetly closed. A person would never suspect...

Except there was a funny feeling in the room and Philippe's ring started vibrating the moment we walked in. I glanced over at Cassandra but she'd already picked up on it, sensing the presence of the unnatural, *spook stuff.*

Mayhew saw our reactions and grimaced at his security chief.

They'd talked it over and decided to play it coy with us. They "vaguely" recalled the death of the Baron and the human bonfire in St. Andrew's Park but expressed little interest in the two incidents.

"You already know that the Baron and I were...associates." Mayhew sat in his big chair, acting very calm, every inch the legitimate businessman. "But, speaking frankly, over the past few months we'd sort of drifted apart."

"Just two ships that passed in the night," I offered, trying to be helpful.

Mayhew scowled. "Ed said you also mentioned Paul Briere. Again, I haven't spoken to Paul in ages. Have you seen him?"

"Sort of," I acknowledged. "But you wouldn't have recognized him. He's changed a lot."

Mayhew was about to say something but reconsidered. Dealey peeked at his watch, anxious to eject our asses and look good in front of his boss. Cassandra saw what he was up to and suddenly switched tacks:

"Where's Aristotle, Allan?" she asked. I glanced at her. She caught my eye and held my gaze for a beat or two. "Odd that he's not here."

The box, Nightstalk.

"Yeah, where is ol' Ari? " I moved toward the desk. "I need my horoscope read and I hear he's just the man for the job."

Mayhew tried to smile but it didn't quite work. "Mr. O'Leary is temporarily unavailable."

"Temporarily taken leave of his senses? That wouldn't come as any surprise." I was zeroing in on the box when Dealey swept past me, scooping it up. He stood with it cradled in his arms; his jacket was open, I could see his shoulder holster.

"What's up, Eddie?" I inquired cheerily.

"I believe there's something in that box," Cassandra said, sidling up next to me. "Maybe we should have a look inside and find out—"

Allan Mayhew rose to his feet. He was not, as I said, a physically imposing man and came close to caricature with his padded suits and giant furniture. But when he stood, a surge of power and authority halted us in our tracks. "I think that's enough for tonight. You two, get out while you still can. Ed, put down that goddamn box and take this pair—"

Cassandra held her ground. She leaned on his desk so that she was eye level with him and let him have it with both barrels. "I *know* what's in the box, Allan. And I know what Aristotle meant to you. We *both* know who did this and why. Aristotle was advising you to back out of the Working, wasn't he? He was no dummy, he knew what would happen if Skorzeny and Fischer succeeded. And that in the new world they were creating there wouldn't be any need for self-made business tycoons. But they got to him and at the same time sent you fair warning, saying if you don't play along, there's a box waiting for you too. Does that about sum things up?"

We all stared at her.

I prepared to die.

Mayhew fell back in his chair. He looked *gutted*.

Dealey didn't like what he was seeing. "Okay," he barked, "that's it: *out*." He set the box on the floor by his feet and prepared to give us the bum's rush.

"Aristotle was right, Allan." Cassandra persisted. "Right to resist them. He saw through their lies. Did he convince you to meet Philippe? Was that the last straw as far as they were concerned?" Her voice softened. "All the security and protection in the world won't save you and you know it. But maybe we—us, the Old Man—can help. Give us a chance." I stayed close in case Dealey tried to put the grab on her. "If there's something we can do, we're at your disposal. If you need confirmation, pick up the phone and call the Old Man. But right now it's important that you level with us."

For a second or two I thought she'd hooked him. Then I saw him smile, a real one this time. "My dear, you are a peach. Truly. I applaud your sterling effort. But, unfortunately," the smile fading, "I must reject your offer. Although please tell your employer I was...tempted."

Then it was my turn. "Aristotle was a genuine adept. You relied on him as a clairvoyant, a seer, whatever you want to call it." Then giving him the bad news: "But his Gift didn't keep him out of that box." Mayhew's head jerked toward me. "Right now *nobody's* safe. That's why we need to work together."

Dealey hovered, ready to summon the dynamic duo from the hallway to do his dirty work. Something they'd relish. "Boss?"

"Let's hear what they have to say," Mayhew decided at last, "I'd like to find out how much the Old Man knows."

"More than us," I admitted, "as usual we seem to be playing catch up."

"Just don't say anything incriminating," Dealey begged, sagging gratefully into the nearest seat.

"That might be difficult for someone in my position," his employer remarked. "Besides, these two have no powers of arrest. And you've already checked them for wires so there's nothing to worry about, right?"

"I still say having them up here is a bad idea. What if--"

"Ed," Allan Mayhew said, "my oldest and dearest friend Aristotle O'Leary is dead. That's a fact. They *Fed Ex*-ed me his head in a fucking box. Murdered him and did it in a way that was meant to put a scare into me. And it worked, by god." He stared hard at Cassandra and me. "This conversation doesn't leave the room. It's a figment of your imagination, got it?"

I bobbed my head but Cassandra wasn't so easily intimidated. "Was I right? Was Aristotle telling you that the Working was too dangerous, that you shouldn't take part?"

He nodded. "Ari thought Skorzeny was a fool and crazy to boot. They were dabbling in stuff we wanted nothing to do with. Others agreed. Paul Briere, the Baron, Vivien. Somehow they found out we had doubts. First Paul disappeared, then the Baron got killed. And look what they did to what's his name, Esch. There's no sense of proportion with these people! Then I guess they decided it was my turn. At first, I thought I was imagining things. There was something here, in the office. You could sense it moving around, almost catch it out of the corner of your eye. Ed felt it too—"

"Fuckin' creepy," Dealey confirmed with a shudder.

"I dig black magic, I've been interested in the stuff since I was a kid. But that's playtime compared to what these assholes are up to." He pointed at us. "You're the ones who should be worried. At least I'm laying low, not running around playing detective."

"Is that your strategy, Allan? Dig yourself a hole, hope for the best?" She sounded more disappointed than angry.

He raised his hands. "What else can I do?"

"What about revenge?" I spoke up. "You're gonna let these fuckers do that to your buddy and get away with it?"

Dealey stirred himself. "Stay outta this, asshole."

"Listen to me, sonny, and you listen good." The power was back on again, the force of Allan Mayhew's personality filling the room. "If you and your lady friend came here looking to join forces or whatever, you're shit outta luck. Not only that, you do *anything* to endanger me or cause Skorzeny to come after me, I'll be all over you. Got it?"

"Thanks for the warning." I pretended to suppress a yawn. "If the best you can come up with is Eddie here and those hormone cases propping up the walls downstairs, I got nothing to worry about."

Dealey stood up. "This conversation is over."

Mayhew was shaking his head. "You still don't get it, do you? Let me put it this way: if I thought there was the slightest chance I could bury Skorzeny's head in the same box as Ari's, I'd do it in a minute. But I'm outta my league. Compared to that evil fuck, I'm just a crooked businessman with a mean streak." All the fight had gone out of him. "Ed, show these people out. And, Ed? They have safe conduct, understand?" He raised a hand in farewell. "Call it…one last goodwill gesture." Dealey was herding us toward the door when Mayhew spoke again. "And if you do somehow manage to stop them, maybe even kill a few of the fucks, come back and see me. I wanna hear all about it."

Saturday, May 29th

Time to pay another visit to the Diogenes Club and check on Holmes' progress.

"You will be pleased to learn that I've managed to infiltrate some of my Irregulars into the Fischers' fête as bus boys and service staff. This despite some rather stringent security measures, I may add." He blew on his fingernails and polished them on the front of his velvet smoking jacket, hamming it up for us. "Luckily, I was able to prevail upon my fellow club members to assist me. Most of them retain close ties to the law enforcement fraternity. Which is fortunate." He looked exasperated. "Several of my best operatives have somewhat lengthy criminal records for, ah, a variety of offenses. A standard background check would have almost certainly disqualified them for employment at the upcoming extravaganza. Or anywhere else, for that matter."

"How will we know which are your people?" Cassandra inquired.

"Easy," I explained. "I just go up to every waiter and ask them if they know where I can score some decent blow. The ones that say 'yes' are probably our boys."

Holmes frowned. "*Really*, Mr. Nightstalk. If I were you, I wouldn't be so quick to look a gift horse in the mouth. Right now our side is looking decidedly thin in terms of manpower so I should think you'd be happy for whatever assistance is offered."

"You're right," I agreed, meanwhile playing with Philippe's ring, kind of rotating it on my finger. It was silver and plain, no inscriptions or designs. Not just silver. *Pure* silver. The purest, most unadulterated silver in the world. Nothing but the best for the Brethren. "I spoke brusquely and I apologize for my crudeness. I'm sure your associates will be invaluable when the time comes." I stopped playing with the ring and glanced up at them. They were staring at me. "What?"

"Are you all right, Nightstalk?" my partner asked, her concern evident.

"Absolutely. Never better." And it was the truth too.

"As I was saying," Holmes continued, "there will be at least four Irregulars on hand to lend assistance. I emphasize, these will be my best people so do not hesitate to use them. As a diversion, for instance, should you require one."

"Great, when can we meet them?"

His face fell. "Ah...yes. Actually, they were supposed to be here by now. I can't imagine what's keeping them."

"Great," I noted, "so at least we know they're reliable."

Cassandra frowned at me. "Never mind, we'll use some kind of prearranged signal if we have to. Mr. Holmes, you've done a terrific job and we're in your debt."

He scurried over, beaming, taking one of her hands between his. "My dear lady, it is a privilege to work with you and your stalwart colleague." A nod in my direction. "I only pray our efforts will prove to be sufficient when the final outcome is decided."

"No shit, Sherlock," I mumbled.

I'd been *dying* to say that.

Sunday, May 30^(th)

A rare evening off. Cassandra insisted. We were both tuckered out and needed a break.

Stayed home. Wanked. Talked to myself. Tossed and turned. When I did sleep, I found myself back at the Black Tower again.

Climbing, always *climbing...*

Monday, May 31st

"*Gadgets*, Mr. Nightstalk?" Professor Edwin Fuchs was offended by my choice of words. "The devices I spend months, sometimes *years* designing and creating with my own hands are not *gadgets*. They employ state of the art technology and adhere to the strictest scientific principles—"

"Yeah, yeah," I said, cutting off the lecture before it got started, "just tell me if you got anything that's *useful*, something that won't give bogeys giggling fits if I wave it in their faces."

Cassandra took pity on him. "My apologies, Professor Fuchs. My partner's formal scientific training began and ended with the chemistry set he got when he was twelve."

"I asked for brass knuckles," I added, for the record.

We were in his workshop, which was adjacent his office. It appeared to be a converted storeroom and Fuchs confirmed as much, bemoaning his lowly status within the academic hierarchy. "No space, everything packed in tight," he muttered, pushing aside stacks of books, assorted tools and styrofoam takeout containers, looking for...something.

"This isn't another one of those ionizers, is it?" I asked suddenly. "Because that spook at the Belasco house nearly stuck the last one up my--" [31]

"No, no," he said. "You indicated you were looking for something that might be used under particularly dire circumstances."

"Kind of like...Cthulhu repellant," I suggested. Fuchs was talking to himself again, clearly frustrated at not finding whatever it was he was seeking. "Something that's going to *work*," I emphasized.

Fuchs paused, regarding me morosely. "Mr. Nightstalk. *Theoretically* my inventions should function with a high degree of reliability and effectiveness. Unfortunately, the only opportunity I get to field test them is

---

[31] As related in "The House on Haunted Hill" (*The Casebooks of Zinnea & Nightstalk, Vol. III*)

through the efforts of individuals like you and your lovely--*Aha!*" He stumbled over a box on the floor and crashed into a table. An object the size and shape of a small egg rolled toward the edge but he managed to reach out and snag it before it fell. He straightened, appearing quite pleased with himself. "I, ah, rather think this 'gadget' might be just what you're looking for, Mr. Nightstalk." He flipped the egg in the air and caught it. Repeated the motion while I tried to get a good look at it.

"What is it?" I asked. "It looks...sort of like a grenade."

Professor Edwin Fuchs giggled. "I commend your powers of observation."

Cassandra was dubious. "So it's a bomb?"

Fuchs nodded. "Yes, my dear, but *what* a bomb..."

IV

"And when he had opened the seventh seal, there was silence in heaven..."

Revelations 8:1

In the days leading up to the big bash, when we weren't planning or doing research or consulting with what few allies we had left, there were the *exercises*. Gawd, how I grew to hate and dread them.

At first, I was pathetic. Absolutely useless. I could pick up general impressions and moods, that was about it. I could tell when Cass was hungry (or horny) but couldn't read specific thoughts.

She would do stuff like hide things around the office and get me to try and probe her mind to discover their location. I'd sit across the desk from her and do my best to block everything out, staring at her until my eyes watered. Then I tried it with eyes closed. *Nothing.* Not so much as a whisper. The key with telepathy is *focus*—letting go of niggling thoughts and problems and tuning in to the right mental wavelength.

Concentrate, let everything else drop away, she kept telling me.

And then one night, after a half hour of sweating and straining, something clicked. I looked at her and I *knew* she had her library card tucked in her brassiere. I went over, reached into her blouse and plucked it out. Instead of slapping me, she jumped to her feet and hugged me so hard I squeaked for mercy. Success!

But telepathy is a slippery skill. I was always better in the first hour or so, when I was fresh and sharp. After that my accuracy dropped off dramatically.

Ditto with psychometry. Sometimes I'd hold a spoon Cassandra snitched from a restaurant or some other found object she produced, and I'd get an *inkling* if there were strong feelings attached to it, fear or guilt or anger. Flashes of contorted, shouting faces, disjointed scenes from places I'd never been, featuring people I'd never met.

As far as psycho-kinetics went, well, the less said about it the better. I could make a marble roll across the desk or cause an orange to tremble in anticipation but that was the extent of it. I wasn't what you would call a quick study.

"Once a 2nd Degree, always a 2nd Degree," I concluded with a shrug.

"But with the ring you should be doing better than you are," she insisted, clearly mystified. "Your admittedly modest abilities should be enhanced to a far greater degree than what you've shown so far." This conversation occurred a few nights before the party so we were both feeling keyed up and on edge. "I still think it's a matter of maintaining a sustained level of concentration—"

"Will you *quit* saying that?" I cut in. "I'm doing the best I can."

"Well, it's not good enough," she shot back. "We're going to need every possible advantage Saturday night. It's up to you to bear down and make some real progress for a change."

"Are you accusing me of not trying? If you are, you're nuts! Lady, I've been busting my hump doing your stupid practices and drills and the only thing I've gotten out of it is a sore head. Fuck these exercises of yours! Will you give it up already? I don't have what it takes, all right? I'm not Gifted, I'm not an adept, I'm only me and if that isn't good enough for you—" I gestured with my arm, either in dismissal or defiance—

--the papers on the desk between us were swept up and flung in every direction.

We watched, dumbstruck, as a mini-blizzard of pages fluttered down around us.

"Sonofabitch," I grunted.

Cassandra was grinning. "Well! I'd say your particular Gift is somehow tied to your emotional state. It appears you need to have the equivalent of a temper tantrum in order to tap into it. You're not Popeye anymore, Evvie. You're the Incredible Hulk."

"I always liked him," I confessed. "Like me, he has a low tolerance for bullshit combined with a truly lousy disposition."

"I'll go along with that," she agreed. Her eyes twinkled merrily. "Do you think you'll be able to get mad enough Saturday night to wreak some serious havoc?"

I laughed. "Darlin', *that* I guarantee...."

--and then, though at first I don't trust my senses, I realize I've reached the last step.

Unbelievably, I've made it to the top of the Tower! Lucky thing, too, because I'm winded, semi-delirious with pain, my poor ankle swollen to the circumference of a grapefruit.

As if in recognition of my achievement, an ominous silence descends. The exaggerated stillness has an unnerving quality to it, giving the impression that it's only a matter of time before the imposed calm is shattered--

The sky overhead is rent by a flash of lightning, accompanied by a shout *of thunder that almost deafens me. The storm is directly above the Tower and its perilous height makes it a natural lightning rod, the air around me sizzling with exotic energies.*

And then the rain comes down, a deluge that drenches me in an instant. The icy downpour helps rid me of some mental cobwebs, by-products of my arduous climb. I shake my head...and once my vision sufficiently clears and I take in the scene before me, the cold and pain are instantly forgotten, driven from my thoughts.

Cassandra Zinnea has been secured to a stone altar, though she resists her bonds with admirable ferocity, bucking and heaving against them. There are grooves and runnels carved into the rock slab, narrow channels with one obvious, practical purpose.

Standing directly over her is a figure in a long, black cloak and as I look on, another jolt of lightning illuminates them in stark, white light. A gust of wind whips the hood from the high priest's head and it's unmistakably Victor Skorzeny...only it's not. His eyes are gone except for two malignant pinpoints of light.

I make myself move, willing myself forward.

Cassandra continues to struggle against her restraints and when the next flash comes, she sees me. Her eyes widen and she starts to call out to me, either a greeting or a warning—

Skorzeny raises both hands above his head and I see a glint, a stabbing point, poised to plunge down and pierce her magnificent heart.

NO! I lunge toward them, intending to intercept that leaping blade, at the very least shield her with my body--
But I slip.
Here, on the summit, the black rock is polished, smooth as glass, the rain pooling on its flat surface. And it's one of these puddles that does me in. My weak ankle buckles and my feet skid out from under me. Arms windmilling...and then a slow motion, backwards tumble, suspended in mid-air, watching helplessly as the knife penetrates her breast and—

I rolled off the couch, then rose in one swift movement, yelling and flailing my arms. Floundered around the room, colliding with a stack of DVD's, sending them clattering to the floor. Panting, searching about wildly...until I recognized the familiar surroundings of my apartment. In my panic, I'd disturbed Tree, who snapped at the air, instinctively seeking out any assailant within reach. I muttered an apology and staggered into the bathroom, splashed cold water on my face until I was fully awake.
Enough is enough.
I started a bath, then went to the kitchen for a box of salt. I wasn't sure of the measurement to use, ended up dumping a cup or so into the tub. Found a few withered garlic bulbs in the crisper, broke them open and placed a clove or two in various spots around the apartment.
When the water in the tub was deep enough, I lowered myself into it. Tried to remember some of the mantras and prayers Cass had taught me. Gave up and simply implored the gods and stewards of Creation who happened to be awake at that hour: *hear this humble sinner and forgive my many transgressions. Above all else, preserve Cassandra Zinnea from injury or harm, now and in the days to come...*

Saturday, June 5th

I started getting ready around the time I usually had supper. Eating was out of the question, of course, the fast now in effect for more than twenty-four hours. I didn't have much of an appetite anyway. Nerves. My guts really giving me the gears.
Once I'd retrieved my father's suit from longterm storage, the first thing I did was try it on. Not a bad fit and after I had it dry-cleaned and the neighborhood tailor made a few minor adjustments, I thought it looked pretty sharp. The sleeves were a tad short and the vest somewhat snug. Other than that, I pronounced myself pleased with the final result.

For the sake of nostalgia, I tucked Pop's old pocket watch into the front slit pocket of the vest. The watch hadn't worked in years but it would serve as a useful prop. Whenever conversation got dull, I'd whip it out, gape at it in disbelief and hurry off as if I was late for a private appointment with the Pope.

I'd gotten my hair cut extra short for the occasion, buzzed almost to the scalp at the sides and back, the way I liked it. Part of *my* ritual, you might say. Long hair is a disadvantage in a scrap. You don't want to give an opponent anything to grab on to.

Before getting dressed, I took an indecently long shower, likely using up every last drop of hot water in the building. I scrubbed myself raw, splashed on lots of cologne and nearly wore out my deodorant stick to compensate for my notoriously over-active sweat glands.

Under the strict terms of the fast, I was allowed *no* food and only enough water to keep hydrated. Cassandra insisted we had to purge and purify our systems, prepare our bodies, minds and spirits for the coming battle. If nothing else, the hunger would sharpen my wits, not to mention make me even crankier than usual.

I lit an incense stick and sat on the couch. Closed my eyes, ran through some relaxation exercises. When they didn't work, I tried staring at a candle but after about ten minutes was forced to admit defeat.

It was hard to get my mind to stay *still*. I was distracted, wondering what the end result of this evening's fun and games would be—life or death? Victory or an invasion of million-eyed bogeys from Dimension X?

I tried to stay positive but niggling doubts kept surfacing, pestering me, preventing me from achieving that peaceful, easy feeling the Eagles sing about.

Was it the dream? What I witnessed on the summit of the Tower, the lightning, the rain, failing her so utterly and completely—

I let go of the thought, watched it drift away like an errant balloon. An old meditation trick. Trying not to think of something makes it impossible to think of anything *but* that annoying and persistent image or idea. Better to name and acknowledge worries and fears and then release them.

I found myself praying again, basically offering up my pitiful soul in return for Cassandra being spared and making it out of this mess alive. It was an open-ended offer, payable to any god, regardless of denomination or cultural origin, who agreed to the exchange.

I was sweating like a junkie and tempted to take another shower. Instead I swabbed on more deodorant and another helping of cologne, hoping that would do the trick. The cologne was a gift from my partner, marking our very first Christmas together. She told me that my regular stuff should be used as tear gas at the next anti-globalization rally. *Ha ha.*

Certain things about the suit were starting to annoy me. The shirt collar seemed over-starched, chafing my throat and the freshly shaved area on the back of my neck. The vest was even tighter under the arms than I'd first thought. It affected my range of movement. The pants were too long but I could tolerate that because the cuffs covered my cheap dress shoes (equipped with steel toes, all the better to stomp you with, my dear). The whole thing sat kind of *heavy* on me, a worrisome development.

I wanted to check the time and pulled out the pocket watch, chagrined when I remembered it was busted. Was I *that* strung out?

Tried the meditation thing again but the same thought loops kept playing and replaying *ad nauseum.* Vacillating between the best and worst case scenarios.

I almost broke my fast with a good, stiff jolt of Jim Beam. Just to rinse the bad taste from my mouth.

To distract myself, I took inventory of the various defensive charms Cass had given me to wear. She spent many long hours deliberating over the proper combination of talismans and amulets. The hardest part, she told me, was trying to anticipate what sort of nasty banes or hexes Skorzeny *et all* might cast our way.

I fingered a small, silver disk on my throat that was some kind of ancient earth symbol. On a second, shorter chain, a rune that supposedly acted as a ward against—*damn.* She told me but I'd forgotten. Of primary importance was a small pouch on a rawhide thong that I had to wear close to my heart for reasons my partner claimed were too complicated to explain. Once I donned the proper gear, *in theory* I should have at least some measure of protection from any malicious spells directed my way.

Truthfully, I had my doubts that our preparations and tactics stood much of a chance against beings older than the Canadian Shield. I didn't have any illusions on that front. I had Philippe's ring but what good was it if I couldn't use it properly? It was like handing an iPod to an armadillo.

Time dragged by. I thought about putting on some music but couldn't find anything to match my mood. Usually when I was about to rumble, I liked to slap on some Eminem or this old House of Pain CD I salvaged from a bargain bin. That night, neither seemed appropriate. Same with TV. Even porn failed to excite my interest.

I couldn't stop pacing. The guy below me must have thought I'd joined a chorus line. Finally, I *made* myself sit on the couch, sweat dripping from my armpits and running in thin rivulets down my back.

Until at last it was nine o'clock.

Time to go.

I went to the door, turned and took one last look around. Raised a hand to Tree. "So long, you nasty fucking plant. Look after yourself."

I heard a rattle of leaves as I opened the door. Maybe she was saying good-bye. It was hard to know.

I went down the hall, took the stairs to the foyer.

By the time I reached the front entrance, I had my game face on. Win, lose or draw, those Cabal bastards would rue the day they were dumb enough to tangle with me.

Yea though I walk through the valley of the shadow of Death, I will fear no evil for I am the meanest motherfucker in all creation...

It could have been false bravado or a touch of hypoglycemia, but at that moment I really believed we would pull it off.

Werner was waiting with the Taurus. It felt good having him along. The fucker was hound dog loyal and, as a bonus, he had his own scores to settle and wasn't the type to forgive and forget.

The burns on his face and hands must have hurt like hell but he never let on. Kept them well covered, the dressings fresh; must have taken about a mile of sterile gauze. I wondered when he would begin treatments--I assumed there would have to be skin grafts, plastic surgery—but lacked the *chutzpah* to ask him.

I climbed in front beside him. We exchanged nods. Our upper bodies were so wide, our shoulders kept rubbing together. After a few blocks, he turned on to the avenue, merging into the traffic, going with the flow. It had rained earlier and the humidity was still high, creating a thin, low-lying mist.

A few minutes passed and then I cleared my throat to get his attention.

"So what do you think of my suit?" I asked, a hint of a challenge in my voice. Werner glanced at me and raised an eyebrow, the one that hadn't been burnt off. "I'll admit," I went on, "I'm a bit worried it might be kinda heavy but it's only early June, right? Technically still spring. And the place is bound to have air conditioning." I felt the material critically. "Actually, I'm wondering if this isn't wool. I couldn't find a tag. And that would make sense, wouldn't it? Bloody thing has to be umpteen years old." I tugged at the collar. "Christ, I'm sweating like a fucking pig, d'you know that? Shit. *Shit.* What was I thinking? I should've just rented a tux. Or tried to get away with a nice blazer, a short-sleeved shirt underneath. Fuck!" I pounded on the dashboard. "This keeps up, I'm gonna have to wring out my underwear." Did Werner's eyes crinkle, signifying amusement, or was it only my imagination? "Oh, well, it's too late to do anything about it," I concluded. "I'll just make it part of the whole purging thing. Uh, I think they're still working on Finlayson so you might want to take a different, y'know, route or whatever. Just a suggestion." But Werner didn't need the reminder and shot a reproachful look in my direction. "Sorry..."

She was coming out of her building when we pulled up. It was like a scene out of a fairy tale and she was the enchanted princess, our Cinderella of the south side. In a cream-coloured, sleeveless gown with long, white gloves. A vision, the most gorgeous thing I'd ever seen.

As soon as Werner rolled to a halt, I hopped out and opened the back door for her. She stepped in daintily, careful not to brush against the rust stains on the side of the car. "Your carriage, m'lady," I announced. I closed her door and reclaimed my seat in front, shrugging apologetically at Werner. "You snooze, you lose, my man." Thank God he couldn't speak, the glare he was giving me was bad enough.

She was fretting with her hair in the rearview mirror. "It's not too much, is it?" she pleaded. "Too Bjork-ish, if you know what I mean?"

"No!" I cried and Werner shook his head as vehemently as his damaged skin would allow. "If someone isn't sizing you up for a glass slipper and a dream castle in Monaco by midnight, my name ain't Evgeny Davidovitch Nightstalk."

"I've always suspected that's a pseudonym."

"No way," I said. "I'll show you my birth certificate. The Nightstalks, I'll have you know, are an old and noble line."

"I think you're feeding us an old and noble line," she replied with a giggle. I saw Werner nod in agreement.

"You people don't recognize class when you see it."

"Oh, come on, Nightstalk. You're a peasant if I ever met one."

"Ye-es," I allowed, "but a *proud* peasant." I heard a snuffling sound to my left and realized it was coming from Werner. He was laughing, the big bastard, keeping his face averted so I wouldn't notice. I hope it cost him dearly.

City police were stopping and diverting traffic two blocks from the Leiber Building. We showed our invitations and picture I.D. and were eventually cleared to proceed (though our chauffeur's Claude Rains-like appearance definitely attracted extra attention and scrutiny). Werner dropped us off outside the front entrance, departing with a wave of his bandaged hand.

We passed through metal detectors and were subsequently wanded and frisked by uniformed rent-a-cops. I don't know what Fuchs' egg was made of but, thankfully, whatever it was, it didn't trigger any alarms. Cassandra had to submit to having her bag searched and I could tell the flunkey assigned the task wouldn't have minded an intimate tour of her body cavities as well.

Security was tight and there were various stations set up to waylay gate-crashers and *paparazzi*. Lots of guys standing around wearing ear pieces and vigilant expressions. Overhead cameras scoping everything out for unseen eyes. With all the gadgets and beefcake, that tower *should* have been the most well-guarded, stringently protected environment outside the counting rooms at Fort Knox.

So how come I didn't feel the slightest bit *safe*?

People were milling about the front lobby, shaking hands and getting acquainted. We killed time by chatting with a pleasant Arab gentleman, who intimated that he belonged to the ruling family of some filthy rich emirate—

--suddenly, without even thinking about it, I knew his game was industrial espionage and that his reputed wealth came largely from the treasury of the People's Republic of China. When I informed Cassandra of my findings, she squeezed my arm. "You're excited, keyed up, it must be having an effect on your abilities. This is encouraging. No, it's *wonderful*. Keep it up."

While we waited for an elevator to become available, we were offered a tasty-looking champagne punch. I could've sucked back that sweet champers all night long but we kept to our fast and turned it down.

I felt sharp, a combination of lack of food and Philippe's ring. Ready to take on the world, if need be. Cassandra slipped her arm through mine and that was the icing on the cake. I thought we made a dashing couple, although she still hadn't said anything about my increasingly waterlogged outfit.

Finally, it was our turn to ride up to the 66th floor. As I stood in the crowded elevator car, watching the illuminated numbers mark our ascent, I tried to get readings from other passengers. Most were quite transparent. They were power-hungry, looking to get ahead, make the right connections, join an upper-echelon network. Others were thrill-seekers, chronically bored, searching for anything that offered diversion or added spice to their joyless lives. I was still flitting from person to person when the door slid open and the festivities *really* got underway.

I was amazed at how the Fischers' personal domain was laid out. For one thing, it was *huge*, taking up the entire floor, thousands of square feet of prime real estate, boasting a 360-degree view of Ilium's skyline. Workers had hauled in chairs and couches, loungers and love seats. They also installed fully stocked bars at various locations, so you never had to go far for a refill. There were long tables laid out with an ever-changing assortment of fancy *hors d'oevres*, delicacies that included caviar and seafood spreads and more colours and varieties of cheese than I'd seen in my entire life.

We wandered around and I felt as conspicuous as a pimple on a supermodel. Everyone seemed so elegant and successful.

My suit drew funny looks, which only added to the flow of salty sweat that was rendering the seat of my pants a soggy mess. We found a gallery of paintings housed in a long, narrow chamber, discreetly lit and watched over by slow-panning security cameras. Two of the works were by an artist named Spare[32] and they severely creeped me out.

Shortly afterward, we came across the entertainment room with its extra-large screen HDTV and theatre quality, surround sound system (*oooo*, wouldn't it be great to watch skin flix on a set-up like that?). You could even check out the guest bedrooms, touch the hand-made comforters or admire the four hundred-year old matching dressers.

"So...this is what it's like to be filthy, stinkin' rich."

"Impressive, isn't it?" She did a slow turn, taking everything in. "Maybe *overwhelming* is a better word."

"When I die," I stated, "I hope heaven looks like this." She tried to hide her smile. "What? Don't think I'll qualify for admission?"

There weren't any reporters or camera crews in evidence, no coiffed, blow-dried idiot jamming a microphone in your face, looking for an insipid sound bite. It was clear the fourth estate weren't welcome here. I can't say I missed them.

Waiters circulated with more of that scrumptious champers. I wasn't sure but I thought I recognized Ratfuck. It was hard to tell. If it *was* him, he'd cut off his mohawk and managed to make himself look fairly presentable. I wondered if Shit was part of the crew. And how they went about disguising the massive bolt hole in his nose.

The acoustics were dicey, similar to the inside of an airline terminal. The place had hardly any walls, much of it open space, its designers employing partitions and screens to delineate certain areas. The result was

---

[32] Austin Osman Spare (1886-1956)

a hubbub of voices, music and outbursts of laughter, an incomprehensible soundtrack. We made our way through the assembled company and she kept her arm in mine, attracting the attention of everyone we passed.

"I might as well be a mannequin," I complained. "Look at these toffee-nosed bastards. Not a single one of them will remember my face five seconds from now. *You*, on the other hand, they'll remember forever. The fairy tale vamp with the killer tits. God, how I *despise* you." She laughed and clutched my arm tighter.

"How could they forget you?" she pointed out. "The man in the antique suit."

"I prefer to think of it as *vintage*. And you still haven't said if you like it."

"I..." She paused and I couldn't tell if she was being diplomatic or simply at a loss for words. "I would have to say I--I hardly recognize you. You look very...I think *distinguished* is the right word." I basked in her praise. "But it's wool, isn't it? Don't you find it terribly *hot?*"

"Not at all," surreptitiously blotting my forehead with a wad of kleenex from my pocket, "it breathes quite well actually."

"It looks like something a British banker would wear in the 1930's," she observed. "The pocket watch is a nice touch too."

"My dad left it to me. Like him, it's broke most of the time. But it's just about all I have to remind me of him, other than a few odd pictures." I brightened. "Y'know, I have to say, it's kind of neat getting duded up like this. I may do it more often, you never know."

"I'm glad." Her smile vanished, replaced by a look of apprehension. "*Nightstalk...*"

I felt it too: a wave of dark energy, an invisible current flowing through the building. The Brethren ring started vibrating like a tripped alarm.

"Over there."

"Yes, m'dear, I see them." Four large men in tuxedos, built like the linebacking corps of the St. Louis Rams, posed menacingly before a set of double doors. "Wow, this ring is something. My whole arm is *throbbing*. I'd say behind those doors is definitely where the action is."

"Those nice gentlemen seem determined to prevent anyone from going in."

"And it isn't the Fischers' bedroom, that's somewhere over on the other side." I eyed the goon squad. "There could be, what, a couple thousand square feet of space back there. How much room do you need for a working?"

"Size, setting, I told you, they're not important," she reminded me. "What's essential is having the wording right and making the proper offerings."

"People are writing their names down and putting them in that big drum." I pointed. "See?"

"It's some kind of draw."

"I'll ask this gent." I stopped an old fart who looked like Colonel Sanders with a bad case of rickets. It turned out that at some point in the evening thirty lucky guys and gals would have the honour of being taken into that guarded inner sanctum, where they would receive a special surprise.

"Yeah," I muttered, "some bogey ties their ankles together and makes a tampon out of them."

"What did you say?" His beard bristled with indignation. "I'm certain I didn't hear you correctly."

"You heard me, pops, now *blow*. And if I were you, I wouldn't sign up for any raffle tickets tonight. Not if you wanna make it back to the green hills of Kentucky with your nuts still attached."

I felt a tug on my arm. "Behave yourself," she warned. "As far as anyone here is concerned, the draw is a huge deal."

"You think we should sign up too?"

She chuckled. "I would say that particular list of winners was likely compiled some time ago."

"And we're on it?"

"Definitely."

"Great," I bitched. "I *finally* win the lottery and first prize turns out to be a one-way ticket to the boneyard."

I didn't see any of the Stones stumbling about, looking for something to shoot, snort, smoke, drink, gobble or fuck. Sirs Elton and Paul weren't in attendance either, though I was certain I recognized George Hamilton and Pia Zadora. There appeared to be lots of jet-setters and more politicians than you could mow down with an Uzi (unless you'd had the foresight to bring extra clips).

We smiled, nodded, exchanged pleasantries, politely waving away the various concoctions and canapés we were offered. Meanwhile, we kept our eyes peeled. Driving ourselves crazy imagining what was going on behind those closed doors.

"I say why wait, let's rush 'em," I urged, sizing up the hired muscle. "There's *only* four of them. We crash in there, break things up before it goes too far and—"

"There are bound to be all kinds of banes and booby traps," she pointed out. "You might get past the guards but you wouldn't make it much further. We've got to bide our time until they let us in with the other winners. That's when we make our move."

"Yeah, but what are we supposed to do 'til then?" I was fidgety. "C'mon, Cass, we have to do *something*."

"In that case, I vote we dance."

"Dance?" I asked stupidly.

"Love to." Her victorious smile said it all: *gotcha*.

We danced. All kinds of hell about to break loose and...we danced.

For two songs. We weren't Fred and Ginger and wouldn't have gotten high marks for style or artistic merit but...it was nice. At one point during the last number ("Torn Between Two Lovers", can you believe it?) she pulled back and looked down at me and I saw she had tears in her eyes. It shook me up, my guts going into free fall.

The piano player's name was Sam...Sam Schulman.[33] He played "Time After Time" for us and "With a Little Help From My Friends" (even I sang along to that one). Everyone else in the vicinity was doing their best to ignore him but he was bloody *good*. Cassandra and I hung out with him for awhile, leaning against his piano and requesting one golden oldie after another. He did an absolutely *killer* version of "MacArthur Park". Blew Bill Shatner's right out of the water.

Sam told us that he'd been born thirty years too late and that he *adored* (he used that word a lot) the music of the 70's and early 80's. Did we like Motown? He could do all those great Supremes and Smokey Robinson standards like he'd learned them at the feet of Berry Gordy himself.

"You know what's going down here, Sam?" I asked at one point, ignoring an admonitory nudge from my partner.

He started playing again. "It's a party, isn't it? And it pays good coin, I know that. I got a student loan to pay off and my share of the rent to kick in so I'm not complaining, know what I mean?" His fingers moved fluidly up and down the keyboard, a slow, syrupy number, real lounge lizard stuff. Sounded a lot like Dan Hill's "Sometimes When We Touch". Cripes, this guy really knew his corn.

---

[33] "Sam Schulman: The *Real* Piano Man. For engagements, call 584-3383"

"You haven't heard about anything planned for later? Something *special*?"

"Is that what they're having the draw for?" He shrugged. "It's supposed to be a deep, dark secret. Whoever wins gets taken inside for a special show. You signed up yet?"

"Not that bullshit story about the Stones doing a private gig?" I scoffed.

"Who knows?" Clearly he didn't. "There's big bucks behind this shindig so we'll have to wait and see. Hey, you guys wanna hear some Captain and Tennille stuff? I *adore* 'Love Will Keep Us Together'. Shall I?" I would've preferred having my face shaved with a high-speed belt sander, but my partner nodded agreement so the Captain it was.

We hung around the general area of that private chamber, keeping tabs on things. The smell of food was starting to get to me. There was a grill set up nearby; you could order flame-broiled steaks, cooked to your taste. And kebabs and juicy, succulent breasts of chicken...and if I didn't find something else to occupy my mind, I was going to start salivating like one of Pavlov's prize pooches.

"Are you suffering as much as I am?" Cassandra groaned.

"Everything carries in this place, including some truly amazing smells."

"You look like you're about to tear someone's arm off and eat it."

"Not a bad idea..." Pretending to look around for a suitable candidate.

As it drew closer to midnight, people started drifting toward the doors to the inner sanctum. The word went out: at 11:45 the names of the thirty winners would be announced. And it was semi-official, those chosen would have front row seats to a massive fireworks display right outside the floor to ceiling, bulletproof windows.

"That's stupid," I observed. "Fireworks? All that hype and suspense for fucking *fireworks*?"

"The winners will believe it, that's the important thing."

"And they'll go right on believing it until something that looks like boiled broccoli has them for a midnight snack," I predicted.

The excitement built as 11:45 approached.

I turned to say something to Cassandra and, to my shock, spotted Werner making his way through the revellers. He was dressed in a waiter's monkey suit, his face concealed behind one of those novelty masks (Nixon? George, Sr.? it was hard to tell) but his size and build gave him away in a second. People were so intent on the outcome of the draw hardly anyone gave him so much as an upward glance.

"Hey, it's Werner..." I chuckled, watching until he'd moved off out of sight. "I should've known he wouldn't miss out on the fun."

"I'm glad he's here," Cassandra said. "If, by any chance, we don't make that list, we're going to have to do it your way and force our way inside." She scanned the growing crowd. "I wish I knew which are Holmes' people. We have to be able to signal them if we need their help."

"Maybe we should rethink our visual cue or whatever. I don't know how many times I've done *this*," tapping the side of my nose with my finger, "and so far all I've gotten back are funny looks. I think some guys thought I was hitting on them."

"I believe the nose tapping was *your* contribution," she pointed out.

"Yeah, well, let's see you—"

Just then overhead speakers hummed and crackled and the people around us went *shhhh* so they could hear better. Gregory Fischer's voice came through loud and clear. He welcomed us as honoured guests and urged us to indulge ourselves at his expense. Then he got to the point. "Don't worry, I'm not going to drag this out. I'm sure you're all dying to know who our thirty lucky winners are. I have the list here and I congratulate you, one and all."

Then he read the names.

The mayor made the final cut, as did a retired air force general, a filthy rich industrialist, several has been actors, various influential political types, a few big shot lawyers, etc.

The roster included Cassandra Zinnea.

It did not, however, contain the name of yours truly, Evgeny Davidovitch Nightstalk.

"Now don't go and do anything stupid," she warned.

"What, like pull somebody's fuckin' head off and use it as a football?" I glowered, my mood homicidal. "They're trying to separate us—"

"Of course."

"You are *not* going in there without me, is that clear?" She bit her lip, looked away. "Forget it, Cass, it ain't gonna happen."

"We *need* someone on the inside," she explained patiently. "Have you seen Skorzeny tonight?" I shook my head. "That's because he—or should I say *Aiwass* is already in there, performing the Summoning ritual. This time they're going to get it right. He'll make certain of it." I could see her withdrawing from me, mentally distancing herself. "You can sense the energy building, can't you? It's only a matter of time. Those thirty people are just the first of many to come."

"All the more reason for both of us to go," I insisted.

"Evvie," she said, "*don't do this*. While I'm trying to pull the plug on the Working, you can be out here, coordinating with Holmes' people and Werner. If something goes wrong, make sure everyone makes it to--"

"*Bullshit*." I was furious with her. "You're acting like you don't need me in there."

Her gloved hand brushed my cheek. "Don't be silly. Now give me a hug and wish me luck." When I didn't immediately comply, she grabbed me, pulled me against her, then turned and walked away. Went over to collect her special red pass and join the other winners. People were laughing and waving their passes jubilantly--just ordinary red envelopes, from what I could see, with their names printed on the front, a simple, elegant calligraphy.

Hmm. An idea was forming and while I waited for it to coalesce, I stood there, fiddling with Philippe's ring, turning it around and around on my finger...

"Hey! Hey! I'm a winner, where do I go? Who do I give this to?" I shouldered my way through the throng, a big, stupid grin plastered on my face, holding my red envelope up for everyone to see. The last of the thirty were trickling past the cordon of thugs. I figured there might be enough excitement and confusion to prevent an accurate head count or maybe someone hadn't heard their name called because they were passed out or off fucking in one of the richly appointed guest rooms. With luck, I might be able to slip through.

I'd given some thought to simplifying matters by popping one of the winners and stealing their pass but decided against it. It wasn't that I had moral qualms, it was just that an opportunity never presented itself. Too many people around, a good number of them disappointed and pissed off, correctly assuming that the fix was in and not taking it well.

So I was forced to improvise. The lining of my suit jacket was red--well, redd*ish* but it would have to do. The trouble was I didn't have a lot of time and was distracted by the noise and hubbub. I focussed hard on seeing an envelope, an actual envelope in my hand. Not cloth but *paper*. I stared at it, trying to filter out everything except that slip of lining, concentrating, bearing down hard...

The ring tingled and—

"I won," I whispered. "They just called my name, a last minute addition." Holding my envelope aloft in happy disbelief, a bright, red envelope with my name on the front. I was fucking stoked: *I never win anything.* But this time I'd hit the jackpot and now I had to hurry, I didn't want to miss the fun, the fantastic fireworks that were due to start any minute--

Two of the goons were preoccupied with a couple of belligerent drunks who seemed intent on forcing their way inside. I felt a twinge of irritation: *their* names hadn't been called, why should *they* be allowed in with the rest of us? *The nerve of some people.* I could tell the seemingly indifferent bouncers were hoping one of the inebriated gatecrashers would step over the line and do something stupid like take a swing at them.

"Could I see that please?" I found myself automatically handing my envelope to someone nearly twice my size. He glanced at the name on the front, started to step aside—

A look of puzzlement crossed his face. He took another long look at the envelope, which seemed to be dissolving around the edges, losing clarity. I blinked and now it was just a torn flap of cloth, hardly red at all. He closed his massive fist over it, straightened to his full height.

"Hey..." he said. "I've been waiting for *you.*" I planted my feet, intending to get the first shot in before they swarmed me. But instead of signaling the others, he was waving me past. "Enjoy the show, sir." I stood there for a few seconds, trying to absorb what was happening, hardly daring to believe my good fortune.

Then he spoiled my moment of triumph by grinning.

And tapping the side of his nose.

Aiwass feels waves of sublime terror emanating from those present. That energy is put to good use, he draws on it as he recites the most critical stanzas of the Summoning. It is a multilingual rite, utilizing a variety of ancient and classical tongues, some decidedly non-Terran in origin. Cassandra said a literal translation of the lengthy incantation would be almost impossible. It would come off sounding like bad Lovecraft:

"Lurkers from beyond the stars
Spirits of the immortal deeps
Arisen and awaiting
Returning to their ancestral keeps..."
Etc.

Aiwass has painstakingly arranged the words into their proper sequence and speaks them clearly, enunciating with care.

For this auspicious occasion he has reunited most of the original members of the Cabal (those who still survive). Perhaps vestiges of Victor Skorzeny's personality remain, remnants of his overweening pride, a desire to flaunt his power. Most came willingly, although some required...persuading. Vivien Vickers withers under his fierce scrutiny. She is clad in a hooded black robe, like the others, and more frightened than she's ever been in her life.

*While the thirty decidedly un*lucky *winners wait on the other side of the tall doors at the far end of the chamber, Aiwass completes the ritual, fulfilling his function to perfection:*

"Terminat hora diem; terminat Author opus.
Consummatum est!"

He lowers his arms and awaits the result of his foul labours.
It doesn't take long.
Inside the sanctum, the air pressure begins to fluctuate, falling rapidly and then rising just as quickly. A sharp, dry clap of thunder booms *from overhead and arctic gusts sweep through the room. Vivian can endure no more. She breaks away from the circle, racing about in her bare feet, crying out for divine mercy until she falls in a heap, sobbing inconsolably. Allan Mayhew is babbling away in some strange dialect, his eyes rolled back so that only the whites show, oblivious to the drama unfolding before him...*

The air is rippling, creating an out-of-focus, mirage-like effect, and lights throughout the building flicker and dim.

Aiwass is ecstatic, having set in motion a process eons old and virtually unstoppable. With an audible whoosh, *the ageless avatar bursts into flames, burning blue-white and as cold as deep space. The mortal body he previously inhabited is simply vaporized, revealing the outlines of his true form: a long, bulbous head and a tangle of writhing, rubbery limbs and grasping pincers. Definitely not of this Earth.*

"SEND IN THE OFFERINGS!" He shouts from the midst of the chill, brilliant fire. The force of that amplified roar drives the others to their knees, howling in terror and anguish, the sonic pressure wave gathering force as it rushes outward. The heavy doors are blown to pieces, creating a fusillade of wood splinters and lethal spears. The effects on the revellers lined up outside are, predictably, horrific. Screams and groans create an unholy din, a feast of suffering and terror and chaos that Aiwass the Opener gorges on.

It also acts as a catalyst for the final stage of the Summoning, a blue spike of energy shooting from his flaming column and where it impacts, a split or rip appears in the middle of the air. There are loud sucking and tearing sounds as material reality is breached, accompanied by more thunderclaps, an overture of what is to come...

She couldn't believe her eyes. "Nightstalk! Holy Diana, how did you—" She laughed and hugged me. Then she held me at arm's length and gave me a stern look. "You didn't hurt anyone, did you?"

"Actually, I used this." I held up the ring.

At first she was puzzled but soon caught on. "You *didn't*! I had no idea you'd progressed so far."

"I just flashed a piece of this," showing her my lining, "and they let me through. No problem." Conveniently neglecting to mention the Irregular manning the door.

She shook her head in admiration. "I have to stop underestimating you, my friend. You constantly surprise me." She indicated the rest of the merry men and women. "What do you think? Do these people qualify as suitable offerings? Look at Judge Winter over there. I know some people who claim he used to chum around with Oliver Wendell Holmes, *Senior*."

The lights dimmed and the building seemed to shudder.

"Listen, you," I told her, "whatever happens, we stick together, right? None of that hero shit."

"I'll be right beside you," she said. "For as long as I can."

"What's that supposed to—"

"Nightstalk, look!" She pointed at a portrait mounted on the wall by the inner doors. Her voice shook with excitement. "I saw this earlier. Do you know who that is?"

I glanced at it. "Sure, that's what's her name...Fischer's bimbo wife."

She groaned. "And you spotted the resemblance right away. Sometimes I wonder if I'm half as smart as I think I am."

"So what's the big deal?"

"The big deal is that's *not* Charlotte Fischer." I took a closer look at the plaque affixed to the bottom of the frame.

Alice Foyle Whittaker
June 5, 1928 – August 14, 1992
"'Release the Fiend that lies dormant within you"

"Nice sentiment," I commented. "But who the fuck is Alice Whittaker?"

Before answering, she drew me further away from the others. It was almost midnight and people were lining up, expecting those doors to swing open any moment. "Alice Whittaker and her husband Albert founded the Children of Baphomet[34]. Heard of them?"

"Satanists?"

"Hardcore. Albert disappeared, no one knows what happened to him, and Alice assumed leadership a short time afterward. She died of cancer but in case you didn't notice, today would've been her birthday. All *this* is meant to honour her."

"I still don't see—"

"Evvie, if Charlotte is related to Alice Whittaker, as the resemblance would suggest, then we may be dealing with something completely—"

At that instant, the thick, heavy doors blew apart, filling the immediate area with high velocity shrapnel.

When we regained our bearings, we found ourselves in the midst of a scene right out of Dante. People were screaming, off their nuts. As far as I could tell, at least half the company were either dead or incapacitated by flying debris, the rest running or staggering about, trying to find an exit so they could escape the horror show. The lights had dimmed again so people were crashing into each other, pummelling one another, fear and shock over-riding basic humanity.

Cass and I were lucky, we'd been standing off to the side while we conversed and avoided the full brunt of the blast. In fact, we didn't have a scratch on us, a miracle in itself.

Others hadn't been so fortunate.

Constance Willcott, the newspaper heiress, was lying no more than six feet away, nearly decapitated, her blue blood looking very red, even in the reduced light. Anthony Deering, the superannuated senator, stared in incomprehension at a piece of wood the diameter of a fist sticking out through the front of his chest. He looked around, trying to make sense out of what was happening then, as I watched, slowly sank back and expired.

The floor around us was literally awash with blood. A few good souls were doing what they could to render comfort and assistance, while the rest

---

[34] For further information on the Children of Baphomet and Alice & Albert Whittaker, check out Charles Fugate's *Hell Spawn: The Story of the Scariest Cult in America* (Felker Books; 1994). Interestingly, Fugate's book makes no mention of a daughter or any other offspring; however, he does note that Charlotte was previously married, a short-lived union that took place in the late 1960's.

flung themselves about the anteroom in a frenzy of fear. Survivors were hammering on the outer doors, clamouring for their release. The doors remained locked, sealing us in despite that frantic drumming of fists.

Something was in the air, literally. My ears twinged as the pressure suddenly spiked. Another strange current surged past and Philippe's ring shivered, alerting me to imminent danger. All at once the floor no longer seemed solid beneath my feet, the glass tower appearing to shift or sway on its massive foundations.

"It's beginning," Cassandra breathed. "They've broken through." Cripes, where was the *thunder* coming from? A low rumble at first, gradually growing in volume until it was a regular John Bonham drum solo and then...silence. *"Uh oh..."*

"Do I take it we're too late?"

"Come on," she urged, hurrying forward, "there might still be time."

But it sounded like she had her doubts.

"Come, my friends," Aiwass invited them. *"Greet your new masters..."*

Gregory Fischer, looking windblown and concussed, blood leaking from his ears, tottered forward. He seemed compelled by some irresistible force...the same force that suddenly cut his legs from under him so that he landed in a heap not far from his wife. He crawled forward, dragging himself hand over hand until he was close enough to drop his face to her feet...and *lick* them.

Charlotte Roper-Fischer looked down expressionlessly as her husband abased himself. She raised one shapely, muscular leg, her foot grazing his back, moving up to the nape of his neck—

--driving her heel down sharply on the spot where his skull met the top of his spine. Fischer twisted and squirmed like a pinned insect, but she bore down mercilessly until his upper spine finally snapped. Disconnected, his body twitched and shuddered for a few seconds as the life leaked out of him. Then all movement ceased.

Turning to Aiwass, Charlotte held out her arms. "Master! I have been your most devoted servant. Now I demand my rightful reward."

Aiwass nodded and instantly complied. Her hood smouldered and erupted into flame, igniting her hair, the fire flowing down her body like spilled tar. The robe charred and dropped from her, the blue flames absorbing and digesting her mortal form, revealing the contours of her malign and corrupted soul.

"*Yes!*" Herman Rache shouted. "*Send for the banished ones! Summon those great princes from their cruel prison...*" His oiled hair was smoking and his eyes were melting, bubbling in their sockets.

Charlotte moved forward, the other two flanking her. The bright, cobalt glow of their etheric flames washed over everything, giving the room a ghastly hue, the colour of a dying man. The cold fire reduced the surrounding temperature, adding a wintry aspect to the proceedings. The air in the chamber crackled as silver-blue bolts leapt between them, joining them in a common circuit.

They floated toward the portal, growing brighter and brighter...*then simultaneously discharged their combined energies, arcs of blue light directed at the dimensional rift.* When the flow cut off a few seconds later, an eerie silence ensued. The three entities remained at their stations. Those Cabal members still conscious roused themselves, reeling about in the semi-darkness, groggy and insensible.

Long, scaly tentacles leapt from the portal, seeking out and snagging Allan Mayhew and Kali Brust and hauling them toward the bulging, distended gash. Something was pushing and straining at the tear from the other side, forcing and widening it, spacial membranes threatening to rupture as the creature's birth throes intensified...

--which was right about when we showed up.

At first it was hard to see, the air was full of dust and plaster, the lighting so crappy you couldn't make anything out.

"What's that burning smell? Are you getting a whiff of that?" As I spoke, I noticed I could see my breath.

She sniffed. "Incense. Dried nightshade, henbane, datura..."

It was a creepy place to walk into, especially when you knew there were going to be bogeys about. As the air cleared, I began to see the care and attention to detail the Fischers had lavished on their black temple. The walls were covered with murals and even in the lousy light you could make out some of the images. It was ugly stuff: mutilation, rape and inter-species sex. A depiction of the Last Supper that was highly scatological (to say the least). There were a number of statues too, most of them toppled over, missing heads or limbs. The majority of the figures represented a variety of alien-human hybrids. Some I recognized from my sojourn in Chorazin.

"These people don't just wanna *raise* Cthulhu," I commented, "they want to fuck him too."

We heard screams and watched, transfixed, as two robed figures were dragged by powerful, reaching tentacles into a split or tear that hovered about four feet off the floor.

It was, hands down, the most fucked up thing I'd ever seen. A ragged, vertical slit just hanging there in mid-air. The man and woman were stuffed inside and what looked like an enormous *beak* started grinding them up. You could hear their bones cracking and everything. It was fucking horrible. Their bodies jerked and twisted so you knew they were being eaten alive by whatever was in there. I'd be hard-pressed to describe the creature. It was like a cross between a feral parrot, an acid nightmare and an ancient god from fuck knows where.

"Ho-ly shit," I said. "Darlin', we're in *big* trouble." Cassandra barely had time to acknowledge my assessment before a sizzling bolt lashed out in our direction. I caught a glimpse of three blue columns floating a short distance from that bizarre slit. We dove for the floor, partially shielded by the rubble and debris. "Did you see that? It fucking *ate* those people." Now there were three, no, *four* slimy tentacles as thick as my arm lashing the air above our position, dipping and darting toward us, scoring some near misses. They had emerged from that slit, attached, I assumed, to that parrot-faced motherfucker.

"This isn't exactly going according to plan, is it?" An understatement, if I ever heard one.

"We'd better come up with something fast or we're dog meat."

"I'm open to suggestions, *partner*," she fired back.

"You're the brains, remember, *partner*?" We glared at each other.

Then I noticed that the Brethren ring was nearly vibrating off my finger. Almost simultaneously, one of those purple tentacles swept down toward me. I raised my right arm, attempting to block or deflect it. Sparks flew from the ring and the tentacle was withdrawn in a hurry, thrashing and jittering in apparent pain.

Cassandra whooped and grabbed my arm, which had gone numb from the impact. "Way to go, Nightstalk!" Then she looked apprehensive. "That's bound to get their attention." It did seem like the atmosphere in the room had changed and when we peeked, we saw that one of the fiery blue pillars had detached itself from the others and was moving toward us. The remaining two stayed where they were, perhaps serving as critical conduits for all the dark energy in the room. "We have to split up to give them more to think about."

"No way!"

"Listen to me." She had that no-nonsense tone again. "The plan stays the same. You distract those things while I figure out a way to close that bloody portal. Look at it. *It's getting bigger every minute.* Do you want to wait around and see what comes out? I sure don't. We've got only one chance at this, babe."

"Who's gonna be watching your back—"

"We'll work this together. You do your job, I'll do mine. And one other thing: get *mad*, will you? It's the end of the world, for Diana's sake." She gave me a shove and moved away, keeping low, using whatever cover was available. A couple of blue spikes darted after her but her amulets and protective spells warded them off. A positive sign.

I went in the opposite direction, grumbling under my breath.

There was no real method to this madness. I was supposed to play hide and seek with the bad guys, hopefully not getting killed in the process, while she tried to prevent the Working from, well, *working.* I knew she wasn't all that confident with the counterspell she'd come up with. It was a hodgepodge of various banishing and binding incantations and there hadn't been an opportunity to test it beforehand. If we didn't stop this extradimensional invasion with our first shot, we were toast.

Something was happening to the detached column. It flashed and shimmered, eventually assuming the form of Herman Rache, easily recognizable despite the electric blue tan. At the sight of him, I guess I sort of froze and he spotted me. Not good.

"*You,*" he growled. "*I shall dispose of you once and for all.*" He opened his flaming suit jacket and the two ferrets unfolded and dropped to the floor. "Kill him," he instructed them. "*Now.*"

They were so fast, it defied belief. I saw a blur of movement and then one of them was clamped to my back, legs wrapped around my middle, his razor sharp teeth fastened to the side of my head. I felt my left ear begin to rip away from my scalp. I yelped like a scalded monkey.

But I had to let him worry that ear a second longer.

I was watching for the other one. It took self-discipline, it took patience (not to mention the pain threshold of a brachiosaurus). I figured he'd go for my legs, the soft meat of the thigh. To them, I was the equivalent of an old wildebeest they expected to carve up in the time it took Tree to digest a quarter pounder.

Motion...but this time I was ready, snagging the second ferret in mid-air, like a hot line drive. No doubt surprised that his buddy had been captured so easily, the one gnawing on the side of my head momentarily relinquished his grip on my mangled ear. In a flash, I had him in my other hand.

"Uh," one began.

"Oh," the second one finished.

I bashed their heads together and from the slippery thud their noggins made, I'd say I inflicted serious cranial damage, possibly reducing them both to a permanent vegetative state. I felt bad about that.

I'd meant to kill them.

Before I had a chance to savour the ass-whupping I'd just administered, I nearly got zapped by another one of those murderous energy bolts. I heard the dry crackle as it whipped past my head. At least having most of my ear bitten off hadn't affected my hearing. I pushed the flap of skin back into place so it wasn't hanging down. Luckily, I'm not much of a bleeder.

Emulating my partner, I used the sporadic cover to conceal my movements. I scurried and crawled until I was within about fifteen feet of the three bogeys, as close as I dared get. Without giving much thought to the consequences, I picked up part of a fallen ceiling tile, stood and flung it at the trio. It sailed like a frisbee, colliding with some kind of force field about a foot from them. I saw the air ripple from the glancing impact and the Rache-thing spun about, regarding me with something akin to disbelief before pointing a rubbery limb in my direction--

--crooked arrows of energy lashed out, slicing through the air toward me. I dove out of the way but one of the bolts changed direction, zeroing in on me with unerring accuracy. It wrapped itself around me before I hit the floor...and then it was like someone was applying lit matches to every single nerve ending in my body.

I suppose all the protective doodads I was wearing helped. Some. Still, it wasn't any spring picnic, I'll tell you that. It was worse than being electrocuted,[35] more like being burned alive. I have no idea how long that thing stayed coiled around me. Likely only a few seconds. I was dimly aware of convulsing, doing the funky chicken, arms and legs flopping, my head thumping on the carpeted floor with each full-body spasm.

My right hand must have somehow made contact, Philippe's ring brushing the blue bolt. The stream of energy leaped away from me, crackling in agitation, flickering out of existence. Once again the Brethren ring had announced its presence. I was woozy but certain I saw the air

---

[35] *See:* "Dr. Dekker's House of Terrors" (*The Casebooks of Zinnea & Nightstalk, Vol. I*)

around the three entities sparkle and change colour, as if some new development was being relayed and debated.

I rolled over and found myself not far from Vivien Vickers. She was nearly catatonic with fear and shock. I wasn't sure she recognized me but as soon as I was within arm's length, she grabbed me and held on tight.

"—*please, God, help me, I am deeply sorry for having offended thee, the sin on my head, sweet Jesus, Lord Protector, save me in my hour of need*—"

"Vivien," I gasped, "let go of me, damnit!" I freed myself from her stranglehold and pushed her away. At that point I wasn't feeling very cuddly. "And save your confession for church. The important thing right now is getting out of here in one piece. So you'd better start clueing in fast or you're parrot feed." I peered around the heavy marble pedestal that was providing most of our cover.

The Rache thing was floating in our direction. Clearly he/it had been appointed watchdog. I sensed keen interest, maybe even the beginnings of unease. I squatted down beside her "Time to bust outta here, kiddo. I want you to make for those big doors and don't look back."

"I...I can't. Those things will get me and—and--" She was in danger of going off the rails again. I headed her off at the pass.

"*Bullshit.* You ran track, remember? You were some kinda hotshot amateur athlete. I saw you interviewed on one of those stupid entertainment shows." I gripped the hem of her robe and tore it up the side to give her more leg room. "University of Arizona, right? C'mon, Wildcat, let's see if you still got it."

She rallied herself. "I'll try..."

"Never fear," I assured her, "they won't even notice you. They'll be too busy dealing with the shit storm I'm about to unleash."

"What are you going to do?"

I smiled.

It was time for the perfessor's bomb.

I'd only half understood Fuchs' explanation of the science behind his "ghostbuster".

"It is essentially a directed and concentrated electro-magnetic pulse. Once activated, it disrupts certain very *specific* wavelengths, confined, er, for the most part, to that particular spectrum favoured by beings inhabiting the spiritual realm. This prototype is still in its early stages so the blast radius is, admittedly, quite limited. However, I can tell you with absolute assurance that when this little baby goes off, any anomalous entity in the vicinity will be obliterated. I'll stake my reputation on it."

All very well and good, I pointed out at the time, but what effect would it have on any *human beings* who happened to be occupying the same general area?

"Absolutely none," Fuchs declared confidently. "The EMP burst, by design, is one hundred per cent harmless to flesh and blood creatures. There isn't the slightest possibility of adverse or...that is..." Something occurred to him. "You don't, by any chance, wear a pacemaker, do you?"

I dug the device out of a secret pocket I'd sewn into the lining of the jacket. Showed it to her. "I'm gonna to throw this, all right? I chuck it at those assholes and meanwhile you *run*, run like you haven't run since you were senior state champ or whatever. Okay? Vivien?"

She took a deep breath and nodded. "Okay...let's do it. What have I got to lose, right?" She squeezed my arm. "I'd kiss you for luck but I can't stop my teeth chattering."

"I throw this thing, you go for it. On three." I hefted the grenade. "One... two..." When I got to "three", I thumbed the switch, arming it.

Right, you fucker, I thought.

I stood and sensed Vivien making her break and never mind those lethal energy bolts and the smoking ruin of my dad's wool suit and the trippy after effects I was still experiencing thanks to my recent 5000-volt enema...

I was mad.

"*Come on, motherfucker!*" I shouted. I lobbed the grenade at the nearest nasty, the critter formerly known as Herman Rache. It bounced off the Rache-thing's defensive screen and fell to the floor directly in front of him. A javelin of energy darted after Vivien but she'd gotten a good headstart and evaded it, moving with swiftness and agility, vaulting through the shattered doorway, escaping with her life.

For now.

"*Nightstalk...*" He definitely had the voice down pat, truly demonic and bowel-loosening. Rache turned the full force of his attention on me. His body was wreathed in flames, that unholy blue fire. He extended some sort of appendage and picked up Fuchs' bomb. Examined it for a few moments and then...began to laugh. I assumed it was laughter; the chamber echoed with an unpleasant croaking, like a bullfrog with its throat cut. "You are a *fool*..."

Okay, that's when I got really, *really* pissed off. Fed up with taking shit from bug-eyed monsters with delusions of godhood. And

Fuchs...Fuchs had let me down yet again. Worthless little twerp. Clusterfuck egghead. Leaving me standing there, holding nothing but my dick. Then I thought about the trail of destruction these evil-minded scumsuckers had left behind them. Eva and the Baron, my buddy Glen, Arturs Esch...not to mention the fucking cats. And now tonight, the people lying in the ante-room dead, missing arms and legs--

Fuck the old gods and anyone who served them. Death was what they deserved and *death* was what they would get. I reared back, sucked in a long, ragged breath and *screamed.*

I don't know what I intended or what I hoped the result would be. Maybe I was trying to access buried reservoirs of strength and ferocity. I've even toyed with the idea that it was a combination of my primal war cry and Philippe's ring that triggered the detonation of Fuchs' device a moment later. Who knows?

All I can say for certain is that there was a *flash* of white light and I immediately realized what it had to be.

"Yeah!" I shouted gleefully. "I got you! I got you, you--"

The Rache-thing blew up. It was only about fifteen feet away, and though the explosion didn't put off any appreciable heat or kinetic energy, *something* went through me, a blast wave invisible to five of my six senses. Hot bits of his shredded carcass were hurled in every direction, creating a gruesome rain of carbonized bone and mangled, multi-coloured flesh.

Aiwass feels the loss of his associate and also a sudden, perilous depletion of dark energy. He glances over to determine the fate of his colleague and sees its remains scattered in the vicinity of a short, stocky man who seems vaguely familiar. What has this unimpressive creature done to inflict such damage?

This has not been foreseen. Will this new wrinkle put the entire venture at risk? There is something else, a strong presence of Old Magic somewhere in this ruined chamber. An unseen magus weaving a spell of considerable skill and power.

Aiwass sweeps the area, seeking the mage responsible—then he spots her, not thirty feet away, crouching in the centre of an improvised magical circle. There are grumbles of complaint from inside the portal, low, bass notes of disapproval that set the floor to shaking.

"No," Aiwass growls, launching himself across the exploded room. "I know what you are doing, human, and you shall not succeed." He levitates through the air toward her, furious and poised to strike. "You shall not succeed!"

The bogey made a bee-line for Cassandra. I hollered a warning but she'd already sensed the approaching threat and was inscribing mystical patterns in the air, chanting a spell of protection, invoking her personal guardian angel. I knew the two keys to any effective spell are concentration and willpower and in those departments my partner was without peer. Sure enough, her opponent was wavering in midair, abruptly veering toward the ground. From inside the portal, guttural croaks of anger. The parrot creature crammed its beak into the opening, forcing it, trying to hasten the progress of its beleaguered minions.

The blue meanie rose again, wobbling, its flames much diminished, transparent in places.

"Dea della luna
Protect io e mio—
Selene, Artemis, Hecate
Isis, Great Mother!
Diana, Queen of Heaven!
Heal this terrible wound
Prevent these unclean things from their—"

There was a tortured cry from the tear and was I seeing things or had it *shrunk*, the counterspell more effective than we'd dared hope?

I scrambled toward them, the ring getting warmer the closer I got. I knew she hadn't had time to properly prepare and consecrate the circle. Yet she didn't flinch from the creature bearing down on her, undeterred by its impending attack.

What a gal.

"Foul creature, return from whence you came!
Fugiat hinc iniquitas vestra!
You are an Abomination and forever banished!
Ecce conclusionem vestram, nolite fieri inobedientes…"

I chanced another look back and saw the rip contract again, despite the insistent beak, which continued to chew and snap at the opening, maddened by this unexpected reversal of fortune.

The blue column flared up again and somehow I knew that this time it meant business. "Hey, asshole," I yelled, trying to get its attention. I held up my right hand: it was wild, my entire hand was *glowing,* encased in a bubble of yellow-white light. "It's *me* you want, isn't it?"

But Cassandra was closer or maybe it perceived her as more of a threat. I'll never know. It dismissed me and spat a zigzag bolt of pure lethality her way, a jagged lance that crackled, I thought, with extra energy, extra potency, a killshot.

She kept chanting her counterspell until the last possible moment. The bolt played up and down the bubble of protection around her, seeking a weak spot. Her magic shield glowed yellow, then green, then took on the same bluish tint as the deadly energies besieging her.

That's when she looked over at me, only for a second, but the connection was crystal clear, her mind speaking directly to mine:

Finish it, Nightstalk.

Her shield was breached and the blue bolt passed through her chest and out the other side. The attacking entity flickered, the expenditure of energy momentarily draining it. The cobalt glow faded and the flames tapered off, revealing a grotesque, ungainly being with an over-large, banana-shaped head perched atop a ridiculously thin stalk of a neck. Fucker looked awkward, comical even.

I sprinted toward it and when I reached it, I didn't hesitate, drawing back my right fist and letting fly. Just before it connected, I sensed the bogey's fear and confusion.

What is this--

The force of the punch cracked my knuckles and jarred my wrist but the results were gratifying. Thanks to the ring, I easily penetrated its defenses, my fist striking the brittle skull with sufficient force to shatter it, bursting through to the cranial muck beneath. I wrenched my arm free and the meanie simply folded up and sagged to the floor. And then a desolate wail as its departing essence was captured and sucked greedily into the rift.

It was evident the thing on the other side was weakening, starved for dark energy...in its hunger, it began feeding on the last surviving column. The effect was immediate: the power drain caused it to sputter and flare up, and in the midst of the angry fire I saw Charlotte Fischer's face, contorted by agonies beyond imagining. Her column was ablaze, burning brighter and brighter. It was a ghastly immolation, fuelled by living flesh, and it continued until her blighted soul was wrenched free and dragged into the portal, consumed by the creature inside.

I hastened to Cassandra's side but one look told me there was nothing I could do. She could barely muster the strength to speak, so I got down next to her, close enough to feel her lips brushing my ear.

"—hurry…hurry Nightstalk do it don't wait do it—"

"What?" I was confused. "What do you want me to do?"

"…go…leave me…go…"

I stood and began to walk toward the portal. Not caring any more; *numb.* Somewhere along the way, I bent and picked up a chunk of cement or plaster. Maybe from one of the sculptures.

When I got within ten feet of the slit, it reacted, two purple tentacles darting out, rushing through the air toward me. I swatted them aside with my glowing right hand and they were swiftly withdrawn, yanked back inside.

At last, I was directly in front of the portal. It was only about six inches in diameter, a wound in the dimensional fabric, a flapping hole in creation.

"To *hell* with you, you sonofabitch…"

Again, I'm not sure what I was thinking. I wasn't exactly what you would call *sane* at that point. I took that chunk of plaster in my right hand and *rammed* it into the opening. I think my intention was to plug the hole but I misjudged its size and my hand went right through, the momentum burying my arm almost to the elbow.

It was the weirdest sensation, neither cold nor hot. A wet, slithery feeling, like reaching into somebody's living guts. The usual reference points didn't apply. It was as if my arm had the consistency of taffy, flowing and bending, doubling back on itself.

"That was for *you*, Philippe," I whispered. I started pulling back as the hole began to blister over and close—

--*something seized hold of me inside the portal.* I felt the ring tumble free and an instant later my hand was spat out like an unwanted bone.

Minus the ring. Left somewhere in that maw. Along with my most of my pinkie and a joint from both my ring and middle fingers. I was backing away, the portal collapsing in on itself, all of that dark energy compressed into an infinitesimally tiny point, requiring some sort of release—

I found myself *catapulted* through the air, somersaulting to a halt a short distance from my stricken partner. I landed awkwardly on my left side and felt something snap. That sensation was accompanied, not surprisingly, by excruciating pain. My fucking fingers were killing me, my head was ringing like a bell and now I could add a couple of busted ribs to the tally.

So I was in pretty rough shape as I gathered my remaining strength and dragged my sorry ass over to where she was lying.

"Cass, Cass," I murmured. Pressing my forehead to hers. "We did it, baby. We stopped them."

She was weak, barely hanging on. "—good…you did good, Nightstalk…"

"I love you," I told her. Kissing her perfect face. Wiping away the tears and streaks of blood I left behind.

"—love you too, you—dear man…"

"Stay," I begged, "please stay."

"Tell me…what happens at the end…of your dream." I didn't know what she meant. "The Tower…"

"I…slip. I get to the top and I try to save you but…ah, *shit*, Cass. I'm sorry. I said I'd protect you and…" Then I got this flash, a mental image of sad-eyed Addie, her scissors poised. "It's those sisters, isn't it? Putting the paradigm right again or whatever."

"*Shhh.*" Pressing her fingers to my lips. "Listen. I…want to tell you something. I lied. I read the *Casebooks*. Thanks for…making me look…so grand."

"I didn't make anything up. You're the best." I felt helpless and bereft.

"Can you…take me outside, please…"

"What?" I wasn't sure I'd heard right.

"I want to…see the moon. Are you able—"

I was busted up, on the brink of keeling over, but I did it. Somehow I did it. Gingerly slid my arms under her shoulders and thighs, lifting carefully so as not to jar her, ignoring the complaints from my wrecked ribs. My efforts cost us both dearly but I managed to struggle to my feet. I carried her out through the ruined doorway and then kept going.

Holmes' Irregulars, with a big assist from Werner, had wrested control of the situation from the goons. People were tending to the wounded and waiting for help to arrive. The mood was subdued, everyone huddling for comfort and reassurance.

A path was cleared for me, knots of spectators looking on as I bore her past them, making for the balcony. The sliding doors were open and I stumbled through them, out onto the enclosed deck. I was having trouble breathing, wheezing badly. I could taste blood and the edges of my vision kept creeping in.

My luck held true to form. The moon, three or four days from fullness, wasn't visible from that side of the building. I was too far gone to take another step. There were only the lights of the city and whatever stars and planets were bright enough to compete with the artificial glare. Her head was resting on my left shoulder and she looked bad, nearly as bad as her outfit. Her beautiful dress was filthy, melted and still smoking around her mid-section. I couldn't bring myself to examine her injuries too closely. She could no longer speak, *sending* the words instead. *Can you see it, is it there?*

"Yeah," I lied. "Shining like—like—oh, *fuck*." Weeping uncontrollably.

—me see, let me see—

There was nothing there, no matter how I hard I wished for a fat, gibbous moon to slip between the tall buildings and shine down on her face one last time. And yet...when I looked at her, she was *smiling*, gazing up at something beyond my range of vision.

Thank you, Evvie. For...for...

"No sweetheart," I sobbed, "thank *you*. It's been an honour and a fuckin' privilege knowing you. I will love you forever and ever and *ever*."

And then she died in my arms.

That's all I remember.

Well. Not quite.

My recollections beyond that point are sort of like flash photographs, moments of brilliant clarity followed by patches of absolute oblivion:

--a close-up view of Werner's ruined face, not a pretty sight.

--the sensation of being carried, cradled like a sick child, down many flights of stairs, numerous detours to avoid police tactical teams, floating through an echo-filled underground parking garage...

--unceremoniously dumped into a trunk, the lid thumping closed above me. No ambulance rides for Evgeny Nightstalk. Guess I should've signed up for Blue Cross.

Lifted out and carried again, achieving breath-taking new heights of pain, a burning spear thrust between my ribs.

Another blackout.

A voice, insistent and annoying, asking me stupid questions. Name. Age. Birthday.

No nonsense, skilled hands binding my ribs, the pain so agonizing I lost consciousness again...

Awakened by music from another room, a burble of distant voices. Hard to tell if it was actual people or a television program. I didn't hang around long enough to find out.

Pain was my constant companion. Some of it physical.

I think at some point I took a swing at someone.

Another needle, this one providing blissful release from worldly cares and woes, a reassuring warmth that sped through my bloodstream to the remotest parts of my body. I slept on a bed made of clouds and had utterly realistic dreams of flying. And falling.

Then...

Rising up toward consciousness again but *fighting* it, unwilling to abdicate my cloud kingdom without a struggle. But it was no use and all at once I found myself blinking at the yellow smear of illumination cast by a bedside lamp. My eyes were doing weird things but I was certain there was someone in the room with me. Not one of my minders, that much was certain. I got the impression of immense age, power and authority.

"Mr. Nightstalk," the Old Man said. "I'm pleased you've decided to rejoin us." I knew the voice, of course, but my eyes were still playing tricks on me. I thought I was looking at a dark-haired woman cradling a lyre.

"Sir," I croaked, "my partner—"

"Gone," he replied and that one single word did me in. I wept, and never mind my dignity and self-control. I wanted to kick and scream and puke and shit myself. I didn't care any more. At that moment all I desired, my one and only wish, was to be dead.

"No, Evgeny," the creature with the head of a jackal said gently. "You're not going to die. Right now your heart is broken but you *will* live to fight another day."

"Fuck you," I groaned, my ribs flaring up again, making it hard to breathe. "You don't know. She—she—" But I ran short of breath and, anyway, it would have been impossible to put into words what I wanted to say. It would've come out sounding trite, like a bad eulogy.

"Thanks to Ms. Zinnea's courage and selflessness a great crisis has been averted. You, too, played a significant role and suffered grievous injuries as a result."

I closed my eyes. "How grievous?"

"A severe concussion, several broken ribs and a punctured lung. And your fingers of course." I groaned again, raising a heavily bandaged hand to my eyes. It wasn't nearly bad enough. He was right, I was going to make it. *Shit.* "My main concern right now is not your physical state but, rather, your mental and spiritual well-being. You paid a dear price for your involvement in this affair. If it's any consolation to you, I believe you conducted yourself with great distinction and I commend you, sir." His voice softened. "The two of you really did save the world, you know." I didn't say anything. Eventually, he got up and left the room. I thought I heard the clop of hooves as he departed but it could have been my imagination. I waited for him to come back but he never did.

I'd been brought to a private residence (safe house?) at some undisclosed location in Ilium. I was being attended to 24/7 by a cadre of rotating nurses who saw to my every need and a first-rate doctor who stayed in a room adjoining mine. I was getting the best possible care. No complaints there.

They asked me if I wanted to talk to a shrink or spiritual advisor. I declined and saw them shooting looks at each other but nobody pushed it.

I soon tired of lying around, doing nothing, and made an honest effort to exert myself and hurry the healing process along. After nearly a week of their constant attention and mollycoddling, I'd had enough and badgered them into discharging me from their care. They didn't need much convincing. I make a lousy invalid.

I still had a lengthy period of recuperation ahead of me. My head felt like it was stuffed with ten pounds of cotton batting and, thanks to my beat up ribs, every breath was a sharp reminder of the frailties of the flesh.

Someone must have fed Tree in my absence because when I opened the door to my apartment, she made no attempt to eat me. Just rustled her branches in greeting then settled down and let me be. I watched a lot of porn but it was more out of habit than anything else. I didn't find it the least bit arousing. Completely dead below the waist.

I went in with Arnie Beddoes to give my official statement to the cops. I likely could've managed it alone. Basically, I told them that the past five or six weeks were a blur. I had no memory of the night of the party. Undoubtedly the result of a head trauma suffered during the course of the evening in question. Arnie read a letter we'd drafted ahead of time and produced a doctor's certificate to back it up but they didn't appear anxious to press the issue. My "amnesia" was accepted at face value because it was convenient for all concerned. No one was looking for needless complications.

One day I discovered a check in my mailbox. The amount was so large, I wondered if it was some kind of severance package, a golden handshake from the Old Man. Something to help ease the suffering.

And I *was* suffering. Grieving so hard it was ripping my guts out. I had no interest in food and what little I did eat I couldn't keep down. It got so that the only thing my system would tolerate was mineral water with a squeeze or two of lemon or lime juice. I subsisted on that for *weeks*.

I found that there was no one I could turn to, no one to help me deal with everything that had happened. As previously noted, I didn't have a large, supportive community of friends and when it came to grief counseling, Tree didn't really qualify. The best I could do was the nutty perfessor, Edwin Fuchs, and I ended up consoling *him* while he blubbed his eyes out, cursing the unfairness and cruelty of fate.

Mostly I stayed close to home, shut up with my misery, drinking too much, just getting through the days. Sometimes, fortified by a fistful of painkillers, I went for walks, long, solo excursions around the city. Wandering in endless circuits until I was footsore, blisters bubbling up on my heels, thighs and calves knotted with cramps...

Once, I found myself across the street from the Diogenes Club. I arrived without a member to sign me in but George Simmons didn't seem to mind. He gripped my shoulder, his eyes bright with emotion. "Mr. Nightstalk. We were, every one of us, shocked by the sudden and tragic death of your colleague and friend. My profoundest sympathies." I nodded. "I am proud to say that all of our members attended the memorial service, an indication of our high regard for her—and, of course, I am not referring solely to her formidable investigative skills. Ms. Zinnea was one of the finest individuals I have ever..." The tough, old ex-cop was too overcome to continue.

"Uh, thanks, George." Both of us were having trouble holding it together. "I know she would have been, y'know, humbled or whatever by what you just said. She thought a lot of this place."

"It was a terrible, terrible, thing," he said. "So much loss of life."

The events of the night of June 5th were still shrouded in mystery, the subject of much rumour and speculation in the media and among the general public. Despite the lack of physical evidence, the feds and their local counterparts were sticking to the story that a bomb had somehow been secreted on the premises by a person or persons unknown. Initially, some anti-corporate fringe outfit was blamed but although numerous arrests had been made, no charges were forthcoming (surprise, surprise).

The prevailing wisdom was that the tragedy could've been much worse. After all, the mayor survived unscathed, as did any number of other power brokers. political fixers and bagmen.

But Cassandra hadn't been as fortunate. She willingly gave her life, sacrificed herself for the rest of us pitiful, selfish, undeserving bastards. The pain of losing her, not only the love of my life, but a good and decent person who represented the very best humankind could offer up, was just about unbearable. I lost her, I lost my faith...and I lost myself. I must have been a pretty sorry sight, literally a ghost of my former self, it was plain from the way Simmons was treating me, the concern I detected in his eyes.

"Is he in?"

He nodded. "I think you know the way. I'll start a pot of tea."

"Thanks."

"Think nothing of it." He scowled. "After all, it's what *he* would expect. Honestly, the man treats me like some sort of indentured servant..."

Holmes was in his usual spot in the library, scrutinizing a document with a magnifying glass only slightly smaller than his head. He bounded off his chair and approached me, hand outstretched. "Deepest commiserations, dear boy," he said, his sharp eyes fixed on me, making a shrewd and expert evaluation of my current state. "I looked for you at the service but, sadly, you were still recuperating from your injuries."

"You actually made it out the front door?" I was impressed. "For the first time in, what, nearly a year. Way to go, Holmes."

"Well...the cause was a good one." He regarded me thoughtfully. "It was a most interesting and illuminating experience. Once I was out of sight of this building, I was perfectly all right. It became an adventure of sorts. I saw the city through new eyes. It was a rather brutal epiphany, I'm afraid. So much squalor and decay. Not entirely dissimilar to London at the height of the Victorian era, come to think of it."

I nodded. The comparison fit. "It gets worse every day. There's no industry, no jobs, so the crime rate's going through the roof. Young people are leaving and who can blame 'em? The cops are useless, the criminals are crazy and ordinary citizens don't give a fuck."

"But certain people—Ms. Zinnea, for instance--don't despair. Their duty is clear, to protect the weak from the strong, punish wrong-doers and preserve the public good. For her sake, in her name, we *must* go on. Continue the battle."

"She'd appreciate that. Especially coming from you."

"Pah," he waved a hand dismissively, "I'm just an egotist who makes the occasional good guess to redeem my inflated reputation."

"No, Holmes." I shook my head emphatically. "I mean, when she first brought me here I thought—well, you know what I thought. But you convinced me. You may not be the real deal but you're pretty damn close in some ways. The important ways."

"Thank you, Mr. Nightstalk. Your praise is much appreciated." He cleared his throat. "I confess my merits, real or imagined, have been much on my mind of late." Holmes hesitated. "I shall be candid, sir. After the memorial service, your employer contacted me and inquired about my availability. In short, the Old Man offered me a job."

I was stunned. "You'd...you'd be a real practicing detective? Sherlock Holmes, on the case?" He looked hesitant but I laughed, for the first time in ages. "I think that's *great*. It'll put the bad guys on notice: the master detective has returned."

"Be that as it may—"

"You'll be this great symbol, a crime fighter with a name everyone knows and respects. Hell, man, you'll be the toast of the town!"

He wasn't so sure. "You don't think...isn't there a likelihood I might be viewed as something of a laughingstock?"

"Not once you prove your worth and earn your stripes. I bet the media loves you."

"And perhaps with you by my side, there might be fewer naysayers. You have a sterling service record, your name possesses a certain—"

"Mr. Holmes."

He blinked. "Ah. I perceive I'm getting ahead of myself. I'm sorry to have brought it up. I could think of no politic way of broaching the matter. I can assure you that whatever future relationship we develop in the course of our professional capacities, you will retain the same degree of autonomy you enjoyed with—"

"*Mr. Holmes.*" That finally stopped him. "Thanks for the offer but right now I'm on a leave of absence and...I don't think I'll be returning to my former position with the agency. I'm sorry."

"Oh." He looked crestfallen. "I'm sorry as well." He was struck by a thought. "Might I inquire if your services are being courted by other organizations? If so, I am certain our employer would almost certainly--"

I held out my left hand. "It was good to see you again, Mr. Holmes."

He took it, held it between both of his. "Feel free to drop by any time. Farewell, Mr. Nightstalk. Until we meet again..."

George Simmons was equally kind as I took my leave. The Diogenes Club, he informed me, was considering a motion to confer upon me the same special "associate" status held by my ex-partner. It was not anticipated that it would meet with serious opposition. What did I think of the proposal and did I have any objection to joining their somewhat odd fellowship?

"I'd be...honoured," I told him.

He grasped my hand and this time I didn't bother hiding my tears.

It was inevitable that sooner or later I would end up back at the office. There was some personal stuff to collect but mainly I think I wanted one last look around *After Hours Investigations*. I suppose I was seeking closure or something. I don't know.

Maude Dreyfuss, in the midst of getting *The Tool Shed* shipshape for its grand re-opening, corralled me before I had a chance to sneak by. Threw her arms around my neck and when she drew back, her face was wet with tears.

"Nightstalk..."

"I know, Maude. It's tough. It's really fuckin' tough right now." That only made her bawl harder and I finally had to steer her back toward her door, promising that we'd get together for coffee some time and reminisce, when it didn't hurt so much. I forgot to ask how things ended up with the insurance company. The investigator's initial report blamed her fire on the same serial arsonist who incinerated Gillette's book store, so Maude scored a lucky break there. I guess Tara must have seen fit to alter her story. Smart girl.

My key still fit the lock. When the door opened, I stood on the threshold for a moment or two before going in.

I found myself assailed by memories. The Old Man hadn't touched anything. It was like we'd just stepped out for a few minutes, off on one of our junk food runs.

It was *eerie*.

She was still there, all around me: sitting on her side of the desk, reading aloud from a book or painting her toenails as she lectured me on Lautreamont or Mirbeau. I hardly knew where to look. Everything provoked a memory, a fond recollection of some silly or sublime moment we'd shared.

I went over and sat in my chair, swivelling it around so I wouldn't face toward her, where she usually sat. It was too much. There was no way I could work there again, even if it meant passing up a chance to play Doc Watson to the great Sherlock Holmes. Too bad.

I regretted missing the memorial service. I'd heard from people who attended that it had been a low-key, dignified affair and I was glad. I knew for a fact that was what she'd wanted.

One of the first things a person did after hiring on at *After Hours* was fill out a document that let the Old Man know what arrangements to make, should they happen to suffer an untimely death in the line of duty.

I dug out her personnel file, flipped through it until I found her D.O.R.[36] form. I'd seen it before, of course (all in the interests of being her unofficial biographer), and was familiar with its provisions. She wanted her body donated to science, once any viable organs had been removed for transplant. Except for her eyes, which I always found curious. She declined any kind of religious service and specifically prohibited any post-mortem viewing of her body. I guess to her mind it was morbid or something. She wanted to be remembered the way she was, vital and beautiful and full of life. Likewise, she forbade any attempts to contact her after her death. From what I'd seen of the dissipated revenants that usually showed up at seances, I didn't blame her.

For next of kin, she listed only one person, a brother, Alessandro Zinnea, professor of marine biology at Costa Rica's National University. She'd never mentioned him to me.

As for the service itself, it was to be kept simple. Musical selections: Yo Yo Ma playing Bach and a song by a punk rock group called The Slits. Readings from Dion Fortune's *The Cosmic Doctrine* and Tom Robbins' *Another Roadside Attraction*.

Stapled to the D.O.R. form was something I hadn't seen before. An undated sheet of notepaper and on it, written in her hand:

Finally, I would like my dear friend, Evgeny D. Nightstalk, in that distinctive growl I've come to know and love, to read Christina Georgina Rosetti's poem "Remember". *And to take its wise words to heart. C.Z.*

She'd printed the poem underneath. I started to read silently then stopped myself. Stood up. "Okay, Cass, you wanted it, you got it."

Out loud then. Let's hear it, Nightstalk.

> "Remember me when I am gone away,
>   Gone far away into the silent land;
>   When you can no more hold me by the hand,
>   Nor I half turn to go yet turning stay.
> Remember me when no more day by day
>   You tell me of our future that you planned:
>   Only remember me; you understand
>   It will be late to counsel then or pray.
> Yet if you should forget me for a while
>   And afterwards remember, do not grieve:

---

[36] Disposition of Remains

For if the darkness and corruption leave
A vestige of the thoughts that once I had,
Better by far you should forget and smile
Than that you should remember and be sad."

She told me that certain writers and artists helped sustain her belief in things that couldn't be; they were prophets, shamans, *sorcerers*. One of her heroes, William Butler Yeats, remained convinced of the power of magic to his dying day, and was a charter member of the legendary Order of the Golden Dawn. Blake talked to angels, Goya conjured monsters and Conan Doyle had a soft spot for fairies.

I suppose in my own way I was similarly deluded. *I* chose to believe in a place not far from here and a time in the not so distant future when I'd see Cassandra Zinnea again. I didn't know what the circumstances would be; I wasn't a big fan of the afterlife and certainly didn't subscribe to the notion that heaven is Central Park without the muggers and dogshit. I didn't hold any strong religious views and, as she astutely pointed out, was somewhat deficient in the faith department.

But, let's face it, I'd seen more than a few odd things during my lifetime, witnessed some bizarre and improbable events. So I couldn't completely rule out the possibility that somewhere down the road, Cass and I might be reunited to solve one final Mystery together, the greatest and most enduring riddle of all.

Knowing my friend and partner Cassandra Zinnea, I hadn't the slightest doubt that she was already on the case, well on her way to coming up with a unique and altogether brilliant solution.

End

Acknowledgements:

Those wishing to read more about the magickal (*sic*) collaborations of John Parsons and L. Ron Hubbard are urged to check on-line. I discovered a lot of *very* interesting sites relating to the occult in cyberspace—babalon.net was a big help to me. That's where I found Michael Staley's "Jack Parsons: Beloved of Babalon", Richard Metzger's "John Whiteside Parsons: Anti-Christ Superstar", Alexander Mitchell's "The Babalon Working", etc. I also recommend Russell Miller's biography of Hubbard, *Bare-Faced Messiah,* and two books on Parsons that were invaluable to my research: *Strange Angel* (George Pendle; Harcourt Inc.) and *Sex & Rockets* (John Carter; Feral House).

I would like to make special mention of several other volumes: Nicholas Christopher's loving homage to film noir, *Somewhere in the Night* and Lawrence Sutin's *Do What Thou Wilt: A Life of Aleister Crowley.* Any writer investigating the supernatural or otherwordly is indebted to Colin Wilson—his books *The Occult* and *The Psychic Detectives* came in especially handy. Rosemary Guiley's *The Encyclopedia of Witches and Witchcraft* was a most helpful resource, as were two little handbooks on the *Kaballah* and *Ritual Magic* (Llewellyn Publications; St. Paul, MN).

I nicked the details from Joe Duthie's monologue on the destruction wrought by American forces in Panama from Martha Gellhorn's article "The Invasion of Panama" in *Granta* (Spring, 1990).

My profound gratitude to Ado Ceric for providing the gorgeous cover art, "Midnight Randevous", and I urge you to check out his website (http://www.adoceric.com) for more examples of his work.

A tip of the hat to S.T. Joshi for the Lovecraft snippet that leads off *Book II* and for saving me from the embarrassment of using a quote falsely attributed to HPL.

In the midst of writing *So Dark the Night* I learned of the demise of the original Nightstalker, Darren McGavin. *Requiescat in pace,* Kolchak...

As part of my preparations for this book, I watched innumerable film *noir* classics: *Kiss Me Deadly, D.O.A., The Seventh Victim, Postman Always Rings Twice, The Usual Suspects*...their moods, shadow play and stark streetscapes permeate *So Dark the Night*. To get myself up to speed, I read quite a bit of Hammett...but to my mind Raymond Chandler is a far more interesting writer. From *The Lady in the Lake*: "There was the doorway with the green curtains across it. Never sit with your back to a green curtain. It always turns out badly. Who had I said that to? A girl with a gun..."

You can't beat that.

Special thanks to Sherron, Liam and Sam, for sharing me with Cassandra & Evgeny for the past three (+) years. Sherron is the best editor I could possibly ask for...and I couldn't have gotten this book ready for printing without her. Her patience, love and faith were sometimes the only things that kept me going.

C.B. (April, 2010)

Cliff Burns lives in western Canada with his wife and two sons. His previous books include *Sex & Other Acts of the Imagination* (1990), *The Reality Machine* (1997) and *Righteous Blood* (2003). *So Dark the Night* is his first novel.

316

317

LaVergne, TN USA
30 June 2010
187965LV00001B/15/P